THE FORGOTTEN WORLD

The Forgotten World

The Forgotten World Series

ANGELA BASTIEN

Library of Congress Control Number: 2024902835
ISBN: 979-8-9902023-1-3 (Hardcover) / 979-8-9902023-2-0 (Paperback)

Editor: Kourtney Schmiedeke/Heartfelt Editorial Services LLC

Second Edition 2024.

~For my mother, the strongest woman I know.~

Part One

The Beginning

Chapter One – Ashanti

I lay in bed crying quietly, tears flowing freely but silently. Careful, even while being held captive in the chaos that is my mind. I was awakened as always by nightmares. They plague me now. I hate the night. Nowhere to hide in the quiet darkness. My pain so intense I swear it will swallow me whole. How badly I want it all to stop. How I beg in the dark for it to stop. "Please take me from this nightmare... I can't love him anymore," I whisper in a voice barely heard by my own ears. I close my eyes and inhale deeply.

I've never been a religious woman but rather spiritual. Tonight, in my torment I pray to my own ancestors, whispering the words aloud, hoping the universe hears them and finally answers. *Have my ancestors abandoned me?* The warm summer breeze blows gently across the balcony causing my curtains to dance as if in response to my thoughts. *No.* Even in my distraught state, I know they listen. I know I must find the strength to choose my own path in this turmoil, but my heart aches in ways I never thought possible.

Tiny footsteps steal my focus and bring me out of my own mind. I glance at the small red digits on my tabletop alarm, 5:36 a.m. I quickly wipe my tears and fix a warm smile that feels fraudulent on my face, as Isaiah quietly pushes open my door and peeks his tiny head in. Eyes much too big for such a little face, full of excitement for the day look up at me, causing my fake smile to quickly turn real.

"Hi, little monster," I whisper. I watch as he runs to my bedside at the sound of my voice, carefully climbing up to hug me. I welcome his embrace and squeeze him tightly.

"Mommy!" he says through uncontrollable giggles. "Mommy I'm hungry."

"Yeah, yeah, little one! I know!" I tease. "Let's go brush our teeth. "I struggle to roll out of bed. My belly causing me to rock side to side to gain enough momentum to pull myself upright. I stretch as I stand and wince at the soreness near my lower back. I realize yesterday's madness has left me bruised: Adam's drunken tirade that ended with him pushing me into the dresser. I recognize the floral scents of my favorite perfumes, their aroma still filling the room, a further reminder of our dysfunction. As I look at the broken bottles that now litter the floor, I make a mental note to clean that mess up before he gets home. Even at seven months pregnant I'm not safe from his anger. Sighing, I adjust my oversized nightgown, quickly pushing those memories out of my mind. How good I have gotten at burying memories now! An impatient Isaiah tugs at my hem, once again pulling me out of my own thoughts.

"Come on, Mommy," he urges me, as he pulls me down the hall. Isaiah excitedly rushes through our morning routine of brushing our teeth together, and getting dressed, after giving him his morning shower. Downstairs, I sit his breakfast on the table and begin preparing Adam's plate.

"Eat your waffles," I say, briefly stopping from making Adam's plate, as I watch my toddler blow bubbles into his almond milk. We both hear the car door slam shut at the same time. Isaiah tenses and sits up straight in his chair, looking down intently at his plate. My heart breaks seeing it, but before I can react Adam bursts into the door, one hand carrying a wilted bouquet of flowers he picked up at the local gas station, the other holding a coffee. I notice he's dressed in clothing he didn't leave dressed in the night before, no longer hiding his betrayal. His beautiful smile and carefree eyes shine brightly once he spots me in the kitchen. No traces of the cruel vicious man from just a few hours before. It's almost as if he has an evil twin, a Mr. Hyde hiding beneath his kind Jekyll-like personality. I smile back, hoping it looks genuine. I quickly think of the glass I haven't cleaned up in our bedroom and begin to worry he might go upstairs.

"Good morning, babe," Adam says, towering over my 5'4" frame due to his 6'4" stature. I stand on my tiptoes as he leans down to kiss me.

"Good morning, honey," I say sweetly, and set his plate of waffles, bacon, eggs, and fresh fruit in front of his usual place at the head of the table. I relax a little when he sits down.

"You're too good to me," he says as he pats my butt. I sit in my spot beside him, across from Isaiah, careful not to wince when my lower back presses against the back of the chair. It would only upset him. Adam leans over to ruffle Isaiah's curly afro, as he giggles.

"Good morning, Daddy," he says, smiling up at his father. Adam picks up his fork and starts shoveling food in his mouth.

"Eat your food," he says sternly. Isaiah quickly begins eating waffles. He peeks up at me, and I flash him an encouraging smile. A silent team. *Don't upset Daddy,* an unsaid pact. We eat quietly as Adam scrolls through his phone, checking his emails.

"Okay, I'm going to head to the office," he says, pushing away from the table. A quick kiss on the forehead and he grabs his work bag by the door and leaves. We listen quietly as the car starts and drives away, both of us relaxing at the retreating sound. I spend the remainder of the morning getting ready for our day, dropping him off at school, and running the few errands I have. I spend several hours cleaning the house thoroughly. I was once a teacher at a private school, what felt like ages ago. But Adam insisted I quit when I became pregnant with Isaiah. I needed to "relax and enjoy motherhood." At the time I thought it was the sweetest thing. He wanted to be the provider, and protector. Looking back, I see it was the beginning of the web of isolation he was creating for me. An unexpected knock at the door scares me out of the thoughts I seem to be lost in so often lately. I set down the dirty dishes in my hand and dry my hands on the dish towel. Peeking out of the window with just my eyes visible I see what can only be described as the most beautiful woman I have ever laid eyes on. Long, curly jet-black hair frames her face, and sits just past her shoulders. Large almond-shaped green eyes with thick long lashes, a full heart-shaped mouth, no more than 5'0 tall but an hourglass-shaped figure, visible even through the loose blouse and pants she has on. Her complexion a beautiful shade of mocha. I murmur "Wow," and I realize I am staring openly at her when I make eye contact with her. I audibly gasp and blush from embarrassment as she smiles. Did she hear me? How? I shrug the feeling away as I open the door.

"Hi!" She exclaims brightly in a voice that calmed my last thought. I smile at her feeling silly.

"Hey!" I respond, her cheerfulness contagious. I look past her and see a moving truck in my neighbor's yard and men carrying furniture into and out of the house.

"My name is Sarah! I am your new neighbor." She smiles as she points at the house across the street from my own.

"That's funny, I didn't know the Williams family were moving," I say confused. *Hmm, surely Janet wouldn't have just up and moved so quickly without saying goodbye? I mean, we weren't insanely close, but we are her neighbors.* I try to remember the last time I saw them and realize it's been over two weeks. *I hope everything's okay with them.*

"Yes, they said they had an important family emergency and had to sell quickly. We happened to be looking for a place and it just lined up perfectly. They practically moved out overnight. I believe they mentioned going home to Hawaii," she explained with a confident smile. I relax a little at this explanation. *Well, that makes sense.* I recall the several conversations Janet and I previously had about Ben's mother being sick and getting worse each day. I watch as large men in matching commercial t-shirts unload the truck.

"Well, welcome to our little neighborhood," I say with a welcoming smile.

"Thank you," she says, her perfect smile never wavering. We stand quietly for a moment, "Well I better get going. Those movers haven't a clue where to put things, but please once we're settled in, you'll have to meet my sister, Erin."

"Of course," I say as she waves and hurries off to her new home. I make a mental note to call and check on Janet. *They must be having a really hard time.*

That night as I lay in bed still sore from the bruises covering my back, Adam's heavy arm draped over my chest. I wonder when things changed for us. I stare at the man I've loved for over a decade. His long, neat dreads in a messy bun, his facial expression so peaceful. Seeing him sleeping like this, I can still see remnants of the gentleman he used to be. My life was so different before him. He saved me from all the turmoil. Having to grow up in the foster care system as an orphan. I lost my mother in childbirth. She was so young, and beautiful. She was an orphan herself. My father could have blamed me for her death but instead, my loving father raised me alone. He never raised his voice, or hand to me. Gentle parenting long before it was a trend. He raised me by example, working hard and always being good to everyone he met. He never let on how badly we were struggling. If the power went out, we'd "go camping" in the house. Candlelight as campfire, scary stories all night, and hide and seek. How unfair it was when he was snatched away from me at just 9 years old. Cancer stealing his youth, and mine as well. Watching my 6'5, 300-pound gentle, giant father shrink, and wither away as I tried to care for him as just a small child. I feel my eyes fill with tears. How I miss my father. My life would be so different. Foster care was a nightmare. Being bounced around, home to home, alone and scared. Everything we owned was snatched away from me. I ran away at 14 after being sent to yet another abusive home. I ended up in Tallahassee, Florida. I slept on the street, at bus stops, shelters, anywhere, doing whatever was necessary to survive, until 16. That's when I met Adam. I was so close to giving up. I smile remembering him smuggling me into his dorm room. His best friend, Chris, helped us keep the secret. Adam kept me safe, and fed. I felt so loved after so many years of fighting to survive. He reminded me so much of my father back then. Always patient, kind, and gentle. I had no one, and he's reminded me often that he was my family now. He would protect me. All we needed was each other. I'd remind myself of that throughout the years, whenever a red flag was raised. When I turned 16, I went back to school, got my GED, then my Bachelor of Art Education. All the while my Adam protected me, and took care of me. He used his father's connections to get my art into galleries, plan beautiful getaways. We were a team back then. So, in love. He'd show up at my school in between classes just to sit in the grass and eat lunch with me. We'd drive hours and hours along the deserted highways at night just so I could see the stars at night, as I did back home with my father as a child. He really saved me. We married shortly after I graduated college at 22, and just under a year later, just after my birthday we found out about our Isaiah. After Isaiah, he changed. It wasn't drastically like in the movies. No, it started off so small. I mean he just *loved* my long natural curls, so he suggested I stop cutting my hair short, above my shoulders back then. I easily agreed. I mean, I wanted to make him happy, and I was so self-conscious with my constantly changing body during the pregnancy. Then came the perfume. He disguised it as a gift. "*This one smells amazing.*" He said it so excitedly. I didn't want to disappoint him. So, I wore it often, then I only wore that one. I think back to the day we discussed my early retirement from teaching. I loved that job, the kids. I worked so hard for that degree. The way Adam described his vision of our happy family, coming home to his wife and kid each day. His fear of my postpartum mental health. So many women had such a rough time after childbirth. He couldn't imagine another person, or a daycare raising our baby. The idea of missing first steps, or first words. It just made sense. He was the breadwinner, and I would enjoy being home with our little one. I could paint and focus on what I love and be there for my family. It sounded beautiful. I could rest, and enjoy motherhood because, *"He got us,"* as he said so frequently back then. The first time Adam hit me, was also the first time I caught him cheating on me. I trusted him so fully back then. Before that day I hadn't even realized how stuck he had gotten me into his web. Isaiah was 6 months old, and Adam had changed. He stayed out late, claiming to be with clients. He was often cold towards me. Snapping at me for things beyond my control. One day I wanted to surprise him at work, so I packed his favorite food, ribeye steak, homemade garlic mashed potatoes, and asparagus. I packed up little Isaiah and went to his office, remembering all of our lunches on the grass near my school. He works at an advertising company, their star employee. I knew something was wrong immediately. Charlotte, his secretary, immediately tried to stop me from entering his office, and his blinds were closed. I pushed past her as she was quickly giving him a warning through the intercom on her desk. I walked into the room just as he was buckling his belt. A young blond standing beside him, adjusting her dress. My heart broke in a million pieces as I sat Isaiah's car seat and diaper bag down, our bag of lunch sliding onto the floor. My vision turned red, and my blood boiled.

"What the FUCK!" I scream. Adam finally looks up at me.

"Don't make a scene Ashanti," he said it so irritated, as if I was being unreasonable, as if I disrupted a normal meeting.

"Adam, are you crazy?" I continue to scream. The bimbo runs a nervous hand through her hair and collects her purse and jacket. Adam, seeing my attention has turned to her, walks over to me, standing directly in front of me and blocking my line of sight to her.

"We were just having a meeting. This is a client, Helen," he explains it slowly, like I am a small child. I stare at my husband, his long dreads loosely falling over his shoulders. Hearing him speak her name, it feels similar to a knife twisting into the pit of my stomach. My pain quickly turns to anger. No, he promised to protect me.

"How could you?!" I yell, "We're married!"

"Go home Ashanti, you're being unreasonable. We'll talk when I get home." He stated and stepped backward, away from me.

"I'm done Adam! I'm taking Isaiah and we're leaving." I start to pick up my bags, but Adam grabs me.

"Don't ever threaten me! Are you stupid? You have nothing Ashanti! I'm all you have! Don't forget that!" He says gripping my arms too tight. I try to break free.

"Get. Off. Of. Me!" I say angrily, "FUCK YOU!"

He slapped me hard and quickly. It took a second to register what had even happened. I just stood there holding my face, crying, as the crowd that made their way into the hall near his office quickly dispersed as if no one had seen anything. They simply turned and went back into their offices. The bimbo, Helen took this opportunity to quickly exit.

"Now go home." He repeated. This time slowly, looking me in my eyes, gripping my shoulders, to ensure I understand. I went home and contemplated a million different scenarios of leaving but where would I go? He was right, I had no one to turn to, no money outside of what he provided, and a newborn. That was when I realized what I had done. So eager to please this man, my savior, I had given myself away. My independence. The 16-year-old girl who survived years on the street alone was gone. In my desperation to be saved, I had given this man everything and left myself empty, weak. Adam came home late that night, drunk but pleading. He begged and cried, promising so many things that I wanted to hear. So, I forgave him, entirely too quickly, with no consequence for his actions at all. He showered me with love, and attention. He went above and beyond to show he was back to my Adam. My sweet, kind husband. I once again let my guard down with him after months and months of changed behavior, but once again things started to change after Isaiah's first birthday. I don't know when drinking became a problem. He started slowly. A drink after dinner, here and there. After-work dinners with clients, a few times a month. Then it became a once-a-week thing, then daily. He'd often come home too drunk to climb the stairs after those dinners. I tried talking with him about it one night. Explaining how it was unhealthy, that conversation ended with his hands around my throat. So, I stopped bringing it up. He'd get angry over little things, Isaiah's toys on the floor, dishes not done quickly enough. After about a year he received a promotion at work, and he stopped coming home most nights, blaming it on out-of-town conventions, or business trips. Just when I would be ready to pack up and leave my Adam would appear. He'd shower me and Isaiah with gifts, and trips to exotic places. He'd be loving and kind, and stupidly I'd stay. I don't know what makes me stay. I guess wanting to believe my Adam will reappear and stay one day. That things would go back to how they were, and we'd be happy again? I contemplate quietly why he has so much anger for me, especially when drunk.

"Ashanti?"

The sound of Adam's whispered voice scares me and I jump at the sound. I look over to see him awake, staring at me, a concerned expression on his face.

"Are you okay babe?" He sounded so worried. I realize I'm crying, as he reaches over to wipe a tear and pull me closer to him.

"Yes honey," I say laughing, "pregnancy hormones, I was just remembering the old days. Remember how you'd smuggle me into your dorm?" He smiles and closes his eyes, remembering.

"Those were the days!" He laughs quietly. We stay awake cuddled close together, reminiscing about our younger days, and planning our future. I cuddle closer to him, happy to have my Adam back, even if it was only for this moment. I doze off thinking how much I love this man.

Chapter
Two – Asim

"Asim! Are you listening to me?" Heqet says in our native tongue from so many years ago, her voice too low for human ears. I glance at my longtime companion— genuinely beautiful, inside and out. She stares at me concerned, her thick mane of hair pulled into a smooth bun on top of her perfectly shaped head, her glasses perched on her nose, just for show, of course. We have no need for such devices of improvement; our senses heightened to an extreme.

"Of course, I hear you, little sister." I smile teasingly at her as I speak in a normal tone. She rolls her eyes at me, annoyed.

"We must be careful, Asim! I enjoy this peaceful town. We have not lived amongst humankind in many years. We cannot make irrational, hasty decisions. It has only been two days! That store clerk did not deserve your wrath. You must control your temper—."

I tune her out, focusing instead on the passing humans walking busily by our small table outside the tiny café we chose to idle at. This town is so much smaller than we normally choose. Heqet loves keeping appearances, and I love Heqet, so I indulge her with these small stops every few decades. So many millennia she has stayed loyal to me, by my side as my companion, my sister. Not a droplet of hatred or resentment towards me after I so selfishly turned her all those years ago, out of pure loneliness. She has just always been there, always patient, kind, rational. Her hope nor her faith in me has ever wavered in all the time I have known her. I've lost count of how many of my messes she has cleaned up for me. My dislike of humanity growing stronger with each passing century. I was once known as their great protector. Now, that time in my life has left me as simply a myth to them— a Goddess that once existed. As I watch these creatures rush past, ignoring the beauty of the earth around them, some shouting into phones, or worse, at each other, I sigh deeply, already longing for the jungle, or perhaps a deserted island they have yet to find, or ruin— anywhere far away from these absurd creatures.

I look over at my sister. She smiles brightly, a glow of pure joy engulfing her, as she looks at a small baby in a stroller at the next table over. It smiles back and giggles. Yes, I will stay in this agony for her. *What are a few years in comparison to eternity?*

"I apologize, little one," I say as she scrunches her face and sticks out her tongue. She hates my pet's name for her, referencing her smaller height of 5 feet and her small frame compared to my 6'4 stature and athletic build. Even with this drastic difference, we both have the strength of more than 100 men. I smile at her, before continuing, "I over-reacted earlier. I will keep my temper under control during the remainder of our stay in this lovely town."

This placates her, and she smiles approvingly at me. "Thank you. Now," she rubs her hands together happily, "the details of our stay"

I turn back to people-watching as she plans our entire stay, periodically murmuring trivial questions about things I may want to try. I smile at her happiness. Just a few years won't hurt, I promise myself.

"Asim, are you really okay?" Heqet asks, her worry pouring out with every word. I smile without hesitation.

"Of course, little sister. All is well," I say affectionately. I add teasingly, "After all this time, you still try to mother me." She rolls her eyes and smiles before turning serious once again.

"I know we are not the same as we once were. Time has been as cruel as she has been merciful at times. I believe our pain is not in vain. We are needed now more than ever. I still have faith in humanity. Our ancestors would not lead us through so many millennia to abandon us now." She stares into my eyes, trying to will her faith into me. I smile widely.

"Vibe killer," I mock a teenage child. "I hear you, Heqet, truly. Perhaps we can lighten the mood and explore a little?" As I expected, this offer distracts her temporarily from her mission of fixing me, as her eyes light up with excitement, and a grin spreads across her face.

"Yes! First, I must take care of our sleeping arrangements." She quickly pulls her phone out and makes several calls. Within minutes, we are in our car heading to our first destination. We spend the remainder of the day exploring little shops and driving along the few roads in town. I'm careful to keep my temper in check and even feign empathy towards the humans, which thrills Heqet.

We are careful to avoid the busiest places, keeping our distance from the humans, and mingling when absolutely necessary. In a town this small, we are noticed easily; luckily, time has made a masculine dressing female a normality, and the few stares we receive are mostly due to my height or Heqet's beauty. The humans, while interested, give us our space after a brief conversation or a passing hello. Luckily, the shops close early, and we check into our small hotel room that Heqet has arranged.

"Today was nice, thank you," Heqet says, smiling as she quickly zips around the room, installing small security features and putting away our belongings.

"Anything for you my love," I say while lying on the twin-size bed, too small for my frame. I lay perfectly still, preparing to meditate. While sleep is unnecessary, we are capable of a dreamlike state. Older beings of my kind can meditate and dwell in a realm not quite of Earth, a separate dimension where our ancestors can speak plainly with us, if they so choose. Our kind's strength comes with age, mental and physical, and only the oldest amongst our kind can achieve this state. Heqet and I are among those capable. We have come to call this state simply sleep, although our descriptions of this realm rarely match. Heqet's visions are always cheerful— a sunflower field, a child's playground, a beach— while my own have become increasingly more solemn than the last. Visits have stopped completely from my ancestors; even my own mother has ceased communication. Heqet believes my refusal to walk in my purpose has deeply offended my ancestors. I was given this gift of eternity a very long time ago, swearing to my ancestors I would use this gift to protect all women, with Heqet making a similar promise to protect children. I shrug off the thought, thinking of how little our same ancestors have protected our loved ones. Hazel ghost eyes flash in front of me. *No, humanity does not deserve our protection.*

"Are you asleep?" Heqet whispers to me.

"No," I sigh.

"Do you want to hunt?"

"Not tonight," I reply, eyes still closed.

"I will return shortly," she says and quietly leaves, knowing I need space and quiet.

Once again in my sleeping state, in an empty field, the sky is gray. I sit alone, in front of a barren tree, quietly remembering thoughts I fear while awake. I remember past loved ones and heartbreaks. My mother's face is full of stubborn determination as she decides to sacrifice her life for my own. The wind on my face as I run with all my newly given strength, running from the smell of fire. Her last words to me still ring too loudly in my ears, *"Run."* My mother so strong, so kind. Far too kind of a soul to remain tethered to this planet. She used her gift of magic and prayed to our ancestors to grant her only daughter protection from man. My youth was a time when women were condemned without proof of crime, savagely attacked by men, and left beaten, violated, or murdered. I spent my human years training and protecting women in my village.

One night after my mother completed a ritual for protection, a soft-spoken, beautiful woman approached her hut. She was tall, taller than me by several inches, with long dreads piled high on her head resembling a crown. She spoke softly but assertively.

"I am Nwt." She spoke to my mother, but she said it in a way that made me want to bow. She was powerful, and it radiated from her body and voice. She continues in our native tongue, "I am told you are a woman of magic?"

"Yes," my mother, always calm, suddenly visibly shaken. I sensed what she felt. This was no human in our presence. I move closer to my mother. Nwt's gaze focuses on me.

"Do not fear me, child," she says, her appearance suggesting she may be younger than me, "I mean no woman any harm."

"What do you need, dear?" My mother asks, her voice still trembling.

"A village I hold close to my heart was attacked. My sisters need help. I can heal them, but I do not wish to curse them with eternity."

My mother's eyes widened with understanding, "you have the gift, then?"

"Yes," Nwt responds simply.

"Bless my daughter," my mother suddenly begs, taking me by surprise. My mother was a proud woman; I had never witnessed her beg before that night.

"Mother, what is this?" I ask, turning her small face to look into her eyes.

"She is blessed, Asim! The ancestors have granted her protection from death for all of eternity. She is free from illness, free to live without fear of man."

Nwt shakes her head gently, "No Mother. I am free to watch my loved ones perish as I no longer age, free to relive this grief, the anger for all of eternity."

I watch her closely. She is strong, much stronger than her youthful appearance would suggest. I think of all the women I could protect if I were willing to make this sacrifice— never joining the ancestors, never having that peace.

"Give me this gift, and my mother will help you." My mother nods in agreement and quickly adds, "Please, I wish to protect my child."

Nwt looks at me, directly in my eyes, her own soft and pleading. "You do not understand that in which you ask."

"This is our condition," I say as sternly as I can muster. For one brief moment, a deep sadness crosses her face— a sadness I would never have understood in my short human life.

"So be it."

She moves quickly, eager to return to her village. She closes the small distance between us before I can blink. She bites her own flesh at her wrists, drawing blood that drips down her arm onto the dirt beneath her. She holds her wrist out towards my mouth," Drink."

I hesitate, disgusted by the thought of drinking blood, but she quickly forces her wrist to my mouth, knocking my own hands away as if I were a small child when I try to protest. The metallic taste flows into my mouth, burning down my throat. I force myself to swallow gulps as she continues to hold her bleeding wrist to my mouth. She watches me carefully.

"Turn your head, Mother," she says gently to my own mother. My mother obeys, and my world suddenly goes dark. I awaken in the dark. It takes several moments for me to realize my mother is cradling my head, and holding my hand. Her hands feel hot, as if she has a fever. I quickly realize my senses are no longer that of a human as I hear and see things I have never experienced. My attention focuses on Nwt standing tensely at the mouth of the cave we stand in. My body senses danger, and I realize I will not have time to adjust to this new life tonight. Four elderly women huddle close together near Nwt. I smell my mother's herbs and realize these women must be Nwt's sisters.

"Sisters, we must go," Nwt warns them, "they are close."

"Who?" I jumped up. My movements took me by surprise. I ran to Nwt's side within a second, moving too fast. She reaches out without looking at me and stops me, steadying me.

"The men who attacked our people."

My newfound strength and speed make me arrogant. "Then we will stop them." I prepare to fight, my mind working quickly.

"No. They have creatures with them I have never seen. Strong as a hundred men, fast and gifted. We cannot fight so many. These creatures can turn into great beasts I have never seen." She turns to her sisters, "We must run now. Come, sisters."

I watch as she runs at a pace much slower than she is capable of, to stay at pace with these elderly women. She must love them. My instinct in this new life is to preserve myself, sensing a danger I cannot overcome. My body tightens, preparing to run away as fast as I can. I look over at my mother. I reach for her.

"Mother, we must run as well," I say, looking back to see the glow of torches growing closer.

"No, my love. I will slow you down. My life has been one of much love. But I am ready to go now, in peace knowing you will be safe."

I stare at her determined face, confused, "Do not be silly, Mother. I am strong. I can carry you on my back and move quickly." She stubbornly shakes her head.

"No, Asim, I will choose my own death. I wish to go now, protecting you. I have no strength left to fight any longer.

I wish to join our ancestors," she says, her hand resting on my cheek.

"Mother, please," I beg. Sadness pours from my soul, but no tears came. I cannot cry any longer in this life. She smiles at me lovingly.

"No, my love, I will distract them. This gift you possess must live on. You can run, live, save our people."

I try to argue and plead, but she holds steadfast until I can smell the fire from their torches. She hugs me tight," I will see you again, my love."

We hear the shouting of men not far from where we stand.

"Run."

I pull myself from my sleeping state, unwilling to experience my mother's death again. I look around the dark room. Heqet is nowhere to be found. I sit up and go to prepare a bath in the tiny tub, hoping to wash the memories away.

The next morning, we again travel to town. Heqet is busily texting on her phone, making the necessary arrangements. I periodically answer the questions she asks me and smile at passing children, much to Heqet's pleasure. We stop at a restaurant to keep up with our human appearances and order steaks, forcing ourselves to eat.

"You need to hunt tonight," She reminds me, "but keep your promise, please. We cannot draw attention to ourselves."

I innocently raise my hands, "I promise." We explore the woods outside of our town, allowing me to run alongside my companion. I smile as we race and laugh, checking for any signs of other beings, our kind or the others. Thankfully, we find nothing and return to our room.

As night falls, I leave Heqet in our small motel room. Careful as always, Heqet insists we stay in cheap motels when we are amongst humans, even though we have significant wealth in various checking and savings accounts under various names. Any one of those dozens of accounts holds enough funds for anyone to live comfortably for generations. But once again, we stay on the outskirts of town, this one in Alabama, that Heqet took notice of so many decades ago as we passed through. I promised her then that one day we would return and stay, and thus, that day apparently coming far quicker than I anticipated. As I leave, Heqet again makes me promise not to feed near the town or drain any human completely. I promise and leave quickly.

After walking slowly and inconspicuously into the nearby woods, I listen carefully. Satisfied that there are no humans nearby, I take off, running full speed through the woods, climbing trees, and jumping from branch to branch. Happy to be free of the constraints humanity places on our kind. After running until my inner beast is satisfied, I find a bridge with a few homeless drunks passed out underneath. I find one on his own, out of sight of the others, and quickly feed on him, careful to bite where these humans typically inject drugs, the crease of his elbow, making sure not to drain him. Once I feel the fullness of his blood, the warmth spreading through my body, I stare deeply into his eyes.

"You fell asleep; this was a dream," I say simply, knowing this excuse and his drunkenness will cause him to forget me. My entrance, as always, works, and I watch as his eyes glaze over.

"I fell asleep; this was a dream," he repeats, as if hypnotized.

I smile, running through the woods back to our small prison of a room. I allow myself time to roam as I enjoy the feeling of being slightly drunk from his intoxicated blood. The feeling will pass soon as my body processes what it needs. Trees blur past me as I quicken my pace. Mother Moon embraces me as she shines through the trees. I slow down, realizing I am approaching civilization, hearing the laughter of a child seemingly safe in his home, a mother bribing him to sleep. I climb silently to a tall pine tree at the edge of the woods, much older than the neighborhood it grows in— a small cul-de-sac, with only three homes within it.

I listen in to a nearby home with an elderly couple as they whisper in the dark, concerned for a sickly motherly figure far away. The third farthest home is quiet, with two humans fast asleep, slightly snoring within it, and a dog noisily digging through a trash can. A car swerves on the street and pulls into the driveway of the mother and small boy, parking haphazardly, partially in the grass. The breeze carries the scent of alcohol as a tall man trips out of the car, muttering obscenities to himself as he stumbles up the stairs to the wrap-around porch of the home. He drops the keys several times before finally unlocking the door and stepping inside. I snarl with disgust. As low as my patience with humans, men specifically have always fallen lower still. No matter the species, the arrogance of males always sickens me.

I listen into this male's home. The child suddenly stops giggling as the front door bursts open. "Shhhh, go to sleep, little monster," the mother says gently. Quickly, she dims the lights in the child's room and closes the door. Hurriedly, she makes her way into what must be the master bedroom and gets into bed after dimming her own lights. *Ahh, a tormentor in his own home,* I think to myself as I realize his family fears him. She stays quietly in this dark room, her breathing low. The male noisily opens and closes cabinets downstairs before loudly stumbling up the stairs. A door slams open, and the light of the mother's room turns on brightly.

"Ashanti!" he yells.

My heart skips a beat at the name. Those haunting hazel eyes stare at me in the darkness, tormenting me with my lost love. So many, many years ago, I stared into those loving eyes. I long for her instantly, and my heart aches in the next instant. *No, she is gone.* I shake the thoughts from my mind as I focus on the commotion coming from the bedroom.

"Adam, please, the baby," she pleads quietly. A mother afraid for her child. I quickly focus my attention on the young boy's room, quietly in bed crying as he listens to his parents fight as well. A growl escapes my lips, taking me by surprise. *Is it empathy for the child, or anger for this man,* I wonder.

"You wanted this baby. You think I care," he says, words slurring as he speaks. *She's carrying a child?* The thought has my muscles tightening, the branch whines and cracks under my grip. I loosen my hand and move to a higher branch. A loud thump follows his belligerent rant, and I hear the sound of glass breaking, and I hear the soft cries of the woman. I watch a few moments later as the drunken coward storms from the house and drives dangerously from his home. I contemplate following him, but I stay still, remembering my promise to Heqet. Although, Heqet may be forgiving if she saw this scene. I stay perched on the branch, listening with unexplained interest to the mother's soft cry, until she picks herself up and quietly makes her way to the child's room. The child pretends to sleep, calming his breathing. The mother goes back to her room and settles into bed. I listen to her cry herself to sleep. It's the name, I reason with myself, feeling stupid and illogical as I quietly jump down from my hiding spot in the tree. I quickly run to the home of my interest, no whispers or laughter to be heard. The neighborhood finally asleep.

I reason I will just peek at their faces, then return to my prison of a motel room with Heqet and dismiss all of this curiosity as the madness of an old vampire. I peek into the room of the small child as I effortlessly climb to the second story of the small home. Innocently clinging to a stuffed animal, worry showing in the furrow of his brow, too serious for such a small face. I push down thoughts I thought long buried about my own childhood. *Not tonight,* I think to myself, as I quietly jump onto the balcony of the master bedroom.

I notice the broken glass first from the fight a few hours before. A broken perfume bottle lying on the floor near the dresser. I scan the large room before my eyes settle on the wooden bed. A large bump rising and falling under the blanket. She is heavily pregnant, I realize, and again shake with disgust. The blanket covering part of her face causes me to creep closer.

Just a small peek. She moves slightly, and I flash to the shadows of the room. Excitement causing venom to flow into my mouth. I swallow hard and settle myself. *Just a peek.* Unsure of what I was hoping to see. *Traces of my Ashanti maybe?* I ignore the thought and quickly move to her side.

My tall silhouette casting shadows across her bed. I gently pull the cover away from her face and examine her face.

I freeze, unprepared for the rush her beauty gives me. Even asleep, I see she is not by any means of average looks. Long, curly reddish-brown hair freely cascades around her face and pillow. Her smooth mocha complexion is so clear and youthful, eyelashes so long I swear they could rest on her chubby cheeks, full from pregnancy weight. I look further down past her nose slightly spread from pregnancy but yet still fitting for her face and stare at her perfect full lips, slightly parted and breathing quietly. She is beautiful. A brief moment of sadness comes and passes as I realize there are no traces of my Ashanti within this beautiful woman I am admiring.

I step back, feeling silly. So much interest in this young human. No more than 30 years of age, compared to my 4000. Still, If I must stay in this hell-like place, it is better to find a harmless source of entertainment. The woman begins to stir in her bed, and I quickly make myself scarce.

I allow myself to smile freely as I run home. *Ashanti.* I feel a small tug in my spirit as I recall her features. *I wonder what color her eyes are.* I think as I run. I recall the male bully, "*Adam.*" Long ago I was known as "The great protector," of my village. A guardian. In a time where women were incapable of protecting themselves, the ancestors saw fit to grant me a gift capable of saving many from man's cruelty. I spent the first few centuries of my new life with Nwt, my creator.

At the time, after her own heartbreak, she decided to create a new world. I was a witness to just how impressive her many powers were as she created a safe realm for all beings of magic. I helped her build our realm, strengthen it. Afterward, we would travel between the Earth and Forgotten World realms. I traveled to every corner of the earth, saving as many women of humanity as I could. I taught these women how to protect themselves, how to make weapons, and set traps.

As I traveled, before Heqet was born into her previous human life, I came across a small village in what would be present-day Haiti. I found a small village there, and a woman who seemed to run it. She was the oldest daughter of the chief there. She spoke, and everyone listened; even the chief himself respected this woman. The chief's wife died in childbirth. She was raised by the compassionate chief and the women of the village. She grew up to care for the sick, and elderly, advising the chief on matters of food, the weather, and advocating for the women of the village, even in war. I stayed there longer than any other village I had come across, and the chief asked me to work closely with Ashanti. While I spent most of my time up until that point protecting women from men, Ashanti was insistent that I train all of the villagers. Fear of savages in the woods outside of town that often practiced black magic and sacrifices. She was compassionate, hoping to one day teach these savages other ways of life. Her view was that if we raise young children to be strong, and intelligent, to be compassionate with each other, we could avoid another generation of savage men and fearful women. I grew close to her; we spent every day together, caring for her village and any village nearby.

After several months, our work together blossomed into a friendship. We grew to trust one another fully. So much so that one day while we were out exploring, I shared my secret with her. The fear I felt of rejection I had not felt in so many centuries. I watched as she laughed in disbelief at first, assuming I was teasing her.

Eventually, I showed her my abilities. Her face went from laughter to fear briefly, then admiration. She accepted me wholly. I found myself deeply in love with this human. She confessed her love for me, and we dated in secret. I was happy for so long.

One day the chief asked me to travel to another village, not far from our own. Apparently, this village's chief had fallen ill, and he wanted to extend a helping hand. I said my goodbyes and traveled to this village. I watched for a night, not wanting to appear too quickly and raise suspicion. I was able to help him quickly, using my mother's herbal concoctions I had learned as a small child alongside her.

Excited to return to my love, I left within three days of my visit, after ensuring the chief was improving. I ran full speed back to my Ashanti. I heard the screams before I saw the village. Then I smelled the fire. Screams of pure agony. I pushed myself to run faster. *Were we under attack?* I barely slowed to a human's pace as I reached the village. I quickly scanned the village, searching for danger for my Ashanti, the chief. I find the chief wounded near the opposite edge of the village, lying with his head in the lap of his youngest daughter. I rushed to his side, and his youngest son was kneeling beside him. He quickly filled me in on the scene that took place in my absence.

His second daughter wandered alone into the forests near the village. The chief forbade wandering alone because of the savages living within them. There was a truce between the two: the villagers did not wander into their lands, and the savages did not enter within the village. However, the second daughter wanted to prove herself. She knew of herbs that grew in the forests and wanted to gather them for her people. The savages took her as an offering. The chief's eldest three sons and some villagers all entered the forest in an attempt to reason with the savages, but they were slaughtered along with the second daughter. These savages could not be reasoned with when they accepted an offering; they did not return what was given. They took it as an act of war.

In a fit of rage, the chief attempted to attack the savages, but these savages were too strong and adapted to the forest the chief entered. Even as the chief retreated, they followed him into his village. Ashanti, seeing this, tried to save her father, but the savages cut deeply into the chief with a spear and took Ashanti.

Hearing my Ashanti was in the hands of these savages clouded my vision with red. I saw no one and heard nothing, just the faint screams as I took off at an inhumane speed after my love. I followed her scent and the scent of blood and came upon the vicious savages within minutes. I let out a vicious snarl and jumped into the center of the ritual they were already in the midst of. A bowl made of a turtle's shell, full of blood, fell to the ground as they screamed and ran. I slaughtered anyone within reach as I looked for my love. I found her quickly, lying on a falling tree, her simple clothing stained with blood. Her throat had been cut open; her head barely attached. My heart shattered, and my legs gave out. I sank to the floor before her and remained there for many days.

Eventually, her people found me there, knelt before her body, still as stone. I knew she would want a proper burial, so I did not protest when they took my love away. I stayed long enough to witness her final burial place, allowed it to burn deep into my memory, and I took off.

I stayed within that forest for nearly a century, only venturing out to visit my Ashanti and help her village when they were in dire need. I became a legend as the years passed and the villagers alive to know me all left this earth, my faith in humanity dimmed. It was during this time that I returned to Nwt's realm, tired of all of the disappointments of humanity. I remained there until Nwt was gone. I left for many centuries and returned when a new queen emerged.

After much time, I decided to return to the woods where I once held my Ashanti. Despite the passing years, I had neither healed nor forgotten my true love. Living there for many years, I wanted to be close to her, even if only in spirit.

One day, as I ran and lived amongst the animals, as I had been doing for many decades, I wandered further than I normally would. There, I heard a young woman yelling. Approaching quietly from a high tree, I watched as this young woman, no more than 25 years of age, stood before a pair of young boys, maybe 3 or 4 years old. She held a knife out towards a group of men, shouting for them to leave her and the children alone, or she would kill them all. I observed this woman no more than 5 feet tall with wild curly hair and fierce eyes, staring down these men. She had no fear, just anger and confidence. She would die protecting these children if necessary. I watched curiously as the men laughed at her. Watching this scene, I grew angry, feeling my need to protect growing within me. I remained still until the man closest to her took a step forward. In a blur, before I could stop myself, I jumped from my tree and quickly ended the men terrorizing this poor woman. She gasped, taken by surprise, but she did not retreat, she did not fear me. She stood before me for one moment, then knelt before me as if to pray. *Thank you, Goddess.*

That is how I met my Heqet. Nearly 2000 years after starting my new life, I was broken, lost, and wandering further from my purpose, and I found her. She was strong and accepting, she saved me from absolute darkness. My little sister. Humanity broke my heart very long ago. I realize I was running at a human pace as my thoughts return to the present day. I think of this new Ashanti, unsure of her character, her thoughts, or her morals. *How could this small, frail human spark this feeling?* I quicken my pace. Heqet would have insight. My companion of nearly 2000 years. She always knew what to say. She knew me in ways no one had ever known. She could reach into the darkness that threatened to swallow my heart and find light.

As I reach the edge of the woods, I listen carefully. Heqet was in the motel room talking to two men. They were discussing the forged documents she requested and the payments for them. I sat patiently waiting for this transaction to end. I hurry at an infuriating human pace to our room.

"How was your hunt?" she asks, examining our documents carefully. I smile widely, but she doesn't notice.

"Promise intact," I say happily. She looks up to say something sarcastic but stops when she sees my face.

"What has happened?" She asks suspiciously," Why are you so.... Happy?"

I pause at her question, the word 'happy' causing me to think to myself. *Happy? Am I happy?*

"Nothing has happened, little one." I tease, suddenly nervous, causing her to scrunch her nose in the funny way that always makes me laugh. Her face continues to grow suspicious, but she does not press. Instead, she watches me carefully. I ignore her curious stares and pick up my new driver's license, "Erin Brown? You're joking."

Her annoyance distracts her for just a moment, "Maybe you should join these meetings then, instead of lurking at the edge of the woods."

I roll my eyes, "Erin it is then."

I pick up her driver's license and smile, "Sarah Brown huh?"

She pretends to organize the paperwork, uninterested, "Well yes, I rather like that name."

I think of Sarah. Heqet's most recent love. She met her when she worked as a nurse in the mid-1800s in America. Sarah was dying of Smallpox, and Heqet took care of her until her death. Since her death, Heqet found creative ways to honor Sarah with each new identity.

"I like it," I say, smiling at Heqet. She looks at me with a soft smile,

"Thank you."

I flip through one of the books on the table and hum to myself. Heqet stops going through her paperwork and looks at me, arms crossed, "Okay, now I know something has happened. You have not hummed in... in decades, I believe. Tell me *now*!"

I sit on the edge of the small bed closest to her, as she curls up into the armchair next to the table. I tell her every detail of my night as she makes faces of disgust at the drunk man I drank from and growls when I describe Adam and the small, scared child. Periodically smiling as I describe Ashanti's beauty in detail. Nodding along as I give my theories and concerns. When I finish describing my night, she sits quietly, head resting in hands as she thinks everything over.

"And you felt that tug of interest at the sound of her voice initially?" She asks thoughtfully.

"Well, not really, I heard the child first, I was just passing by and heard several voices. I wasn't specifically interested in her until I saw the male, and heard the name, " I say feeling silly again.

"Hmm, and after you saw her face, you felt a connection?"

I think of the moment I saw her face. She was beautiful indeed. And hearing her cry, it awoke something within me.

"What does this mean?" I ask Heqet, unsure.

"I believe this is good, Asim," she nods her head, agreeing with her own assumption. I look to her, waiting for her explanation.

"Our ancestors guide us. They protect us. They send gifts at times. I believe the ancestors have not forgotten you. This could be their gift, their own way of guiding you back into your purpose. We were given this life as a gift. But with this gift comes a burden— Our purpose. So many, many years ago, you swore to protect all women, and I, children. That was our promise. We have faced many heartbreaks in this long life. I have lost and loved many people, some of our own kind, others as well, but you, my light, you have loved one. You have given your heart to one. So many years on this planet, and to only feel the gift of being in love once. This may be the gift the ancestors have given you." She says this with confidence, knowing she is right because she feels so, her intuition telling her so, and Heqet's intuition has never led us astray. I think over her words carefully. I remember Ashanti's curly mane of hair, her full lips, and soft voice. The sound of her laughter with her child, and the pain in her cry. A small snarl escapes my lips as I remember this drunken fool of a man, Adam. How his cruelty left her broken and crying. Heqet is right; something has awoken inside me tonight. Heqet stands and whispers something about "taking care of details" and is gone. Leaving me to my own thoughts once again. I lie back and allow myself to drift into a restful state, knowing I will know more about this Ashanti soon.

Chapter Three – Ashanti

I sit cross-legged in the sand, smiling with my face towards the morning sun. I look over and watch Isaiah playing happily with his beach toys on the wet sand beside me. We sit like this for hours, happily eating the sandwiches I made and enjoying our play day. I smile at my son, not a frown in sight as he focuses on the left side of the castle he's building— always so much happier when Adam is away. *Is staying the right thing*, I wonder ruefully. *Maybe keeping our family together is more traumatic than my children growing up with a single parent.* Adam would never let me leave anyway. *He'd probably kill me before I made it out the door*, I think jokingly. I shiver thinking about it, realizing it's probably closer to a reality than a joke. I shrug the thought out of my head and focus back on Isaiah.

As the sun sets, Isaiah curls up beside me to sleep, wrapped in his favorite dinosaur blanket. I pick up my favorite novel, about a vampire who falls in love with a young goddess, and read quietly, every so often snacking on some grapes I packed.

"It is so beautiful here."

I jump and drop my book, quickly looking towards the source of that voice. I look up to see green eyes staring back at me, "Oh! Sarah? What are you doing here?"

She smiles her calming smile and points towards the ocean, "I have never seen such a beautiful beach. We have been busy moving in, and I just wanted a little break."

"Oh, yes, I noticed you guys are all moved in now. How are you liking Bastiville? Bored yet?" I ask with a laugh.

She laughs with me, "Not yet. I have found it to be the exact opposite actually. The people here fascinate me. So many families, and everyone is so nice!"

"Good ole fashion country hospitality," I say smiling.

"Yes, we are so used to living in the big cities! No one has time for anyone. It is a profound change of pace," She explains.

"Do you guys move a lot?"

"Well, yes. We have an adventurous spirit I guess you can say."

I look at Sarah. She looks no more than twenty-five if even that. *I wonder what my life would look like without Adam, or children.* I look over at Isaiah, sleeping closely beside me. *No, I found my purpose within this child of mine.* Sarah gestures towards Isaiah, "How old?"

"He's 4, turning 5 in September this year." I say smoothing his curly afro, then volunteering his name, "Isaiah."

"He is adorable. I'm sure he's just the sweetest." She says lovingly, "How far along are you?"

I rub my belly, smiling as I look down at it, "Seven months."

"Do you know what you're having?" She asks excitedly.

"Yes, a little girl!" I say. I look up at her and realize the sun is setting, "Wow I didn't realize how late it has gotten."

I rock back and forth, preparing to stand up, and realizing what I'm attempting, Sarah offers me her hand. I laugh with embarrassment, "I'm afraid I'll drag us both down at this point."

She shakes her head at the statement, and wiggles her fingers, insisting I grab it, "Don't be silly, trust me I'm stronger than I look, and you are perfect love."

I grab her hand and she easily pulls me to my feet, her smile never wavering. So smoothly, I'm left speechless, "Please share your workout routine one of these days."

"You are just not as heavy as you think love," she says as she helps me gather my belongings and carries Isaiah to my car.

"Thank you so much Sarah, really. You know if you have a free moment, stop by tomorrow! We can have some sweet tea and chat. I'm usually home all morning by myself, with Isaiah in pre-k, and Adam at work." I say as I load the car.

"That would be lovely, I hope you wouldn't mind if my sister tagged along. Her name is Erin," She says it in a hopeful voice, "She doesn't get out much and some social interaction would be nice."

"Of course, I can't wait to meet her." We say our good-byes, and she stands off to the side, watching me back out of the parking space.

"Drive safe!" she calls out. As I drive away, I look back in the rearview, and she's gone. *Hmm, she sure is quick,* I think to myself. Once I get home, I get Isaiah ready and settled into bed, and clean up the house before I get myself ready for bed as well. Cuddled in my big empty bed, I call Adam. No answer. I check my messages, and voicemail to find he hasn't called since before we left for the beach. Sighing deeply, I lay down and drift off to sleep, hoping he'll call tomorrow.

"NO!!" I scream, running as fast as my legs will take me through the endlessly dark forest. I can hear Isaiah calling for me, over and over but with each step, my legs only feel heavier.

"Where are you!" I yell, my legs beginning to shake from the exertion.

"MOMMY!" he yells again in response to my voice.

"I'm coming Isaiah! Mommy's coming!" My legs give out beneath me. I reach down to protect my belly from the fall and realize my stomach is now flat. Sobbing, I begin to crawl, crying as I claw my way to the sound of his voice. A distant light comes into view ahead, and I crawl faster, begging the universe to give me strength to get to my child. As I reach the edge of the forest, I climb to my feet and burst into the light. There is a small stream a few feet ahead, and Isaiah is standing in it barefoot. He looks at me and smiles brightly.

"Mommy!" he exclaims, and I look to him confused. I feel relief and joy as I watch him smile at me. *He is okay!*

"You're okay, little monster. Mommy's here." I begin walking to him but stop cold, as a giant panther comes into view behind him.

"Isaiah, baby run!" I try to say calmly. He looks at me confused but doesn't move, "Baby, you have to run to mommy now; there's a big panther behind you." I reach for him, but he's still too far away. He looks behind himself and smiles.

"No, Mommy, she's, my friend!" He says and continues to stand in the stream, unmoving. As I move closer, prepared to grab him and run, the panther leaps from behind him. I scream and jump to cover him, but the panther leaps over us, and crashes into a black bear I had not seen behind me. I jump up from my sleep, covered in sweat.

"What the hell!" I sigh, wiping my forehead. I look over at the clock sitting on my nightstand. 4:27 am. *Great! I'll never get back to sleep!* I wobble over to my bedroom balcony, needing some fresh air. The nightmare causes my heart to race. The cool breeze feels soothing against my warm, damp skin. *I hate these hormonal dreams! I guess it makes sense. I've been worried about Isaiah and Adam for months now.* I try to reason my dreams as I think of all the stressful things I have put off thinking about. My thoughts are cut short as movement across the street catches my eye. The new neighbors must be awake. A light peeking through the blinds of what must be the master bedroom turns on, and a tall, slender figure steps out. Even with the dim lighting, I can see it's a woman, although her frame leans more towards athletic than curvy. I realize this must be the sister Sarah has spoken of, Erin. I try to make out her features, but she's too far away, and it's nearly impossible with such little light. I make out her long dark dreads, even longer than Adam's, as they rest just below her waist. She's very tall for a woman, and athletic, muscular even. *Maybe a basketball player?* I squint, trying to see her facial features, and realize she's watching me. I feel the blush rising to my cheeks as I wave a quick hello. She waves back. Embarrassed, I retreat to my bedroom, knowing I look like the neighborhood's nosy creep. I laugh at myself. *This pregnancy definitely has me loopy.* I begin cleaning my already clean room to keep myself busy, then go downstairs to prepare breakfast for Isaiah and myself. Once Isaiah wakes up, I quickly get him dressed and off to school, stopping by the market to grab a few things for dinner. As I pull onto our street, fear sweeps over me seeing Adam's car in the driveway. I quickly shake the feeling off. It's my husband after all. I should be happy. I grab my grocery bag and make it into the house.

"Honey!" Adam says sweetly and helps me quickly with the bag, "We have company."

I look to the couch to notice Sarah and what must be her sister Erin, standing to greet me.

"OH! Hello! I'm sorry; I completely forgot about our get-together today." I say apologetically, embarrassed I forgot our meeting, "Let me go set my things down, and I'll be right back. I quickly grab the bag from Adam and head to the kitchen.

"No, no, It's fine! We are here a little early," Sarah calls from the living room into the kitchen, "But we did meet your lovely husband, Adam."

I can hear the smile in Adam's voice as he speaks sweetly to Sarah, "I'm so glad you guys came by."

"Thank you so much, Adam. Is there anything we could help with?" Sarah continues to call into the kitchen.

I shake my head no, knowing she cannot see me, but reply, "Thank you so much, but it's just a few things for dinner." I quickly put away the few things I purchased and return with a pitcher of cold iced tea, and a few cups.

"As promised," I say and begin pouring some for every-one. Sarah gestures towards her sister, and she stands to greet me. The first thing I notice about her sister is that she is attractive. Where Sarah is the epitome of feminine beauty, her sister is attractive in a masculine sort of way. She without question a woman but exudes a masculine aura that I cannot place. Her features, while clearly those of a woman, are also strong and attractive, beautiful even. She towers over me, and with her long hair piled on her head, she seems taller than Adam. She smiles, and my heart leaps. She reaches her hand out to shake my own, and I feel electricity radiate from her hand up my arm. *Safe.* I feel safe suddenly as she touches me. I look into her chocolate brown eyes and see she's fully focused on my own. She looks at me, smiling her beautiful smile, and I blush, deeply. I hear Adam clear his throat and realize we both were standing there looking into each other's eyes for a few moments too long. I slowly pull my own hand back, but Erin continues to hold my hand tight.

"It is so nice to finally meet you, Ashanti. Sarah has mentioned you and your adorable son several times." She says as she continues to hold my hand. Heqet clears her throat, and Erin reluctantly lets go.

"Yes, I uh- I've run into Sarah a few times now, I think." I sit down beside Adam and can feel his irritation with our little scene.

"Yes, we have. I'm so glad I have finally met the whole family. Adam, you've been avoiding the new neighbors."

Her mention of Adam's name distracts him, and he's back to a giggling schoolboy, "No, of course not. I just have a pretty full work schedule. I actually just got back from a work trip this morning, and I'm heading out in a few minutes actually to a conference in Ohio."

I frown at this news, but say nothing, not wanting to upset him in front of the neighbors, "Yes, Adam is practically running the show at his company." I brag for his benefit.

He beams as I say it, "Well, yeah. I've put in a lot of time there."

"That's great!" Sarah says, smiling at us both. Adam looks at his watch.

"Wow, I actually better get going if I plan on making this flight." He stands quickly.

"So soon, honey?" I pout slightly, hoping this approach will work. He kisses my forehead.

"Someone's gotta bring in the big bucks to fund all your hobbies." He smiles at his own joke, "It was really nice meeting you, Sarah, Erin."

"I'll walk you to the door," I say, attempting to get up.

"No, it's fine. You'll have to climb your way out of the couch at this point." I blush with embarrassment at his fat joke, as he grabs his already-packed luggage and leaves once again.

"So..." Sarah says, "How long have you lived here?"

"Oh, it's been just under 6 years now, " I say, "We purchased this home after we found out about our Isaiah. It's a great town to raise a family in."

"Yes, I can tell already just from exploring, lots of young families here," Sarah says.

"Do you like it?" Erin asks, finally speaking again.

"Well, yes, Adam really put a lot of effort into finding our home, and it's not too far from his job. Isaiah loves his school," I try to avoid her eyes. *Why am I so nervous?*

"But what do **you** like about it," she pries deeper.

"Oh, umm, the quiet?" I say, stumbling over my words, "Especially at night, you can see just about every star from the balcony at night. It's peaceful."

"Yes," she says, "I saw last night, it was really beautiful."

I look over at her and see she's staring intently at me. *Is she flirting?* Sarah clears her throat again, "Well, I do believe we have taken up enough of your morning. I think we better get going, we do have a few errands to run."

"Oh, of course. I appreciate the company." I say setting my cup down. I begin rocking back and forth to stand up, "Let me walk you guys out."

Sarah stands and reaches towards me, wiggling her fingers like at the beach. I grab her hand without a fuss and she again, easily pulls me to my feet.

"You really are strong," I say jokingly, as I pull my maternity sweater down to cover my growing stomach. She makes a muscle and laughs.

"It was nice chatting with you, Ashanti." She reaches down and grabs her sister's hand, "we'll have to catch up again sometime."

"Of course. It was nice finally meeting you, Erin."

Erin smiles warmly at me, 'and it was nice meeting you as well."

I spend the rest of the day childishly peeking through the blinds as I busy myself with household chores, hoping to catch a glimpse of Erin again. I roll my eyes at myself after peeking through the blinds for the 100th time. *A silly crush at twenty-nine!* I plop down on the couch, and flick on the TV. Curiosity still getting the better of me, I log into my social media to search for the neighbors. I quickly realize I won't get anywhere without a last name. I laugh at my own silliness and give up, going to get Isaiah.

The rest of the day is completely peaceful. I give in and allow Isaiah to have burgers and fries for dinner, while I make myself a simple alfredo pasta. Afterward, we build blanket forts in the living room, giggling as we make shadow puppets with an old flashlight.

"I like it when it's just you and me, Mommy," Isaiah whispers as we wind down. He's curled up with his blanket facing me, his eyes barely open.

"Yea, why's that, little monster?" I ask, running my hand through his hair.

"Daddy's mean sometimes."

My heart sinks, "Yes baby, I know. Daddy's job just has him a little stressed out lately, and it makes him a little tough. It'll get better soon."

After he falls asleep, I leave him in our fort and sit on the porch. The quiet, cool breeze makes a perfect night, as I lean back on our porch swing, eyes closed, and sway back and forth.

"Are you okay?"

I jump up, startled awake. I look over to see Erin, partially up our stairs leading to the porch, a concerned look on her face.

"Oh!" I giggle nervously," I must have fallen asleep."

"You've been out here for quite some time; we grew a little worried, so I decided to come check on you. I'm sorry if I scared you."

"No, it's fine. Just a tired pregnant lady," I say smiling.

"Glad you're okay then, mind if I?" she points to the seat beside me on the swing.

"Of course," I try my best to move over, giving her space to sit. We sit quietly for a moment, just swinging back and forth, listening to the grasshoppers chirping.

"So, where are you from?" She asks quietly.

"A small place called Reading, Pennsylvania. Have you heard of it?" I ask.

"Actually, yes, I have. I've been there once or twice." She says smiling.

"Really? What would bring you there?"

"We just move a bit; Sarah loves a good adventure."

"I believe she mentioned that to me." I say, "So where are you from originally?"

"Oh originally? A small village near Egypt."

"Wow, Africa?" I say, "How long have you been in the US?"

"Quite some time. Seems like another life I was in that village."

"You weren't kidding about adventures, huh?" I say, thinking of the few places I have been.

"Mommy?" I hear Isaiah call for me from the living room.

"Oh, excuse me a moment," I say and hurry inside. I get Isaiah to bed. Feeling silly as I hurry to the porch, I peek out the door and see Erin, still swinging quietly on the porch.

"Sorry about that," I say as I walk outside.

"No, of course. The little one needs you. He sounds sweet." She smiles, and again, I feel my heart skip a beat.

I smile back at her, "Yes, he is the best kid."

"I hear you're having a girl?" She says, pointing to my belly.

I rub my belly while we swing, "Yes, I hope she's half as sweet as Isaiah."

"I bet she will be. You seem like a great mother. They'll both be great kids."

"Thank you, that means a lot, Erin." The baby begins to kick, and I rub the spot where she kicks.

"Can I?" Erin asks, her hand halfway reaching towards my stomach.

"Sure," I take her hand and ignore the butterflies I feel touching her, and place it on the spot where the kicking has intensified. She sits quietly for a moment, feeling the little kicks.

"Wow, that is really beautiful," she says and looks at my stomach in wonder.

"Isn't it? Women's bodies are amazing, how we can create life."

"I agree," she nods.

"Do you have any children?" I ask. She shakes her head sadly.

"No, not me. My sister, Sarah adores children but unfortunately, she cannot have her own," She explains sadly, still rubbing my belly. She leans in closer, as if she's listening for something, or might speak directly to my stomach, and just stays there. My breath catches with her face so close to my own. She looks up at me, her brown eyes staring deeply into my own. I close my eyes and breathe slowly. Feelings I did not expect stirring within me. *What is happening? I am married, and heavily pregnant.* I talk to myself as I try to calm myself.

"Are you okay?" Erin asks, concerned.

I open my eyes, and she is so close I can feel the warmth radiating from her. I nod wordlessly. Her eyes searching mine, concern showing in the furrow of her brow. I smile to reassure her.

"I am okay."

"Should I go? It's pretty late, I'm sure you need rest?" She says, but does not move.

"Yes," I say quietly, "I guess I should." But neither of us moves. We sit there quietly, staring into each other's eyes, unwilling to move. Finally, she looks away, and slowly gets to her feet.

"I'll help you to the door."

I let her help me to my feet, and I stand in the doorway of our front door as she leans a few inches away.

"It was really nice, talking with you, Ashanti." She says in a voice filled with something I can't quite place.

"You too. I don't get much social interaction over here. It will be nice having a friend."

She nods, "Yes, it will be."

We stay there just another moment before she leans down and kisses my cheek so softly, then turns and walks back to her home across the street as my heart does somersaults in my chest.

Chapter Four – Asim

"Heqet, please!" I say, begging her to stand still for just a moment, as she paces quickly, flashing from one side of the room to the other. "It will be okay. Just stand still so we can discuss—"

"SHE IS WITH CHILD!" Heqet shouts loudly, stopping briefly to face me before returning to her pacing. I stop speaking, shocked. Heqet has not raised her voice in many years. "Can you genuinely not see the danger your actions put her in? She is with child, a mother, and married to a demon of a human. This will not end well if we are not careful. We cannot take unnecessary risks."

"I am aware of the dangers, Heqet, truly. It was just one night. She *IS* human. She has already forgotten, I'm sure," I say quietly, my heart aching, hoping my words prove untrue. Heqet stops pacing long enough to face me so I can witness her expression of annoyance as she rolls her catlike eyes.

"Do not insult my intelligence, Asim; she has watched this house relentlessly. Her blinds have a dent where she has peeked through them every hour. She has not forgotten."

I smile at the confirmation of Ashanti's interest, "You think so?"

"ASIM!" Heqet says exasperated. She flops down on our couch and rubs her temples to emphasize her frustration.

"I thought you wanted me to pursue it?" I say, annoyed by her unusual pessimism.

"I thought we would take our time. Her husband is dangerous to her. Let us not antagonize him."

A low growl escaped my lips at the thought of him harming her. Heqet ignores it and continues, "This vile human male is important to her."

I sigh deeply, "Yes, yes, no harm, no killing," I say, tired of the conversation. "I won't bother her, Heqet. I'll be an angel." It's a lie, which, of course, Heqet immediately sees though. It is her turn to sigh deeply, the frown so deep it seems permanently etched on her face.

"Asim, I know you are finally interested in humanity again, or at least *this* human. I am grateful nevertheless; our ancestors have finally answered my many prayers. But we must move slowly, and rationally. She is married, heavily pregnant, and in danger." She looks me in the eyes, unmoved by my growls.

"I can simply remove the danger," I say quietly, just below a whisper. Heqet pauses patiently, "And how will this human respond to the death of her husband? Do you think she will think you a hero? Her savior?" She asks me. I sit quietly, thinking of Ashanti crying, holding Adam's lifeless hand, hysterical.

"It was one night. One conversation," I say.

"You think me a fool? I have been your companion for many centuries, millennia; I feel the shift in your energy. I see the look in your eyes. We are different. We are intense creatures. I beg of you, please. Let us move slowly. For the sake of the children."

I nod in agreement and lay back on the recliner, eyes closed, defeated. She sits quietly for a few moments.

"Good. Thank you," she says finally, "I will leave you to your thoughts."

I listen as she quickly flashes upstairs into her bedroom. I know, as always, Heqet is right. I must move carefully. Ashanti is unaware of my world. There are small children involved. As easy as it would be to remove Adam, Ashanti surely would not respond with joy to the murder of her husband. I look out the window and listen to her home. She's playing with Isaiah, water splashing. It must be bath time. I continue to listen in as he laughs hysterically, as she makes animal noises. I picture her kneeling next to the small bathtub, smiling. The image frustrates me in ways I cannot describe. I listen in, finding the third heartbeat away from the mother and son. I listen to his snores and the sound of the television near him. I picture him drunkenly, sprawled across the couch, watching his movie, feet propped up in his recliner. Resting peacefully, while his heavily pregnant wife is on her knees trying to wrangle a small human in a bathtub. Atrocious. *She* should be resting. I eavesdrop this way, listening intently into their home for hours. I listen as Ashanti lovingly reads Isaiah a bedtime story, a classic story about three bears and an entitled golden-haired child. She patiently answers his never-ending questions. I listen to her step into her shower, as she whispers her prayers to her ancestors. My heart soars, knowing she is also spiritual and knows to honor the elders before her. My pride in her knowledge is interrupted as Adam stirs from his place on the couch. I listen to him drunkenly call for Ashanti and make his way up the stairs when she does not respond. He falls on his way up and curses the stairs as if it is its fault for his misstep. He makes his way into the bathroom, Ashanti's quiet gasp of surprise as he opens the door. I stand quickly as I hear his quiet murmurs and drunken kisses. I take off running, unable to listen to this intimate moment between the two. I picture him touching her as I run and immediately push the thought from my head; instead, I focus on ways I can remove him from this world. From *her* world.

I concentrate on this as I run aimlessly through the woods, planning every minuscule detail, until I can feel his blood on my hands. Smiling broadly, I hunt.

I return home long after Ashanti has gone to sleep, I walk into our home to find Heqet sitting in the living room, surrounded by more piles of books she has found. She looks at me, confused by my mood—a mixture of anger and happiness from planning my adversary's death. She no doubt had heard the very moments I fled to avoid.

"I'm okay," I say, smiling as convincingly as I can muster, drawing on thousands of years of practice. She smiles back at me, seeing through my act.

"What have you been up to tonight?"

"Just running to clear my mind, hunting," I say as nonchalantly as I can.

"Anything exciting?"

"Not at all, " I say, plopping down on the recliner across from her. She immediately puts her book down and smiles excitedly at me.

"Let me tell you all I have learned about the townspeople." Her eyes light up with excitement as she feels me in on trivial gossip. I listen and show interest where needed, not particularly interested in the gossip or townspeople...

"And let me tell you this! Apparently, Adam, Mr. Narcissist over there..." I sit up and listen intently; all things Ashanti interest me, infatuated in ways similar to a teenager and her first crush. It could consume me. "I heard the women in that café downtown, yes, they were going on and on about a tall blonde that lives right outside of town. They frequently see Adam with her."

I knew he was unfaithful. I knew it from the moment I saw him drunkenly falling into his home, before I laid eyes on Ashanti. He just seemed the type. Combine that knowledge with him never being home, and it's almost obvious. I frown, poor Ashanti.

"Yes, apparently, she was a client of his. Some big-shot heiress or something. She owns a few beauty salons and hired his company for advertisement. It's been going on for years!" Heqet says this with disgust dripping in her tone. "What a vile man."

She continues with her gossip, and I listen as I always do. She describes infidelities, corrupt politics, teenage pregnancies, and scandalous flings. She loves humanity, so much so that even their flaws excite her. We sit this way for hours, her describing individual residents and their troubles or successes, and I add my adlibs or questions to encourage her to tell me more. We speak of our many past lives and experiences we've shared, laughing at careless mistakes, having a much-needed girls' night.

"Heqet?" I say hours later as we sit quietly. Heqet is reading a stack of the town's history books, flipping through the pages quickly. She pauses briefly to look over at me when I do not continue.

"Do you think she would accept it? – Our world, I mean," I ask quietly. Her expression softens as she considers my question. A few endless moments pass as I sit, hoping she'll say the words I want to hear, but knowing Heqet will only ever tell me what I *need* to hear.

"I cannot predict humans; by nature, they are sporadic, spontaneous, irrational. One may accept our world, settling naturally into it even, while another may go mad with just the thought of the supernatural being a reality. The only guarantee we are given in this torturous eternity is if we do not pursue our dreams, our deepest desires, then *Never* will always be our prison. We fail what we do not attempt every single time. Ashanti seems intelligent, kind, and patient. She has lived a short, painful life, met monsters scarier than those her kind are unaware of lurking in the shadows, and she has loved them.

You, my beautiful sister, are no monster. You are worthy of the deepest love, the happily ever after kind of love. I pray to the ancestors this is that love for you."

I close my eyes, trying to will the universe to give me this one thing. So many lifetimes sacrificed in the name of our ancestors. Allow me this one gift. In my focus of manifestation, I slip into a deep sleep-like state. A large barren field surrounds me, grey skies as always. The quiet swallows me whole. I lay still, eyes closed, picturing Ashanti with me in this place, but it does not fit. Surely this field would be filled with flowers, sunflowers as far as one could see, bright sunny skies, and pretty butterflies fluttering about. That picture would be more befitting for my Ashanti. I smile as I picture us, hand and hand, walking through the sunflower fields, the sun shining on her pretty face.

"My child."

The words cut through the air like a sword. My eyes pop open, and I sit straight up, immediately recognizing the voice as though I heard it yesterday rather than centuries ago.

"Mother?" I call, looking around for the source of the voice. I spot her sitting beneath an unfruitful tree, on an overgrown root. Her long dreads braided on top of her head in a crown, small and frail in stature, her beautiful face full of wisdom, shown in the wrinkles deeply etched in her face. I run to her instantly, dropping to my knees, head in her lap, tears streaming endlessly down my face. "Mother," I whisper once again, relief traced in the word. "How I've missed you! So many centuries come and gone since you've visited me last. Why have you abandoned me?"

"Hush, child," my mother says gently in our native tongue. She affectionately wipes the tears from my eyes and raises my head to peer into my eyes. "Come walk with me." She stands, and holds out a small, wrinkled hand, in a way a mother would for a small child. I eagerly hold on to that hand as if my life depended on it. So many centuries without her in this barren land. My heart could implode at this moment, looking down at my mother's face, feeling the touch of her hand once again.

"I've missed you," I say again, as she pats my hand.

"And I, you—" she says walking slowly with her walking stick. I frown at this.

"Mother, with so many forms you can take in this realm, you prefer to age?"

"Age is a gift; have you not come to understand this lesson as well."

I nod quietly, thinking of Ashanti, how in time she will age, perish, and I will remain unchanging.

"You have grown quite attached to this girl," my mother says, as she stops at a tree, lifeless, and greying, quietly inspecting it.

"Yes, this human is special, Mother," I say, watching her intently examining the tree.

"How so?" She asks, focusing on the roots of the tree, pacing around it, periodically touching one.

"Umm, she gives me hope. I feel that deep desire to protect. I feel alive again near her."

"Hmmm," she mumbles, now focused on a low branch.

"What are you doing?" I ask, frustrated, 'We have not spoken in many years, Mother, yet your focus is a tree?"

She ignores my question, simply sucking her teeth as if I frustrate her, and continuing her inspection, now completing a second circle around this tree.

"Where do you think you are?" She asks me suddenly.

I look around; as long as I can remember, I have known this realm as the final resting place of our ancestors. I remember back to my earliest years finding this place, and my ancestors referring to it as "the resting place."

"It is the final resting place of our people," I say confidently, confused by the question. She sucks her teeth once again.

"You think yourself so powerful that you can drain the life of the sacred resting place?" She looks at me in disbelief, then looks back to the tree.

I pause, "I brought dishonor to our people, abandoned my purpose." I whisper the words, ashamed of admitting this to my mother."

She stops her inspection then, turning to look me in the eyes, "Oh sweet child. Come." She pats a large overgrown root, and we sit together side by side as she holds my hand in her own.

"Mother, what is this place? I remember being told it was the resting place."

"It is *YOUR* resting place, child. The burden of eternity is great. The ancestors granted you the mercy of rest long ago. What you see here is not dishonor. It is heartbreak. Your heartbreak, dear. Your family has never abandoned you. We watch you carefully. We have all fallen off our path, stumbled, given into our anger. You have shut us out for so long, child. You are still The Great Asim, Protector of Women, The Warrior. Eternity is so extraordinarily long, child. You were granted the gift of immortality, strength, speed, so many gifts, but perfection was not one of those gifts. Mistakes are important. They teach us life lessons; that words would never explain. I know your heart aches from loss of love, loss of family, and the disappointment you have experienced from the very ones you are meant to protect. It shows in the barren trees and lifeless grass. But you must heal. You must carry on with your purpose. Your gifts come with a heavy burden, my heart. Loving humanity and watching so many move on to their final resting place. But this is your destiny. I've prayed for joy in your life. Now this special woman appears." She smiles slyly at the last part, as if she's in on a secret I do not know.

"What is it, mother?" I ask wearily, remembering that smile from so many, many years ago.

"Nothing, child," she waves off my question as stands, staring up at the trees, "I cannot reveal all secrets tonight." She nods, with a knowing smile, "Yes, you will be fine."

"Are you sure?" I ask worried, hoping for my mother's reassurance, her comfort. I watch her smiling, facing the gray sky, under the dead tree, "Yes, love, I am sure." She nods towards the tree, and a single flower has blossomed. I stare at it, so far up and small I take a moment to understand what I am looking at.

"Mother?" I say hopefully, looking back towards her, but she's gone once again, a single sunflower in her place.

Chapter Five – Ashanti

"Pass Mommy the apples," I say watching Isaiah struggle happily carrying the bowl of freshly peeled green apples. He smiles brightly as he makes it to me without dropping it.

"So strong," I say cheering him on. It's another quiet night for us with Adam gone on an extended business trip, again. We busy ourselves making dinner and dessert: homemade mashed potatoes, pot roast, and apple pie for dessert. A knock on the door interrupts our chaos, and I quickly check to see who it could be.

"Erin?" I say, unable to hide my surprise as I open the door. She stands there awkwardly, half-smiling at me.

"Hey..." She says simply.

"Umm, hey, how are you?" I ask, suddenly nervous for some reason.

"Me and Sarah were at the market, and we came across this, and thought of you." She holds up a bottle of what looks like wine, with a pregnant belly on the label.

"Wine?" I ask, smiling,

She smiles in response to my smile, "Yes, it's umm, alcohol-free wine, for pregnant women." She points to the label where it says alcohol-free, "I thought you might like it."

The pit of my stomach warms and tingles in response to her thinking of me, "Oh! How thoughtful! Thank you!"

"I see you're cooking. It smells wonderful; I'm sorry to interrupt." She says apologetically, handing me the bottle.

"Oh, no it's okay. Ummm, would you like to join us?" I offer, holding up the bottle, "I'll share." We both laugh.

"Sure, " she says, smiling widely. My heartbeat quickens at the sight. As I step back to allow her to enter, I catch my reflection in the mirror on the wall. I'm covered in flour and random food bits. My hair is in a loose, messy bun, tangled at the top of my head. I blush in horror and try to brush the flour from my clothing.

"You look lovely, " she says suddenly. I look up and see she's watching me, making me blush deeper. I tuck a loose piece of hair behind my ear nervously.

"Thank you," I say, trying to ignore the zoo now doing flips in my stomach.

"I, uh, I hope I'm not intruding," she says, following me to the kitchen.

"Oh, no, it's no bother; my son Isaiah is helping me cook, " I say as we enter the kitchen. Isaiah looks up and smiles at us, his mouth full of apples.

"Are you sneaking apples?" I say and tickle him. He squeals and struggles to get away, "Miss Erin, wanted to join us for dinner, is that okay with you?"

He nods and smiles at her, "Yes, ma'am."

"Hi, little guy!" Erin says cheerfully, reaching out to fist bump Isaiah, who happily bumps his fist to hers.

"Hi!" He turns to me, "Momma, can I go play now?"

"You don't want to help me anymore?"

He shakes his head quickly, "I want to play."

I ruffle his hair, "Fine, go play, love."

He takes off running, without hesitation, upstairs. Erin chuckles as the sound of his little feet fades.

"I guess I'm on my own," I laugh. She rolls up her sleeves.

"I can help."

I smile, "You can cook?"

"Oh, I've been in a kitchen or two. I'm sure I can keep up," she says with a smile. She casually walks over to the sink and washes her hands, turning to face me, "So what are we cooking, boss?" She asks with a smile.

Our eyes lock, and we stand there, smiling at each other for much longer than we should. I break away first, picking up the apples.

"Umm, so we were making apple pie, the pot roast is already in the oven, " I say, focusing on the bowl of apples.

"I love to bake!" She says, taking the apples from me, "Why don't you sit down, and I'll prepare the pie?"

"Really?" I ask, surprised. She points to the barstools pulled up to the kitchen island.

"Please, relax, I've got this, " she says and begins cutting up the apples in the bowl.

"You're the best!" I say, struggling to pull myself up onto the high barstool.

"Thank you!" She says, beaming at my compliment, "How are you feeling?"

"Like an overstuffed meatball." I sigh, rubbing my belly.

She laughs at my comment, "Well, you are carrying very well. I'm amazed at how busy you keep yourself."

"What do you mean," I laugh, "You barely have visited me. I've been so lazy around here."

She laughs, "You're right. I just assumed you keep busy because your house is so spotless," she explains.

"Oh, thank you. Isaiah has been super helpful with cleaning up behind himself. He's a great kid. I'm lucky." I say, smiling at the thought of my little guy.

"Yeah, I can tell. He's so smart!" She says, smiling at me. *Butterflies.*

"Ummm, so how about you? How are you feeling?" I ask.

"I'm having a great night." She says, still smiling. I laugh.

"Of course, I mean, I am great company," I say sarcastically.

"You really are."

I blush and look down at the placemat in front of me. Using my finger, I start tracing the design on the mat to avoid eye contact.

"But really, I am having a wonderful week. I reconnected with a relative I haven't spoken to in quite some time, " she says, "We got to catch up, and she gave me great advice."

"Really? That's so great! Family is so important."

"I believe the same." She smiles to herself as she begins pouring flour into a bowl.

"Oh, I have pie crust," I point to the store-bought premade dough. She shakes her head instantly.

"No, I'm going to make it from scratch," she says, smiling.

"Really? You don't have to go out of your way."

"In all of my time, I have never used premade dough. I will not start tonight, especially when I'm baking for you!"

I smile at her comment, " All of my time? You speak as though you are sooo much older than me. You can't be more than 30."

"You'd be surprised. What is the saying? Black doesn't crack?"

We laugh together briefly, and I again try to guess her age.

"Seriously, how old are you? 31?" I ask, genuinely curious. She doesn't look old enough to even be in her 30s.

" I'm ancient." She smiles at her own joke.

"Okay, okay. I guess never ask a woman her age, right?" I say, giving up.

"Just know I'm grown." She says and winks at me with a mischievous smile, sending tingles up and down my spine.

"Mmm-hmm, I manage to murmur.

I sit and watch her bake, and we casually talk about our favorite things and future goals. I watch in amazement at her baking skills. She never measures anything and whirls around the kitchen with ease. When it's time to eat, she insists on making both myself and Isaiah's plates.

"Mmmmm, mommy this is good!" Isaiah says in between big bites of pie. I wipe some filling off his cheek.

"Miss Erin made it all from scratch!"

He looks at her with big eyes, "I love it,"

She smiles at him brightly, "Well, that means so much to me! Wait until you taste my pecan pie!"

He lights up at the offer of more pie and continues scarfing down his dessert.

"Slow down!" I say laughing. She reaches over and pours more of the alcohol-free wine into my wine glass and lifts her glass as if saying cheers. We continue chatting while we eat, Erin telling jokes to Isaiah as he laughs happily at the silliness. As I sit and watch their interactions, I can't help but to compare the stark contrast of this happy care-free little Angel, laughing and talking to our normal family dinners. I look at Erin, or *Rinny* as Isaiah began calling her at some point during dinner, and smile, grateful for this moment of peace she has brought us, even if it only lasts for the night.

After dinner, I take Isaiah upstairs to clean him up and settle him into bed.

"Mommy?" He says sleepily, as I tuck him into bed.

"Yes, my love?"

"I like Miss Erin. She's funny, and she makes the best food."

I smile at him and smooth his curly hair, "Do you now?"

He nods and pulls his blanket up to his chin.

"Well, I love you!" I say touching the tip of his nose.

"I love you too Mommy."

"Goodnight." I kiss his cheek and turn on his nightlight before leaving his room to join Erin, who's waiting for him downstairs.

"Have I been upstairs that long?" I ask astonished by the clean kitchen, "You cleaned everything?"

"Well, I wanted to keep busy while I waited and help out."

"Wow, you finished so fast! You really didn't have to do that!"

"I'm pretty fast." She says smiling.

"Sarah's strong, you're fast. Your parents must have been superheroes."

She laughs at this, while she dries her hands on a kitchen towel.

"You keep this up, and I may have to kidnap you!" I say laughing. She grabs two wine glasses and walks to the porch, and I follow. She helps me onto the porch swing, and we sit together, swinging in the quiet night.

"Are you close to your parents?" She asks.

"I was close to my father. He passed when I was young. My mother passed when I was born, " I explain.

"Do you have siblings?'

"No," I say simply. She sits quietly with this information before saying, " I'm sorry you experienced tragedy so young."

I look at her as she stares up into the sky, a thoughtful expression on her face. She looks sad, I realize. I reach over and hold her hand in my own.

"I have a feeling we have that in common, huh?" I say as I hold her hand a little tighter. She looks down at me and smiles as she pats my hand, " I'm afraid so."

We sit in silence for a while, thinking of our own traumas and enjoying each other's company. After a while, she looks toward her house, as if she heard something.

"I didn't realize how late it has gotten, " she says as she stands up.

"Oh, I guess it has, " I say not able to hide the sadness in my voice at the thought of her leaving. I bite my lip, pregnancy hormones threatening to make me cry. She smiles at me, and my insides warm again.

"I'll come visit soon." She reassures me, making me smile brightly.

"Promise?" I ask, childishly but unashamed in the moment. She laughs at this and nods.

"Promise."

She hesitates for a moment, and I think she might kiss me, but she instead waves gently and jogs over to her home. *Why do I feel so sad she didn't try?* I try to shake off my complicated feelings and push them to the back of my mind as I head inside to shower.

Once I'm in the shower, I can't help but think about Erin. I would be in denial to say I don't find her attractive. I have never found myself attractive to women before, but

I haven't had much experience outside of Adam with love. I was just trying to survive in my youth when most people were figuring themselves out. I think of Erin's smile and how perfect her hand felt holding mine, how I wanted to soothe her worries when she suddenly looked sad. Isaiah's happy face and carefree laugh cross my mind. He was so happy today. Genuinely happy. *Maybe staying with Adam is the wrong choice?* No, I'm being silly. Erin could just see me as a friend. Her only friend in the neighborhood, and I'm any day away from giving birth. It's just a silly crush. I laugh at my silliness as I shower and climb into bed, but it's Erin's face I fall asleep thinking about.

"Mommy!" I open my eyes to see Isaiah standing next to my bed, covered in red marker.

"Isaiah..." I say as I rub the sleep from my eyes, "What have you gotten into?"

"I painted you a picture." He says, clearly proud of himself, "Come see."

I climb out of bed and follow my now red child into his room, where he shows me the 30 pictures he drew all scattered around his floor. I look at the clock hanging in the hallway.

"Baby, it's 6:00 am... how long have you been awake?" I ask, still half asleep.

"I woke up before the sun." He says proudly.

"Okay, let's go brush our teeth, huh?"

I help him brush his teeth, wash the red marker off of him, and get him and myself ready for the day. I try Adam's cell, as we eat our cereal, but he does not answer.

"Well, it's Saturday, so how about we make it a park day?"

"YES!" Isaiah spoons his last bite of marshmallow cereal into his mouth before running to get his favorite toys and his shoes. I pack a few drinks and snacks, and we hurry out of the house.

"Heading on an adventure?"

I look up to see Erin and Sarah walking past our home. I smile too widely at them and scold myself silently for looking so eager.

"Just heading to the park," I say, as Isaiah happily shows them his plastic dinosaur.

"We were actually just going on a walk, can we tag along?" Sarah asks, smiling at Isaiah.

"Sure, it might be a little boring though, just a bunch of kids running around."

"Oh, I don't mind, I love children," she says reassuringly. We walk as a group, Erin walking beside me. Sarah holding Isaiah's hand and pointing out birds and butterflies.

"So how are you feeling today?" Erin asks, taking the bag I packed from me to carry.

"Thank you! I'm okay, my energy is a little low today so I figured a day at the park would tire little man out." We both watch Sarah and Isaiah now chasing a butterfly.

"She's really good with kids." I say smiling.

"Yeah, she's had a way with kids as far back as I can remember," Erin says with a smile.

We reach the neighborhood park, and Isaiah runs off to play on the slide. Sarah, Erin, and I sit facing him on a nearby bench.

"Miss Sarah, look at me!" Isaiah yells climbing down a ladder.

"Wowwww!" She says loudly, walking over to praise him.

"Isaiah seems to have taken a liking to Sarah," I say watching as she encourages him to climb back up the ladder.

"Yup, she's like a child whisperer, " Erin laughs, "Never met a kid she hasn't won over."

I rub my belly as the baby kicks repeatedly, " I guess someone woke up."

"Do you mind?" She asks, hand outstretched.

"Oh, no, go ahead," I say, blushing for some reason. She gently places her hand on my belly, exactly where the baby is. She smiles happily as she feels the kicks, one after another.

"Amazing, " she says, looking at me in awe. I feel my pulse quicken, and my insides melt in response to her stare. Erin smiles, and I quickly look down. *Am I blushing?*

"You are quite beautiful," she says. I look up to see she's still looking at me with that look of awe.

"Thank you, I find you to be beautiful as well, " I say shyly. She smiles widely at my statement, making me wonder if she feels the chemistry between us too, " Can I ask you something?"

"Of course."

"Umm, do you... do you like women? Romantically, I mean, " I ask, blushing from embarrassment at my question.

She gently removes her hand from my belly and straightens, looking at Isaiah and Sarah playing, "Would that make you uncomfortable if I do?"

"No, no... I'm sorry; I didn't mean it to sound that way. I'm very open-minded about that sort of thing. I mean I... Well, I don't mind who you love. I know everyone around here isn't as open to that sort of thing, definitely not Adam... I mean I had.... well, I think..." I wring my hands in embarrassment, " Ugh, no, it does not make me uncomfortable, " I finally say and look down again.

"Have you ever found a woman attractive? In a romantic way, I mean, " she asks me, repeating my question back to me. My cheeks burn red.

"Not until recently, " I say staring intently at my feet. She remains quiet, and I look up to see her sitting quietly, staring up at the sky, thoughtfully.

"Do you find me attractive?" I finally ask after a few agonizing moments of quiet. I avoid looking at her, afraid of her answer. *Why did I ask that?*

She cups her hand under my chin, gently forcing me to look into her eyes, "I find you to be the most attractive woman I have met in a very, very, long time."

My entire body melts into a puddle, and my breathing nearly stops. All I can think of for the moment is she is attracted to *me*. She lets go of my chin after a moment. She opens her mouth to say something but stops suddenly.

"Mommy! Look! Look!" Isaiah screams as he runs up to me excitedly, something in his clenched fist. I quickly turn my attention to the wide-eyed, smiling child running to me.

"What is that?" I ask smiling brightly, arms outstretched. As he gets closer, my smile turns to open-mouthed horror, " A frog?!"

Erin, recognizing my fear, jumps up and intercepts Isaiah, distracting him with her own excitement.

"Oh, my goodness! That's a huge frog!" She says, kneeling in front of him, " Did you catch that on your own?"

"Yup, Sarah showed me how!" He says, smiling and looking back at Sarah happily.

"He's a fast learner." She says, smiling back at him.

"Can I keep it, Mommy?" He asks in his sweetest voice. I cringe.

"Well, what if he has a family? We wouldn't want to make them worry, would we?" Sarah says, winking at me.

"Oh, yeah! We should put him back! His mommy might miss him." He grabs Sarah's hand and pulls her back to the grass they caught the frog in.

"So, frogs huh?" Erin says with a soft laugh.

"Anything slimy!" I say, shuddering with disgust.

"So, no pet snakes?" She laughs.

"Abso-fuckin-lutely not." I laugh.

"Somebody's hungry," Sarah says as she and Isaiah walk up to us together. I sanitize and wipe his hands and pass it around to everyone.

"I've made sandwiches; there's enough to share?" I offer the sandwich to Sarah and Erin, but they shake their heads no.

"Oh no, we have a big dinner planned tonight, gotta save some room," Sarah says with her comforting smile.

"Oh, going out?" I ask, wiping crumbs from Isaiah's face.

"No, I'm making dinner at home tonight." Sarah says, kneeling beside Isaiah to help me as I struggle to bend over to clean him, "Wow, Isaiah, aren't you a messy eater, huh? Is it good?"

Isaiah laughs as she wipes his mouth for me.

"Thank you so much, Sarah. You really have been a huge help today," I say. She shakes her head and waves off my thanks.

"Oh no, I love kids, really, and we are neighbors. We should look out for each other, right? Don't mention it, " she says ruffling Isaiah's hair, "plus this little guy is awesome sauce."

Isaiah beams up at her compliment, "Awesome sauce?"

She leans down and smiles at him, "The most awesomest sauce of all awesome sauce." She fists bumps him, and he can barely contain his thrill at her compliment.

"Well, you are a saint; he adores you."

"He's the coolest, like his momma, huh?" Erin high-fives him, as he nods in agreement. I smile at Erin and Isaiah. He really is a different child away from Adam. With Adam gone so often, Isaiah seems to be just a carefree little boy, and I genuinely feel happy. Erin and Sarah really bring so much peace to our family. I remember praying to the ancestors after Adam and I had a huge fight not so long ago. *Is this their answer? My new friends?* Erin turns and smiles, one of her knee-weakening smiles. My new *love*?

"You, okay?" Erin asks, concern showing on her wrinkled brow. I nod yes and smile.

"Just a little tired, I guess." She frowns before she straightens up and puts Isaiah on her shoulders. He immediately starts giggling and holding his arms out as if he's a plane.

"Look, Mommy, I'm so high."

"I see, please be careful, " I say, reaching for him. Erin shakes her head quickly.

"Don't worry, pretty eyes, I got him," she says, and something about her little nickname sends tingles through me once again, "why don't we head back? Sarah makes great lemonade. "

"I love lemonade!" Isaiah squeals, smiling at Sarah.

"You do?! Well, I make the best lemonade in the world. Or at least that's what I've been told." She laughs as she gently elbows Erin. Erin laughs with her, and Sarah grabs my bag.

"Come on, Momma, " she says, reaching out a hand to help me up. She pulls me up without hesitation, and I am still amazed at her strength. She's inches shorter than me and has such a tiny frame— *how?* I'm still thinking about her unusual strength when she loops her arm through mine, and we start the slow walk back home. Erin and Isaiah have a foot race down the block, while Sarah chats with me about nursey ideas. It feels perfect in that moment. My life which had been filled with so much turmoil lately felt absolutely perfect for a moment. I smile and discuss monkeys vs turtles. We share a laugh, and I look up, and my world stops. I see a car swerving towards us. It's going too fast. I realize it's my car, and at the same time, I make out Adam's angry face in the driver's seat. He's home early, and drunk.

"I have to go," I say quickly, removing my arm from Sarah's arm. Erin, is firmly holding Isaiah's hand, staring straight at Adam approaching. I quickly reach Isaiah, " Hey little guy. It looks like Daddy made it home."

For just a second, fear dances across his eyes, and my heart breaks. Before I can comfort him, I hear the tires screech to a stop behind me.

"Why aren't you home?!" Adam yells, before he's even out of the car. His slurred speech confirms he's drunk. I breathe in and exhale before planting a fake, wide smile on my face.

"Honey? I'm so happy you made it back early! I just took Isaiah to the park. I would have cooked if I knew you were coming home!" I quickly hug him. He swats me away.

"Yeah, well, I came home hungry, so let's get it going."

"Hello, Adam," Sarah says smiling, but this time something about her smile scares me. She looks like she could kill him, or rather she's debating it. Adam, oblivious, smiles and sways up to her, pulling her into a much too-tight hug. I look away embarrassed. Sarah clears her throat and politely untangles herself from Adam's hug, " I offered to cook tonight for your family. I hope that's okay?"

Adam brightens up, "Of course, I'd love to have a beautiful woman in my kitchen."

I see Erin take a step towards Adam but stop herself, before turning to Isaiah, " Hey kiddo, why don't we race the rest of the way there?"

Isaiah lights up and nods in agreement.

"No, I can drive my son home, " Adam says, glaring at Erin.

"It's only half a block. I don't mind, " Erin says tightly.

"No, don't you have your own kid or something?" Adam says, "Isaiah, come here now."

Isaiah looks sadly at Erin, then slowly jogs to Adam.

"Honey, He was having so much fun, couldn't he just--"

"SHUT UP" Adam yells in my face, making Erin react in a way I didn't expect. She walks straight up to Adam, close enough that she leans down and whispers something to him. I'm close enough to touch her but I can't make out what she's saying in her low whisper. I watch as Adam stiffens before whispering something back to her. His stance changes. He stands up straight before removing his hand from Isaiah's shoulder.

"I think Isaiah should jog. It's better, " he says simply, then turns and gets back into the car.

"Adam? Are you okay?" I ask, shocked by his sudden change. He ignores me and just drives off. I watch him drive the opposite way he just came from, confused. I turn to ask Erin what she said, but I notice Sarah and her staring intensely at each other. I watch their silent exchange before Sarah quickly turns to me and smiles.

"Well, that was eventful, " she says, " I guess he decided to go calm down maybe?"

I look from her to Erin, who is seething, her face contorted into something I can only describe as pure fury, while Sarah takes Isaiah's hand and begins walking towards our home.

"I'm sorry; I thought he would be out of town today. I should have sent him a text... He just worries when he doesn't know where we are, " I say as apologetic as I can, praying he didn't just scare off the only friends I have. Erin flinches, then looks at me with soft eyes, so sad. My heart aches. She walks up to me, close enough I want to reach up and touch her frowning lips. She stares into my eyes for a moment, then closes her eyes and exhales, before opening them again.

"Ashanti," she says, and my heart leaps hearing my name come from her lips, " Please, do not apologize for his actions. Nothing you could ever do would warrant such vile behavior. You are the closest to perfection I have ever met. Sometimes people are cruel, and there is no reason for it." She tucks a loose strand of hair behind my ear before tilting my chin up to look me in my eyes and smile.

"You calm my spirit, " she says it simply, but the magnitude of those words sears deeply into my heart. She takes my hand without hesitation and leads me to my home, and I can't help but to feel safe with her fingers twined around my own.

Chapter Six – Adam

"You promised me, Adam," Helen pouts and tosses her long blond hair over her exposed shoulder. I look over at her, young and beautiful, her soft cream- color skin flawless. The money I spent enhancing her lips, breasts, and behind was money well spent. Her shape is similar to that of a 90s video vixen, her straight long blonde hair cascading down her back. I toss my own dreads out of my face and smile brightly at her.

"Baby, come on. I can't leave her now. You know she makes me look good down at the office with all those old family men. She's about to have my child. What about Isaiah?" I reach for her, and she pulls away, folding her arms like a spoiled child.

"But it's been so many years now, and you're always here anyway. Why can't you stay? Isaiah would love me!" She pouts again.

"I know, baby, he will love you. I just have to get rid of my wife, *AFTER* she has the baby, and it'll be me, you, and the kids, just like I promised." I say, reaching for her again. She smiles, finally done with her tantrum, and throws her arms around my neck, pressing her naked body close to mine.

"I'm so excited! I hope it's a girl! I want to wear matching outfits."

I nod, "Yeah, babe, that'll be great. Now come take care of me." I push her head under the blanket and lay back.

My phone rings loudly, bringing me out of my sleep. The morning sun peeking through our curtains, telling me I overslept.

"Yeah," I answer, tossing Helen's arm off of me as I get up, pulling my boxers on.

"Umm, good morning, Adam. It's uh Brady. You know, from down the street. You had uh asked me to keep an eye out on your home... remember... uh, in case anyone suspicious was hanging around."

I roll my eyes as I pull up my sweats. *What is this idiot going on about?* "Yeah, Brady, I remember you. We have been neighbors for a while now. What's going on?"

"Oh, yes, of course. I was just worried because we don't really get to hang out, like you suggested. You know I found a great golfing spot just out of town. I thought--"

"Brady, my house?"

"Oh yeah, sorry. Well, I didn't want to say anything, because, you know. I know you and your wife have a very loving relationship. But, uh, those sisters across the street. You know, the short one with the curves and the pretty eyes? I mean, the curves on that one, eh-"

"Brady, I'm kinda in a rush. I know the sisters, Sarah, and, uh, Ellen."

"Oh, yeah, sorry. Well, the shorter one, she's been introducing herself to everyone in the neighborhood, real nice. But the taller one, she's been kinda friendly with your wife, and, you know, I think she's *gay.* Now, you know I'm not phobic or anything. Everyone can do what makes them happy, but we don't see that much in our town so--"

I clench my teeth; this idiot is going to make me snap. "Friendly how?"

"Oh, yeah, well, I've seen her talking to your wife out on the porch, and I swore she went inside one night, and stayed a while, *without* her sister, and just now, I saw the whole lot of them, with your son heading to the family park at the end of the street here."

"Just now?"

"Yep, they were walking and laughing together."

"Okay, thanks."

"So, about that golf day-"

I end the call, and throw on my sweater, and retrieve my travel bag still in the trunk, maintaining the story of a last-minute conference I told Ashanti. Helen is still fast asleep. I write a quick "I love you note," and send my secretary a text to have flowers delivered, then start the drive back home. It takes about an hour, given the speed I drive, to make it home. I swing by the park, but don't see anyone due to the dense trees lining the street. Pulling into my drive-way, I take a quick hit of the coke conveniently stored in my armrest. I jog up the stairs, open my door, and, as Brady stated, the house is empty.

I crack open a bottle of whisky and take a few chugs, walking around examining my home. The dishwasher is full of unloaded dishes, and her hair products line the bath-room sink. *This hoe thinks she can cheat with some dike bitch after I pulled her out of the gutter?!* My fury rises as I take a few more sips from my bottle. I look at the clock, realizing another hour has passed. I set the bottle on the counter and grab my keys.

As I speed to the park, I see my son, laughing and running with the he she, or whatever it is, and my wife arm-and-arm with Sarah. *So, she thinks she can make alliances to leave me?* Probably told Sarah all kinds of nonsense to turn her against me. *I'll show them how crazy and useless you are. No one's going to need you. I worked too hard getting those stupid ideas out of her head.* She spots me and drops arms with Sarah, reaching for Isaiah. *Too late. You're caught!* I pull up beside her and get out of the car.

"Why aren't you home?" I ask as calmly as I can. I observe her fake smile spreading across her clearly guilty face.

"Honey! I'm so glad you made it back early. I just took Isaiah to the park. I would have cooked if I knew you were coming home." She tries to hug me, but I push her away from me.

"Yeah, well I'm hungry. So, let's get it going."

"Hello, Adam."

I turn towards Sarah, offering a smile as she reciprocates with her best one. My eyes immediately roam over her petite figure, and I pull her into a hug, needing to feel the contours of her body against mine. We embrace for what feels like forever until she reluctantly pulls away.

"I offered to cook dinner tonight, for your family. I hope that's okay?"

I imagine her bent over my kitchen counter, my hand over her mouth, " Of, course, I'd love to have a beautiful woman in my kitchen." I wink at her, and I swear she blushes.

"Hey kiddo, why don't we race the rest of the way there?"

I look back to see the tall, muscular woman smiling at my only son. Fury rips through me again. *Who the fuck does this clown think she is?*

"No, I can drive *my* son home." I assert. She looks at me as if I annoy her.

"It's only half a block. I don't mind."

"No, don't you have your own kid or something?" I ask, ready to wipe that annoyed look off her face. "Isaiah, come here now." I watch my child look at this woman as if seeking permission. *Has she turned my own child against me? I married her, provided a life her poor, foolish father could never offer, and she turns my own kid against me.*

"Honey, he was having so much fun, couldn't he just..."

Hearing her speak as though my son doesn't want to come with me sets me off.

"SHUT UP!" I yell before I can compose myself. Ashanti takes a step back, and I turn to grab Isaiah, but Ellen is in my face before I can blink. She's taller than me, I realize, and her eyes are black— so black. *Shouldn't there be some white in there?*

Suddenly, I feel weightless; looking into her eyes makes me feel weightless. She's saying something. Something important. I listen closely because suddenly, this information feels urgent. *Have I forgotten something?*

"You will leave. Isaiah coming with me is a better idea. You need to clear your head. Go to Helen's house and stay for a week. Stay away from this house until then."

She's right. Of course. Isaiah walking is a great idea. I do miss Helen. I need some air for sure.

"I think Isaiah should jog. It's better." Everything gets hazy. *I must have drunk too much, or maybe I'm having a bad trip off that coke? I just need to go. I need Helen.* I get back into the car and drive. The faster I get there, the better.

Chapter Seven - Asim

"You could have exposed us!" Heqet yells for the 10th time in the last hour. I watch my companion as she paces, much too fast for the human eye to see, back and forth throughout the house, angered by my blatant use of our abilities in front of Ashanti.

"I was in control, Heqet. I didn't kill him. I simply sent him away and kept them safe," I say, also for the 10th time in the last hour. She doesn't stop to show me the eye roll; I can sense she's giving me.

"The child was there! Do you think he would not fear us if he knew our true identity? What we truly are? Do you think Ashanti would thank us once our lies are exposed? We could have handled the dimwitted human without the risk of exposure!" She stops pacing now, turning to me with pleading eyes. "Asim, I have never, in all the millennia we have spent together, felt regret for the gift you have given me. I have accepted the sacrifices that must be made for the sake of our purposes, and given all I am without hesitation--"

"I know, Heqet--" I say, cutting her off, but she holds up her hand, silencing me.

"When you met me so very long ago, I was a mother. Maybe not in the sense of a birth mother, but I cared for many children, babies, without families. I took all of them in and I loved and cared for them all without hesitation. I accepted then that would be the closest I ever came to a family. That they would be my children, and I was happy. Truly. But I love that child," she says as she points towards Ashanti's house, "I love that little boy, and I love Ashanti, and I am excited to meet the child within her womb. I feel like we have a chance here. A real chance our ancestors have finally granted us the gift of a *family*, Asim. Can you not feel it? A chance at happiness? I beg you, please, we must do this correctly, we must do this with care. I cannot bear to lose them. Please."

I look at Heqet, who somehow seems smaller in her fear. She stands before me, eyes wide and pleading. I realize she has bonded with my love and her child in an extraordinary way. I took away her ability for children in a selfish fit; I cannot risk taking away her chance at a family now. "Heqet, I love them too. I am sorry for reacting without thinking it through. I will not make such mistakes again, " I say, trying to comfort her. But sadness radiates her in such a way I get the overwhelming feeling she is crying without tears, incapable of such a thing. I quickly reach my sister, my best friend, and embrace her so tightly it would crush a human.

"We cannot lose them, Asim. I cannot bear it. I almost feel human again. Finally. I love that child. She has created a change in you I have never witnessed. I beg you, move carefully."

"I understand, little sister. I feel the same. We cannot lose them."

We sit quietly, contemplating together how to move forward. Periodically, we listen into Ashanti's house to check on them, as well as, hopefully decipher if she has any suspicion.

Heqet frowns suddenly while flipping through pages of a history book.

"What is wrong?" I ask, listening but also enjoying the sound of Isaiah's laughter as Ashanti plays tickle monster with him, as she tucks him into his bed. Eavesdropping into her home for the millionth time. Heqet puts down her book, and I focus my attention on her worried face.

"Isn't it curious?" She asks, tilting her head to the side as she recalls something.

"What?" I ask impatiently.

"Ashanti, she has called no one. Adam acted so strangely; shouldn't she have called a friend or relative to discuss it by now?" She asks perplexed. "Given our study of the human race, surely she should have called someone. Is that not their natural reflex? Discuss their suspicions?"

I pause and recall our conversations and interactions, " I believe her vile husband has alienated her from all she held affection for. That is typically how abusers work, is it not?"

She nods in agreement. " Well, we shall change that. I believe it is time for me and my future sister-in-law to bond." She smiles and sits back, her decision made.

I pace before stopping at the window to peek out at her home. She has not left her home at all today; surely afraid her husband will return. I growl, frustrated and angered by the fear this pathetic man has placed in her. I will show her she is not alone.

Thirty minutes later, Heqet and I are knocking on Ashanti's door, two of the one hundred bottles of non-alcoholic wine I purchased, and Heqet holding the walnut brownies she made, still warm, and three horror movies, she swears humans love. We listen to Ashanti walking quickly to the door, and Isaiah fast asleep, softly snoring in his bed. The blind moves slightly, and we listen as her heartbeat quickens as she sees us. I try to remain neutral, but a smile spreads across my face at the thought of her becoming excited to see me. She takes a deep breath before opening the door.

"Well, hi!" She says, the excitement in her voice evident, "What are you guys doing over here?"

Heqet playfully pushes past me, "Girl's night!" She says, holding out the brownies. Ashanti giggles, before reaching out for the brownies.

"Oh, my goodness, they smell so good!" She looks at me, "And what do you have there?"

I hold up the bottles, and she steps to the side, "Come, come."

We laugh together, and walk into her home, Heqet stopping to kiss her cheek, "You glow more every day, I swear!"

Ashanti pats her belly and frowns, "More like grow every day! I feel like I'm gonna pop if this child doesn't come out soon."

"It must be any day now, huh?" Heqet says cheerfully, as she plops down on the couch. I reach out to help Ashanti sit down, as she slowly sits, before leaning back and propping her swollen feet up.

"Thank you so much," She says, blushing and smiling at me, "yes, any day I'm hoping."

"I hope you don't mind, but I picked up a few things, and I was hoping to drop them off tomorrow?" Heqet says, smiling, " I just love children, and I couldn't help myself."

"Oh, wow, that is so sweet, Sarah. Absolutely bring them over! You guys are really my only friends, so it'll be the closest I have to a baby shower." She laughs, but I can hear the sadness in that statement. Heqet frowns slightly but corrects her response before Ashanti notices and laughs with her.

"Well, we are your friends, 100 percent so you can count on us."

"Always, " I say, smiling at her.

She smiles back at me before patting the spot next to her on the couch, " Erin, why don't you sit down? I thought this was girls' night?" She says it calmly, but the change in her heart rate and breathing say otherwise. *Is she nervous?*

I sit next to her, my arm brushing her soft skin, and she leans into me slightly, wanting our arms to touch. I hear her heartbeat quicken at our touching and place my arm around her on the couch, casually, as if I were just getting comfortable. Heqet glances at me quickly before asking Ashanti how Isaiah's day was. They chat about their day and plans for DIYs they have.

"Oh my god, Erin is so handy! You should see how quickly she can build furniture, " Heqet says, beaming at me. Ashanti turns to me, impressed.

"You can build furniture?" she asks, eyebrows raised.

"I can do small projects, yes. Sarah has an obsession with antiques, and she constantly has me building replicas of things she's seen, " I say, laughing, "She's a bit bossy."

In response, Heqet sticks her tongue out at me before laughing too. Ashanti stares at me for a moment longer before turning back to Heqet,

"You have to help me design my nursery. I've done some things, but I just hate it, to be honest." She says, frowning at the thought of it.

"Can I see it?" Heqet asks, excited at the thought of designing a nursery.

"Sure, let's go, but we have to be quiet; Isaiah wakes so easily these days." She says and leads us upstairs. I remember peeking into their windows the first night I saw her and feel guilty as she points to rooms, giving us a brief tour.

"So, there's an office connected to our bedroom, and we turned it into the nursery, so this is my bedroom, " she says opening the door at the end of the hallway. I look around the room I was in not too long ago, noticing how spotless the room is first. The bed perfectly made, everything lined up perfectly, almost compulsively done. I glance at Heqet, and notice the slightly worried look, behind the smile she is forcing. *Has this male abused her so badly that she is terrified of imperfection?* We both smile and comment on how beautiful the room looks. I think of her swollen ankles and rounded belly, struggling to make this king-size bed, and I have to restrain the growl threatening to escape my lips.

"You must work so hard to keep everything this organized! Lord knows we could never, " Heqet says, knowing our home is inhumanely clean due to Heqet cleaning obsessively. At her inhumane speed, she cleans the entire home in minutes most days.

Ashanti smiles, "Thank you, Adam likes everything in its place." She opens a door in the corner of the room, and we walk into a smaller room. It's simple. White paint, and a changing table, a plain white crib, a few baby toys, and boxes of diapers piled in the corner. I watch Ashanti as she looks down embarrassed, nervously tucking her hair behind her ear.

"It's lovely, " I say reassuringly, "I can see Heqet brainstorming ideas already."

"Oh, my goodness yes! I love it!" Heqet chimes in, with her typical cheery enthusiasm.

Ashanti looks up, embarrassment fading into excitement as well. Heqet has this amazing ability to light up rooms and bring even the saddest person to a hopeful place. I smile, glad Heqet has Ashanti, as much as Ashanti now has Heqet. Heqet starts pouring out ideas and pointing to places, periodically calling out tasks she has now charged me with. Build a crib, changing table, dresser. Ashanti looks at me bemused.

"How on earth can you get all that done before the baby is here?" She asks, "Maybe we could find what you're looking for online?"

Heqet looks appalled, "Oh my, absolutely not. This baby needs a special room to match how special they are!"

Ashanti giggles at Heqet, not realizing she is serious. I roll my eyes, "it's too late to reel her in; she's not going to stop."

Heqet sticks her tongue out at me once again and continues with her rambling of ideas. I make mental notes of what she's saying as I imagine Ashanti and I in this nursery. I picture her in a rocking chair, feeding the baby, while Isaiah and I play nearby. We both look up and make eye contact before smiling and continuing with the children. It seems so perfect. I watch Ashanti and Heqet giggle and discuss decor possibilities. I listen in as Ashanti describes things she's always wanted in a nursery, making mental notes. *I wonder what crib she had as a child?* I will ask Heqet to look into her childhood.

"I'm gonna run across the street and get my paint swatches!" Heqet hurries out of the nursery without looking back.

"Well, you've started a monster; there's no stopping her now, " I say, picking up a colorful teddy bear.

"This is gonna be so fun!" Ashanti says, smiling so brightly; I smile with her.

"How are you feeling?" I ask as her heart rate increases suddenly. *I wonder why?*

"I'm okay, " she says, very interested in the crib against the wall. *I wonder what she's thinking.*

I walk over to her, closing the short distance in the small room quickly, "What are you thinking?"

She jumps at my sudden closeness, "You scared me; I forgot how fast you are."

"I'm sorry; are you okay?" I hold her gently by the waist to support her. Her heart takes off, "What's wrong?"

"Nothing...nothing. I'm okay," she says, inhaling and exhaling, calming herself.

"Tell me what you're thinking, " I say quietly, still holding her waist, enjoying the closeness of our bodies. I lean closer to her, knowing how angry Heqet will be but not caring. I just want one moment of closeness, to enjoy her being near me. She leans into me; *maybe she wants this closeness too? Does she crave me too?* I inhale her sweet scent. It sends tingles over my body. Yes. Heqet was right; the only way to describe this feeling is to feel alive. Ashanti gives me human feelings I thought were dead to me so exceedingly long ago. She leans on her tiptoes; *is she trying to kiss me?* I lean closer, our lips inches apart. She lingers, allowing me to take the next step. I hesitate only briefly before giving in to my desires. I will hear Heqet's qualms later; now I just need Ashanti. Her lips are soft and warm. She tastes like honey. I want more. I let go of her waist and wrap my arms behind her back, gently holding her tighter to me, slightly lifting her off the ground. She runs her hand up my back before wrapping them around my neck, hungrily sucking my bottom lip and running her tongue along it. Knowing I cannot allow this to go too far, I slowly separate from her, setting her back on the ground but embracing her. She buries her face into my chest.

"I don't know what's happening," she says, her face pressed into my body.

"What do you mean?"

"I have never felt so deeply for someone I just met. I shouldn't feel this way. I'm *married.*

But I cannot stop thinking of you. You send trembles through my body. I want this," she explains.

"I feel the same. I want you. You are all I think of."

"Even though I'm...like this?" She separates to gesture to her pregnant stomach.

"You look beautiful. I adore Isaiah, and I would adore this child as well."

"I don't know if I could leave him, " she says this in a whisper, but it cuts through me. If my heart could beat, it would stop hearing this. But I know this is normal. She has been beaten and battered. It will be a challenge getting her to see I could provide a better life, and I am up for this challenge.

"I am not asking you to choose right now. I know the situation we are in. I will wait until the end of time for you, " I say. I look into her eyes and see the tears forming.

"What is wrong? Was it something I have said?" I ask worried. *Have I hurt her feelings somehow? Caused her stress?*

"You just are wonderful. Really, really wonderful, and you say the sweetest things."

"We will figure this out, love. I promise," I say, brushing her hair out of her face.

We both separate as we hear the door close. Heqet giving a heads-up for Ashanti's benefit. Ashanti steps away from me and wipes her eyes, adjusting her clothing.

"I got swatches!" Heqet comes in just as excited as when she left, "Sorry it took so long I could not find these for the life of me." I know this is a lie. She simply gave us a little privacy.

"Oh my, this blue!" Ashanti says, holding one of the swatches out to show Heqet. They spend hours going through the swatches and drawing possible furniture. Two bottles of pregnancy wine and a plate of brownies later, and I carry a sleeping Ashanti to her bed. Heqet checks on Isaiah. We leave their house and go to our home, knowing Heqet will make me begin at once on her ideas.

"Could you look into her childhood? I want to know her favorite childhood items, " I ask Heqet, as we settle into our usual places in our home.

"That's a great idea, Asim! I will look into it immediately." Heqet jets off without another word, as she always does. I lay on the couch, thinking of my newest interaction with Ashanti. My body feels as though it has warmed, as hot as the sun, and I smile. *She is truly special.* I replay the image of Isaiah and me playing while she feeds the baby. *Yes, I will fight for her.* I close my eyes, concentrating hard on this prayer. *Please, ancestors, I beg of you. Grant me this little piece of joy. Allow me this.* A warm breeze on my face forces me to open my eyes. In my concentration I have returned to the sleep realm, as I often call it. My resting place. Only, now it has changed. Sunflowers have sprouted up sporadically throughout the once-barren field. Grass has grown, covering the dirt, blue skies peek through the dissipating clouds, the tree my mother sat on not too long ago, covered in leaves. It reminds me of springtime in the northern states of North America. Quite beautiful. New life, growing and shining through. I guess that is how I feel at this moment. *New.* I walk through the field, enjoying the quiet hum of my resting ancestors. A hum I have not heard in a very long time. They have returned to me, letting me know they are here, with me. I smile as I rest on the wet fresh grass, watching the clouds pass. Feeling as though this is the most perfect my life has been in such a long time; I barely can remember the words to describe the feeling. Closing my eyes, I hum along with my people. Allowing their blessing to rain onto me through their song. *So, this is peace?*

Chapter Eight – Ashanti

"Ashanti, please, " Sarah says impatiently, " You have to wait; it is a surprise!"

"I just want to peek!" I say, pouting. It has been a full week since I asked Heqet to help me with the nursery, and after Erin's warning, I now see the monster I have unleashed. Sarah has worked endlessly, arriving before the sun and leaving well into the night. She installed a lock on the door to prevent me from ruining her surprise. She has carried box, after box, sometimes taller than her, or Erin has carried weirdly shaped packages. All were seemingly too heavy for them to carry, but they refused any of my offers to help, preferring to struggle with the many trips of loading and unloading. She locks the door and quickly places the key into her pocket.

"I promise it will be miraculous, phenomenal; you will be listed as this year's most beautiful nursery." She brags, while heading to the stairs, unmoved by my pouting and pleas.

"We have much work to do, before the little love muffin arrives, and no, I cannot let you peek." She blows a kiss and hurries out the door. I laugh to myself as I watch to ensure she safely makes it home. She hurries across the street, stopping to wave before opening her door and disappearing inside. I wait for a moment, hoping Erin will come outside.

Ever since the night of our kiss, after Sarah leaves for the night, Erin slips out of the house and comes over. We sit on the porch or on the couch and watch movies, talk for hours on end, sharing our tales, whispering what-ifs to each other.

I laugh at myself, standing in the doorway, hopeful I might see her slip out the door again. How quickly I have gotten attached to this beautiful mysterious woman, and honestly Sarah too. She's the closest to a best friend I have had in a very long time. I bite my lip. *Should I close the door?* This is silly; we never made plans; it just has kind of happened these past few nights. *Maybe she's asleep.* I start to close the door, but a light from her porch catches my eye. I swing the door open, then reprimand myself quietly for being too eager. Erin walks outside, her hair loose and swaying over her shoulders. Her tall, lean physique looking even more muscular in the moonlight. She looks at me, giving a little wave before hurrying across the street.

I open the door and step back, allowing her to come in. I smile, trying to hide my childlike excitement. She stops, her tall figure hovering over me in the doorway. She reaches down and gently cups her hand around my neck, pulling me into a slow kiss that sets my insides on fire. I'm left breathless when she finally pulls away.

"Good evening," she says with a smirk. I blush, looking down. She has such a huge impact on me. I tuck my hair behind my ear and close the door, making sure to lock it as well. She holds out her hand, and I hold it as she leads me to the couch. Tonight *feels* different. Like tonight we might just take things to the next step. I swallow hard at this thought. *Am I ready for this?*

"Are you okay?" Erin asks, patting the seat beside her on the couch.

"Oh, yes, I'm okay," I sit down next to her, as she rests her arm lazily behind me on the couch.

"So how was your day?" She asks, playing with a strand of my hair behind my back, "Did Isaiah keep you busy today?"

"You have no idea! That little monster is quick!" We both laugh in agreement.

"Yeah, he really is a ball of energy. I love it though. Kids have a way of making you feel alive, you know?"

I smile at her, happy that she loves children, more importantly, *my* child. "Absolutely! It's like some days he just drives me crazy, and all I can think of is when is bedtime?! But most days he's the sweetest little gremlin. He hugs me, and it all feels worth it. Like I have a real purpose here with him."

"I hope to experience that one day."

I look up at her thoughtful face and wonder what she is thinking. She almost looks sad.

"You will," I say and cuddle up a little closer to her, hoping to get a smile.

"I hope we get to experience that feeling together, " she says quietly, while looking into my eyes.

"I don't think you understand the burden you are trying to volunteer for," I say nervously, twisting my hands in my lap. She places her hand on top of mine, stopping me.

"What burden is that?" She asks seriously. For a brief moment, I feel what I can only describe as anger radiating off of her. My heart quickens as I feel.... fear. I shake off the feeling, feeling silly for it. I peek up at her, but her face is sad, frowning.

"Well.... I mean I'm obviously older. Even though you won't tell me your age. You don't look much older than 25, and well, the obvious," I wave my hand over my round belly, "and I also have a toddler..."

She sits quietly, so quietly I think she must be holding her breath. After a few moments, she turns me gently to face her, cupping my face in between her hands so that I look directly into her eyes.

"Ashanti..." She starts to say and hearing her say my name sets a burning deep in the pit of my stomach.

"Ashanti, you are not a burden." I start to interrupt, but she holds her hand up, asking me to wait, "This is important. Hear what I say, you are not a burden. I know life has not been easy for you. I know this may not be the life you pictured as a small girl. I am not blind to the situation you are in. I see the battles you face within these walls. At times it may not seem so, but you *are* worthy of love. You deserve happiness. The lessons we learn through our experiences, good, bad, and sometimes ugly, do not devalue us. You are brilliant, you are beautiful. You light every room you are in. Your presence alone has made my life better. Having children does not devalue you or make you unworthy of happiness. I would love you *AND* your children as my own. I would love you through your rough days *and* your best days. More than that, I *want* to. Nothing about you or this package deal says burden to me. I have prayed for you every day for as long as I can remember, and if you allow me to, I can love you into believing that. Just let me love you. I need you near me, always."

I sit in silence, speechless by her words. My eyes blurry, and my throat burning. Tears threatening to spill at any moment. *How can anyone be so perfect? Is this what I prayed for when I asked for peace?* I look at her, sitting in silence with me, giving me time to consider her words. Her forehead is wrinkled with worry.

"In my heart, I know this is right. I don't know how, but I just know we are right for each other. I can feel it. I wish we met a few years ago," she begins to interrupt, but now it's my turn to hold my hand up, "I wish we met before I met Adam, and we had a chance to get to know each other without so many obstacles. I don't want to hurt you or be hurt myself. I know I shouldn't even be doing this right now, but being away from you feels worse. It's going to take time, maybe more than is fair to ask, but I do want to pursue this. I want to put my faith in you and try happiness. I just don't know when or even how I'll ever be able to leave Adam."

"I understand love, I truly do, but we will figure all of this out together. We will go through any and every obstacle before us together." She says and kisses the back of my hand she is holding, "I love you."

"I love you too." As the words leave my mouth, I realize how true they are. I reach up and pull her face to mine, pressing my lips into hers. She kisses me back, slowly first, then slipping her tongue between my lips. She kisses me in a way that creates a pool between my legs. Slowly, she rubs my back while bringing my body closer, somehow lifting me and sitting me on her lap. She grips a handful of my hair, pulling it back to expose my neck as she trails kisses down it.

I reach in between us, trying to pull my oversized shirt over my head. She breaks from kissing me long enough to pull it over my head and tosses it across the room, quickly returning to kissing me. I reach behind my back and undo my clasp, allowing my ample breast to bounce free. She moans softly seeing this and helps me to stand, removing my pajama bottoms and panties. I stand before her completely undressed, covering myself, feeling vulnerable, conscious of the stretch marks that have recently appeared.

She stands and picks me up as if I weigh nothing. I gasp in surprise, but she smiles down at me, carrying me up the stairs carefully. We quickly reach my bedroom, where she lays me down and begins kissing each stretch mark, reaching up to tease and pinch my sensitive nipples. I moan quietly, enjoying every touch, every kiss. She positions herself between my legs, gently rubbing my most sensitive spot, causing me to arch my back in response to the pleasure. She begins licking and kissing as if she has already memorized every part of my body, slowly sliding her fingers in and out of me. My body begins to shake and tremble, I try to wiggle free, but she locks her arms around my legs, speeding up the pleasure she is causing. All I can do is moan and say her name over and over as my body releases, and I feel the lake of wetness forming where her mouth just was. She looks up at me, smiling widely, as I gather my senses, unable to speak. She goes into the bathroom and comes back with a wet rag, wiping the mess I've made off of me. We cuddle for a while, whispering promises to each other. She helps me change my bedding, and lays with me until I drift off to sleep.

I awake to the smell of bacon, and Isaiah laughing. Sitting up, I check my alarm clock. 8:36 am. I quickly get up, realizing I'm wearing a nightgown I don't remember putting on. I head downstairs, confused.

"So, you get to fly?" Isaiah asks excitedly.

"No, I can't fly," Erin says, laughing. I walk into the kitchen to see Isaiah sitting on a stool with his toy cars lined up in front of him on the counter, and Erin cooking breakfast. Her long dreads are pulled into a messy bun atop her head. She looks up and smiles.

"Who can fly?" I ask, ruffling Isaiah's hair and smiling at Erin. Isaiah giggles and squirms away from me.

"Erin! She's a superhero!" Isaiah says happily.

"Shhhh! That was a secret!" Erin says, winking at him. Isaiah, realizing he shared a secret, quickly looks up at me.

"Mommy, it's a secret, okay?"

"Of course, little monster," I say with a serious face.

"See, mommy keeps secrets good." He says to Erin.

She nods her head in agreement, "You're right! Mommy might have to keep all my secrets for me!"

"Breakfast?" I ask, looking over the spread of eggs, bacon, biscuits, and grits.

"I thought you guys might be hungry this morning, and I know you're tired."

"Thank you. This was really nice, " I say, stealing a piece of bacon as she playfully swats me away. Isaiah sits watching us, laughing.

"Did I miss breakfast?" Sarah asks, surprising us.

"Oh! I didn't hear you walk in! Come, Come. Erin was just making this huge spread, " I say.

She smiles, looking at everything, "Wow, impressive sister, I thought for sure you had forgotten how to cook."

"Doesn't she cook at home?" I ask. Sarah laughs.

"Let's just say, the last time she cooked, the pyramids were a new attraction!" She says, laughing at her own joke. Erin rolls her eyes. I laugh at their sibling banter, watching them stick their tongues out at each other like children. As I'm watching, so suddenly I swear I might be imagining it, they both lock eyes, their expressions changing into a serious stare, as if a silent exchange was happening. It only lasts a second or two, and then Sarah sits next to me, smiling. I look confused between the two of them, unsure what I just witnessed, but Erin smiles and tosses a blueberry into the air, catching it before it has a chance to fall. Isaiah laughs and claps and begs to try. I shrug off the feeling, assuming my pregnancy hormones must be making me crazy.

"So, Ashanti, me and Erin are heading out of town later. I found an antique piece of furniture I must have," Sarah says casually, winking at Isaiah, as he smiles.

"Oh really? I hope I'm not causing you guys too much of a hassle. How much is it? I can transfer you the money," I say worried about what the cost of this nursery is going to total when she's finally done.

Sarah rolls her eyes, and waves her hands, dismissing my statement, "Oh please, Ashanti, it's a gift from us. I love this sort of thing, and Erin wouldn't even hear of accepting payment for anything from you."

"What? There's no way I can put this on you guys! You've already done so much!" I sit arms folded, determined to pay for it.

"No love, we got it. Let us do this, please. I want to help," Erin says in a stern but somehow soft voice. The sound has me unfolding my arms.

"But it's really too much to ask," I say again, softer this time.

"That's okay 'cause you're not asking, love." She says it in such a final tone. I find myself just sitting there quietly. *What has this woman done to me? Am I really giving up this easily?* Erin places a little plate in front of Isaiah. She managed to arrange his food into a smiley face, and he is excited about it. Next, she hands me a plate overflowing with food, but I accept it, thanking her. Sarah stands up walking into the kitchen to help Erin clean the kitchen as we eat.

"You guys aren't eating?" I ask, savoring the best biscuit I have ever tasted.

"Oh no, I never eat when I cook," Erin says washing the dishes. Sarah continues scraping the pots into the trash.

"I had a big breakfast before I came over, I wish I knew Chef Erin was over here, though," she says, laughing as she teases her sister.

The sound of a car door closing causes me to tense up. *Adam?* I look around, worried I haven't cleaned up yet. I stand and hurry to the living room, but everything is spotless. *Has Erin cleaned too?* I make a mental note to thank her, as Adam walks into the front door.

"I'm home!" he calls as he steps inside. I plaster the biggest smile I can manage and walk up to him.

"Hey, honey! I've missed you!" I say, kissing him. He quickly pulls away looking around suspiciously.

"What's been going on around here?" He asks.

"What do you mean?" I ask, confused. Sarah walks into the room with Isaiah drying her hands on a paper towel. Isaiah, noticing his father tenses slightly before also smiling and running to his father.

"Daddy!" he says, hugging him. He reaches down, pulling him into a half hug.

"Hello son," he says, barely looking at him, instead focused on Sarah, "What are you doing here?" His cold demeanor towards her catching me, and her off guard.

"I was here helping Ashanti," she says, maintaining her smile, almost as if she doesn't even notice how cold his voice is. I say almost because there was a very brief moment before she spoke, I swear her eyes went black. Not her pupil but her eyes. I blink a few times and rub my own eyes, realizing I must be tired, as Erin suggested earlier. I look at Sarah again, and see the soft, cheerful woman she always is, smiling brightly at Adam, oblivious to his flaring temper and cold glare.

"Ummm, honey. How was your trip? Did it go as planned?" I ask, hoping to divert his attention from the small, defenseless woman standing a few feet away. This, of course, does catch his attention. He frowns, but the gesture is an act I know well. He tosses his long hair behind his shoulder and shakes his head sadly.

"Actually, it didn't go as planned. I'll probably have to go back soon to seal the deal," he says as he looks everywhere but my eyes. I look sad as well, a conversation we have had often.

"Oh no, honey, I'm so sorry!" I say, rubbing his arm, consoling his fake sadness. Erin walks into the living room, casually, exuding the confidence and calmness of a Queen, as if Adam's presence doesn't bother her in the slightest. Adam, however, tenses immediately upon seeing her. His temper flaring again, sadness forgotten. If I wasn't terrified of what was about to happen, watching his sudden change in emotion would be almost comical.

"What are you doing here?" He repeats his earlier question, but this time directed at Erin, his voice dripping with venom. His fist clenched, and for a brief moment, I think he might attack her. Sarah, normally cheerful and calming, twitches, her smile fades as she turns her head slightly towards her sister. No one speaks for a brief moment. I clear my throat, fearful of things escalating.

"Actually, honey, Erin and Sarah have been helping us with the nursery. They are a bit of a dynamic duo when it comes to decorating, and they were nice enough to help out since the baby will be here any day." I try to keep my voice even and cheerful, but my fear betrays me, and my voice shakes. Erin turns to look at me and Adam sees her concern.

"We don't need help, " he says angrily, swatting my hand away from him. Erin steps forward, and Sarah steps towards her, holding her hand and turning to smile at us.

"Well, I bet you two have a lot of catching up to do after such a long time apart. We were just heading out actually." She pulls Erin with her and heads to the door, "I'll chat with you later, Ashanti."

As the door closes, Adam turns to me but speaks to Isaiah, "Go play with your toys son.

Me and your mom need to talk."

My stomach drops as he talks. *Will he hit me?* Isaiah hesitates, afraid, before running quickly upstairs. *Please protect my child,* I think silently to whoever may be listening. As Isaiah's door closes, I take a step back from Adam, hoping to reason with him in his sober state. He surprises me by walking into the kitchen. I hurry in to explain the mess, but as I walk into the kitchen behind him, everything is spotless, as if we had not eaten a huge breakfast five minutes prior. I exhale the breath I was holding.

Adam walks over to the fridge and grabs a soda out of it. I can't help but compare the change in the atmosphere between now, with him home, and when Erin was standing in his place a few minutes earlier, Isaiah laughing hysterically.

I frown before pushing the thoughts out of my mind. I need to stay present, Adam hates it when I'm not focused on what he's saying, and I need to keep him calm.

After grabbing a soda, he leans against our counter and gestures for me to sit. I comply immediately, hoping my eagerness to please him satisfies his anger. He takes a sip, enjoying the fear and anxiety he is causing before finally speaking.

"Since when do we have strangers in our home?" he asks. Confused, I think over the last few days, he must mean Erin and Sarah. I've had no one else in our home.

"Well, honey, our neighbors aren't really strangers, are they? I mean, I've become friends with them since they've moved in."

"Friends? With the whore and the dike? That's who you want around our children?" He says, laughing in appalled disbelief.

"Adam! Why would you say that? Sarah has been the sweetest to both of us, and Erin has helped a ton. They are good people. I didn't think we were the type of people to judge anyone so viciously."

He rolls his eyes, "Please, Ashanti, that Sarah girl is *too* nice, and her sister is just sniffing around, hoping to get some desperate housewife to fuck her."

"And I'm that desperate housewife?" I demand, his words stinging.

He makes a point to look around, then turns to me, "Obviously, you're the only pregnant bimbo around here, entertaining some gay he- she that doesn't know what they are, all times of the night." He looks at me angrily, "Yeah, I know all about your late-night rendezvous with that bitch."

I stand up too quickly, and I feel a sharp cramp in my stomach. I stop for a moment to catch my breath, "I really don't know what has gotten into you Adam. You come home, after disappearing for a week without even a check-in and come back accusing me? I'm going to go for a walk. When I get back and you're feeling better, we will talk."

I expect him to stop me, but to my surprise, he lets me go. I quickly walk out of the house in time to see Erin and Sarah walking out. Sarah waves to me as they both get into the car, Erin waves slightly, concern obvious on her face. I nod at her reassuringly and go for a 20-minute walk, taking several breaks, and thinking over my last few days.

By the time I get home, I have decided to tell Adam I'm leaving him. I take a deep breath, and walk inside, ready to have the talk with him. I turn to close the door, and suddenly someone pushes me into the door. I slam into it, my stomach smashing into the thick wooden door. I fall backwards, bouncing off of the door, landing hard on my back. Pain begins to shoot through my stomach, as my world begins to turn black. The last image I see is Adam standing over me, his eyes wild with hate.

Chapter Nine – Asim

Furious. That is the word that best describes my emotions at the moment. I contemplate simply opening the door of this small prison Heqet has trapped me in and running back to Ashanti's side, tearing off Adam's pathetic head in the process.

I look at my companion. She taps happily along to the car radio, and of course, it is blasting her favorite music from the 60s. Just moments ago, Heqet was so full of rage that I feared she might rip Adam's head off herself. As always, she quickly gained control of her emotions. Heqet, once a fiery, lioness of a woman, unpredictable and always ready to strike to protect, has softened over the years.

Perhaps it was because of my careless, spontaneous nature; one of us needed to be rational, and she naturally fell into that role. I prayed to the Ancestors many times to allow Heqet to feel my rage over the years, especially when humanity became increasingly disappointing. Mass shootings, and torture of children, but Heqet simply mourned for the world. Always there to reel me in, and keep me from going too far off the deep end.

For just a moment, in Ashanti's house, as Adam's demeanor became increasingly threatening, I thought the Ancestors had heard my pleas, and my comrade would bend, just this once, but as quickly as the rage appeared it was capped, replaced with her carefully crafted persona. I grit my teeth, remembering Adam swatting Ashanti away as if she were a mere fly, the disrespectful way he spoke of my Heqet. My hand gripping the door, ready to break out of this horribly slow contraption and finish him once and for all. Heqet symbolically locks the car door, bringing me out of my internal rant. I look at her, facing the road, but her attention is clearly on me.

"We did the right thing," she says simply.

"We left her alone, unprotected," I say furiously.

"If we had stayed, even a moment longer, you would have exposed us, and murdered him," she says, still calm as ever.

"And," I say, still contemplating the very scenario.

"Ashanti would not take kindly to finding out the woman she has fallen for is not only not of this world but also a murderer, " she says, switching lanes to avoid a car going much too slow for the left lane.

"Ashanti hates him, I'm sure of it. She stays for Isaiah, and out of fear, " I say.

"Whether that is true or not is irrelevant. Introducing her to our world in such a brutal way would turn her from us forever. It is better to follow this lead and continue winning her over than to push her further away," Heqet tries to reassure me, unsuccessfully.

"Heqet, she is unprotected, left in the hands of that animal. She is small, frail, and with child. Isaiah is small and frail, unable to stand a chance against that horrid example of a human." My hand twitches at the thought of any harm coming to my soon-to-be family. Heqet exhales, the thought of harm coming to them upsetting her as well. She shakes her head.

"Do you honestly think me an idiot? Of course, I did not leave them to his brutality. I left them in capable hands." She says confidently. I stare at her bewildered. *What does that mean? What has she done?*

"Heqet? Please elaborate as to what that means. Surely you did not invite one of our peers into the town of my love? Surely you did not lead them to this town and point them to them?" I say, speaking each word carefully, trying to control my anger. Heqet would never do such a thing. While we are able to exist in civilization, most of our peers cannot. They prefer the wild, chaotic life of the darkness, only interacting with humanity to feed.

She sucks her teeth at my assumption, "Thousands of years, and this is what you reduce my intelligence to. Of course, I have done no such thing. I would never endanger our new family in such a way. I called on Cairo the moment I found the "Crafter". I heard he was within the States, and he assured me he would arrive within a night," she says, smiling.

This news calms me slightly. While I would prefer to be near her, to protect Isaiah and her myself, Cairo will be sufficient. The only male in all my years, both Heqet and myself have come to trust. I am unsure of his age, although I believe he is older than even me. He is an intelligent man, an admirable warrior, and a protector of humanity. He fell in love with Heqet many years ago, but Heqet never saw him as more than a longtime friend. Nevertheless, when Heqet calls, he has always come. He is not of our kind, but something far more mysterious. His strange DNA grants him the ability to transform into any creature he witnesses, in person or in pictures. He has not aged since I have met him, and I have never seen him so much as panic. Death escapes him, although I have heard rumors of his attempts to meet his maker in the past. He simply wanders the earth, blending into wherever he chooses to be in that moment. His only identifier, no matter the form he chooses, is the sun-shaped mark that appears on his right hand in human form. I have often wondered if his human form is his true form. He has never spoken of it, and no one dares to ask. Yes, Cairo will provide great protection to my loved ones in my absence.

"When should he arrive?" I ask her, checking the time. 10:22 am.

"I called him last night, so he should be there before noon," she says.

Okay, I pray silently, may our ancestors wrap their arms around them until he arrives.

We arrive at our destination several hours later. Cairo messaged Heqet shortly after his arrival, assuring me Ashanti was home, asleep in her bed. The home before us is modest, a small one-floor shack with a small garden in front and a leaning mailbox near the dirt road, with no neighbors in sight. Heqet gets out first, as always, and knocks on the door. I listen into the home. Someone is inside, watching a news program; the chair creaks as they get up with a huff. Slowly, they shuffle towards the door. Their heartbeat is frail at best. An elderly woman, maybe in her 90s, opens the door. Her hair is combed into a long gray braid, her age causing her light brown skin to pale.

"Why are you here?" she asks suspiciously. "Are you one of them?"

"I'm sorry to disturb you ma'am, my name is Sarah, we spoke yesterday on the phone?" Heqet says politely, ignoring her question.

"Oh, yeah. I remember ya. Come on in and tell that one out in the car to come too, " she says, leaving the door open and walking back inside. I get out of the car and follow Heqet inside. We stand quietly in the small living room. A recliner sitting in the corner in front of a TV, while every other space available is cluttered with boxes of papers and machines.

"Well, go ahead and sit down," she says, gesturing towards two small chairs tucked in between stacks of boxes. We both wordlessly go to the chairs and sit. She makes herself comfortable in her recliner, putting on her reading glasses before turning to us.

"So, I'm guessing you're like the rest of them... you know... from The Forgotten World, " she says, surprising both of us. *How could she have knowledge of The Forgotten World?*

"I'm sorry, ma'am, The Forgotten World?" Heqet asks, feigning ignorance.

"You know, vampires, werewolves, shapeshifters, unicorns. All the creatures that once ran the earth, now all but forgotten, " she says, as if this is common knowledge. I look at Heqet. This is a strange elder for the modern world. *She knows of us, yet keeps this knowledge to herself?*

"Yes, ma'am," Heqet responds honestly, "And you are the crafter?"

"That's what they call me. I must say, I'm surprised you came to me directly. Typically, you have humans doing your bidding no? It's a rare moment when I come face to face with one of you," she says, looking at us over her glasses.

"Yes, ma'am, but we needed complete discretion for this. We couldn't risk anyone else knowing, " Heqet explains.

"Well, I guess I can understand that. Forgive my suspicion. Gots to be careful in this line of business. I have created identities for probably a million others by now. Some were up to funny business, and I told them absolutely no funny business under my watch," She explains, pointing a shaky finger. She surely was a force to be reckoned with in her youth, meeting the scariest creatures on earth and telling them no, yet being respected enough they allow her to live.

"So, my companion here has fallen in love with a human. She is in grave danger from another human, and we mean to help her escape. Her, her child, and her unborn child as well, " Heqet says.

"She's with child? Do you plan on moving her before the birth?" she asks, raising an eyebrow. Heqet looks to me.

"I, uh, I'm not sure, to be completely honest," I say. She nods.

"Do you have the things I asked you to bring?" She asks Heqet. Heqet nods and hands her the bag she has with her.

"Hmmm," she says looking into the bag of money and documents she asked for, "Okay, well give me 24 hours. I'll be done with it, and you can come pick it up. Don't tell anyone you dealt with me directly, though, and no offense, but lose my number," she says as she struggles to rise from her recliner, signaling us to leave.

"Oh, okay, of course," Heqet says as we both stand.

"Can't have the Loch Ness pulling up to my door now, can we?" She laughs at her own joke. We thank her again and leave.

Once inside, I sigh with relief. Just a few more hours, and I'll be back with Ashanti, able to watch her myself. Heqet insists we stay overnight and leave once the documents are completed. I contemplate leaving Heqet for a moment but decide against it. I could never abandon Heqet with a woman like the Crafter. While old and frail, she knows too much, and this could simply be a trap. We park a few miles away from the Crafter's home, off-rode, deciding to feed in the woods and stay nearby. I call Cairo shortly after we find a pair of campers a few miles into the woods and make it back to our vehicle.

"Hello, Cairo," I say anxiously.

"Ah, Asim! Haven't talked to you in a while, eh? How are you, my friend?" Cairo asks happily.

"I'm doing well, brother. Ready to return to my home."

"Home? I've never heard you call any place but our homeland home; this woman must have left quite the impression on you."

"Yes, yes, she has. How is she?" I ask, anxious to hear she's well.

"She is fine. I am watching her, and the small boy play in the yard now. The child is catching fireflies," he says, "I must say, she does seem rather tired from the pregnancy; she is wobbling around here. Due any day, huh?"

"Yes, she is, and that human male there works her to death," I say, aware of my anger rising with just the thought of him.

"I see, well, it's all good right now, chief. She's playing with the kid, and I don't see the moron anywhere. He must have taken off," Cairo says, "Heqet says I should only observe from a distance? Would you like me to take a closer look?"

"No, no, unless something happens, keep your distance. I do not want to risk her becoming alarmed, " I say.

"Of course, well, rest easy, I will keep an eagle's eye on her." He assures me. I thank him and end the call.

"I told you; she is fine. We will be back tomorrow, and all will be well." Heqet says, settling into the car to scroll the internet.

I lay back in the car, deciding now would be a suitable time to rest. I close my eyes, meditating, finding peace amongst all my chaotic thoughts. The breeze on my face welcomes me first. I open my eyes to see the field once barren, now turning green with fresh grass growing, the tree sprouting leaves. I smile at the sight of several sunflowers blooming. I wander over to the tree I sat under with my mother not too long ago. Sitting in the same place she once sat. After sitting for a few moments, a cat appears and sits beside me, meowing. I look up at the sky, admiring the clouds.

"Hello, grandmother, " I say in our native tongue, "I was wondering when you would appear."

She hisses before taking her human form. She sits beside me, preferring to take the form of animals than humans.

"Hello, child," She responds. Her human appearance changes often, always at different periods of her life. She now appears as her youthful self, no older than 30. She sits, cross-legged on the grass, pouting "You never were much fun."

"I apologize. You look wonderful as always," I say smiling.

"Of course, I do, child. It's in our blood!" She laughs, patting the grass beside her. I sit down, leaning my head on her shoulder. My father's mother. Grandmother struck fear in men and women alike. Tall, taller than me, and strong. She never bit her tongue, but her humor often kept her in trouble. She would often help my mother with me when I was a small child, while my mother healed the members of our village. My father died when I was just a girl, protecting our village from savage rebels, whose intentions were to steal the young girls in our village and take them as child brides.

"How is father? He does not come often," I ask, knowing the answer.

"Your father is well, your father, child; he comes and goes as the breeze blows. I could not tame him in the waking realm, and I fear there will be no taming him in this one either."

We share a laugh at my father's madness before my grandmother sighs deeply.

I fear this choice you have made will not be an easy one," she says finally.

"I know; my choice remains the same nevertheless."

"I know, stubborn as your mother, " she says, shaking her head, "Our protection can only go so far. There are lessons you are destined to learn, lessons that even I cannot protect you from."

"I am prepared to learn these lessons, " I say.

"Child, believe me when I say, we cannot prepare for all the lessons we are forced to learn. Some come from true heartbreak, heartbreak in all your many years walking amongst the living, you could not fathom."

"If I must endure every torture possible, physical or mental, I will for her, grandmother. I have never loved another as I do her."

"You are strong. I remember the fear your father felt. He knew you were different even as a small child. He feared our bloodline would end with you. To think, our bloodline will never die, because of you. You make your ancestors proud, child. Even in your stubbornness, even when you doubt your purpose. We hold our heads high, proud of you." She pats my hand, as if in confirmation before she stands and stretches, "Well, I cannot prepare you for everything you are going to endure, but I can warn you of it. I leave the rest up to you."

"What if I am not enough?" I say, afraid of my failure. She cups my chin, forcing me to raise my head.

"You are of my blood; you will succeed or die trying, beloved." She kisses my forehead, "Now I am sorry, but you must awaken. She needs you."

"What? Who?" Before she can answer, I feel my body being pulled, shaken. Someone is trying to wake me up in the living realm. I open my eyes, sitting up suddenly, conscious of Heqet yelling.

"Wait, what? What has happened?" I demand. Heqet sounds frantic, as she screams Ashanti's name. My heart stops as I grab Heqet by the shoulders.

"Tell me now, what is wrong!" I say, forcing her to focus.

"Ashanti is hurt; Adam has attacked her in her sleep. Cairo could not reach her in time! He has taken her to the hospital; he said she was bleeding badly!"

My world crumbles, "And the boy? Where is Isaiah?"

"He is safe; Cairo has taken him with Ashanti." She says, already driving, swerving back onto the dirt road.

"On foot is faster," I say, grabbing the door handle.

"You know that is not true. This car can go just as fast, if not faster; we will be there soon. I worry for her too." She drives faster, pressing the pedal to the floor and swerving past the few cars on the road this late. I sit back, unable to control my emotions. *Is this what grandmother warned me of?* Fury swallows me whole as I think of Adam. *Today will be his last day on this earth,* I promise myself. We are at the hospital within 3 hours, faster than the time our trip to the Crafter had taken. I can barely control my speed as I rush into the hospital. Heading straight for the room number Cairo provided us moments before. Heqet appears before I make it to her door, and we both enter.

Cairo sits in the recliner, Isaiah fast asleep in his lap. He tries to speak, but I raise my hand, silencing him. I have no time to talk. Ashanti lies in the bed, her face battered, tubes, and cords everywhere. The monitor showing her vitals beeps; her heart rate is steady but low. I sink to my knees beside her bed, wishing I could cry. *How this hurts, I cannot describe.* I hear Heqet hiss.

"The baby, " she whispers, her voice so low that humans could not hear, but the agony laced in those words is palpable. I realize her once-round stomach is noticeably flatter, and no baby monitors are hooked to her. I listen, but only hear one heartbeat coming from her. My heart breaks further. I cannot stand; *how could I face her? I swore to protect her.*

"How could this happen?" Heqet asks Cairo.

"I am so sorry, Heqet. All was quiet; he was gone. I must have drifted to sleep, and when I awoke, he was in the home. I heard her yells, and I rushed there. I attacked him as a wolf, but after seeing the blood, I transformed and brought her here. They were able to save her, but she lost the baby, " he explains, looking down in shame.

"You fell asleep?! Cairo, I trusted you! How could you do something so stupid?" Heqet says angrily. "Where is Adam?"

"I left him bleeding in their home, " he explains.

I cannot move from her side; I hear Heqet leave, but I have no urge to stop her. Adam must be dealt with. Heqet will not kill a human, but she will ensure he cannot escape so I can do what needs to be done. After Heqet leaves, Cairo stands, gently laying Isaiah on the chair he was sitting in.

"Asim, you must believe, I thought she was safe. It had been quiet for hours! I watched her carefully all day, well into the night. I only drifted off when she was fast asleep, and the boy too, " Cairo pleaded.

I remain silent, kneeling beside Ashanti, unable to move or think, watching her swollen face, her eyes closed, listening closely to her weak heart.

"You will make this right, Cairo," I say, my eyes remaining on my battered love.

"Of course, anything, " he says, eager to do anything to fix this.

Knowing Cairo, he blames himself as much as I do in this moment, deep down I know he isn't to blame. He has needs remarkably similar to that of a human. When we asked him to protect her, we had no way of knowing what he had suffered or endured up until that moment. At times, Cairo has gone as long as a week without rest, always trying to save kidnapped children, or battered women, always on a mission of his own. As unfair as I know it is to blame him, seeing Ashanti battered, and unconscious, her heart struggling to beat, my blame lies with any and everyone, myself the most.

"This is what I need...."

Chapter Ten – Ashanti

Black. Everything is so black. I struggle to open my eyes, but nothing. *Have I died?* I try feeling around, but my arms won't move. I panic, *is this what death feels like? Just nothingness?* I try to think of the last thing I can remember. I remember Erin. Her smile as she cooked us breakfast. I feel my heart beating faster as I remember her. *Surely, I cannot be dead with a heartbeat?* I think harder, trying to remember something.... anything? The back of my head throbs. I try to touch it, but my arms will not respond. Adam. I remember our argument, going for a walk. Adam attacked me as I closed the door. I didn't stand a chance. I internally flinch remembering the feeling of the bat hitting my head. The sound of it hitting my skull. I thought I was dying. He knocked me unconscious, and I awoke in our bed, Adam gone. I remember Isaiah, afraid. I tried to let him play outside, but the pain was too much. I fed Isaiah and tucked him into bed early, trying to sleep off the pain. I remember an owl, strange. *An owl on my balcony, watching me?* No. I must have dreamt it. It was not there when Adam woke me, dragging me by my hair out of bed. I remember the pain of him ripping my hair from my head, as he slammed me over and over. His fist hitting my face, he stomped me. The wolf. My body goes cold as my memories return. The wolf. *Was that real? The giant gray wolf that somehow appeared in my home?* I remember hearing its growls as it lunged at Adam, tearing him away from me. Adam's blood-curdling screams as it bit him, over and over. Someone was screaming. Me. I was screaming. Screaming as I saw my little Isaiah running towards me, afraid. Run. I screamed for him to run. The wolf turned to me. Looked me in my eyes, and suddenly a man stood there. I tried to scream, but my body was too weak now. I blacked out as I saw his scarred hand reach for me. The sun scar. Fear rips through me. *Where is Isaiah? Did this... this werewolf hurt my baby? MY BABY?* I try to feel my stomach, but again my stubborn arms won't move. Please, please, my babies. Let my babies be okay. *Where am I?* I try to focus. Push my fear down. I need to try and listen. *Maybe I can hear Isaiah nearby?* I try to listen, focusing on my surroundings, but I hear nothingness. I search through my mind, hoping for anything. *Shouldn't there be a light?*

"Shhhh, it's okay, love."

At first, the words are so low; I think I imagined it.

"It is okay." I hear a woman speak clearer this time. *Am I going crazy?* I begin to panic again, *voices in my head.*

"Focus, my child. You have to focus." The voice says again.

"Focus on what?" I ask, but my question is met with silence.

"Focus, " The voice repeats after a moment. I focus on the darkness, trying to will my eyes open. After a few moments, I give up, instead focusing on trying to find a light, anything but this darkness. After a few moments I see a shimmer, but it's so far in the distance I can only assume there is something there. I focus on this, forcing my mind towards it. After a few moments, I notice it growing brighter. There is definitely something there. My mind begins rushing to it, hopeful I'll get out of this nothingness. It's not until the light has almost overtaken the darkness that I realize maybe I shouldn't go towards the bright light. *Is this death?* Realizing I don't have much of a choice, I force myself through it. Shocked, I realize I've stepped onto a beach. I must be dreaming, but the breeze feels so real. I look as far down the beach as I can see and realize I am alone. I reach to rub my stomach, and finally, my arms move for me, but rest on a flat stomach. *Am I dreaming? Did I have my baby?* I sit near the water, allowing the beach water to run over my toes. I decide this must be a dream. Everything feels so real here.

"It is beautiful here, no?"

I jump at the sound, quickly recognizing the voice as the woman who had spoken to me in the darkness. I look up to see a woman so beautiful, I could only dream of her. Her dreads piled high on top of her head like a crown, taller than anyone I have ever seen, even taller than Erin. Her clothing is similar to what I would imagine an African goddess would wear, her feet bare. Her flawless brown skin, almost glowing with power. Her presence brings me comfort, and I take that as a sign I can trust her.

"I am Nwt, " she says simply. She holds out her hand, offering it to me. I reach for it, and she helps me to my feet.

"I am Ashanti, " I say, although something tells me she knows everything about me, "Where am I?"

"Come my child, let us walk and talk. I find that helps."

I walk beside her in the sand, and occasionally a wave splashes against our feet. Finally, she speaks, although she continues looking forward, her head held high like a queen, or maybe a God?

"You are in your resting place."

"I've died?" I ask, my feet freeze, and I turn to face her, fear spreading cold shivers down my spine.

"No, you are still very alive in the waking world. This is simply the place your ancestors have created so your mind can rest. You have endured much in your short life, and so much more will come. Your body needs time to heal, and your mind needs to rest. You can stay here in this realm until you feel safe enough to return, " she explains.

"But Isaiah? My baby?" I ask, fear preventing me from moving another step. She stops, taking my hands into hers.

"Isaiah is fine, my love. He rests, protected by many beings of the forgotten world, " she reassures me. My heart breaks, realizing she has avoided discussing my baby.

"And my baby?" I ask knowing the answer but needing to hear it.

"I'm afraid she is resting now. We welcomed her not long ago. She is safe with us. She will grow in this realm, she will be happy, and loved. She will remain with her family here."

My knees give out as I sink to the ground. My baby is gone. I will never see her little face.

"You will see her again. No one truly dies. We just meet again in a new place, at a different time. Come, I want to show you something." She reaches her hand out again, lifting me from the ground and leading me further down the beach.

"Who are you to me?" I ask, "Are you God?"

"No, no, I am not our creator. I am one of your ancestors. I lived very long ago in Africa, a small village near what would be Egypt. I was what you would call a vampire in your time."

This revelation stops me cold, "A vampire? Is that what you meant when you said the forgotten world?"

"Yes. There are many beings, outside of vampires living in the waking realm. I lived many, many lives there, praying for years to our ancestors and the creator to grant me rest, and here I am. They finally granted my wish."

I think over what she is telling me, "And you said Isaiah is safe because these beings are watching him?"

"Yes, no child on Earth has ever been more protected."

"Who is he with?"

"Asim, and Cairo, at this moment."

"Who are they? The wolf that attacked me and Adam?"

"The wolf you are referring to is Cairo; he attacked Adam to save you. He is a shapeshifter and takes many forms. While his protection came a little late, he did save your life. Asim asked him to watch over you and Isaiah."

"And who is Asim? A relative? An ancestor?" I ask.

"No, you may know her as Erin."

"Erin? No, Erin isn't some mythical creature. I know Erin. She is a normal woman. She walks in the daytime. She cooked with garlic."

Nwt laughs gently, "The legends you have heard are wrong, meant to give comfort to children. Vampires do not have these limitations. We walk in the day and can swim in garlic if we choose. Asim is a vampire. She has been for a very long time. I met her many moons ago. Her mother once helped me. In exchange, I gave Asim the gift of eternity. Since that day, she has spent her time protecting women and wandering the earth."

"You changed her?"

"Yes, so long ago, it seems fate has a sense of humor. Asim and you are now in love, no?" She asks.

I think of Erin, or Asim. Her teeth long and pointy, her eyes red, "I don't know."

"I understand. This is so much to accept. Learning the monsters of bedtime tales are real. Knowing you have loved one. Asim is a good being. She has saved many people. She loves you and Isaiah. Even now, as we speak, she kneels beside your bed, your hand in hers." I look down at my empty hands, "Even if I could get past that knowledge. She lied to me. I let her into my life, around my child, and she is a... a *vampire*? Is Sarah as well?"

"Sarah is Heqet, and yes. Heqet has been a longtime companion of Asim."

I walk quietly with this new information. Unsure of what to do or feel. So much has happened, and yet, I am walking on the beach, with my ancestor, feeling the ocean at my feet, in another realm.

"Here, I think there is something you must see, before you make so many decisions," Nwt says. I look up to see a small, rundown house. My home from childhood.

"How?" I ask in wonder, the home exactly as I remember it.

"This is YOUR resting place. This home brings you comfort." She says, climbing the stairs. She waits at the front door for me, "Why don't you go in? I will wait here."

I hesitate at the door but she smiles and nods with encouragement. Walking inside, the first thing I recognize is my old rundown sneakers at the door, kicked off as if I just ran inside. I hold my breath, realizing this is a place for my ancestors. I walk slowly into the living room, afraid he may not be there. The sound of the old tv makes me pick up my pace. I turn the corner and look where his old recliner used to sit. Sitting there, just as much of a mountain as I remember, my father.

"Daddy?" I say, my voice cracking with emotion. He looks up, and smiles at me, holding his finger to his mouth, telling me to be quiet. On his chest a newborn baby. I cry out, tears streaming down my face as I rush to my father. My baby girl snuggled with him.

"Now, now, don't go shedding no tears for me, " he says, wrapping his arm around me.

"I missed you so much!" I say, sobbing.

"I missed you too, little monkey."

I laugh at his old nickname for me, "So much has happened."

"I know, I know. I wish I could have been there with you through it. But some lessons have to be learned the hard way, and I couldn't protect you from it, no matter how badly I wanted to. They're real strict round here about stepping in." He chuckles to himself, "You bet I tried though."

My daughter coos, and I look down at her, totally mesmerized.

"Well, hello, " I say, reaching for her. My father hands her to me, and I hold her close, "I'm so glad I got to meet you." I rock her while I hold her tightly, silent tears running down my cheeks, "I'm so sorry I couldn't protect you, little one."

"You protected her just fine. This wasn't your fault. Things happen as they do. We gotta just roll with it. Even the hard stuff. You lost a lot of people, Shanti. More people than most. I'm afraid you gonna lose a few more in your lifetime, but good is coming. You come from a long line of stubborn women. You fight to get back there to that little guy, and you're gonna be alright."

"I don't want to leave you! I just got to hold her." I say, "Can't I stay here and just be near y'all for a little while longer."

"You'll be here with us soon enough; no need to rush it. I'm gonna stay here with this little one. She'll be fine here. I promise you that."

"But I don't know what to do about Erin, or Adam. I'm scared, Daddy," I say, sitting in the rocking chair next to his, holding my baby girl close.

"Do you love this, Erin?" He asks.

"I thought I did, but I don't even know her."

"Of course, you do. So, her name is different. So, she's different. She kept you safe. That's more than that Adam has ever done. You go on back there, and you talk to this Erin, or Asim, or whoever, and you figure this out. Isaiah needs you."

"I love you so much!" I say, getting up and hugging him close.

"I love you too, little monkey. Now let's name this little one, so you can get going where you belong."

For some reason, this request takes me by surprise, "Name her?"

"Yes love, you have to name your daughter."

I look down at her, memorizing every feature, her scent, the chubbiness of her cheeks.

"What about Isis?"

"Isis?" My father repeats, "Like the goddess?"

"Yes, Isis, it's a queen's name, " I say.

"Okay, Isis. Come back over here to Paw Paw, and let's give your momma the boot."

I hug my dad as tightly as I can, and snuggle my daughter until my father reminds me, I have another little one waiting. Walking out the door, I see Nwt waiting.

"Are you ready?" She asks, patting my arm comfortingly.

I inhale and exhale deeply, "I want to see Isaiah."

"Good."

We walk back to where I walked out of the darkness. I peer into the tunnel, afraid, remembering the feeling of nothingness.

"You have to focus, child, remember what you are fighting for and reach towards it." She says this as if she is not just speaking of the tunnel.

I nod, "Will I see you all again?"

"Of course, this is your resting place. You'll be back when it is your time."

I nod, inhale deeply, and step into the darkness.

Chapter Eleven – Adam

"Who the fuck are you!" I yell. I again attempt to wiggle my hands-free, but the rope is too tight. I look around in the darkness, trying to make something out. However, it's too dark. I try to squirm, but the ropes dig into my torn side. I recall the wolf that attacked me before I blacked out–Ashanti. That stupid bitch. She's the reason I'm here. I hope she's dead. Did she genuinely believe she could leave me for another woman? Embarrass me in front of my peers and parents?! I'll escape from here and find Isaiah; together, he, Helen, and I will fix this. But first, I have to get out of this mess. Ashanti doesn't have friends or family. Who would care enough to do this? Erin. It has to be Erin. Did she pay some goons to tie me up while I was unconscious? I look around again, hoping to make something out, but every-thing just blends in. I realize that what I thought was sweat is actually blood. I'm bleeding heavily, and it starts trickling into my eyes, burning them.

"WHO'S THERE!" I scream again. "They'll be looking for me. Let me go now, and we might not kill you."

I hear movement in the corner. I squint, hoping to see something. I make out a silhouette of someone, or maybe something. It doesn't make a sound, just walking slowly and quietly towards me.

"Who...Who's there," I ask again, my voice betraying me with a quiver.

"I thought all humans deserved life," the silhouette says. The voice sounds familiar, but I can't make it out. As it continues to speak, "I have fought for so much of my existence for even the worst of you to live. But you... your kind. I have never understood. We are considered the monster to your people. But how? How could we be the monsters when you and your kind are here? Polluting the world. Hidden in plain sight. Preying on innocent souls."

A light suddenly turns on, blinding me temporarily. As my eyes adjust, I recognize the voice finally. "Sarah?"

I laugh to myself, relaxing in my seat. "Look, I don't know what kind of kinky shit you're into, but this isn't how you get alone with me, love."

Sarah smiles at me and continues walking slowly to me, but it's not her usual cheerful smile. This smile sends shivers down my spine, my stomach twists and turns. "What do you want?'

She stops directly in front of me, her small frame just a few inches taller than me sitting down. I flinch as she raises her hand to caress my face, her features soft, like she's thinking of something.

"Do you know where we are, Adam?" she asks quietly. I look around, unfamiliar with the room I'm in. The best I can make out is a basement of some sort.

"I don't know, love, a basement?" I try to remain calm; this bitch is obviously a lot crazier than I gave her credit for. "Why don't you untie me and show me around."

Without hesitation, Sarah stops caressing my face, instead digging her nails into my cheek. I scream out in pain as her nails slice through my cheek like knives. To my horror, she pulls her nails out of my cheek and licks them, frowning.

"You even taste disgusting," she says, wiping her hand on my ripped shirt.

"What the fuck is wrong with you, Sarah? This shit can't be about my ho-ass wife. You barely knew her." I say, feeling the blood leaking down my face. Sarah rolls her eyes.

"My name is Heqet, you idiot. He-qet," she says slowly, as if I annoy her.

"Heqet? Who the fuck is that?"

"Ugh, me!" she says. "And that ho ass wife you are referring to is my family, unfortunately for you. I love her like a sister. Isaiah like a nephew-"

"Look, you crazy ass bi-" I start to scream, but she grabs my lips, digging her nails into them until they are dangling from my face. I scream, my body violently shaking in response to the pain.

"Like I was saying. They are my family," she continues as if nothing has happened. "I love them. I am a peaceful being. While I detest men, I have always felt humanity deserved a chance. But seeing what you did to her... in front of your own son? How could you be so vile? That poor baby, gone. She never got to see her face!" Sarah, or Heqet, says, angrily, shaking her head in disgust.

"Look, just let me out of these; we can talk," I say, hopeful I can reach some sane part of this delusional woman.

"How could you kill your own baby? How could you traumatize your own son? Attempt to kill your wife?" She drags an empty chair until it is right in front of me. "I haven't been forced to kill a human in a long time. I've locked that rageful monster deep inside for longer than you have cursed this earth. But I am convinced I would be doing this world a service with you gone," she continues on with her rant, and I try to loosen the rope tied around my wrist. She's clearly insane. I need to find a way out of here. "I'm going to take my time with this, Adam. I'm going to let those thoughts I buried deep take over for once. My family means everything to me. Everything. You hurt all of them, so I'm going to make sure you feel a piece of that hurt too. Okay?"

"Listen, I don't know what you're on right now, but we can talk this through," I say, but she holds her finger to my mangled lips. I scream out as she presses into them.

"Shhhh, save your energy."

I look in horror as her eyes turn black, and her lips curl back, exposing her teeth. My last thought before she sinks her teeth into my throat: *I'm going to die.*

Chapter Twelve – Asim

"Asim?" Cairo whispers to me as I sit beside Ashanti, firmly grasping her hand. I look over at Isaiah, coloring in the new notebook one of the nurses brought him. He looks up at me and smiles before focusing back on the picture he is coloring. I smile back at him, thankful for this child. He is the only reason I have not burned the city to ashes.

"Asim?" Cairo repeats impatiently. I look towards the door of the small hospital room; Cairo stands in the doorway, dripping wet from the pouring rain outside.

"Yes, yes. I am coming." I softly rub Ashanti's hand, hoping this small gesture somehow wakes her from her coma. She continues to sleep peacefully, "I will be back, love," I whisper to her.

"What have you found?" I ask Cairo as we step into the hallway.

"Heqet has taken Adam; she has been torturing him since Ashanti... since that day Adam harmed her," Cairo says.

"Have you spoken to her?" I ask. I knew Heqet would find Adam and take him. It was expected. Ashanti is her family too now, and Heqet has never been more vicious than when her family is hurt. I look anxiously back into the room.

"Yes, but Asim... she is not well. I fear she has snapped. She has allowed her inner monster, we thought long buried, to rampage freely. She needs you. When she calms, this will not sit on her spirit well," he says, worried for his love.

I look back into the room, checking on Isaiah. It has been three days since his mother was gravely hurt at the hands of his father. Children's Services attempted to remove him and place him into the system, but with the help of The Crafter, Cairo was able to obtain documents allowing me to gain power of attorney over Ashanti in an event such as this, and temporary custody of Isaiah. Ashanti has endured several surgeries in an attempt to repair the internal damage that was done; so far, they seem to be successful. All that can be done now is to wait and pray for her recovery.

"I cannot leave them alone," I say, torn. I cannot abandon Heqet, nor Isaiah, and Ashanti.

"Allow me this time to repay my debt. I will watch them, and I swear on my life no harm will come," Cairo pleads.

I stare at him in disbelief, "Cairo, your previous failure nearly cost me the love of my life and traumatized Isaiah. I cannot put them back into harm's way."

"Asim, you know me; I can do this. I was arrogant, I got comfortable, thinking I can handle a mere human, and I failed. I will not fail you again. I swear it."

I stand there, unsure what to do. My heart belongs to Ashanti, to Isaiah, but I also love my best friend dearly. Every second, I know she draws closer to a dark hole she will not be able to climb out of.

"Cairo... I beg of you. Please. Watch them as if it was Heqet in that bed. As if it were your own child in that chair," I plead with him.

"I swear to you, Asim, they are safe."

"The moment she awakes, you are to contact me. ANY change, and you are to contact me," I say. He agrees quickly. I return to the room and kneel beside Isaiah.

"Hey little one," I say, smiling gently at him.

"Hey, Rinny!" He says happily, "I'm drawing a picture for mommy, when she wakes up."

"That's great! You are doing such a good job." I ruffle his hair, and he giggles. "So umm, I have to run a quick errand and grab Sarah so she can come here with us to wait for mommy to wake up," I explain. At the mention of Sarah, Isaiah lights up.

"Yesss! I love Sarah!" He says, smiling widely.

"Great, so Mr. Cairo is going to stay here with you and keep you company until I get back in a little while. Okay?" I ask. Isaiah nods his head while peeking at Cairo. He then signals for me to come closer. I lean over so he can whisper in my ear.

"Will he turn into a wolf again?" He whispers, afraid.

"No. I made him promise, no more wolves." I look sternly at Cairo, and he nods in agreement, putting up a scout's honor hand gesture.

"I promise," he says seriously.

"Okay then," Isaiah agrees, hesitantly.

I stand and walk over to Ashanti, bending down to kiss her forehead. "I will return quickly, love." As I turn to leave, Isaiah calls my name. I turn to see him running to me, before throwing his little arms around my legs, hugging me.

This gesture breaks me in a way I did not expect. I hug him back, tightly.

"I'll be back, little guy. I promise," I say and hurry from that hospital room, unsure what I am hurrying towards.

I knew when I heard of Heqet's disappearance exactly where she would go. It was our safety net. In case everything went to hell, and we had to go into hiding. I quickly drive out of town and deep into the surrounding woods, turning onto a dirt road, and parking out of sight. I run on foot for a few minutes, slowing when I hear the muffled screams of Adam; the screams are too low for human ears. He's deep underground. I follow the screams until I find the cabin we built not long ago. At first sight, it appears abandoned, left to decay, the roof intentionally made to cave in, shattered windows, and a sunken porch. Once inside, under the fridge, down the hidden stairs, we built a cellar, or a bunker really. I walk slowly down the stairs, knowing Heqet can hear me approaching. I hesitate at the door, not bothering to knock.

"Come," Heqet says simply. I walk into the room and immediately realize Cairo was right. Heqet is not well. I stare at my companion, covered in blood, Adam's ear in her right hand, the nails of her left hand dug deep into his chest. Adam, whimpering, on a table. I look in horror, realizing he is not strapped to the table. Heqet having broken his ankles, as they dangle off the table at odd angles. I look at my longtime companion, concerned. Heqet has given in to her monster, falling so deeply into the darkness...

"Hey, Heqet," I say quietly.

"Asim," she says through her teeth; even three days of torture has not satisfied her monster.

"What are we doing, little one?" I ask, ignoring Adam's pleas for help. My inner monster giddy, seeing Adam broken and beaten, at the edge of death.

"He deserves this," she says, as she looks at me, her eyes pleading with me to understand.

I smile, an encouraging smile at my best friend.

"It's okay, love. Let me finish it," I say, reaching for her hand. "Here, let's put down... his...uh... ear. Yup, right there." I set his ear next to him on the table. I pull Heqet into a hug. "It's okay... Shhhh, it's okay." I hold her as she crumbles. "You did good."

I soothe her, patting her hair, and allowing her to grieve, the loss of a child, the innocence of Isaiah. I knew that would hurt her the most. "I'll finish it. Wait upstairs."

"No, I need to be here." She says, her voice firm, "I need to know this monster is gone."

I nod in understanding, walking over to Adam, barely alive, so weakened his eyes remain closed, his breathing ragged. I listen to his weak heart as it falters. So close to death, I can smell it.

"Help," he whispers.

I dig my own nails into the hole that was once his ear. "Open your eyes."

Adam's eyes flash open as he screams in pain. I lean down, whispering close to his remaining ear, "Ashanti lives. She will heal and feel love. She will travel, paint, and prosper. I will love her *and* Isaiah. He will grow old and forget your face. The world will forget you existed. They win."

He tries to say something. His lips quiver as he tries to build the strength to say it, but I do not give him the courtesy of last words as I snap his neck. I look down at this lifeless, insignificant human, who has wreaked havoc and turmoil in the last few years of Ashanti's life. I remember the night I sat in the tree, Isaiah lying in bed, crying silently as we listened to his mother's cries as this swine beat her. "He is gone," I whisper. Heqet steps closer, standing beside me as we both stare at his body.

"May he rot," Heqet spits.

"Are you okay?" I ask her, still staring at Adam's body.

"I am now," she says, "How is Ashanti?"

"Still asleep," I say. We stand still for a moment, trying to wrap our heads around our current lives. Without speaking, we begin cleaning our mess. Quickly, using the cleaning chemicals we stored here to remove of any traces of Adam. As we put away the chemicals and inspect our work, my phone rings.

"Yes," I answer quickly, "Are they okay?"

"Ashanti's heart rate is dropping; you need to get here," Cairo says, panicking. Heqet and I take off running, making it to the car within a few minutes.

"She will survive," Heqet repeats to herself, as if chanting. I tune her out, as I pray to my ancestors and hers. *She cannot die. I cannot bear it.* The drive back to the hospital seems to take an eternity, but we finally reach the entrance to the hospital. I leave Heqet, as she quickly changes her blood-stained clothing in the car. I hear the commotion before I see the room. Nurses and doctors rushing in and out. She's struggling, losing the fight to live.

"Ma'am, you cannot go in there." A nurse attempts to stop me, but I push past her. I must see her. I listen to her heart rate as I approach her; it is much too low. I grasp her hand tightly, scarcely aware of the nurses demanding me to leave.

"Ashanti," I whisper, as I lean into her hair, inhaling her scent, "Please, Ashanti. We need you. You must fight. I know you are scared. I am too. Please, please...fight for me. Fight for Isaiah. We need you."

"Asim," Heqet calls to me, her hand resting on top of my own and Ashanti's, "We must allow the doctors to work. Ashanti will come back when she is ready. She will not die here."

Heqet says this so confidently, that I turn to face her, "How are you sure?"

"Because she is a fighter; she will not leave Isaiah alone, nor you. Believe in her; she will return."

I contemplate this for a second, part of me wanting to snatch her up and run. Surely, I know more than these human doctors. But Heqet is right. This is her mind protecting itself. She must fight to live. I lean down, kissing her forehead, "Live for me."

Heqet holds my hand as we walk out of the room, allowing the nurses and doctors to continue to attend to her.

"She inhaled deeply, then her heart rate plummeted, I don't know what happened," Cairo says, holding Isaiah tightly in his arms.

"Sarah!" He practically shouts, squirming to get out of Cairo's arms.

"Little one!" Heqet swoops him into her arms and hugs him tightly.

"Mommy is sick!" Isaiah sobs, his face buried into Heqet's shoulder.

"It's okay. She will be okay." Heqet comforts him, rubbing his back softly and pacing with him, "Why don't we go get some hot chocolate while the doctors work to make Mommy better?"

"Okay," he says quietly, still crying as she walks away with him.

"Is it all taken care of?" Cairo asks quietly, once Isaiah is out of earshot.

"Yes, she seems okay," I say, focused on the room. Cairo nods and exhales. His love is safe; he can relax. I feel a tinge of jealousy. I watch as the love of my life is worked on by these strangers, barely holding on to life. I wish for the days we sat in her living room, laughing, the touch of her lips against my own. *Come back to me, Ashanti.*

"Erin Brown?" A doctor steps forward, calling over to me from the room. I quickly reach her, maybe a little too fast. She blinks a few times, stepping back surprised.

"Yes?"

"Oh, eh hmm," She clears her throat, trying to compose herself.

"How is she?" I finally impatiently ask her.

"She has stabilized; she gave us a scare there for a little while, but her heart rate is climbing, and she has even had some movement. Her hand has been moving slightly. She's not fully out of the woods yet, but we were able to stop the internal bleeding, and she seems to be on the road to recovery now. All we can do is continue to monitor her, and allow her the time she needs to fight through this," She explains. "She's a tough cookie; I'm sure she'll be up and running behind her little one soon."

"Thank you. I'm grateful to you for saving her life. She means everything to us," I say. The doctor nods.

"She's lucky to have so many friends that care. Too often we see victims of domestic violence who have no one; they get out of here and go right back to their abuser. I'm glad she has people she can lean on once she recovers."

She places her hand on my arm, trying to comfort me, and walks away.

"You okay, chief?" Cairo asks, appearing beside me.

"I'll be better when she's awake," I say, watching her from the doorway. I listen to her heart, stronger but still beating too slowly.

"I'm gonna head over to the café, check on Heqet, and the little guy," Cairo says, patting me on my back before leaving. I smile at his eagerness. We both know Heqet has long loved women. In all the time I have known Heqet, while rare, Heqet finds herself romantically interested; those interests have only ever been shown to women. She has made these feelings abundantly clear to Cairo; nevertheless, he has pursued relentlessly. *How many centuries until he gives up?* I smile to myself as I take my place next to Ashanti. The feel of her hand in mine settles my anxiety.

"I am here, my love," I whisper in her ear, resting my chin beside her. I watch her chest rise and fall, praying she will awaken with each breath. "What are you doing in there, love?"

I lose track of how long I sit in that position. Nurses come and go as they check her vitals and IV bags. Heqet comes, letting Isaiah say goodbye. She has made arrangements for an extravagant hotel outside of town, allowing Isaiah some fun, far away from his home of horrors. Cairo takes his leave with Heqet, offering his much-unneeded protection. Night falls, and I remain unmoved, watching her breathing, listening to her heart.

"Can you hear me, love? I miss you. Please come back," I whisper. "We have so much to discuss, so many adventures to go on. Isaiah misses you," I say. Her heart rate fluctuates slightly, catching me off guard. "Ashanti? Can you hear me, love? Squeeze my hand if you can hear me?"

I stare at our hands, hoping to feel a soft squeeze; minutes pass slowly, but nothing happens. I settle back beside her, realizing sadly, that it was probably a coincidence. As I reposition myself beside her, resting our hands on the bed, I feel the softest squeeze.

"Ashanti?"

The squeeze becomes stronger. I jump up. "Open your eyes, love; it's me. I am here with you."

Her lips part, as her heart rate spikes. I watch in shock as her eyelids flutter; then, Ashanti opens her eyes and stares directly into mine, smiling.

"Asim."

Chapter Thirteen – Ashanti

"I am okay," I say, swatting Heqet's hand away. Since I woke up yesterday, Heqet or Sarah as I have known her, has hovered nonstop around me. "Please, Heqet. I am okay, I promise."

"Hearing you say my true name will always be shocking to me," she says, laughing gently, as she continues to smooth my hair and monitor me.

"Where is Asim?" I ask, surprised she left my side.

"I am here, love, just getting Isaiah a snack," she says, walking into the room holding up a kid's meal with Isaiah in tow.

"Mommy!" Isaiah yells as he rushes up to my side.

"Hi, little monster," I say, trying to sit up. Heqet quickly gently pushes me back onto my pillow.

"Absolutely not!" she scolds. "You have to heal."

"Guess what, Mommy?" Isaiah says happily, as Heqet positions him to sit at the foot of my bed.

"Yes?"

"Sarah took me to a hotel! It had a huge pool, and a giant bed, and I got to jump on it! She said it was okay," he says, smiling brightly as he takes a bite of his burger.

"That sounds amazing! Sarah must have taken good care of you while mommy was sleeping," I say, smiling at Heqet. She looks guiltily away.

"Heqet?" I say, confused. Asim holds my hand, momentarily distracting me.

"Why don't we talk about what we all did when you were asleep later, hmm?" she says, smiling at me. I look back to Heqet.

"Okay, we can all talk later," I say, focusing back on Isaiah, as he tells me all about his drawings and his fancy hotel room.

"It's a secret, but Mr. Cairo can change into animals," Isaiah says, leaning over to whisper to me. "But he won't turn into a spider. I think he can, but he said he can't."

Asim, and Heqet chuckle as Cairo blushes.

"Well, little one, everyone has their fears, no?" Heqet says elbowing Cairo as they laugh. I make a mental note to ask about that inside joke.

"How are you feeling?" Asim asks me softly, brushing loose hair from my face. I press my cheek against her hand. I cannot believe I ever doubted this feeling. I love her. I look at Heqet, playfully tickling Isaiah as he giggles, and squirms. They love us. I feel safe; there's no way these gentle beings could hurt a fly. I look at Cairo, the image of that vicious wolf flashes across my mind, and my heart rate spikes, the monitors betraying me.

All three of them look at me at once.

"What's wrong, love?"

"What happened?"

"Are you okay, Ashanti?"

I nod, "just thought of something."

Asim frowns as she follows my eyes to Cairo, piecing together my thoughts.

"I know this may be overwhelming, love, I am in shock how well you have handled all of this. I promise I will explain everything once you are well enough to leave here," she says, patting my hair.

"Okay, I feel so left in the dark about everything," I say frowning.

"I know, but right now, let's focus on getting you better, then we will focus on catching up," she says. I agree because honestly, I would agree to anything she asked of me. We spend the afternoon talking and laughing. Cairo, who terrified me at first, turns out to be the funniest man I've ever met. He clearly is madly in love with Heqet, who shows zero interest, but he seems to enjoy the chase. I wonder how old they all are. They all seem so comfortable with each other. Asim seems different. *Less uptight?* I guess me being in on the secret is a little less stressful for her. I think of her surprised face when I opened my eyes and called her by her name. She seemed less surprised when I explained I dreamt it. I make a note to ask her if she's familiar with those kinds of dreams. *I wonder if they have superpowers?*

"Ashanti?"

Hearing my name pulls me from my thoughts; I realize to my own embarrassment, everyone is staring at me. *How long have I been talking to myself?*

"Are you okay, love?" Asim asks, pressing her hand to my forehead. I laugh to myself, a vampire checking my temperature. She looks at me puzzled, and I shake my head in response.

"Nothing, just a few silly thoughts," I say smiling. Asim looks as though she is going to press me further, but Isaiah yawns.

"Is someone sleepy?" I ask, smiling at him. He shakes his head no.

"No, Mommy, I'm wide awake," he says, unable to stifle his second yawn. We all chuckle at this, while Heqet swoops him up into her arms.

"I think someone's ready for bedtime," she says gently. He rests his head against her shoulder. Cairo stands, prepared to leave as well.

"Cairo, you know I don't need your protection," Heqet says, rolling her eyes.

"Of course, you do love, you just don't know it yet," he says and winks at me with a smile.

"I want Cairo to turn into a rabbit again!" Isaiah says sleepily. Cairo fist-bumps him, and Heqet surrenders to Isaiah's request.

"Fine, little one, "she says. We say our goodbyes, and Heqet leaves with Isaiah, Cairo not far behind. After they leave, Asim closes the hospital room door and turns her focus back to me.

"Now, what were those silly thoughts?" She inquires smiling.

I pat the bed next to me, and she comes over, pulling her usual chair closer, holding my hand tightly.

"Oh, you know, a vampire holding my hand, a shapeshifter tucking my son into bed." I giggle just saying it aloud. She frowns slightly.

"And how do you feel about that? I know we haven't had a moment alone to talk about it since you woke up this morning. It is still a shock to me how well you are taking everything," she says nervously, as if she is waiting for me to scream at any moment. I smile and pat her hand comfortingly.

"I know it seems like I just found out, but I had this... this dream, and I had time to process everything, and learn a few things," I explain again.

"Yes, I remember you saying that before the nurses and doctors came rushing in. But can you explain this dream to me? If it told you about me, it would seem to be more of a vision," she perks up, listening intently.

"Well... the last thing I remember, before.... before the wolf...umm...before Cairo... well, you know," I say, twisting my hands in my lap, remembering Adam's pain-filled screams of horror, "Everything just went black. I couldn't move. My arms, and legs didn't work. So, I just sat in this like never-ending darkness, for days. Well, it felt like days. Then I heard a voice. This woman started talking to me. I couldn't see her at first, but I heard her so clearly. She told me to focus, and guided me out of the darkness. I ended up on this beach. The wind felt so real. I could feel the mist on my face." I gesture towards my face, reenacting the mist spraying on me, "Then this woman, the voice... She appeared next to me. She was so tall, and beautiful. She called herself... Nwt?"

Asim sits up straight in her chair, "Are you sure? She said her name was Nwt?"

I nod my head, "I'm positive. She's the one who told me about you, Heqet, and Cairo. She said she turned you a really long time ago, before her ancestors granted her peace."

She sits back in her chair, thinking of something, "Did she say who she was to you?"

"She said she was my relative, an ancestor," I explain, "So she really turned you?"

"Amazing," Asim says, squeezing my hand gently, excited, "Yes, she did. I met Nwt in my human life. It was a very, very, long time ago. But please, continue."

"Okay umm, so she walked with me on the beach, and explained to me I was in my...umm... she called it a –."

"Resting place," Asim finishes my sentence.

"You know about it?" I ask, relieved. Explaining my dream makes me feel insane, but her understanding of it makes me feel less silly.

"Yes, I have a resting place as well. I go there from time to time; I have never heard of a human being able to visit there and return." She looks at me curiously, "You are remarkable."

I blush deeply as she looks at me as if I am a masterpiece of art.

"Did anything else happen there?" She asks, encouraging me to continue.

"Well, yes, I learned about my...my daughter," I say, my voice cracking with emotion. Asim rubs my hand, trying to comfort me.

"I am so sorry, Ashanti. I should have never left your side." She says, full of shame.

"No, this was not your fault. Adam did this. He is a monster. A true monster, and one day he's going to pay for this." I say, trying to comfort her. Something flashes across her face, an emotion I don't quite understand, but it's gone quickly.

"Thank you, love. Did you meet anyone besides Nwt there?"

Her question distracts me and I feel myself smiling widely, "Yes! I met her! My daughter! She is so beautiful, Asim. I didn't want to leave her. She was with my father. He promised to raise her there, and she will be safe. I named her Isis, after the goddess. I got to hold her and hug my father again." I say, tears running down my face. "It was beautiful."

"I'm so glad the ancestors granted you that."

I nod in agreement, "Then my father told me it was time to come back, and Nwt led me back to the darkness, and told me I have to fight my way back. When I stepped back into it, I almost got lost again. I could feel my legs going numb, but this Abyssinian cat, you know like the orange ones in the movies in ancient Egypt? Well, it just appeared in the darkness and led me out. I woke up here."

"A cat? Are you sure?" She asks, shocked.

"Yes, does that mean something?"

"I'm not sure," she says.

"This wasn't a dream, was it?" I ask, slowly accepting the reality of my recent situation.

"No, love, it was very much real. It is a realm outside of this one. A place where our ancestors dwell. It is very, very unusual they granted you, shall we call it, a round trip from there. You must be quite special in your bloodline. They have many plans for you, love," she says thoughtfully.

"You mean if I got stuck there...if I didn't find my way out of the darkness, I would have died?" I ask, fear setting in.

"Yes, but you *did* find your way out. You are here, with me, safe, and very much alive," she says, kissing me.

"This is so much to process," I say, laying back against my pillow. Asim gently caresses my face before playing with a loose curl.

"It is, love, I have had a very long time to understand my world, and you have been thrown into it. I apologize for that."

I reach for her, and she brings her face to me, so that I can rest my hand against her cheek. I look into her eyes, searching for any trace of the monsters I envisioned in my dreamworld, but all I find is my Erin, or Asim as I now know her. She kisses the back of my hand and holds it back against her cheek. "I will admit, this new world scares me in ways I can't really even explain, but I feel safe knowing you are in it," I say, a blush creeping into my cheeks as I admit my feelings.

"I would perish protecting you and Isaiah. You are my world now, love," she says, and we sit quietly, enjoying each other's company for a while, laughing at silly jokes. I don't know when I drifted off to sleep, but I'm startled awake by a loud commotion.

"I do not care, wake her up!" I hear a woman yelling from the hallway."

The voice sounds so familiar, I struggle to sit up, but the pain in my ribs forces me back to my pillow. *Where do I know that voice from?*

"This is absurd. Where is my grandson!?"

I sit straight up in my bed, wincing at the pain, but understanding creeps into my mind all at once. Adam's parents are here. I look around for Asim, but she's gone. I listen as the nurse struggles to turn her away.

"She needs to rest, ma'am."

"She can rest after we find my son and my grandson. They could be hurt somewhere. Really, I am sure she is fine. She was always a bit dramatic."

"Asim?" I whisper, unsure how the vampire thing works. *Can she hear me from far away?* I think of all the embarrassing moments she might have heard in my house if that is true, and pray it isn't.

"I'm here, love." Asim says, appearing at my doorway. Blood rushes to my cheeks as I realize she absolutely heard all my embarrassing, most private moments, even with Adam, "It's okay, I'm not going anywhere."

I nod in understanding as Adam's mother continues her tantrum.

"Why can this stranger just go into her room? I'm the only mother the girl has. Seriously. We are her only family."

I roll my eyes. Adam's family has always hated me. His mother made it abundantly clear she saw me as a gold digger the moment she met me. They rarely came to visit, and I would hear them pleading with him to take Isaiah and leave me. They forced Adam to get a DNA test as soon as Isaiah was born. I loathe this woman, but I know how ruthless and persistent they are. I might as well get this over with now.

"They can come," I say as confidently as I can.

"See, she's awake."

I listen to the clicking of her heels on the hospital floor as she approaches my room., Asim takes a seat in the corner, and I smile a thank you, grateful she decided to stay.

His mother enters the room first. Her usually long hair flawlessly straightened and cut into a bob, dark sunglasses covering her eyes, and dark red lipstick standing out on perfectly sculpted lips. Years of surgery have done wonders and has helped her keep the figure of a 20-something-year-old model. Her expression, as always, disapproving. Her husband, never far behind, walks into the room and immediately looks around, disgust clear on his face. Adam is a carbon copy of his father's features. His father preferring his hair cut low, and his mustache trimmed. Years of being catered to have added a few extra pounds around his midsection, which his wife reminds him of often. They both notice me simultaneously turning their heads in my direction, before noticing Asim in the corner.

"Oh! Would you look at you! Pitiful thing!" His mother feigns concern, "I heard you hurt yourself, and I just told Robert we have to go check on her! Didn't I, Robert."

"Yes dear, we were so concerned," he says, sounding uninterested.

She comes to me, and kisses my forehead, barely grazing my skin before standing upright, "So where is my son and grandson?"

I stare at her in disbelief, wondering who called them, "Isaiah is with friends... I don't know where Adam is, but I did not hurt myself--"

"What do you mean he's with friends? He should be with family," she says indignantly, "Surely he should be with family."

"He's fine where he is," I say sternly. My voice catches her off guard. My usual meek and mild-mannered self long gone after enduring everything I have been through. I feel stronger, and the idea of them sinking their claws into Isaiah... never.

His mother waves her hand, as if dismissing what I've said, "Don't be silly dear, you're unwell; they clearly have your meds on high," She laughs at her own joke, "Where is he? We will collect him."

I look from his mother to his father, genuinely confused, "Lauren, do you understand what has happened to me?"

"Of course, I do, you and Adam are having a little spat."

"No. Adam nearly beat me to death, in front of our son, your grandson then disappeared. There is no way my son is going anywhere with you."

His mother adjusts her bracelets on her wrist, annoyed with my refusal to accept her twisted reality, "Ashanti, darling. You have always been a bit clumsy. I tried to teach you more elegance, but unfortunately, with your upbringing, it has been nearly impossible. Being angry with your spouse is normal. Surely, me and Robert have had our spats in the past; however, I have never done anything as juvenile and tasteless as making baseless accusations for attention."

"Please leave," I say, fighting to swallow every horrible thing I could say. His parents are just as deranged as the son they raised, and I'm done with them and him.

"What do you mean?" She asks, confused.

"Get. Out." I repeat, "Your son is a psycho, narcissist, who beat me ALL of the time. You guys knew he was abusive and made me think I was the problem. I am healing, and my son and I are getting far away from you and your son."

"Are you crazy?" Lauren asks before turning to her husband, "Robert?"

"Sweetheart, there is no need to become hysterical. We understand you are upset, and maybe a little confused. I understand there was some possible head trauma. We will come back tomorrow, and maybe you will be in a better mood?" He says this slowly, like he's speaking to a small child or a very stupid adult.

"Respectfully, Robert, kiss my--"

"I think maybe it is time for you to leave." Asim stands quickly, cutting off my statement. She pats my foot gently as she walks by, her face slightly amused.

"Who are you?" Lauren asks, looking her up and down.

"I believe this is the friend Adam called to tell us about, darling," Robert says, eyebrow raised, as Asim ushers them out of the room.

"Ashanti, don't be silly, we both know this won't end well in court."

Before I can respond, Asim leans closely, towering over Lauren as she stares directly into her eyes, "Leave now, and do not contact Ashanti again."

Lauren stares up at her, first confused, then her face becomes lifeless, as she whispers back to her, "I will leave and not contact Ashanti."

Robert stares at his wife, then back at Asim, "What? Honey, are you okay?"

Asim closes the door in their face before turning to smile at me, "Well, your family is lovely."

"That is not my family! Adam's family all reflect exactly who he is! The audacity to show up here and demand my son." I sit fuming; *how entitled, and deranged are these people? How could I be so blind?* As quickly as my rage rises, it falls. I sit in quiet wonder. *Where did that come from? I would never have done that before! Will they really take me to court?* The stress nearly swallows me before Asim interrupts my thoughts.

"It is okay, love, Heqet might swallow them whole if they attempt to take him from her."

My eyes grow wide, "Can she, can you do that?"

Asim laughs out loud, and it is the most carefree sound I have ever heard. I smile listening to her laugh, "What's so funny? I don't know anything about it."

"That is true, love. I do not believe you will hear from them again. I was waiting until we left this horrible place, but I guess if it will make you happy after that event, I can answer a few questions now."

I smile brightly, forgetting my worries, and wince as I try to adjust myself against my pillow. Asim quickly helps me, "You must have questions ready, then, huh?" She asks, suddenly nervous.

"Umm, just a few." I smile, feeling silly.

"Okay, shoot."

Chapter Fourteen
– Asim

I listen intently to Ashanti's heartbeat; stronger than ever as she sleeps. This is what happiness feels like. After a very long four weeks in the hospital, Ashanti will be discharged tomorrow. Heqet, prepared as always, has made travel arrangements for all of us, including Cairo, very much to my surprise. She insists he is traveling along due to his insistent pleading to tag along for a few years, but I suspect Cairo may have succeeded in gaining the affections of a certain little vampire. I smile at the thought of my very new future: me, Ashanti, Isaiah, Heqet, and Cairo. A family. The Ancestors have smiled down on me finally, granting me this path of peace. Ashanti's heart rate spikes, grabbing my attention. I quickly lean towards her, inspecting her body. Her eyes suddenly open, and she gasps loudly.

"Ashanti? What is wrong, love? Are you feeling okay?" I notice the tears flowing silently from her eyes. My protective instincts react, as my eyes darken, and my mouth floods with venom, "What has happened?"

She looks at me, and blinks several times, her eyes trying to adjust. I quickly calm myself, allowing my eyes to return to their normal state.

"I'm sorry, I had a nightmare," she admits looking down in shame. *Oh.* A nightmare was one danger I was not prepared for.

"It is okay, love. Do you want to tell me about this nightmare?"

She curls her legs slowly to her chest. I notice this happy change. Just a few weeks ago, she could barely move. *How quickly her body is healing.*

"It was Adam."

I feel my anger flare. *This demon of a man continues to torture her in the dream realm! Unbelievable.* I think of the ways I could try and remove him from her nightmares, but I know it is useless. Her nightmares are of her own doing; she fears him, so he exists in her mind where I cannot reach him.

"He... He... He came back." She sobs, terrified. I quickly wrap my arms around her, attempting to comfort her. Seeing her afraid hurts my being. *How can I protect her? Would knowing Adam is dead comfort her, or make her fear me?* It is selfish to withhold this information. Whether she fears me or not, knowing he is dead would provide her with closure I cannot give with comforting words.

"You are safe now, my love, it was just a dream," I say soothingly, gently rubbing her back.

"I'm just so scared I will go home tomorrow, and he will be waiting there," she says, wiping her eyes.

"We could go somewhere else," I suggest. Her assumption of us returning to her home takes me by surprise. I assumed she would want to move elsewhere with me and already made the arrangements. *What else have I assumed wrong?*

She laughs quietly without humor, "Yeah that would be nice, to just run away."

"No, really, love. We could. Wherever you want to go. We could be whoever you want to be," I assure her. Maybe I should not have waited to answer the big questions about my life.

"Adam would never let me just leave. Even in hiding, he would find ways, and his family would never give up. They are quiet because they are plotting, believe me," she says. I frown. *Have I not shown her I am capable of protecting her?* I guess I have failed in the most significant way. She may not trust me completely. That is understandable; I need to earn that trust. Perhaps I should be honest with her.

"Ashanti...there are some things I have done... I am not proud. But I feel I should be honest with you--"

"Nothing you could have done would ever make me stop loving you, Asim. You and Isaiah are the only light in my world right now."

"Well, what does that make me?" Heqet says walking in. I roll my eyes; I heard her approach but assumed she would wait, hearing the seriousness of our conversation. Once again, I assumed wrong.

"Of course, I can't forget you!" Ashanti lights up seeing Heqet.

"As long as you both remember I am the light of both of your worlds." She says smiling.

"Where is Isaiah?" She asks disappointedly.

"He is coming, he is making Cairo do magic tricks in the children's unit." She says casually before sitting down.

Ashanti and I exchange looks, "Heqet...magic tricks? Surely you do not mean..."

"No, no, do not be absurd. He taught Cairo a card trick and he is making him reenact it for the children. He insisted they are big enough to do it on their own and sent me here." She says casually, but I detect a slight pout.

I smile and walk over to ruffle her perfect curly hair, "Come now, little one, you are not jealous, are you?"

She playfully pushes me away, "Jealous? No, I am glad Isaiah has bonded with Cairo." She says, but crosses her arms defensively, "Anyway I have made all of the arrangements for tomorrow."

I freeze in my position, having not prepared Ashanti; I prepare for her reaction.

"Arrangements?" Ashanti asks.

"Surely you have spoken to her by now." Heqet looks at me incredulously.

Why is she suddenly so talkative? Is this a side effect of her happiness? I try to silence her with a look, but she rolls her eyes at me, before waving me off entirely.

"Ashanti, I did not realize Asim had not spoken with you yet. However, Asim and I both thought it would be best to disappear for a little while. With Adam's parents making threats, and I assume disposing of them would not be ideal for you," She pauses, giving Ashanti a chance to respond. I stare at her in utter shock.

"Oh...um...no that would not...we probably don't want that option." Ashanti struggles to get out, unsure if Heqet is serious or not. I stare at her knowing she is very serious.

"Well then, yes, leaving would be best then. Do you agree?"

Ashanti turns to me, "Is this what you were trying to say a little while ago?"

I nod, ashamed. I should have spoken honestly with Ashanti regarding our plans. *Why am I so afraid of her reaction to me? She has openly professed her feelings. Is this not enough?* She nods too, as if she is piecing something together. She remains quiet for a few moments. Heqet patiently sits, allowing her to think without pressure. I sit quietly as well, thinking of how confident Heqet is. She has completely opened herself up to Ashanti without hesitation.

"Okay, where are we going?"

"Really?" I ask, shocked.

"You think I'm letting my little Addams family get away?" She laughs at her joke, as I smile. Truly, I am favored.

"Great," Heqet says, as if she knew the answer all along, "We will return home."

"Home?" Ashanti and I say at the same time.

"You mean Africa?" Ashanti asks.

"Heqet, we did not speak of this," I say, worried.

"We never speak of the arrangements. I simply arrange," Heqet says as she rolls her eyes, "Yes, love, Africa. Our home is near present-day Egypt. It is...shall we say a magical place? We thought it would be important to introduce you to parts of *our* world."

"Introduce, not throw into," I correct her, "Heqet, I need to speak with you regarding this."

"Let us speak then." She says, adjusting herself to sit cross-legged in the chair. I raise an eyebrow. *What has gotten into her?*

"Alone?" I suggest.

"Not necessary," She looks at me as if I have missed an obvious detail, "Asim, Ashanti is now one of us; we mustn't shelter her from the world she is now a part of. She needs to be a part of these decisions. They affect not only us but her, and more importantly Isaiah. You will always be Asim, the great protector to us, but we must learn a balance of protection versus control. Ashanti has just gotten out of a very abusive," She pauses to give Ashanti a compassionate smile, "relationship; we need to include her in decisions and get her opinion on what *she* wants as well."

I look at Ashanti, noticing she is nodding in agreement, smiling at Heqet. *Have I been controlling? To Heqet?* I never thought of it that way, but Heqet, as always, is right. I will never control Ashanti as Adam had, "I apologize, Ashanti; that was never my intention, yet I may have crossed that boundary without meaning to. I will include you in decisions going forward. And Heqet?" She looks up at me confused.

"Yes?"

"I am sorry; it never dawned on me after so many years together, I had become controlling. I apologize to you as well."

Heqet looks at me puzzled for a moment, then smiles, "Thank you, Asim; that was unexpected but welcomed."

"So, what makes it so magical? Is it like filled with vampires?" Ashanti asks curiously.

"You've told her nothing?" Heqet asks, appalled.

"Well, Asim has answered a few questions." She says quietly, trying to defend my actions, but now that Heqet has brought my attempts at control to my attention, I wonder silently *if not answering all of her questions immediately was also controlling.*

"No, I haven't told her nearly enough," I admit with a sigh, sinking into my seat like a defeated child. Heqet's scolding was the worst kind. While she bore no children herself, nothing can defeat Heqet's motherly demeanor.

She shoots me a stern glare, while sucking her teeth, and for just a moment, I see Heqet of our ancient youth, standing in the forest, protecting her children, "Let us explain today, so tomorrow isn't a surprise, eh?"

I nod in agreement, realizing quickly she is in fact right. Ashanti, excited as ever, sits at attention, like an eager child.

"Do you need a pillow, or maybe you should lean back?" I offer, concerned, but Ashanti swats my hand away, shushing me.

"No babe, I've been waiting forever for this!"

"Okay, where to begin?" Heqet asks herself, "Hmm, why don't you share what you already know?"

Ashanti looks shyly at me, and I nod encouragingly, "Okay. I know you are older than
America-"

"AMERICA?" Heqet sits up in her chair, shooting me a look, "Really Asim?"

"Let her speak, Heqet." I say, smiling at her annoyance. She sits back, arms folded, and allows Ashanti to continue.

"Okay umm, I know you drink blood, but you do not have to kill to survive; you can eat food but you do not. You can walk in the sun, and garlic doesn't hurt you... or crosses. You two are not really siblings by blood but you have been companions for so long you are family by bond." She explains, and looks to me for praise. I smile proudly. But Heqet makes a sound of disgust.

"Is that all she told you?" She asks her, but stares directly at me.

"Y...yes," Ashanti says quietly.

"Okay, so the beginning then, hmm? I'm sorry, Ashanti, I don't want to be pushy, but this world is not rainbows all of the time. It is important to be prepared, especially because we have that little one with us. You need to be knowledge-able about what we will be facing, and how we will live going forward. It is important that you make this decision with all the pieces of this puzzle, you understand? I know you haven't had a lot of choices in your life but you do now. You are an ancestor of Nwt. Power runs through your veins. You must come out of this stronger, wiser," Heqet explains. Heqet's words resonate with Ashanti. I notice her sitting taller, more focused.

"Okay, let us start with what I know of Nwt. No one knows her age. She appeared to transition into her life of eternity around the age of 25 or maybe 30. Humans call her the goddess of the sky and heavens because it is believed she was the first of our kind. Humanity believed it was her purpose to watch over the dead until they joined the after-life, but truly she brought those on the brink of death to eternity. Her blood is the only true pure blood there is. No one knows how she turned. The tale has always said the sky opened one day and she simply fell from it. Her fall created a great rumble and flash of light. She wept as she fell, and that was the creation of what we know as a thunderstorm. She came to this realm with the strength of 10,000 men, and her senses heightened to unbelievable scales. Tall, and beauty unmatched. Her skin dark as night but glowed in the day. She had the tongue of a snake and could hypnotize anyone, and some say any animal as well, to do her bidding. She is the Queen of our people."

Ashanti sits so still; I grow anxious, wondering if she will remember to breathe, totally engrossed in Heqet's telling of our history. I pray silently she keeps some details to herself. *I wonder what Ashanti thinks of this?* I'm aware of Heqet's dramatic pause, carefully placed as I listen to Cairo quietly approach the door, with Isaiah in hand. Hearing our discussion, he invites Isaiah for morning ice cream and quickly carries him away, giving us more time for our history lesson. I focus intently on Ashanti's reactions, half-listening as Heqet continues, but she continues to pause as a nurse comes in to check Ashanti's vitals.

"How are we today?" she asks cheerfully. *Terrified, impatient, Anxious.*

"Great," I say, with a smile, and Ashanti and Heqet respond with their happy replies.

"Just here to check your readings." She quickly reads her devices, and leaves, sensing she is interrupting a discussion.

"So Nwt, I met in my resting realm is the vampire creator?" She asks, stunned.

"Yes," Heqet says softly, "You are a descendant of the original Vampire."

"And she fell from the sky? Does that mean she is a goddess? That I am a descendant of a goddess?"

Heqet sits quietly thinking, "I have thought of this since you shared your meeting with Asim, who, of course, sought my advice. I have searched. I do not know Nwt origin; it is not written as fact. I cannot provide that answer for you. I am sorry."

Ashanti sits thoughtfully before asking Heqet to continue.

"So, the tale continues that Nwt wandered throughout Africa, saving women on the brink of death. No one knows why she chose to save women over men, or if there was ever a man she found worthy of changing in those beginning times. During those times, our kind interacted openly with humans. We were not feared as we are today but regarded as goddesses, and temples were raised in our honor. Time passed, and Nwt, surrounded by many, felt alone. She stumbles across a small village. After so much time feeling alone, she meets a regular human man, widowed with a small child. She falls for this man, and she decides to stay."

Ashanti looks at me, and smiles. *I wonder if she is comparing Nwt and her love to our own?* Sadly, this story does not have the happy ending she is hoping for.

Heqet notices Ashanti's smile and smiles empathetically, "Nwt stayed in that village for many years; she lived as husband and wife, and helped raise that small child. That child grew into a great man. They say he was as big as a bear, strong as an ox. He loved Nwt dearly. Unfortunately, illness falls over that village, and humans begin to die excruciating deaths. When that illness knocked on the door of that man-child, Nwt could not bear the weight of losing him. She turned him. He grew strong, his illness was cured. But the power he possessed was too much for him. It corrupted him to his core. He began attacking women in the village, eventually fighting with his father over these actions and accidentally killing him. Nwt, seeing her only true love slaughtered, tried to turn him, but it was too late and too much damage. He died quickly. The son, afraid, ran, and Nwt allowed him to. After his death, she came to learn of a blessing the ancestors left her with. A child. Our Queen realized she was with child. She swore to protect her love's village and raise her child there. So, she gave birth to the little girl, who seemed to be more mortal than immortal, and she raised her in that small village. For a while, she found peace there, even found happiness again. She claimed her husband's sisters as her own and loved them deeply. While Nwt found peace, the son who once ran away grew paranoid waiting for Nwt's vengeance. He convinced himself Nwt would come and kill him for murdering his father. He searched for allies for many years, even turning to what he thought were humans and convinced them of a great evil woman, who would come and steal their children, and kill their wives. What he didn't know was this was no ordinary village he had come across. These villagers were cursed with a strange ability. At night, when the moon was high, these humans turned into great beasts, larger than any wolf you have ever seen, strong and intelligent. The son, so thrilled by his discovery, quickly aligned himself with this village. The men allied with this liar of a son, and they plotted her demise. Nwt's daughter, now grown, and married to a human, heavily pregnant with a daughter of her own, was completely unaware of the danger, as was Nwt. She decided to move with her husband to his village, leaving her mother alone with her aunts in her childhood village. That is when the son attacked. Nwt fought, but when her village was lost, she grabbed her injured sisters and ran. She managed to get as far as the next village, where she was told of a great woman of magic." Heqet looks at me with a smile, "Asim's mother."

"Wow, is that how she turned her? And werewolves are real? Vampires can have babies?" Ashanti asks, one question after another. Heqet smiles patiently while she asks all of her questions.

"Yes, that is how Asim met Nwt, and werewolves are very real and dangerous. Aside from Nwt's direct bloodline, no other cases of vampires have ever given birth that we know of." She answers her questions in a row, "Asim, would you like to take over?"

I look at Ashanti, suddenly nervous. *Should I leave parts out? Will Heqet tell her anyway?* Ashanti realizing I will be taking over, turns her body slightly to face me, her eyes intently on my face. I clear my throat, "Well, as Heqet has said, she escaped with her sisters, her daughter already safely away. She came to our village one night when I was still a young woman, barely 30 years of age. She begged my mother to help her. She needed to cure her sisters but did not want to curse them with eternity. My mother begged her to change me, and the exchange was made. I gained eternity that day, but the son had not given up on his quest to kill Nwt and chased her to my village as well. I lost my mother that night." I pause, remembering the smell of fire, and my mother's command to run. Ashanti holds my hand, pulling me from my sorrows.

"I'm sorry," she says softly. I smile at her and place my other hand on top of hers.

"So, I found Nwt, and together we put an end to the son, although it hurt Nwt deeply. She taught me about our world. I followed her for many years until I decided to go off on my own. Nwt had grown tired of this realm, and I needed to live in my purpose." Ashanti raises her eyebrow, questioning me, "to protect the women of earth. I lived alone for some time. I discovered many creatures. I swam with mermaids, and slept in a field full of what you would call fairies. I have seen spiders as big as a horse and spoken to creatures as small as a mouse. In my time here, I have come to realize every myth comes from some truth. Many creatures have been hunted and have become extinct. But where we go tomorrow, many live, the Forgotten World. You are safe with me--"

"With us," Heqet interrupts.

"With us, but it is important you stay close to us at all times. If you choose to come with us, your life here is over. Ashanti Whitel is dead, and Isaiah Whitel no longer exists. We will live under different identities; we will travel to many places. But I can promise you, we will protect you. You both will be happy, loved, and safe. I am not perfect. Our life is not perfect--"

"When do we leave?" Ashanti asks, holding my hand, and smiling up at me.

"Really?"

"Without question love."

We stare into each other's eyes, for just a moment, in love, and at peace.

"Well! I'm glad that's cleared up!" Cairo walks in with Isaiah in tow.

"How long were you out there?" I ask, hugging Isaiah.

"We got ice cream, and I made some friends! Cairo even showed my magic trick to the nurses," Isaiah says, thrilled by his adventure.

"Oh, did he?" Heqet asks, looking at Cairo.

"Oh, come on love, you know you have my heart!" He says, putting his arm around her, as she playfully pushes him off.

I look at my loved ones, all together talking and laughing. Ashanti's hand firmly in mine. For just this moment. I have peace. A family.

Chapter Fifteen – Ashanti

I lie quietly in my bed. My head swirls with all of the new information I learned today. *Werewolves and mermaids?* I think of Nwt, an ancient vampiric goddess, whose very blood may flow through my veins. Asim, as always, sits beside my hospital bed. I can guess that she is aware I am awake by the way she periodically asks, 'if I am okay'. She stays quiet otherwise, allowing me to process my thoughts. I think of just a few weeks ago, how helpless I felt with Adam. *Adam.* My heart rate spikes as I think of him. I remember the fear of being dragged out of bed in the middle of the night on more than one occasion. *Am I really free?* I wonder for just a moment: *where is he? , is he okay?* I know it's stupid to care, but Adam was the love of my life for my entire adult life, and many of my teenage years too. While he turned into my nightmare, he started as my hero.

"Asim?" I ask nervously. My tone makes her lean towards me, concerned.

"What is troubling you, love?" She asks, gently brushing my hair from my face.

"I was just thinking... Well, actually worrying. What if Adam does come back? Will we have to run from him forever?" I ask quietly. She gets quiet, and I look up to make sure she's not upset. Her face is a mixture of sadness, and... guilt. No that's not it. It's like she's contemplating something.

"Love, we are not running from Adam. We wouldn't waste time worrying about something as inconsequential as that. We travel often to avoid suspicion. Also, a lot has happened here. It will be good to go away and let the people forget. Humans never focus on one topic for too long," she says, smiling gently at me, "Now, how do you feel? Ready to travel?"

"I'm fine. Nothing even hurts anymore. I don't know why the doctor insists I stay here for this long. Even my bruises have healed. Well, except for this scar." I say, pointing to the small dark brown line on my side, where Adam kicked me repeatedly.

Asim caresses that spot and smiles, "All warriors have their trophies, hmm? The doctor may be my fault, though, love. I, shall we say, used my gift of persuasion to convince her to let you stay a bit longer."

I stare at her, wondering what she could possibly do to make my hospital stay longer, "What did you do? What gift?"

"Most, umm... mythical creatures? Well, we have gifts, special abilities that are unique to our kind. One of the things we can do is hypnotize our prey into doing, well, I guess pretty much anything we want."

I can feel my mouth drop open, as she explains, "Anything? Have you used this on me?" I try and think back to our interactions, *would I know if it was my idea, or hers?*

"Never. I would never use it on you or Isaiah," she says seriously.

"What about Heqet? Have you used it on her?"

"No, unfortunately, we cannot use it on one another. Although I wish! She can be so stubborn."

"Have you used it on Adam? I remember that day, the one we went to the park. He acted so weirdly, " I say, remembering his sudden calmness. His immediate departure.

"Yes. I have used it on him. But mostly for safety reasons," She says, looking away.

"Hmm, I wish you would have just hypnotized him to leave forever, " I say with a sigh, leaning back against my pillow.

"Would you have been okay with that? I thought you would hate me for it," she explains.

"I guess I would have worried. Wondering if he's okay. I kinda have been worrying now... I know it's stupid, but I've known him a long time now," I say quietly, hoping she'll understand, "Do you think he's okay?"

"I.... I..." Asim stumbles over her words, clearly upset by my questions. I reach for her hand.

"I'm so sorry; I know that was thoughtless. You, Heqet, and Cairo, all helped me so much and saved me from him, and here I am talking about him. I don't want you to think I am unsure of us. You make me so happy, and I want nothing more than to be with you. Adam is just... well, the father of my son, and I've known him for a long time. He wasn't always a monster, you know. I guess it's just going to take a little longer to heal the inside than it did for the outside." I say ashamed, looking down.

"It's not that. You are entitled to feel how you feel. I have been alive long enough to know how emotions are. They don't always make sense. There is something else. Well, not something else. It, uh, it has to do with Adam and I--" Asim struggles to express herself, and I realize I am making things harder right now.

"Don't. Maybe this isn't the right time to discuss this. Let's just put it in the 'things to discuss later' box, okay?" I smile at her, hoping to reassure her. She looks at me hopefully.

"Are you sure?"

"Absolutely."

"Okay, yes, you are right. We have much to discuss later ." She nods in agreement, then seems to relax. Grateful she relaxed, I decide to change the subject and ask more questions.

"So, how old are you exactly?" I ask, curiously. She smiles at my persistent question.

"I guess I better tell you. You are never going to let go of that question, I see."

I shake my head nope.

"I do not know my exact age; time doesn't pass for me the same as you. Years blend together after time, but I would say I am over 4,000 years old."

4,000. Did she say 4,000? That cannot be right. She looks no more than in her 30s.

"How? You look so young, and you speak like me?"

"Well, I do not age. My entire being changed when I was turned, and after so many years alive, I learned to blend in. Heqet loves humanity, so we try to learn the trends of the current era. Heqet is great at staying up to date. She loves to learn, and research things."

"I don't even know what to say. You must know so many things." I say, thinking of everything she has seen. She's older than most religions.

"I would be thrilled to share those things with you." She leans over and kisses my forehead, and I feel those butter-flies like the first time she smiled at me.

"The place I went to... I mean mentally, I guess. When I was in a coma... You said you have a similar place." I say, hoping she'll tell me more.

"Oh, yes. Our resting place. It's funny honestly. I thought for so many years, that it was the final resting place of our ancestors. But recently, I learned it was a resting place spe-cifically for me. So that I can rest when I need. You see, I do not sleep in this realm. I have no need for it, but unfortu-nately, while my body does not get tired, my mind does."

"So, you go there? What does it look like?" I ask

"Umm, okay so it can change. No one's looks the same. I always see a giant field. It stretches as far as the eye can see. There are sunflowers everywhere. Just fields of them, and trees full of fruits. My favorite tree has these over-grown roots, they reach out of the ground, and intertwine like chairs. I sit under that tree and speak with my elders sometimes. It feels like home to me." She explains. I watch her expressions as she talks, and listen to the excitement in her voice, trying to memorize it all. She is so perfect it hurts. So gentle, and soothing.

"How do you get there?" I ask her, curious if I could return to my own perfect place.

"You have to master meditation. Once you master it, it's just a matter of focus, and practice."

"Could you teach me?" I ask, excited. *Maybe I could see my father, and my daughter again.*

"Of course, love. I will teach you everything I know, if you allow it."

We smile at each other, happy to be in each other's presence, before she pats my thigh.

"Okay love, tonight you sleep. We have a lot to do tomorrow, and you will need your rest." She says, and I wonder how I am supposed to sleep knowing that.

"I know! That's the problem. I'm so excited. I can finally be with Isaiah full-time, and we are going to Africa!" I say a little too loudly, so I whisper the end of my sentence. Asim laughs, and gestures for me to lay back. She leans over and kisses my lips softly, but I reach up and wrap my hands in her long dreads, pulling her into a kiss much more intense than she expects. I feel a heat forming in my chest, that slowly travels to the middle of my thighs, where I feel a puddle form, as my most private of areas gently throb, begging for release. I continue kissing her as I guide her hand, but she stops me.

"Not yet love. This time will be special." she says pulling back slowly, and kissing my forehead, "Now sleep."

"How?" I protest, gesturing towards my vagina, "She won't stop calling you."

Asim laughs out loud, before kissing my forehead again, and sitting back in her chair. I pout for a few moments before she says, "I could always force you to sleep?"

That idea fascinates me more than I believe she expected, "Could you? Would you try it?"

She looks at me with a raised eyebrow, "Really?"

"Yes, just this once. I'm curious how it works." I say, and sit up to face her.

"Okay." She says with a shrug, "I wouldn't be surprised if it didn't even work on you. You are so full of surprises at this point."

I laugh, and pull my hair away from my face, "Ready."

"Okay, so first I stand face to face with my prey. I make eye contact like this," She pauses to kiss my nose, "Then I focus on my intention…"

I watch as her eyes go black, her pupils blending in, as her eyes go completely black, I want to scream but I cannot. No words escape my lips. All I can think of is obeying her.

"You have had a long day, and you want to sleep." She tells me, her jet-black eyes piercing into my soul. I want to turn away but what she is saying is so important. She's right. I'm exhausted.

"I want to sleep." I say, and as I say it, I realize I cannot think of anything else. I'm exhausted and my eyes can barely stay open. I lay back, my head feels like it weighs 1000 pounds. I must sleep.

As I open my eyes, I hear Isaiah laughing. My eyes pop open. The bright light compared to the darkness I was in, what felt like just moments ago, burns my eyes, and I squint to adjust. I notice Heqet first, sitting cross-legged in the visitor chair across from me, smiling down at Isaiah as he laughs watching Cairo change his hand into various animal paws quickly. Confusion sets in. *What happened?* Asim walks towards me, smiling brightly.

"How did you sleep, love?" She says, chuckling to herself. Isaiah notices me and begins jumping up and down.

"Mommy's awake!"

"Hi, little monster, how did you sleep?" I ask, as he climbs up into the bed, hugging me tightly.

"Cairo said we are going to leave today to go see where he was born!" Isaiah whispers happily, "But it's a secret."

"Really? Are you excited?" I ask, ruffling his hair.

"Yes! Heqet says I'm going to see fairies and big flying horses!" He says, gesturing something huge with his arms spread wide.

"Flying horses?" I say, smiling but looking at Heqet confused., but Heqet simply smiles at Isaiah, ignoring my stares.

"We should get ready to go, love. They will be discharging you shortly," Asim says, brushing the stray hairs from my face.

"Will we leave directly from here?" I ask curiously.

"Yes, we will leave here and go directly to our plane. From our plane, we will make our way to our homeland."

"The Forgotten World?" I ask, remembering Asim calling it that.

"Yes," she says, proud of my memory.

"Okay, are you ready, little one?" I ask Isaiah, as he nods excitedly, wiggling and jumping happily.

We leave the hospital in an SUV, with Cairo driving, Heqet in the passenger seat, and Isaiah between Asim and I in the backseat. I smile as the wind hits my face, as we zip down the highway, listening to Isaiah ask Asim a thousand questions, and she patiently answers each one with a smile.

"Are we flying there?"

"Yes, on a special airplane I purchased a few years ago," she explains.

"You purchased?" I ask, stunned. Asim looks at me, puzzled.

"Yes, love, Traveling discreetly is of the utmost importance. It made sense to make the purchase under one of my aliases, and when the time comes, I will sell it to another alias of mine. I learned to fly long ago, and we are able to doctor our logs as needed."

I nod; it makes sense. I wonder briefly just how much Asim, and Heqet have at their disposal. 4,000 years is a long time to amass a fortune.

"We should be there in about an hour, " Heqet explains, turning slightly in her chair to smile at Isaiah. "I made sure the plane was stocked with ice cream and games." She says smiling.

"Really? Mom! Can I have ice cream when we get there?"

"Sure, I might have some too."

Isaiah starts questioning Heqet about the plane, and I settle in watching the trees blur by. I stare at the trees, questioning what else lives in plain sight that I may have encountered in my life. After several minutes pass, Asim taps my shoulder with the arm she has thrown over the back of our chairs.

"Hmm?"

"Are you okay?" She asks, concern showing across her face. I nod.

"Yes, well, a little overwhelmed. A few weeks ago, I didn't know any of this existed, and now we are on our way to a private plane to fly to a world full of mythical creatures. It's a drastic change, and I haven't had much time to adjust. I mean, I know what you guys are, but you all seem so normal... well, maybe not Cairo," I say, as Cairo laughs, winking at me in the rearview mirror, "It's just... what creatures are we about to see? Is it safe for... humans there?"

Asim lightly caresses my face; the gesture calms me, and her touch sends tingles down my spine, "Yes, my love, I understand your concern. The truth is, there is some danger in our world, but you are safe with us. We are respected in our realm. No harm will come to you, as long as we live." She promises. I sit back, secure with her promise, and wrap my arm around Isaiah. He will be safe, as long as I live, as well.

We reach a small airport, within the hour, as promised. It's a small, barely running airport, with one runway and a small hangar. The entire place is fenced in, with a barbed wire chain-link fence, and 'Do Not Trespass' signs hanging as a warning. Heqet quickly gets out, opening the fence for us as we drive in.

"Do we have a pilot?" I ask, looking around the small field as we approach the hangar, "I don't see anyone else."

"You're looking at him!" Cairo says, laughing.

"You're joking?" I ask, unamused.

"It is okay, love. Cairo has flown for many decades and never had an issue. We will be safe with him flying," Asim tries to reassure me, my heart rate climbing the closer we get. Asim pats my hand softly, "You can trust us, love. Cairo can fly this plane with his eyes closed."

"Well, keep them open, please," I say sternly, causing Cairo to laugh hysterically.

"I will be with him in the cockpit. We'll get there safely," Heqet says, lightly hitting Cairo's arm, as if scolding him. With Heqet involved, I feel more relaxed, and I gently hold Isaiah's hand as we pull into the hangar. The plane is a lot bigger than I expected— smaller than a commercial plane, but still big enough to carry maybe a dozen people.

"Wow!" Isaiah exclaims as he hurries out of the car, "It's so big!"

"Wait till you see the inside!" Cairo scoops Isaiah up into his arms and jogs up the stairs into the plane.

"See, it's sturdy and safe. We have it fully fueled, and the plane is in top condition. We will make it to our homeland in about 17 hours," Asim explains.

"It'll be fine, Ashanti," Heqet says, looping her arm through mine and pulling me to the plane. Inside, Isaiah is getting a tour of the cockpit, and Heqet shows me the lavish plane," It looks like something out of a magazine."

"Heqet decorated," Asim says, casually sitting and pouring herself a drink of a red liquid I quietly hope is wine. Seeing me watching her, she smiles apologetically.

"I haven't eaten in a while," she explains. I nod, trying to look unbothered.

"I will get Isaiah so we can depart," Heqet says before disappearing behind a curtain leading to the cockpit.

"So, you drink from a wine glass?" I ask, trying to sound casual, as I walk down the aisle looking at random things.

Asim approaches me quietly, taking me by surprise as she presses against me, running her finger along my throat, "I prefer it fresher," she says before burying her face into my neck, trailing kisses down my collarbone. She lets go of me as quickly as she grabbed me, and before I can blink, she is back in her seat, across the plane, smiling. Isaiah runs in before I have a chance to question her speed.

"It's time to go, mommy!" He says, picking a seat in the back of the plane. I help him with his buckle as Heqet hands him a set of headphones and turns on a screen.

"Would you like to watch a movie?" She asks him, and he quickly agrees.

"Can you sit next to me, Heqet?" He asks nervously.

"How about I sit next to you until the plane is flying, and then Heqet can come check on you? She has to help fly with Mr. Cairo," I suggest.

"Okay..." He says, clearly wishing his favorite vampire could.

"I tell you what! Once we get this plane in the air, I'll be back with some ice cream, and we can see the sky from the big window up front! How's that?" She asks.

"Deal!"

"Deal!"

The plane takes off smoothly, although I grip my seat so tightly, I'm afraid I've torn the fabric. Once we get into the air, Heqet returns as promised with the ice cream and leads Isaiah into the cockpit for a better view of the clouds. Asim slides into his seat.

"So that explains why you are always so fast," I say looking out the window.

"I was fast as a human too," She says, shrugging.

"Really?"

"Yes, I was a warrior. I could outrun anyone in my village. It was important. I trained endlessly to protect my people," She said, her eyes far away as they remember her ancient past.

"Is that where we are going? Your village?" I ask, "you call it your homeland, but you also use words like realm, and world."

"It is not my village, rather before Nwt disappeared. Now I know she chose to leave and join the ancestors, but she convinced all of the magic-possessing creatures to join together and create a separate realm. One is undetectable by humans. All creatures, good and evil, magic-possessing, and not, they live there. Some prefer to return to humanity."

"Like you?"

"Yes. Heqet and I leave our realm often to live amongst humanity. Heqet has never forgotten her purpose, even after humanity forgot us." She says thoughtfully, "And I have never abandoned Heqet. So, we travel often."

I listen as she explains, trying to picture her world, "What does it look like?"

"Hmm, at first... at first, it looks like nothing. A cave, boring, and quiet, but inside that cave, invisible to the naked eye, is a guardian. The guardian only allows creatures of our world inside. Once inside, you enter the realm of magic. There are fields of dancing flowers, and fairies who live amongst them. Giant creatures, taller than your biggest skyscraper. Mermaids, and merman swim peacefully in the lakes and oceans. Flying horses, you call Pegasus, or unicorns gracefully fill the sky. It is a beautiful place, dangerous, yet peaceful. I believe you will love it. We have a home we built there, quite some time ago. No one will bother us there. Cairo's people are there as well. His people are good; we have been connected for a very long time. They will also provide you with protection."

"It sounds amazing. I cannot wait to see it," I say.

Asim tells me more about her world, describing her big house on the hill, and how free she can be there. She describes the different creatures we may encounter, the flowers, and the night sky. A part of me has a feeling she is withholding the darkest part of her world from me, but I know in due time she will share. Heqet explains our new identities, Isaiah keeps his first name, but our new last name is Wright. We relocated from the Americas, specifically California. My name is Patrice Renee, Heqet's is now Sarah Lynn Munson, and Asim is Rachel Ann Munson. They are sisters, of course. Cairo's name now changed to Bryan Lee. We memorize our new lives and questions that may be asked of us. Occasionally, Asim or Heqet will give us a pop quiz on our identities, and Isaiah quickly learns his, much to Cairo's delight.

Our first glimpse of Africa is breathtaking; the ocean so clear, and the structures leave me speechless.

"This is nothing like what they show us on the TV back home," I say, staring in awe out of the window.

"Africa is never given her due praise. She is the center of the world. Almost everything originates here, and yet, she's tossed to the side," Asim says, shaking her head, and admiring her home.

We land as smoothly as we took off, which Cairo brags about as we disembark the plane. The airport we land in is similar to the one we departed from. Small, and in a remote location. A black SUV is waiting for us in the hangar.

"Well love, there is no turning back now, huh?" Asim says, more excited than normal. I buckle Isaiah's belt, and then my own.

"Let's go," I say with a smile, as Cairo pulls out of the airport, knowing today starts the rest of our lives.

Part Two

The Forgotten World

Chapter Sixteen – Asim

What a change from a few short months ago. I watch as Cairo and Heqet hike ahead of us, walking at a maddening human pace. Isaiah laughs as he sits on top of Cairo's shoulders. I feel the gentle squeeze of Ashanti's hand, a quirk I've noticed of hers whenever she's excited or anxious. After landing the plane, we drove around, sightseeing for her and Isaiah's benefit

before parking off-road and beginning our hike to our destination.

"Are you sure you don't want me to carry you, love? It's quite a trek to the cave," I ask anxiously. I have never introduced anyone to my home. Now my dear, sweet love will be there shortly, and I feel...nervous. A new feeling for me, or rather one I have not felt in a very long time. She laughs as she tightens her grip on my hand.

"I've been in bed a long time; I can walk a while. It feels good," she explains. I flashback to her beaten and unconscious in her hospital bed. Yes, seeing her in good spirits, walking, does feel good.

"We should reach the cave next week at this pace," Cairo calls back, teasing.

"We really should pick up the pace, Asim," Heqet says, walking slowly.

"Pick up the pace? We are practically jogging now!" Ashanti says, struggling to match our strides.

"Come on, we'll show you a faster way!" Cairo says excitedly.

"Cairo," I say, warning him. Knowing Cairo, he could turn into a lion or cheetah and take off at any moment. He simply shrugs and continues walking.

"If there is a faster way, we could try it," Ashanti suggests.

"Are you sure? I don't want to frighten you."

She laughs out loud. "I think I've seen enough to handle a little speed."

"Okay."

Cairo immediately hands Isaiah to Heqet and takes off with his backpack, ducking behind a tree. Suddenly, I hear Ashanti gasp, afraid. A few minutes later, a large cheetah jogs slowly from behind the tree, a backpack in its mouth.

"It's okay, love. It's just Cairo," I say softly, as Isaiah claps and runs towards him.

"Isaiah!" Ashanti calls him back as Cairo snuggles up to Isaiah, licking his cheek. He laughs and hugs his neck. Ashanti calms as she watches their interaction.

"Cairo?" she asks. Since the day she was attacked, Cairo has been careful not to fully transform in front of her as she healed mentally and physically from the trauma. Cairo, hearing his name, walks up to Ashanti slowly, carefully sitting a few feet away from her. Ashanti, holding my hand, walks up to him, stopping to look at me for encouragement. I nod and give her hand a tug forward. She raises her hand, holding it out for Cairo. With a mischievous look, Cairo playfully licks her hand as she makes a disgusted sound.

"Eww, Cairo!" she says, laughing. We all relax, seeing her calm. Heqet pulls Isaiah onto her back, and I pick Ashanti up into my arms.

"You're going to run and carry me? Is that safe?" she asks nervously.

"There is nowhere safer for you than in my arms, love," I say, smiling at her.

"Isaiah, close your eyes, and hold on tight, okay?" Heqet says. "Just like we practiced."

Isaiah wraps his little arms around Heqet's neck and tucks his head into her back. Cairo takes off first, a backpack firmly in his mouth; he runs full speed into the trees for cover. Heqet takes off next, Isaiah's laughter loudly trailing back to us.

"Are you ready?" I ask, pulling her closer. She nods nervously, tucking her head as close to my chest as she can. I start running slowly before quickening my pace to match Heqet and Cairo's strides.

"Finally!" Heqet calls to me, laughing happily as the wind whips her hair around. Even in cheetah form, admiration is obvious on Cairo's face as he watches Heqet run freely.

"I got you, love," I whisper to Ashanti as everything whirls past us. After running about an hour, we finally see the riverbank where the cave is located. We slow down as we near the river, and Cairo ducks behind a large boulder, emerging moments later in human form, fully clothed, his backpack across his back.

"Well, that was fun, eh?" he calls. Ashanti peeks her head out, noticing we have slowed down.

"That was so fun!" Isaiah agrees with Cairo.

"That was something," Ashanti says, smoothing her hair back into its ponytail. "I can get down now."

"You could, but I enjoy you here," I say, holding her a little closer. She smiles and snuggles into me.

"Am I not heavy at all?"

"I barely feel you in my arms," I say honestly.

"I will never get used to your insane powers," she says, laughing. We reach the river and approach the cave together.

"I should go last," Cairo suggests too casually. Heqet eyes him suspiciously.

"Why?"

"I, uh, may have..." he stutters, avoiding Heqet's glare.

"What have you done, Cairo?" she asks, visibly annoyed.

"Well, how was I supposed to know the fairy king took a new wife!" he says defensively. Heqet throws her arms up in annoyance.

"Really? How are we supposed to enter through the fairy's cave if you have pissed off the fairies?"

"I hoped they would calm down by now! It's been 30 years!" he explains.

"Cairo, maybe we could have discussed this prior to our arrival?" I suggest, trying to calm the situation. "The fairies have a long memory."

"Yeah, I'm sorry, guys. I was just so excited about showing them our home; it kind of slipped my mind," he says apologetically. Heqet rolls her eyes, and I wonder how much of her anger is true annoyance and how much is jealousy.

"Fine, I shall go first; the fairies owe me a favor, for tending to their troll problem," Heqet says. "Isaiah, remember our game at the hotel? The words I taught you?"

Isaiah nods excitedly as we slowly walk up to the mouth of the cave.

"Okay, ready? Let's say it on the count of three," she says, taking him from her back and setting him on the ground beside her, holding his hand tightly. Isaiah nods, and stands feet apart, back straight.

"What is happening?" Ashanti asks, climbing out of my arms to watch Isaiah, concerned.

"I believe Heqet has taught Isaiah how to enter our world," I say, amazed.

"Watch, Mommy!" Isaiah calls back to Ashanti.

"Okay, one... two...three!" Heqet says. We watch as Heqet and Isaiah chant the words together, shouting them loudly.

"Rishanu mishpa lotzna!"

The ground around us begins to vibrate as the inside of the cave starts to glow. I hear Ashanti gasp as the vibrating turns to shaking, and the glowing turns into a bright white light. After several moments, the shaking abruptly stops, leaving the cave and the bright white light. I squeeze Ashanti's hand for encouragement.

"Isaiah did this?" she asks, whispering. I nod.

"Heqet believes magic runs through his blood, but I did not know he was capable of this," I say, watching Isaiah jumping up and down, proud of his accomplishment. Heqet praises him, and Cairo gives him a high five.

"Okay, let us go," I say, as Ashanti watches her son in amazement.

"Mommy, I did it!" he yells to her.

"I saw! You did so good, baby," she says, clapping for him.

We walk into the cave in a line, Heqet first, holding Isaiah's hand. I walk closely behind him, holding Ashanti's hand to keep her close behind me, and Cairo behind us all, walking with his head down, nervous.

The light dims as we enter, slowly going out. The cave looks normal inside, with rocks and boulders scattered everywhere. The only abnormality is the giant set of wooden doors on the far side of the cave, an emblem of a snake carved into the middle of the doors.

"Humans?" A loud booming voice shouts, echoing throughout the cave, "Why are there humans at our door?"

"No! Can you not sense it? The magic coming from these creatures is not that of a human! It is buried deeply, not yet activated, but these are not mere humans," a seductive feminine voice interrupts.

"Ahhh, I see. It is faint, but it is there. Why have you come here, girl?" The deep voice calls. Ashanti looks at me, frightened and unsure of what to do. I step forward.

"It is I, Asim the protector. We have come home. We seek entrance to The Forgotten World, dear King of Fairies, Grooden."

"Asim? Ahh, that is you, isn't it?" The fairy king says, stepping out of the shadows. His highness is no more than 3 feet tall, with the face and body of a middle-aged man. His copper-colored skin almost glows in the darkness. He has the strongest magic of his kind. His new wife follows closely behind him. Surprisingly, her height is almost 5 feet tall, with long slim legs and pointed ears. Her hair is curly and dark, her features beautifully crafted, while her figure is seductively curvy. Her green eyes light up slightly, recognizing Cairo.

"This is my wife, Lotus," he says, gesturing towards the fairy queen. "Beautiful, eh?"

"Yes, King Grooden, she makes a lovely bride," Heqet says, nodding at the queen.

"Ahh, Heqet! Finally, you have returned! We owe you our lives!" he says, laughing, making his round stomach shake. "She was quite a force against that troll problem we had, love," he explains to his wife.

"Come, come, I cannot wait to hear of your travels! We shall feast in your honor!" He gestures for us to enter, before stopping and pointing at Isaiah, then Ashanti. "Have you found a new type of being?" he asks, curiously.

"We are unsure, King," I say honestly. Ashanti turns to me, confused. I shake my head slightly, warning her against voicing her questions.

"Hmm, okay, we shall have a look then, eh?" The king walks towards the door, as it opens slowly, before stopping abruptly. "And who was that in the back there? I think I recognize him, eh?"

Cairo peeks his head up and waves slightly with a guilty smile. The king grunts angrily as the doors slam closed again. "No, absolutely not! This one is yearning for a beheading!"

Ashanti gasps, and looks back at Cairo, worried.

"King Grooden, your subjects voted to put an end to beheading over a century ago. Cairo has changed since you've last seen him," Heqet pleads. She beckons for Cairo to stand beside her and takes his hand. "I would see it as a personal favor for you to forgive his trespasses, and I will watch him carefully to ensure no further insult comes to the fairy people."

The king eyes Cairo with distaste. "Fine, but you step out of line once, and you'll be exiled so fast your head spins, you hear me, eh? And you best stay away from our womenfolk."

"Yes, King Grooden, I'll be on my best behavior," Cairo says, holding up his Boy Scout salute. The king and Heqet both roll their eyes simultaneously.

"Come on then, enough of these formalities." The king takes his wife's hand, and they walk through the door.

I look at Ashanti as she nervously shifts from one foot to the other. "I have to warn you. This door acts as a portal. On the other side, we take our true form. It can be frightening at times, but it is important you remember we are still ourselves. Okay?"

"Your true selves?"

"Yes, in this realm, we take more humanlike features. This earth possesses magic, but it is mild compared to our world. When The Forgotten World was created, almost all magic was shifted there. Creatures who cross through this portal weaken into a lesser being until they cross back into our realm," I explain, trying to make sense of magic.

"But you will remember me?" she asks nervously, "Isaiah will be safe?"

"Of course," I say, smiling reassuringly.

"It'll be great, Ashanti," Cairo says with a wink.

She takes a deep breath before gripping my hand tighter. "Okay, let's go."

As we walk through the door into blackness, I feel my bones shift as my magic strengthens throughout my body. My shoulder blades separate as my wings grow from them, my fangs sharpen, and my eyes once again turn the darkest shade of black. Ashanti gasps and lets go of my hand. *Is she afraid?* I hear Isaiah yell, and Ashanti's strained voice calls for him, searching. Something is happening, but I cannot see in this portal of blackness. After mere moments that feel like an eternity of falling, we step through the portal and into a field of swaying sunflowers. We are home. Ashanti stumbles through the portal, landing on her knees before I can react. My body has not yet adjusted to the magic that now flows through it. I look at Ashanti in shock.

"Ashanti?" I ask, unsure if it is truly her. She looks up at me, her eyes wide with fear. "It is me, love. It is Asim."

She looks around, her eyes adjusting to the brighter light of our world. Heqet, a foot taller, her pure white wings tucked firmly into her back as she kneels, cradling Isaiah. Ashanti, seeing this, runs to her. Heqet gasps as she notices her.

"What has happened?" Heqet asks, looking at me, confused.

"I do not know."

"The boy will be fine; his magic must have activated when we entered the portal, and his mother's too. His first transformation took its toll on his strength. He shall sleep until his body adjusts to the magic now flowing through it," The queen, who has shrunk significantly to no taller than 3 feet (tall for a fairy), explains, kneeling to brush her hand across Isaiah's forehead. "Yes, his magic is strong. He shall sleep in our castle, as a protected guest."

"What is happening?" Ashanti says, looking at the queen, confused.

"You do not know?" she asks, perplexed, "Surely even on the earth realm, you have noticed you are not like the rest? With magic this strong, I am surprised it has not manifested before."

Ashanti looks at her hands, her nails longer, almost claw-like, her skin glowing, her hair flowing around her, gold wings now sprouting from her back, matching the small gold wings now visible from Isaiah as well.

"Will he be, okay?" she asks worriedly, cradling him closely to her.

"Of course, dear, he is young, and his power is great. All of our bodies take time to adjust to the magic when we reenter this world. The longer we stay away, the longer our bodies take to adjust, and this child has never been here. His power has been activated. He needs sleep and nourishment," she says gently, outstretching her silver wings, preparing to fly.

"Come," the king calls before taking off into the sky, the queen following closely behind.

Ashanti, so concerned with Isaiah, temporarily forgets her own changes to tend to him. Heqet quickly scoops Isaiah up, her own wings spread. "He will be fine, Ashanti. I promise," she says before taking off behind the queen and king. Ashanti attempts to run after her, but I stop her.

"We will not reach the castle on foot, love. We must fly," I explain, "I can carry you until you learn how."

She nods and holds my neck as I once again take her into my arms. "He will be fine. I will ensure it."

The flight to the fairy castle is not long. We fly over fields of flowers and fairies dancing in the sunlight, trees that sway as they dance to the fairy's songs, and Pegasus with horned heads who have stopped at a small brook to drink. Ashanti watches wide-eyed but says nothing, her only concern being her son.

"Wow," she whispers as she spots the castle for the first time. It sits on top of a tree the size of a mountain. The size of the castle is bigger than any skyscraper or mansion on earth, although the fairy people are no larger than a human child in their true state. It is a magnificent sight, watching the magic so potent it appears as small droplets of light dancing around the castle air.

"We will land there," I say pointing to the front of the castle. We land softly, and Ashanti immediately jumps from my arms, running to Heqet's side.

"He is fine, his breathing is steady. He is merely sleeping," Heqet reassures her. Ashanti nods but does not leave Heqet's side as we enter the castle. The fairy people within the castle listen intently to the queen's instructions before leading us to the upper floors of the castle. They leave us in a bedroom I assume is for royal guests.

"The queen has taken a liking to him," Heqet states proudly. "This is the room designated for an honored guest. She can sense it too. He is special."

Ashanti, satisfied with Isaiah's care, turns to me, "What is this?" she asks, gesturing towards her own transformation and Isaiah.

"I do not know," I say ashamed. "The only answer I can assume is you do, in fact, have goddess blood flowing through your veins. That magic is so potent that even after generations, and generations passing, it manifested when you entered our realm, into what you see now."

"Goddess blood?" she whispers, quietly, biting her own lip nervously. "What does this mean?"

"Now that we are here, I can search for clearer answers. We will find out what we need to know," Heqet promises her. Cairo stumbles into the room, no longer in human form, causing Ashanti to scream in fear.

"It's just me," he says, out of breath and annoyed. "You left me." He casually walks over to an armchair and sits, throwing his long, hairy, legs over one of the arms. In his true form, Cairo takes the form of a beast. His upper body bulging with muscles, four eyes in place of his human two, his entire body covered in hair, paws in place of feet, and claws where his hands once were.

"Cairo?" Ashani asks, confused once again.

"Yeah, this is how my people look. Stop being racist; we can't all be princesses," he laughs to himself at his own joke.

"Princess?" I ask, hearing his words.

"Yeah, look at her. She looks just like our Queen," he says, shrugging.

"The fairy queen?" she asks. "I look nothing like her."

"No, no. He means the queen of the immortals," I explain, staring at her. She does resemble her. The hair, the eyes, the wings. The resemblance in this form is easily visible.

"The Queen of the immortals?" she asks.

"Yes, love, Cairo, will you sit with Isaiah? We will find the nourishment the queen promised, and I must show Ashanti our history."

Cairo nods. "Bring me something back; I'll watch over the little guy."

"I will as well," Heqet says. "He will be safe, Ashanti."

She looks hesitant, not wanting to leave her son in this form, in a new place. I take her hand. "He is safe with the fairies. They have long had an alliance with our kind. No harm will come to him while here."

She nods before walking over to her son and kissing his forehead. "Mommy will be back soon, little monster."

We walk hand in hand as I show her the great art room. She wanders from painting to painting, her eyes sparkling as she stares at each beautiful piece. After a moment of admiring their beauty, she looks up at me, finally asking all the questions she was dying to ask.

"Who is the queen of the immortals?"

I gently pull her by the hand, leading her to a large painting of a powerful-looking woman sitting on a throne surrounded by mythical beings of every species.

"Our realm was once united. We all pledged loyalty to our goddess," I say.

"Nwt?" she asks.

"Yes, I was essentially her right hand. Vampires are greatly respected here. We served as the goddess's loyal guard, ensuring the safety of all of her subjects. You could compare us to the police of your world," I explain. She nods in understanding, and we walk to the next painting— an empty throne and grey skies.

"One day, Nwt left our world, which was normal in those days, but she never returned. She simply disappeared. We searched and searched to no avail. I was her stand-in while she was gone, but I did not want to rule. I left after many years passed, and while I was gone," I continue, showing her the next painting— an angry, violent scene from a war, "the once united realm fought for power. It was a tragic time; friends turned against one another, blood filled the streets.

It was during this war our queen emerged," I say as we stand before a new painting. A beautiful creature, her aura seeming to glow, emerging from a cave. "She found us from the earth realm. A being unlike any we had ever witnessed since the time of Nwt. It was with her arrival that a treaty was formed.

So, the fairies, the vampires, and the mermaids held power. Each voted a queen or king to rule their kingdom." I watch her as she views the painting of the three beings meeting along the shore— our immortal queen, a fairy, and a mermaid.

"While she is not a vampire, she is an immortal. Her subjects love her. I returned around the period of her arrival and became counsel of sorts to her. She has held power for a long time. I traveled back and forth from our realm to earth, but she remained here. Once, she left for a brief time, a few years, but returned and has remained in power since." I explain, remembering my brief return years ago. The queen requested I stay as her right hand, but I chose freedom and left to return to the earth realm. I knew if I stayed the queen would expect more than just counsel.

"Do you think she is my relative?" Ashanti asks hopefully, looking at the painting of the queen of immortals sitting on her thrown.

"Considering the similarities, it is possible she is of your bloodline," I say honestly.

"Can we meet her?"

I hesitate, unsure if the queen has forgiven my rejection in our time apart. If she is truly of Ashanti's bloodline, will she take my choosing of her relative as an insult?

"Asim? What's wrong."

"Uh," I stutter. *Should I be truthful?*

"Is something wrong with the queen?"

"The queen has been fair to her subjects. We have a...history," I say quietly.

"Oh."

"She wanted me as her trusted counsel, and I declined. I am unsure how she feels in my absence," I explain. "But we can meet with her. She may be overjoyed with finding someone of her own kind, that she overlooks my slight."

"Is she alone then? She's been alone here?"

"Yes, she is the only known being of her kind in this realm. She is quite powerful, especially as queen. Her power feeds off of the land here."

Ashanti grows quiet, thinking of her newly gained information.

"What are you thinking?"

"How sad it must be. To be the only of your kind, in a world full of beings."

I nod in agreement. "Yes, it can be quite lonely, I imagine."

She continues to walk, looking at each painting, realizing the historic value of each of them. She stops in front of a dark painting: a herd of Pegasus in armor, surrounding a large cube-shaped box, grey mist surrounding the box.

"What is the meaning of this one?" she asks.

"This is the myth of Apep, the god of chaos and destruction. He battled with his brother Ra, the god of power for longer than our universe has existed. As punishment, Ra had him imprisoned. The Pegasus guard him, refusing to allow him to escape."

"Pegasus? Like the ones we saw flying here?"

"Exactly," I say smiling, "you'll have to talk with Heqet. She has a deep love of knowledge. She could tell you details of all of our history and the powers of creatures."

She nods while staring at the painting.

"Come, the kitchen is through here."

We arrive at the kitchen, with fairies busily cooking the feast for this evening, in Heqet's honor. I recognize one of the fairies and call to them.

"Ezra!" I call happily recognizing a friend. She looks up and waves before flying over.

"Asim! It has been so long! Look at you!" She hugs me, excitedly zipping back and forth.

"I decided it was time to come home," I say, squeezing Ashanti's hand.

"And who is this lovely creature?" she asks, taking Ashanti by surprise as she hugs her.

"This is Ashanti; it is her first visit to our realm."

"You are simply divine!" Ezra says, clapping, being her usual bubbly self.

"Thank you," Ashanti says, blushing.

"Are you hungry? Of course, you're hungry! Go on up to your room; I'll have food sent to you right away!"

"Thank you so much, Ezra," I call after her as she quickly zips away to arrange our meal.

"She's fun," Ashanti says, watching her zip around, giving orders, and checking lists.

"Head fairy in charge. She's essentially the queen's assistant. She makes sure this place runs well."

"Oh, I see," Ashanti says, admiring the artwork and statues, placed even in the kitchen.

"The fairies have exceptional taste; they value the arts and knowledge above all. They have always allied with our kingdom. They have a strong aversion to war, but they are quite powerful if needed," I explain, watching her reactions.

"And will I see your kingdom?" she asks, curiously.

"Yes, I'm hoping our queen may know something about your bloodline."

"Oh, right," she looks over her shoulders at her own impressive wings, "this is so...different. Terrifying actually. I mean what am I? What is Isaiah?" she asks worriedly. I take her hand.

"Whatever you are, we will figure it out together, love," I reassure her. She nods quietly, staring at her long nails and glowing skin. I watch her and decide it may be time to distract her from her worries.

"Come, we have a moment or two to spare and I want to show you something," I say, as I pull her gently from the kitchen and towards the courtyard.

"Where are we going?" she asks, looking around at the castle walls, as we hurry down the hall.

"Here." I push open the castle doors, leading to the courtyard, and we step into the damp grass.

"Oh, my goodness." She says, her heartbeat spiking with excitement, "Unicorns?"

We watch as just a few feet away, magnificent creatures, pure white, and black, trot back and forth, drinking from the fairy well, and eating their share of grass.

"Pegasus. They have wings tucked closely to their bodies. They tend to stay in the fairy kingdom. Fairies are notoriously protective of nature, and the sweetest grass grows here. That fairy well is full of magic-laced water. It's known to heal the sick and energize the tired. These guys love this stuff." I say, pointing to the well.

"Wow, I never even dreamed of being this close to anything so beautiful. A real Pegasus!" she says happily, taking a step closer.

"Careful love, they are very skittish, that horn on their head is not just for looks. They prefer to be admired from afar." I explain. She nods understanding, and steps back next to me. We stand for a while, watching them graze and admiring their beauty. One of them looks up and takes notice of us, its pure black coat glistening in the sunlight. It tilts its head, as if examining us, before slowly approaching. Ashanti looks at me nervously, and I give her a nod that it's okay. To my own amazement, I watch as it walks up to her and nudges her, demanding to be pet. She raises her hand slowly, understanding what it is demanding, and runs her hand over its back, then its long neck, as it snuggles closely to her.

"In all my years, I've never seen one so friendly," I say attempting to pet it. It grunts at me and shakes its head, unhappy, "I guess it's a one-woman kind of horse?"

Ashanti laughs as she continues to pet it, "What is your name?" she asks innocently. I stare in amazement, she has no clue what naming a creature will do, and I watch, waiting to see if this Pegasus allows it.

"You look like a queen; would you like to be called Queen?" She shakes her head at the name she has decided, "Yup that's it. Hi Queen."

The Pegasus kneels on its front legs, as if bowing to her, and she looks at me, stunned.

"Naming a creature here is like taming it. If it accepts your name, it's essentially your subject. You have tamed your first Pegasus, which is one of the hardest creatures to tame here. It's rather impressive."

"What? I didn't want to tame anything. What should I do?" she asks bewildered.

"Anything you want love," I say, shocked by her power. She stands for a moment, petting the Pegasus, contemplating what she should do.

"I think I will leave her free. No creature deserves to live in servitude." She pets her for another moment, "You are free, girl." She whispers before walking back beside me. The Pegasus kneels in gratitude before taking off into the sky with its mate.

"They are so beautiful." She says, watching them glide through the sky.

"You are amazing; no one has ever set a Pegasus free. They are incredibly powerful beings." I explain, in awe.

"Incredible beings deserve the freedom to be incredible. I lived the last few years of my life feeling trapped; I won't do that to anyone else." She says quietly, but full of emotion. I wrap my arm around her shoulder and pull her close.

"You are free as well, my love," I whisper, holding her close. We stand that way for a moment listening to the songs of the birds in the trees, and the faint chatter of the nearby fairies, "Come, let us check on Isaiah," I say after a while. We turn to walk to the castle and hear a loud flapping noise behind us. I recognize the sounds of the Pegasus. Ashanti looks back and gasps aloud.

"What's wrong? I ask, turning quickly, and stop in shock, "I cannot believe it."

A small herd of Pegasus, about eight, gathered in the courtyard, led by Queen, the Pegasus Ashanti had just named. Queen walks slowly up to Ashanti, before kneeling before her. One by one, the Pegasus all follow suit, until there was one young buck left, gold and black in color, no older than a few months. It slowly walks up to her, trotting through the crowd of kneeling creatures. As it approaches her, its small wings begin to flap, bringing it to eye level with her. It stares into her eyes, before licking her cheek, and kneeling as well. This small family of creatures, all pledging their loyalty to her. She is truly amazing. I watch as she stands there, in utter shock, tears falling silently from her eyes. She bows before her newly found subjects.

"I don't know what is happening." She says quietly to me, as she watches them slowly rise. They stand still, as they wait for her to speak to them.

"I believe Queen has chosen to serve you and gathered her herd to do the same. They must see something in you, something powerful. I have never seen anything like this, not since...Nwt," I say, causing Ashanti to look at me, a mixture of fear, and excitement on her face, "Pegasus do not belong to any kingdom; rather, they are captured, and forced into captivity, broken like a stallion on the earth realm. This is magnificent to see. They usually refuse taming. The only other time I have seen groups of creatures volunteer servitude would be with the creator of this realm, Nwt." I explain.

"This being is not like the rest." Queen Lotus says, flying into the courtyard. She must have watched the scene play out from a window in the castle, "She is even more powerful than I suspected."

The sound of her voice makes me uneasy. She sounds fearful, and nervous.

"She was unaware of her power before entering our realm. She means you or your people no harm." I say genuinely, "We want no issues with you or your kingdom."

The queen nods at my statement, "I know this to be true; I can sense falsehoods. I do not fear her causing my people harm intentionally. What I fear is her power if it is not properly trained. She needs to discover what power she possesses. As well as, her child. They must learn to unleash this power and to use it, before it overwhelms them, and someone is hurt. There is too much magic in this realm; it will call to them." She says, flying beside me, watching Ashanti intently.

"Will you help me to train them?" I ask, "I do not know what powers they possess; I may not be equipped to handle this level of magic."

"Of course. We will begin once they have recovered from their travel here. They should remain in the castle until we know more. They will not be safe elsewhere." She warns.

"Thank you for your generosity, my queen, I owe you a great debt."

The queen waves her hand, dismissing my statement, "You owe no such thing. I believe it would be wise to ally ourselves with these beings. They may rule one day." She raises her eyebrow in a knowing gesture, and turns to fly away, "Oh, I have checked the child. He is fine. The shift in his bone structure was unusually draining on his life force, but he recovers quickly. He will be awake by morning. Tell his mother not to fret. He is a strong child." With that, she flies away.

"Thank you!" I call behind her; this is good news. Isaiah means the world to Ashanti, and I have grown quite at-tached to him, as if he is of my own blood. I was prepared to trade my life force for his survival if his condition grew any worse.

I watch Ashanti as she walks to each creature, naming it, and showing it affection. After a moment, she looks up and sees me, mouthing, "Oh My God," before laughing. I think to myself, *yes, I will protect this woman and child with my life.* Something extraordinary is happening.

Chapter Seventeen
– Ashanti

I gaze into the mirror, marveling at my transformed appearance. My mocha complexion seems to have been infused with gold speckles, radiating a shimmering light. My long, curly dark hair has grown even longer, now covering the tops of my new wings. *I have wings!* Gold and white, yet devoid of feathers, they feel like the softest silk as I gently touch them. My fingernails have transformed into long, claw-like golden nails. I still feel like myself, but there is an additional presence deep within my body— an unexplainable that resembles an electric pulse, yearning to break free. *What has happened to me? And to my beautiful Isaiah?* His new appearance resembles that of an angel, with his beautiful dark brown skin now glowing with the same gold speckles. His wings, half my size but similar in color and pattern, exude a captivating aura. Shortly after he woke from his long sleep, we discovered another surprising addition: a long white foxlike tail that sprouted from behind him as his body adjusted to the magic flowing through it, shocking us all.

In the past week, so many changes have occurred that I've barely had time to explore my new home. Asim is convinced that these changes are linked to my bloodline, pointing out distinct similarities between me and the queen of the immortals, such as the texture of our wings and our shimmering glow. She insists on giving us plenty of time to rest and allow our bodies to fully adjust to this new world before delving into the discovery of any potential powers or abilities. The prospect of having powers both excites and terrifies me. Thoughts of Queen and my new Pegasus friends bring a smile to my face, and I secretly hope Queen might try to communicate with me, but she has not. Although I do believe she understands when I speak. Asim is adamant it must be the goddess's bloodline.

A knock on the door draws my attention as I adjust the flowing black dress that the fairy queen had made for me, designed to accommodate my new wings.

"Come in," I call, turning away from the mirror.

"Mommy!" Isaiah comes running in, his tail twitching with excitement.

"Hi, baby!" I say, scooping him into my arms and hugging him close.

"Heqet said I can practice flying if you say yes!" he says happily. I look at the door, and Heqet leans against the doorframe, smiling lovingly at Isaiah and me.

"Flying lessons?" I say, concerned.

"It's better he learns early; with his growing daily excitement, I fear his wings may very well carry him off one day," she says laughing. I join in the laughter.

"Will it be safe?" I ask, nervously.

"Of course, love. I will be right beside him, and we will not go any higher than a safe distance."

"Boooo!" Cairo calls from the hall.

"Hush," Heqet rolls her eyes as she shushes him.

"Okay, but you have to promise to be careful," I say to him, holding out my pinky. He locks his pinky to my own and smiles.

"Promise!"

After they leave to begin their new lessons, Asim appears, a big mischievous smile on her face, leaving me nervous and excited.

"What are you up to?" I ask suspiciously.

"Today, you start your lessons too!" she says excitedly, rubbing her hands together.

"Oh no. I thought I would research some more in the fairy library," I say, shaking my head no.

"You must learn to fly; I may not be near always, and everything in this realm is not as friendly as the fairies," she says firmly, holding out her hand for me. I pout slightly before grabbing her hand, knowing there will be no refusal today. She takes me to a small clearing, away from Isaiah and the fairy castle so that I can concentrate.

"Okay, this is perfect." She gestures towards the wide field. "Now, the first lesson will be you must focus. Your wings are just a new limb. You control them. It is like learning to walk or waving your arms. With practice, you will begin to make them do as you wish when you wish, without much effort at all."

I nod along. "Can I fly as fast as you?"

"I do not know the details of your powers. Nwt was very powerful; she could fly faster than any being here, but the immortal queen is very limited in flying. She can fly quickly for very short periods of time before becoming exhausted. She typically flies at a slower, steady pace."

"I see. Okay, what is step two?"

"You take off stance. Spread your feet slightly so that you have a balanced takeoff, straighten your back, and look to the sky. Perfect," she explains as I copy her movements. Her compliment makes me blush as I try to maintain focus. "Okay, now, I want you to flex your back, tighten and release, until you can feel your wings as though they were a limb, such as an arm or leg."

I try to flex the muscles in my back, moving my shoulders up and down. I frown as I realize while I can feel my wings, it is not as easy to control them. I hear shouting in the distance and look back to the castle to see Isaiah flying high above the castle walls. His movements are so smooth; he appears to be floating.

"Well, would you look at that?" Asim says, smiling proudly. "That kid is a genius!" She claps loudly, cheering for Isaiah.

"Is he safe?" I ask, proud but terrified. I watch as his tiny frame soars through the sky, easily 80 feet from the ground. Asim points towards Isaiah.

"Of course, Heqet adores him, and Cairo has taken quite a liking to him. If you look below him, just a few feet, you will see Heqet hovering, and Cairo is that rather large eagle soaring above him. It looks like quite a few fairy folk have also joined in the flying lesson. He is quite popular among the castle staff."

I exhale as I follow Asim's gaze. Of course, Heqet is close. She has become an honorary aunt to Isaiah. I watch as he flies and does a small circle in the air before lowering down, below the castle walls, and out of my view.

"Okay, you got this love! Let's focus on moving those beautiful wings of yours once more!" Asim says, excitedly.

The sight of Isaiah flying must have ignited a fire in her. I smile at her determined face.

"Okay." I rub my hands together, hyping myself up to fly, closing my eyes. I again flex my back, searching for my wings. The sound of wings flapping breaks my focus as I turn to face the sound.

"I will never adjust to this," Asim says, looking to the sky in awe. I watch Queen, the Pegasus, and her family descend to the field we stand in. She trots up to me, tucking her wings to her side as she snuggles up to me.

"Well, hi there, beautiful! How has your day been?" I walk to each of the majestic creatures before me, snuggling each one and engaging in a one-sided conversation.

"Okay, love, come. We must tackle this!" Asim says, giving up on touching Queen as she loudly flaps her lips and turns from Asim. I laugh and walk over to where Asim and Queen stand, winking at Queen as I walk past her. I swear she smiles at me, but Asim begins my lesson, and I don't have the chance to ask.

"Okay, now let's try this. Close your eyes. Hold your arms out, and flap them slowly, as if they were your wings."

I hold my arms out, feeling silly with my eyes closed tightly, but I do as she asks. Moving my arms up and down slowly as if they were my wings, after a few moments, I feel Queen nudging my wings.

"No, Queen, I have to focus," I murmur, keeping my eyes closed. After a few more moments pass, she nudges again, and again. I grow annoyed and wave my arm. "Please, Queen, no!"

Even with my refusal to play, she continues the nudging. Finally, I shout, "QUEEN, NO!"

In my frustration, I swipe her away. I hear Asim gasp and feel ashamed. "I'm sorry, I didn't mean to shout, but -"

"No, Ashanti, your wings. You moved them," she says. It takes me a moment before I realize I did not use my hands to wave Queen away. I look at her, proudly trotting side to side, excited.

"You were doing that on purpose?" I ask her, amazed.

"Amazing," Asim seconds my thoughts. "Try it again."

I try to remember the feeling of swiping Queen, and attempt to move them; they respond immediately. I jump up and down, happily.

"Okay, now move them just like that but faster," Asim directs me. "Perfect! Now jump, just a little jump, and continue swiping them like that."

I close my eyes and jump, holding my breath as I flap my wings as fast as I can. I wait to feel my feet reconnect with the ground, but it never comes.

"Ashanti, open your eyes."

I open my eyes and look directly into Asim's black eyes. Even in their darkness, they seem inviting. The way she stares into my soul warms my core, distracting me, and my wings falter for just a moment. I drop slightly before she steadies me in her arms, but the drop causes me to look down and I see I am at least 20 feet off of the ground. Queen and her family excitedly running beneath me.

"Are you okay?" She asks me, holding my arms tightly.

I nod, "I'm doing it. I'm flying." I whisper it, afraid any loud noises may cause me to crash to the ground. She smiles brightly, her fangs exposed. A look I'm sure would terrify anyone, but my heart skips a beat as I recognize her proud expression.

"You, my love, are flying," she says, leaning into me to kiss me gently.

She lets go of my arms but stays near as she continues her instructions, "Okay, now we need to lean direction. It's rather simple. Lean the way you wish to fly and give your wings one big swipe before returning to the quickened pace; your wings and body do the rest."

She leans back and flies backwards before leaning forward and flying back to me.

"I can do this," I whisper to myself, leaning backward slightly, and suddenly I'm upside down, with my dress around my neck. I scream out, flailing around, "Asim? Where are you?"

"The view is magnificent," she laughs quietly, "I'm coming."

After several long seconds, I feel her pulling me upright. All the blood that rushed to my head while upside down rushes to my cheeks, embarrassed.

"Let us try leaning back slightly. You are still adjusting to your new body."

I nod, and lean back slowly, swiping the air with my wings as hard as I can, and I feel my body lurch backwards as I quickly pick up the pace. I sit upright and hover. Queen, excited, flies up to me. nuzzling me in the air. I get the sense she is proud of me. Asim flies to me.

"I have waited for this moment. I want to show you something," she says, so excited she seems out of breath.

"Okay," I say, simply because "*I would follow you anywhere*" seems too dramatic for the moment. She outstretches her hand, and I take it, and we fly higher. Queen follows behind us, leaving her family grazing in the field. We fly over more fields, and small ponds, with creatures

I've never seen before drinking peacefully, trees shuffling about using their roots as feet. I stare in amazement at what seems to be a herd of dinosaurs eating from bushes below. After several minutes, Asim points to a wooded area, and we begin descending to the ground.

"Wow, it's so beautiful. There are creatures I have never even thought of, existing here peacefully," I say as soon as we land.

"Yes, our home is truly divine," she agrees, squeezing my hand, as her wings retract slowly into her back. "Not all parts of this realm are peaceful, though. I wanted to show you something I know you would enjoy but also warn you of the dangers here. I will protect you and Isaiah with my life, but I also want you to understand this realm to avoid unnecessary issues," she says seriously. I heed the warning and become aware of my surroundings as I make a mental note to ask her how to retract my wings as well. Looking around, I realize we are entering a quiet forest. Queen seems uneasy and waits just beyond the tree line, nervously pacing.

"Stay close," Asim whispers as we walk deeper into the trees. We walk until a large lake comes into view. The water glowing a bright blue. We walk to the edge, and I stare down into the water, as my reflection looks up at me. A moment later, the water begins to tremble and shimmer. My reflection shifts slowly until a beautiful face I do not recognize looks back at me. I stare at this woman confused; something about her feels inviting. She smiles at me and motions for me to join her in the water. I look back at Asim, wondering if she sees this as well. She smiles at me before firmly taking my hand.

"She is with me, Annipe," she says sternly looking towards the water. The water swirls and trembles until a small crown of shells breaks through, followed by the woman from the reflection. She rises from the water until her head and neck are exposed.

"Ah, our protector has returned home." She bows her head, as a sign of respect, "Who is this exquisite being? I sense great power from her."

"This is Ashanti, my love," she says, "I wish for you to meet, so we can come to an understanding regarding her and her son's well-being."

The woman looks at me, her eyebrow raised in curiosity, "Come closer, child."

I look at Asim, unsure of what I should do. *I feel an unexplainable urge to go with this woman. She seems so familiar.* I fight the increasingly gnawing need to be near her and wait for Asim's instruction. She looks at me and smiles reassuringly, squeezing my hand.

"It is okay, love, The Annipe tribe is honorable. You can trust her."

I walk slowly back to the lake, kneeling at the water's edge. The mysterious woman moves closer; the water doesn't seem to recognize her movements and stays perfectly still. She raises her arm towards me, and I gasp as I see the beautiful blue and green scales trailing down her arm. She smiles and gently raises her long fishlike tail out of the water.

"You're a mermaid?" I ask in shock. *How beautiful she is.* I always picture mermaids as hideous, savage-like creatures, with giant black eyes, and seal-like skin, razor-sharp teeth.

"Yes, I am Thalassa. We live in the waters of this beautiful realm. I mean you no harm. A friend of Asim is a friend of mine." She smiles at me, reaching again for me to take her hand.

"It is okay, love; Thalassa has powers unlike my own. She can sense powers. She can see into your past and future. Her people are very gifted."

"Amazing," I say, smiling back at her. I take her hand, and she rises further out of the water. Her upper body exposed down to her waist where her tail begins. Her arms, shoulders, and breasts are covered in beautiful turquoise scales. Her features resemble that of someone of African descent, but her complexion is blue in color. Her hair is a mixture of green and blue shades, forming tight curls above water. "You are stunning," I say mesmerized by her. She smiles, patting my hand.

"Careful, child, my kind cannot control our hypnotizing presence. We are known to have admirers follow us into the depths of our home."

I nod, understanding passing over me. *The curse of a siren. In fairy tales, it's their song that lures men into the sea to drown, but being in her presence I realize it is just seeing them that could lead to the same outcome. They are magnetic.* Thalassa closes her yellow eyes, and I feel the urge to be near her wane. *So, it is her eyes that hypnotize then?* We sit quietly for a few minutes, while Thalassa holds my hand, her expression grows more and more concerned, until her eyes pop open.

"I see," she says, looking at Asim, "She is of goddess blood. A descendant of The Creator, Nwt. Her powers will be our salvation." She pauses, looking directly into my eyes, I feel the urge to jump into the water, to swim away with her, the only sound I hear is her voice, "You will face many hardships in this realm, my love. You must protect your child. The eternal queen will be pleased with your arrival, but not for reasons you will understand. What appears ripe in the light, rots in the darkness."

"I do not understand," I admit, unable to look away from her piercing yellow eyes.

"You are meant to be extraordinary. Your son will grow to be magnificent, but you must protect him. You must tread carefully. Not all mothers know the instinct to protect their youth. Some creatures swallow their young to protect themselves."

I stare at her confused, opening my mouth to ask her to explain, but a small yellow bird lands near us, distracting her momentarily as she drops my hands, "That is all I care to share for now. Take care. You will always find refuge with the Annipe tribe." She backs away, lowering herself as she does, until once again only her head is above water. Several similar faces rise above the water, until at least a dozen yellow eyes stare back at me. She nods at Asim, and all of them disappear below the water. I stare at the lake, so quiet and unmoving, you would never know just seconds ago, a dozen mermaids swam in its waters.

"Where did they go?" I ask searching for the glow I saw moments ago. Asim slips her hand into my own.

"Thalassa and her people are more powerful than land beings; they travel through the water and can open something similar to a portal between different bodies of water. They could be anywhere right now," she explains, "I am amazed at the strength you displayed. Not many can resist the urge to enter the water."

"You felt it too?" I ask, glad I wasn't alone in that fight.

"Yes, but she was intentionally focusing on you, trying to lure you in. She was testing you. You are not easily corrupted or swayed. You have impressed them; you and Isaiah will be safe in the water now."

"Which waters?"

"All of them." She smiles at me, pleased by our inter-actions. She squeezes my hand and leads me away from the water, and the strange little yellow bird that watched us curiously. Once we leave the trees and are back in the open field, Queen gallops towards us, happy to see us once again.

"I wonder why Queen didn't want to come?" I ask as I pet her neck.

"Queen has lost many relatives to the mermaids." She explains sadly.

"What? They seemed so peaceful. I thought they would eat... I don't know, fish?"

"Well, yes, they eat fish, and any meat that wanders close enough. Do not let their appearance fool you. The Annipe tribe are powerful and savage at times. You do not want to offend them; their appearance can just as easily change into that of your worst nightmares."

I shudder, thinking of the old myths I heard, of mer-maids dragging sailors to the bottom of the ocean, "Got it, don't piss them off."

"What she said of you was quite curious, no?" Asim says quietly, more to herself than me.

"I thought all of it was curious. I didn't understand any-thing besides, I must protect Isaiah." I say, after I say it aloud, I stop in my tracks, turning to face Asim, "Does that mean something might happen to him? We have to go back. I need to know what might happen!"

Strong hands clasp onto my arms, "My love, be still. Nothing will ever come to harm Isaiah, or you. Heqet and Cairo never leave Isaiah's side. He has charmed the fairies beyond what any being has ever thought possible in all of their history. The fairy king himself falls over himself to care for Isaiah. He is the most protected child in all of the realms. You have charmed many here as well, most of all me. I would see the eternal fire before I allow a hair on your head to be harmed. You and Isaiah are my life. You are safe. The mermaids speak in riddles. I believe Thalassa believed herself watched, so she revealed very little. We will speak with her again."

"I didn't understand what she said about mothers. Does she think I would harm my own child?"

"Let us return to the palace, hm? Heqet always has the answers I search for."

I nod, Heqet is the smartest person I know. She'll definitely know things like this. Asim lets go of my hand and gestures for me to go first. I close my eyes, and imagine Queen nudging me, after a moment I feel my wings flapping, a jump into the air, and open my eyes.

"I did it!" I yell down to Asim, as she smiles proudly back up at me.

"Yes, you did! You took off beautifully." She says as she takes off behind me, "Let us enjoy a friendly race? First one to the palace maybe?"

"Is it just straight back that way?" I ask pointing towards what I believe is the palace.

"Yes, just a straight path."

"Fine. But if I win, I can choose what we do tomorrow." I say confidently.

"What is it you wish to do?"

"No, no, I'll tell you after you lose." I tease.

"Such a shame, I will never know."

"Whatever! Wait, what is that?" I ask pointing behind her. As soon as she turns, I take off, leaning forward as she taught me. I flap my wings furiously as I head directly towards the path I pointed out moments before. I hear her quickly gaining behind me, and my competitive side screams inside. *There is no way she's going to beat me!* I focus solely on the sound of my own wings and close my eyes. *I have to go faster.* I flap my wings faster until it feels like the wind is gliding me to the palace.

"Ashanti!"

I hear Asim call my name, and I open my eyes just in time to see the wall of the palace. As a knee-jerk reaction, I throw my arms up, screaming for my wings to stop mentally. *How did I get here so fast? We just took off.* A bright white light flashes, and suddenly I realize I'm stuck in slow motion as the wall inches towards me. I watch in horror, unable to stop myself, I collide with the stone wall of the castle. The stones crumble around me, dust covering me, as my world goes black.

"Ashanti?"

I hear Asim's voice calling me, growing closer. I open my eyes and see her hovering over me. Terrified.

"You're bleeding! We must get you to the hospital wing. I don't know what happened! You moved so quickly, it was as if you teleported."

"I...I... I don't know what happened." I say confused, my body hurting. I feel my head, and realize it's bleeding, "Oh, no."

"Come, I'll carry you," she says, concerned. Queen quickly trots to us. She kneels beside us and sniffs me until she finds the wound.

"I'm okay, Queen," I say, reassuring her as I gently pet her long neck.

She whines a little, her eyes tearing, as she leans over me. I watch in shock as her tears spill over, falling on me. My head tingles were the wound is, and I reach up to feel the spot.

"I.. I think she just healed me?" I ask Asim, confused. She checks my head and looks at Queen in awe.

"She did. It is truly rare for a Pegasus to willingly interfere, to heal any species. I have not heard of a case in a long time. They are hunted for their gifts." Asim looks at me wide-eyed, "Come with me, we have to find Heqet."

I wave goodbye to Queen, after thanking her and hugging her tightly. We hurry inside. I immediately begin heading towards Isaiah's room, but a fairy stops us quietly in the hall.

"Asim, she is here," Ezra whispers, fear clouding her once cheerful eyes.

"Who?" Asim asks impatiently, looking around for Heqet. Ezra grabs Asim's hand and flies within her eyesight.

"*She* is here."

Asim stops moving. She stands so still I thought I may have slowed time again. Ezra's eyes dart down the hall.

"Where?"

Ezra clasps her hands together, "She is in the throne room, talking to The King and Queen. She appears happy, but her aura is dark. She is inquiring about *her*." She says as she points to me.

Asim takes my hand, protectively, "Tell Heqet and Cairo, of her arrival, protect Isaiah. We will have to make an appearance so she does not suspect anything."

"Wait, Asim... who is she?" I ask, confused.

"The Queen of Immortals."

"She is here? I am going to meet her?"

Asim turns to face me, looking directly into my eyes, pleading, "Ashanti, we must heed the Annipe's warning. Until we can decipher what it means, we will take it literally. She may mean us harm. Do not volunteer information. Do not mention Isaiah. Try to be as friendly as possible. No matter what she says, do not react."

Seeing her afraid, I quickly assess this Queen may not be as kind as the fairy queen. I adjust my dress and smooth my hair, "Okay, I got it."

"Are you sure?"

"Yes, yes, I can do this."

We walk together to the throne room, Asim slips inside, and I follow behind her. We stay hidden against the wall, behind the fairies standing witness to the meeting of the royals. I stand on my tiptoes trying to look through the crowd of excited, flying fairies.

"My little birdies told me you have a guest here, that I may be interested in meeting," the Immortal queen says. Her voice is familiar to me, but I cannot place it as I struggle to see her face.

"Why would a guest of ours interest you, Queen?" Queen Lotus asks, smiling.

"This guest apparently arrived with a member of my royal guard?"

"My understanding is Asim, chose to decline that generous offer and decided to return to the Earth realm instead."

The queen flinches, annoyed, "Yes well, vampires fall under my kingdom, so she would still be a subject of mine, whether on my counsel or not."

"This is true. What is your interest in our guest?"

"I merely have heard of a new being that has entered our realm and would like a chance to greet this creature," she says smiling back at Queen Lotus, "Surely Asim would like to greet her queen. Is that not correct Asim?"

The immortal queen calls out to Asim, without turning towards us. Asim hesitates for a moment, before smiling at me for a second, "Of course, my Queen. I am grateful for your visit to greet us here." We step forward as the queen turns towards us. I bow, with Asim. I feel a wave of dread flow through me, the urge to take Asim's hand and run to Isaiah. I struggle to stay there, exposed.

She's going to kill you.

She's going to kill you.

The words chant in my head, as I straighten myself. Asim squeezes my hand, and I lock eyes with the immortal queen, terrified. As our eyes meet, I drop Asim's hand, and I feel my stomach drop in shock. *I recognize this powerful woman.* Her strange golden-brown eyes staring back at me. I remember the picture I recognize her from, as if I were staring at it in this very moment, because I have seen it a million times. My father young and smiling, sitting with this woman as she sits on his lap, her arms wrapped around his neck. I step forward, completely stunned.

"Mom?"

Chapter Eighteen
– Asim

"Mom?" Ashanti asks, as everyone in the throne room looks on in shock. The Queen of Immortals looks at her, confused.

"Ashanti?" she asks, taking a step closer, clearly confused by Ashanti's appearance. "What are you doing here?"

"What am I doing here? I thought you were dead. You died when I was born. You've been here this whole time?" Ashanti asks, crying. Her tone a mixture of pain and anger. Without thinking, I step forward, unable to bear seeing her in pain. I wrap my arms around her, trying to offer her comfort with my presence.

"Asim?" The Queen says, her voice a mixture of confusion, and jealousy.

"We have much to discuss, my queen. Perhaps we can find a quieter room?" I suggest, looking pointedly at the crowd of fairies whispering. The Queen adjusts herself, smoothing out her dress, and nods in agreement.

"Well, it appears I do have much interest in this guest of yours. If you would be so kind, I think I shall extend my visit in your kingdom for a few nights?" she says, turning to face Queen Lotus.

"Of course, this is quite an interesting turn of events. Ezra? Ezra, where are you?" Queen Lotus calls.

"Here, your majesty, sorry for my delay."

"Of course, please let's give Queen Marienne and our guests some privacy?"

"Yes, of course, my queen." Ezra bows, and flies quickly to Queen Marienne, "Your majesty, if you'd please?"

The queen nods and follows Ezra to the adjacent room. I look down at Ashanti, silent tears falling from her eyes. Looking into her eyes, I feel her heartbreak. Her eyes ask a million questions, but she remains silent. I grasp her hand, hoping she understands what I cannot say. I am here with her. We will find the answers together. I wish I could share these sentiments with her, but I remain quiet out of fear of offending the queen. I lead her to the room Ezra and the queen disappeared into.

"Thank you, Ezra," I say, as she looks between the queen and Ashanti concerned, before nodding and fleeing the tense room.

"I guess you have questions?" Queen Marienne says after a moment of silence, her back facing us as she looks out the castle window.

"Questions?" Ashanti shouts, walking closer to the queen, "Yes, I have a few questions! How are you alive? I thought you were dead my entire life!" Ashanti continues to yell. I squeeze her hand, pulling her back slightly. I watch the queen, preparing for a response. While her appearance has not changed since our last encounter, there is something very different about the queen. Her presence seems to carry a darkness that was not present before. I fight the urge to grab Ashanti and run from the room.

"I understand your anger. If you allow me to explain..." She says calmly, too calmly.

"Your majesty-" I begin, but stop quickly as she turns at the sound of voice, her face distorted into a dark, enraged version of itself. Her eyes red as fire, so contorted the only word I can think of is *evil. She looks evil.* It happens for just a second, before she turns her head again, inhales deeply, composing herself, before returning to her calmer self. I turn to Ashanti, but she is staring at the floor, crying once again.

"Asim, perhaps it would be best if you allowed my daughter and myself time to discuss family matters?" The queen suggests, so calmly, I contemplate if I imagined her sudden transformation. The request is rational, but after viewing the carefully hidden side of the queen, I would rather die than leave this woman alone with Ashanti.

"My apologies, I will not interrupt again," I say walking to the corner of the room and leaning against the wall. She watches me, the fire burning dimly in her eyes.

"I don't understand. Why would you leave us? Why did my father tell me you died?" Ashanti asks, her hands shaking from her anger and sadness. I steel myself, as my entire being craves to steady those hands.

"I am sorry. You must believe me. I loved your father, and you. I wanted nothing more in this world than to stay beside him and raise you. I went to the earth realm as many of our people do, to clear my head, to live amongst humanity. I went there with no intention of finding your father, but I met him by chance, and I fell in love. I decided to stay awhile. I loved him so much that I thought I could stay there, temporarily abandon my duties as queen, and just love him during his short stay in the living realm. Unfortunately, I learned quickly that the immortality I was granted here, when my power activated, does not withstand the transition back to the earth realm. I couldn't leave my people forever. I had to decide what was best for the realm. I chose all of our people over my dreams of a family." She explains, weeping. I watch her carefully, waiting for tears that have yet to fall. *What has happened to our beloved queen*, I wonder.

"You mean you choose immortality over me?" Ashanti says, her anger rising.

"I can see how you would think that, but it's simply not true. I chose our people, this kingdom. There were tens of thousands of beings within just our kingdom, even more now. What would have become of them? Their families? I had every intention of returning here, I did not know it was even possible to become pregnant at the time. I am so many, many years old. Thousands of years have passed." Marienne walks to Ashanti, slowly, her palms up in a surrendering manner, "Darling, I wished to bring you here with me, but your father loved his home, he had no idea of this realm, of magic. I feared it would do more harm than good to introduce this life to him, and the idea of leaving him there, alone, it broke my heart. I left you there with him because I knew he was capable of loving you, and raising you. He is a good man. I had no qualms about his capabilities of fatherhood."

"He was a good man," Ashanti corrects her, bitterly. For just a moment, the queen seems genuinely shocked.

"He was? Has something happened to Maurice?" She asks, steadying herself on the chair beside her.

"He died when I was just a kid. He raised me the best he could, but he developed cancer, and died before my 10th birthday." Ashanti says, fresh tears streaming down her already-soaked cheeks. The queen looks weak, as she sits in the chair, she held moments ago.

"And you? What happened to you?" She asks, her expression looks as though her mind is in a different time.

"I grew up in foster care, I was moved around, abused, eventually I ran away, and raised myself." She explains, deciding to leave out the horrors of her last few years.

"I did not know." The queen looks at her daughter, shame painted on her face.

"You could not. You left. My father was so convinced you died. He mourned for a long time. Even now...." Ashanti stops herself, then continues, "I bet even in the afterlife he would think about you."

So, she senses it too? She doesn't trust her mother, any more than I do. She carefully left out she saw her father in her resting place amongst the ancestors.

"I am so sorry. Truly, I would have never left if I had known he would... I did not know." Marienne looks away, as tears finally fall. Ashanti watches her, her face a mixture of anger, and guilt.

"He loved you. He told me so many stories of how happy you were together, and he had a picture of you. He told me how you were superstitious about pictures being taken, and you only took one photo for him, at a party."

The queen wipes her tears, smiling at the memory, "Ah yes, the party he insisted on dragging me to, he begged for that picture, and I gave in. I remember his smile, when I finally agreed. He threatened to post it on a billboard, I believe."

They both laugh at the memory of her father, before looking at each other.

"I uh, I know what I did was inexcusable; I never dreamt that my decision would lead to such a horrid life for you. If you allow it, I would like to know you now. Perhaps we could get to know each other?"

Ashanti looks down, wringing her hands, "I guess we could try."

"Perfect, perhaps I could even teach you a thing or two about our magic?"

"That would be nice."

"It's settled then! I will stay for a few more days, and we can begin anew." The queen's mood suddenly shifts to cheerful and she excitedly stands, "Now come along, I wish to show you, my Pegasus. It is just like a fairytale! I just know you will love it. I am the only one in the kingdom that has tamed one, you know! He just trotted up to me one day, and I named him, and now I take him with me everywhere!" Ashanti looks back at me as the queen takes her arm and pulls her along. I give one quick shake to warn her against showing her power to the queen.

For a moment, I am torn; I wish to check on Isaiah, and to update Heqet on what is happening. However, I know I cannot leave Ashanti defenseless against the queen, not until I figure out what is happening with her. As I follow behind Ashanti and the queen, I run into Ezra.

"Oh, I apologize Asim. I am a little out of it. We were not expecting a royal visit today. So much has to be prepared," she says flustered.

"Of course, no worries." I lean closer to her, lowering my voice to a whisper. "Please let Heqet know to keep our guest away; something isn't right, and I must keep an eye on Ashanti."

Ezra nods. "I've noticed something is definitely off. Don't worry; the queen had to force half the fairy guards back to their stations. Everyone wanted to protect the little one. He's charmed the whole castle. No harm will come to him."

I smile. Of course, he has. He charmed me and Heqet just as fast. "Thank you, Ezra. You are a dear friend."

Ezra nods and flies off to finish her duties, and I'm left to focus on Ashanti and her safety. I contemplate hurrying outside first to send Queen and her family away, but as we step outside, I notice Ashanti's family of Pegasus are nowhere in sight. They must have somehow sensed they needed to stay away, or maybe they sensed danger. Pegasus are amongst the smartest creatures in this realm.

The queen walks outside, arm and arm with Ashanti, talking quickly about her kingdom and all of her plans as if Ashanti is an old friend, not a daughter she abandoned years ago. As we near the Queen's carriage, I see her Pegasus. It does look beautiful. Pure white in color, its horn a beautiful gold. *Something seems off, but I cannot place what.* I watch as the queen and Ashanti walk closely to him. *He seems uneasy, and anxious*, but he stands still as Ashanti runs her hands over his neck. I watch as her eyebrow furrows; she must feel it too. Something is not right here, but she remains quiet about her suspicions and continues listening to the queen's tales.

Not once does she ask Ashanti about her current life, instead choosing to describe her castle, her servants, her many powers, and even how beloved she is. I follow behind, listening to the queen's detailed admiration of herself. Every once in a while, Ashanti will shoot me a look of disbelief, before turning her attention back to her mother. I smile to myself, proudly, realizing Ashanti is not as unprepared as I thought. She is wise enough to know when to speak and what to speak of. She keeps the important details to herself, instead allowing the queen to speak endlessly of herself.

After several hours of the queen talking and Ashanti listening, Queen Lotus appears, with Ezra.

"I hope you two have become better acquainted?" She asks, smiling at Queen Marienne.

"Yes, yes, we have learned much of each other. Have we not, darling?" Marienne turns to Ashanti, smiling expectantly.

"Yes, we have," she says, smiling at Queen Lotus.

"That is wonderful. Our chefs have prepared a lovely meal to help us celebrate this splendid reunion," Queen Lotus says, gesturing towards Ashanti and Marienne.

"That is very kind of you. I'm sure it will be a beautiful celebration."

I watch this interaction, the tension so thick I could cut it. *What has happened here in my absence?* My focus has been solely on Ashanti and Isaiah, adjusting. I must have missed something since my return.

"Thank you, Your Majesty," Ashanti says, smiling at Queen Lotus, "You have been so wonderful to me since I arrived. I am grateful for your hospitality."

"You are welcome here as long as you like, Ashanti. It has been a joy." She smiles at Ashanti, then at me, "Asim, why don't you take Ashanti to get ready for our dinner while us queens discuss a few things, hmm?" She says, folding her hands in front of her, smiling brightly at me.

"Oh, of course, please excuse us," I say, quickly grabbing Ashanti's hand and hurrying away from them.

"Oh, my goodness." She says after me round a corner away from the royals.

"How are you?" I ask quietly.

"Honestly, overwhelmed, confused." She says, "I don't understand. She is not the woman my father described throughout my childhood. She's selfish, and rude. He described someone kind, compassionate, and empathetic. Someone who loved everyone. The only thing the queen seems to love is herself."

I nod in agreement, "I am confused as well, I must admit. That is not the same queen I left behind so many years ago. Something is not right." I say. I describe the change in her face as I spoke in the private room. The feeling of unsettledness I felt seeing her Pegasus.

"I agree, something is not right here, at all. I have felt like she has not been truthful since we first spoke. She is definitely hiding something. I think it would be best if we keep Isaiah a secret for now until we figure out what it is."

"Absolutely," I agree. We find Heqet in a hidden hall on the east side of the castle, near the staff quarters.

"Ezra thought here would be best while the queen is here; she wouldn't come here," Heqet explains.

"Smart, I agree. After meeting her, I don't think she'd be caught dead near staff bedrooms," I say, smiling at Heqet, "Is Isaiah already in bed?"

"Yup, we played football in the hall for the last 3 hours. He passed out after eating the small feast one of the kitchen chefs brought up. They adore this kid," Cairo says in his human form.

"We all do," Heqet says, plopping down on the arm of the chair Cairo is sitting in.

"Yes, we all do wholeheartedly," I agree, "Which is why we have to figure out what has happened in the time we have been gone from this realm. The queen is not herself at all, and we need to know why."

"Agreed." Heqet says, nodding, "Whatever it is, it happened after we left?"

"We left about 25 years ago; it was four years after her return to the realm," I look at Ashanti, realizing she did in fact return shortly after her birth. "She was different then as well, but not as she is now. She returned and had a fascination with the abilities of the other creatures in the realm. She wanted to establish her power and strength in the kingdom."

"My father described her as patient and kind. She would stop to help the homeless, and she would constantly bring stray animals home," Ashanti says quietly, sitting in the chair closest to her, "She's nothing like I imagined."

I pull her into my lap, sitting in the chair, holding her close, "I am sorry, love. I never imagined you would reunite with her, especially not under these circumstances. Heqet and I tried to find more information on your family, but we couldn't find any details at all. Your mother was simply listed as deceased, and there weren't many details regarding your childhood until you were put into foster care," I explain.

"How? How does the entire world think she's deceased? Did she just get up after giving birth and walk out of the hospital? I don't understand," Ashanti says, frustrated.

"We have had to fake quite a few deaths in our time. She must have had someone of our kind, or quite a few, to convince so many people without a body," Heqet says, pulling her hair into a bun, as she does when she is thinking, "I wonder who it could have been? You were her most trusted ally, were you not?"

"Yes, she spoke of nearly every detail of her plans with me. All of her troubles, and concerns. I was her advisor of sorts. She thought of me as her friend," I explain.

"Was she in love with you?" Ashanti asks me, her eyes full of questions. *Unsure how to answer*, I hesitate.

"I... I don't think that is a simple answer I can give."

"Try."

"We met during a time of war. Many of the beings I called friends died. I lost a very dear person to me prior to returning here. I was...broken. Nwt had disappeared. I had yet to meet Heqet. Marienne was the only friend I had for a very long time. I loved her as a sister. I believe she cared for me, possibly loved me. But she was also broken when she came here. Her family had died, from disease, slavery, and she clung to me. I became her family. She expected me to stay with her here, in this realm, to rule with her, but after so many years I could not return the affections she needed, so I left."

Ashanti listens thoughtfully, processing what she has learned before turning to Heqet, "I do not trust my mother. When she was talking, she made it seem like her kingdom was a paradise, but I got the feeling from her Pegasus, and the interaction with Queen Lotus that she isn't as kind as she would like me to believe. Something is very wrong."

"I agree," Heqet says.

"As do I," Cairo nods in agreement, "I'm going to try and find some of my relatives tomorrow. The last time I was here, I believe a few were living in the fairy realm, near the marketplace."

"Perhaps, you could take young Isaiah, and Heqet with you? It would be good to get him out of the castle for a while." I suggest. Ashanti looks at me upset.

"For how long?"

"A few days at least, The fairies will protect Isaiah, and Cairo's family, while their means of income isn't the most legitimate, they are trustworthy. Above all, I trust Cairo, and Heqet. They would not put Isaiah's life in danger." I say, hoping my confidence calms her.

"Well, of course, I trust you guys. We are family, but I don't like Isaiah being so far away, in a strange new place." She says, biting her lip nervously, "I guess it would be safer to keep him away from my mother, at least until we figure out what's going on."

"Yes, love. I promise he will be safe. I will talk with the queen and ensure a few of her guards accompany them." I say, patting her thigh.

"I'll watch him like a hawk, Ashanti, I promise," Cairo says, turning his head into a hawk head for a moment, before turning back into his human form. I roll my eyes, as he laughs hysterically.

"Ugh, don't worry, Ashanti, I will be there, watching Cairo as he watches Isaiah." Heqet says, as she and Ashanti both laugh.

A short time later, the fairies deliver clothing that was created for each of us to wear to the celebration. Cairo volunteers to stay and keep watch over Isaiah. As we prepare for our night, Ashanti looks into the mirror, adjusting her hair, her expressions a mixture of worry and sadness.

"What is wrong, love?" I ask, hugging her from behind. She sighs and sinks into me.

"I'm just worried. I mean, I have wondered what my mother was like for so long. Now to find her here, selfish and... and I don't know... Evil? My mother could be an evil queen for all I know."

"Evil, love? That is a strong accusation. Does your instinct tell you she is evil?"

"I don't know. I just got this awful feeling when she touched me, like this nagging urge to run. I truly don't know her. My father described her as this wonderful, kind, Mary Poppins type of woman, and now... I guess it's just disappointing to realize, this woman I've missed my entire life, is a made-up fairy tale." She says, staring at the floor. I turn her towards me, lifting her chin with my hand.

"Hey, no matter what, you grew up to be a kind, wonderful, Mary Poppins type of woman. You are an amazing mother, an amazing artist, and an amazing love. You have conquered much. We will figure this mystery out together, and we will keep all of us safe. It is going to be okay. I promise." I say, kissing her forehead. She nods, giving me a half-smile.

"I am so grateful for you."

"And I, you."

We walk into the ballroom, Ashanti, and Heqet on either side of me, our arms interlocked. As soon as we enter the room, Ezra flies up to us.

"The queen has been asking for you, Ashanti. She is rather shall we say, persistent, that I bring you straight to her." Ezra says, clearly annoyed, but a smile plastered on her face. Ashanti nods, and steps towards her, but Ezra holds her hand up, "And I have every plan of bringing you to her, but my queen would like a word first." She says, gesturing for us to follow her. She takes us into a small room, hidden behind a curtain, behind the queen's table. It is a small room, with a round table and six chairs in it.

"Ah, Ashanti," Queen Lotus says, as soon as she sees us.

"Queen Lotus." We all bow slightly. As the queen waves her hand, gesturing for us to stop.

"Please not now, we have much to discuss and very little time. Your mother Queen Marienne is not what she seems." The queen says, rushing her words in a quiet voice.

"What do you mean, ma'am?" Ashanti asks, leaning over the table to better hear the queen

"She was a kind woman, once. I was just a girl when I first met her; she was already queen by then. She came to meet the prior queen and king and discuss treaty details. This was a very long time ago. We fairies are not immortal, but we age slowly. I am several centuries old myself. Anyway, the queen was different then. Her focus was peace, and the safety of all creatures, not just her kingdom, but all of our kingdoms. She was loved, but that all changed years ago. Several of my trusted subjects stated they witnessed the Immortal Queen going into the forbidden forest to make deals with the corrupted sirens there." The Queen explains.

"Forbidden Forest? I thought the mermaids were good?" Ashanti says.

"No, dear, the Annipe tribe is overall good. They have some questionable practices, but they are not savages. There is another tribe; they broke away from the Annipe and were corrupted after doing unthinkable rituals. They wanted to use their powers to conquer the realm. As punishment, the Annipe tribe locked those sirens into the lake in the forbidden forest. They are unable to leave there and must live in their prison for an eternity."

"And my mother went there?"

"Yes, several times. We are unsure what it is she was after, but with each visit, she changed. She became more aggressive, power-hungry, and self-absorbed. Her personality has changed so drastically; I question if she is, in fact, the same being." Queen Lotus says.

"You think she may be possessed?" I ask, surprised by the comment.

"Or cloned, I don't know. I do not know the extent of the corrupted tribe's powers. But I know they are capable of horrendous things."

"What should we do?" Heqet asks.

"For now, we will watch her. We must find out what is happening. Whatever it is may threaten the realm as a whole," the queen explains.

"I agree, but I want to ensure my son's safety," Ashanti says sternly.

"Of course. I do as well. He will remain under our protection for as long as needed. I will assign guards to him, and of course a tutor, and I think it best he remains within the castle walls for the time being. Queen Marienne has made plans to leave tomorrow evening. He should be safe here, while we decipher what dangers may be lurking."

"I am grateful," Ashanti says.

"I am forever in your debt," I say, grateful once again for the kindness of the fairies.

The queen waves her hand, "Please, this is for the well-being of the realm, and to be honest, your son is quite the charmer. I fear there would be an uprising if any harm came to him."

"I would expect nothing less," Ashanti says, laughing with the queen.

"Okay, please, I beg of you, take care. I expect updates on any findings."

"Of course, your majesty," we all agree. The queen slips out of the door first, immediately calling for Ezra.

"Are you okay?" I ask Ashanti, holding her hands.

"Is it possible? Could my mother be possessed or corrupted in some way?" She asks me.

"I have seen very few cases; the sirens are just corrupted mermaids. They are very powerful and not limited by the moral code the mermaids follow. It is possible they have used your mother in a way she did not intend."

"Then we have to find out. If she's possessed or something, we have to help her," Ashanti says anxiously, looking at me as if pleading. I look at Heqet, who also looks concerned. *She will not like this.* Anything that will put our family in danger she'll be against.

"We will discuss our plans later love, tonight let's enjoy this party, hmm?" I suggest. She nods and adjusts her hair and dress.

"Okay, I'm ready."

We head out of the small hidden room and try our best to blend into the crowd. Ashanti, however, stands out with her beautiful new wings, and Queen Marienne quickly finds us.

"There you are!" She says, as she pulls Ashanti into an unexpected hug, "I began to worry you would not make an appearance."

"We got held up a little." She says quietly, awkwardly hugging her back.

"You look marvelous, let me see! Spin?" The queen says clapping happily, as Ashanti spins for her, "Your wings are so beautiful. The pattern and color are so close to my own. How lovely it is to have another demigoddess in the realm."

Ashanti freezes as her mother finally puts a name to her species, "Demigoddess?"

"Well, of course, my love, you are of goddess blood. We are demigoddesses, as my mother was before me. The goddess Nwt, was my grandmother. Although I never got the chance to meet her. My own mother died when I was a young woman. Unfortunately, she died before she had the chance to activate her own magic; no realm such as this one existed."

"I'm so sorry," Ashanti says, sadness etched on her face. I listen to the queen's story; in all of the many years I've known her, she never acknowledged her history. It seems the bloodline is not as diluted as I originally thought.

"Well, enough about that; I do not like to dwell on sadness. Tell me, what powers have manifested since your arrival?"

Ashanti looks at me, unsure how to answer.

"Your majesty, we have yet to truly study her powers. She is just learning flight." Heqet answers her, smiling.

"What? That is unacceptable. Once you join me in my palace, we will have to find out what you have hidden in there." She says, tapping Ashanti's head gently, with a smile.

Ashanti nods, smiling back, "How is living here? I know you are queen but do you have many friends?"

"Why yes, the realm is like a family. We all care deeply for one another." She says, smiling at Asim while drinking from her champagne glass, "So uh, darling, what about you? Tell me is there anyone in your life? Any children or pets?"

"Well, uh... at the moment..." Ashanti stumbles over her words.

"I am courting Ashanti," I say, "obviously I was unaware of her parentage until recently, but I am quite smitten with her."

Ashanti smiles at me and blushes, but the queen's face flashes angrily for a brief moment, before her smile returns.

"Well, that is wonderful dear. I am happy for you, of course! I never thought Asim would settle down with any-one! Especially after her first Ashanti passed so suddenly," Marienne says, a smile threatening to break through her worried expression.

I close my eyes; of course, she would go this route. She would try to expose me, and try to convince Ashanti that my feelings are not real. I open my eyes to see Ashanti has shifted her body, slightly, but in a way that positions herself between the queen and me. She looks back at me briefly before turning to the queen.

"It was very tragic, but I am grateful we have found one another. We both have a lot to heal from."

I stare at this woman in disbelief. *Is she defending me?* She could have accused me, and demanded answers, but she chose to protect me and remain united. I smile at the queen, "very grateful indeed."

Marienne looks frustrated between Ashanti and me, "That is truly divine. Have you decided when you will be coming home?"

"Home?" Ashanti asks, confused.

"Well, of course, you will move to the castle; you are an immortal, after all. All immortal subjects are to live in the Immortal kingdom. Surely, you do not mean to stay here?"

"I haven't even thought about that. I just met you. I don't know if I want to live with you or anything like that. I thought you were dead until a few hours ago," Ashanti says.

"This is true. I guess I am getting a little too excited to have you back in my life. I did not think I would see you again," Marienne says, wiping her eyes.

"I'm not leaving anytime soon," Ashanti says, placing her hand on top of her mothers, "We have plenty of time to get to know each other, and figure this out."

They both smile at each other, and for a brief moment, Marienne seems like herself again.

"Well, all of this emotion has driven me mad with thirst," she says, snapping her fingers and clapping loudly until the staff rushes over, "Yes, I am parched, please bring me a glass of champagne, and none of that cheap stuff you gave me before. I am not a commoner."

I cringe at her statement; thousands of years of kindness and humility gone. *I wonder what her staff in the palace have come to think of her?* I watch the members of the royal guard who are in attendance with her. To my surprise, I recognize no one. *New vampires? Why would the queen choose new vampires to guard her? Especially, when it is obvious, she isn't the most well-liked royal at the present moment?* I look over and make eye contact with Heqet, who looks pointedly at the door.

"I'm sorry, my love, would you mind if we stepped away for just a moment?" I say to Ashanti.

"Is something wrong?" Marienne asks, looking suspiciously at us.

"No, no, we simply need to tend to a few details for the surprise we have organized for Ashanti tomorrow."

"Oh, I wish I could attend! I love surprises! Unfortunately, I need to head back to the palace. An unexpected issue has come to my attention, and well, the kingdom needs their queen," Marienne says, looking sadly at Ashanti, "I do hope you will decide to return with me. There is so much I could teach you, and we could continue learning one another."

"I will think about it tonight," Ashanti says, avoiding looking her mother in her eyes.

"Well, Ashanti, I think we should dance while the music is good, hm?" Heqet says, reaching for Ashanti's hand, and quickly pulling her to the dance floor before she can protest. Marienne sits quietly watching Heqet and Ashanti dance, and I remain standing watching them as well.

"So, my daughter?" Marienne asks, breaking our silence.

"I did not know at the time," I say, turning to face her. She rolls her eyes, gesturing for me to sit down.

"Oh, please Asim, I know you had no clue I had a child. She looks like her father, aside from her obvious goddess-like features. It's actually humorous. We spend thousands of years as friends, and within what, a couple of years you fall for her? I must admit I'm quite jealous. I had hoped you would settle down and stay here with me, but you could never spend more than a decade or two at a time before you and Heqet would run off again. I honestly thought maybe you'd fall for Heqet once upon a time, but I realized she's nothing more than a sister to you."

I smile politely, knowing if I correct her and tell her I've known Ashanti less than a year, she'd grow jealous. So, I simply smile, "I thought of you as a sister as well. I'm disappointed you didn't share this part of your life with me."

"I must admit, it was fun. Having that secret. Being queen is wonderful. I love our people, but having that private secret, it was thrilling. She was my secret. She belonged to me. I thought about going back, just peeking in on them, or asking the mermaids. I guess I was too scared of knowing. I kept imagining Maurice married, smiling on the porch, our daughter in another woman's lap, calling her mommy. I couldn't bear it. I am a coward," Marienne says, tearfully, before she wipes her eyes and laughs without humor, "Ugh, look at me, a sentimental old fool. I did what was best for the kingdom. If I stayed for too long, I would have perished. I could not risk it."

I nod, although I do not agree. Her choices caused so much harm to so many people, "Still, you could have told me. You should have. We could have figured out a plan."

"I do not have the luxury of regrets, unfortunately. Our lives are far too long to regret choices of the past. All I can do now is move forward."

Listening to her speak, she sounds so normal, with no trace of the awful being that spoke endlessly of herself. No evil aura emanated from her. *Maybe she was simply angry, or hurt, and we misread her?* I watch her carefully, as she watches Ashanti, a small smile on the ends of her lips as Heqet and Ashanti dance and laugh. Just a proud mother, watching her only child. I join her in watching Ashanti. She looks beautiful. Her flawless skin glowing with power, her smile brightening the room as she twirls around holding Heqet's hand. She seems happy. The happiest I have seen her in quite some time. This realm suits her.

"I will take my leave now."

The queen's voice cuts through my thoughts, dripping with anger.

"What has happened? Are you okay?" I ask, watching as she stands up quickly, and her guards rush to her side.

She waves me away angrily, "Stay. I do not care to re-kindle old friendships. I was a fool tonight. Goodnight."

She exits quickly, stooping away like a child throwing a tantrum, as I am left standing at our table, confused. *What happened?*

"What's wrong?" Ashanti says, rushing over with Heqet.

"I do not know, love. She was fine. She sounded like her old self, and suddenly she became so irrationally filled with anger and left."

"Hmm, we definitely need to investigate more tomorrow," Heqet says, watching the empty doorway the queen and her entourage left through. I nod my agreement.

We spend the rest of the night enjoying ourselves. I pull Ashanti in, close to me to dance our worries away, as we glide around the dance floor. We indulge ourselves on the buffet of delicious food the fairies have prepared, and the finest magic-infused wine.

"I really needed this," Ashanti says, downing another glass of wine.

I smile as I sip the glass of blood from our kingdom's annual blood drive on the earth realm. We keep a steady supply for the blood drinkers of our realm. Every year we hold thousands of blood drives in cities all over the world. We collect the donations and hold them in storage through-out our realm so that those who choose to live here can survive comfortably.

"Me too!" Heqet says, laughing. "Perhaps I should bring Cairo a plate of food?"

"You and Cairo have gotten pretty close, huh?" Ashanti says, lifting her eyebrow and bursting into a fit of giggles. Heqet straightens and smooths her dress.

"Well, umm, we have always been close," she says, looking at her hands.

"No, no, no. I mean close!" Ashanti presses, slurring her words.

"Uh, perhaps we have had enough to drink, hmm?" I say, taking Ashanti's hand, distracting her momentarily. Heqet, grateful, nods a thank you before disappearing to get Cairo some food.

"Perhaps not!" She says, laughing hysterically and flagging a fairy for more wine. I have never seen her this level of intoxicated, so I laugh at her outburst.

"My love, we have a busy day tomorrow, why don't I help you to our room?"

She turns and looks at me, her eyes barely open. She stares at me for a moment before opening her mouth and sloppily licking her lips. The gesture would look unappealing on anyone but her. Even in her drunken state, she looks divine.

"You want to come to my room?" She purrs, raising her eyebrow.

I shift uncomfortably. Of course, I find her incredibly attractive, but I also must protect her. In her state, she may cause an unbecoming scene.

"Yes, my love, we share a room. Here, come with me," I say, standing and reaching for her hand.

"Come on, Heqet!" Ashanti says loudly. "Asim thinks we're drunk!"

"Does she now?" Heqet says, laughing, walking back to the table with Cairo's food in her hand. Using her free hand, she takes Ashanti's extended hand. We walk arm-in-arm out of the ballroom. Ashanti remains quiet, occasionally giggling or loudly whispering an inappropriate comment to

Heqet. Until we are near our rooms, once she realizes where we are going, she becomes upset.

"No, I have to check on Isaiah before bed."

"I can run and check, love, you need to rest."

"No, I want to see he's okay with my own face... I mean eyes," she says, straightening her back. "I am okay."

I contemplate for a moment, "Of course love, we will check on him, then rest."

We hurry to the staff floor, and quietly sneak into his room. Isaiah lay quietly snoring in his bed, in the next room Cairo lay across the sofa in the corner.

"How was the party?" He asks, not bothering to open his eyes to look at us.

"It was good, I brought you food," Heqet says, nonchalantly. Cairo's eyes shoot open, smiling.

"I knew you wouldn't forget me, babe."

Heqet blushes before clearing her throat and tossing his food to him, rolling her eyes, "Only because you watched the little one."

"Mmhmm," Cairo says, already stuffing his face.

"He is perfect," Ashanti slurs, coming out of Isaiah's room.

"Yes, he is," we all agree. Ashanti drunkenly falls forward as she walks, and Heqet catches her.

"Okay love, why don't we go to sleep, hmm?" Heqet suggests, speaking as if she is trying to convince a toddler of naptime. Ashanti doesn't respond aside from an incoherent mumble. Heqet, clearly amused, looks at me, "Perhaps Asim can assist you to your room." She says it in a teasing child-like way.

"Very mature, Heqet," I say, but my stomach warms and does flips at the thought of being alone with her once again,

"Of course, I will assist her. Come Ashanti, let me carry you." I pick her up, carrying her like a newlywed across the threshold.

"Mmmmm, so strong," Ashanti mumbles, as she points towards the hall, "Onward!"

Cairo and Heqet both laugh.

"I am glad to finally see her cutting loose," Cairo says, as I walk towards the door, "poor kid's been through a lot."

"She deserves her fun. Asim too," Heqet agrees, "Asim, try and have fun, hmm? I'll stay here tonight and keep an eye on the little one."

I smile, closing the door, as Cairo lifts his arm, and Heqet snuggles in close to him. My companion has finally found her mate. Getting Ashanti to sleep proves to be harder than I imagined.

"I'm not going to do anything!" she whines, as she continues to pat the bed beside her.

"I believe I shall sit on the couch, my love; I do not require sleep," I say, reminding her for the third time.

"I know, but I just want to cuddle, please," she continues to plead. I hate to hear her plead, but I know she is far too intoxicated to give me the consent I require.

"If I lie beside you, you will sleep?" I suggest. She nods excitedly. "Okay."

I climb into the massive bed beside her, wrapping my arm around her waist, pulling her close to snuggle by my side. She smiles up at me before snuggling closer, her hand tracing the buttons on my shirt. Slowly she traces my buttons until she reaches my exposed neck. I tremble as she lightly traces her fingertips along my collarbone. Reaching for her hand, I hold onto it tightly.

"My love, please. You must sleep."

She pouts for a moment before pulling her hand free. We lie still for a moment, suddenly she climbs on top of me. Her angelic face and matching wings leave me speechless.

"Can you teach me?" She asks, trailing her hands along my shoulders.

"Teach you?" I ask, focused solely on how her dress hugs her hips just right.

"Yes, teach me how to tuck my wings, like you? I mean, I have grown to love them, but they get in the way sometimes," she says, touching her wings softly.

"Oh, umm, yes. Uh, close your eyes," I say, thinking of the easiest way to explain it. I watch as she closes her eyes, readjusting herself and straddling my hips. "Umm, it's similar to flying. Feel for your wings."

I watch as she furrows her brow in concentration, and her wings twitch.

"Yes, exactly, now stretch your back, and tighten your upper back; you can feel your bones pushing them in. It will hurt a little at first, but you will get used to it," I say, placing my hands on her hips. She murmurs as she concentrates, stretching her back. I bite my lip as I watch her, her back arching in pain as her wings slowly retract into her back.

"Perfect, love," I say, rubbing her back where her wings once were. I watch as her face lights up.

"I did it!" She says loudly, turning and flexing each way to examine her own back.

"Yes, you did," I say. She looks down at me, her eyes suddenly catlike.

"Now, where was I?"

"You were going to sleep," I say, laughing.

"No, I was not! I'm feeling very... in need of your touch," she says, rocking her hips slowly, "Please, baby."

I close my eyes, steeling my willpower, "I would love to give you all of my touch, my love, but you are intoxicated. I could never disrespect you in that way. Let's cuddle and sleep tonight; tomorrow we can talk about my touch, hm?"

"It's okay! Disrespect me!" She whines, making me laugh.

"No, now come here," I pull her off of me and cradle her next to my body, "You are my queen, and I will respect you always."

"Fine," she gives in, "Tomorrow let's teach Isaiah how to do that with his wings."

"Oh, Isaiah knows," I laugh aloud, "His exact words were, 'his wings are too cool to put away.'"

She laughs with me, "They are cool."

"Tomorrow we are going to the Forbidden Forest," I explain, stroking her hair.

"The Forbidden Forest? Won't we get into trouble?" She asks me, her eyes wide with fear.

"Only if we are caught, love," I say with a mischievous grin. Understanding crosses her face.

"You want to find out what my mom is up to? Do you think the mermaids will tell us?"

"Corrupted mermaids are sirens; there is no telling what they will reveal. However, we must remain vigilant, and take everything they say with a grain of salt. They will not lie, but they will speak in riddles. They aren't bound by the same morals as the mermaids, and we could likely see anything walking into there," I explain. She nods.

"I'll be careful," she agrees, yawning. "We all will."

"Yes, we will. Sleep, my love. I will be here when you wake."

Chapter Nineteen – Ashanti

"Come in," I call as someone knocks on my room door. Ezra burst into my room, a ball of energy as always.

"The queen is coming! Uh, I mean your mom," she says frantically, looking around for any sign of Isaiah.

"It's okay. Heqet saw her first; he's safe," I reassure her. She calms down, and I smile at her concern for my baby. I take her tiny hand into my own, "Thank you. You have been nothing but kind to us, and I appreciate it more than you will ever know."

She blushes at my statement, "Well, Asim and Heqet are my friends, and I can tell you are a good person. I want to help in any way I can."

Before I can respond, my mother, Queen Marienne, barges into my room with several of her guards, looking around with a look of distaste obvious on her face. She smiles as she spots me.

"Ah, darling. I have looked everywhere for you!" She says, walking up to me, grasping both of my hands, "I wanted to apologize for last night. It appears even the queen can get a little inebriated." She laughs at her own comment.

I smile back at her, "It's not a big deal, nothing to forgive. We all got a little buzzed last night."

"True, thank you." She smiles before turning to examine the room, " Is this the best they can give the princess of the immortals?"

The sound of the title takes me by surprise, "I'm not the princess of anything," I say, smiling in apology to Ezra, "This is the most beautiful room I've ever seen."

She waves off the statement, unimpressed, "Wait until you see my castle!" She claps her hands together excitedly, "Have you packed? Are you ready?"

"Ready for what?"

"To go, darling! I must leave today for my kingdom, and I had hoped you would return with me. Our people will be overjoyed."

"Oh, I- uh, I think I still have some things I'd like to do here... but I will definitely come visit once I'm done."

She looks at me bewildered, "What ever could you have to do in fairy kingdom? Don't be silly."

"I'm not going to be able to leave with you today," I say sternly, hoping she doesn't notice how I dodged her question.

"Hmm, well, that was not the expected answer. Well, fine. I won't press, but I am having a grand ball by the end of the week, Sunday. I'd very much enjoy you there."

"I'll try my best."

"Stubborn like your father," she says with a smile, kissing me on my cheek, "I'll see you soon then."

She leaves quickly, her guards hurrying after her. Ezra looks at me sadly, "I know it's not my place, but your, uh mom...she's a bit... well, out of touch...with reality."

I laugh at her statement. I don't know why, but, in the moment, I find it hysterical. Ezra joins my laughter, and we laugh together until Cairo joins us.

"What's so funny?" He says, plopping down on the armchair. His furry legs draped over the arm of the chair. Ezra wrinkles her nose at the sight of him

"Cairo, I'd like to remind you that you are residing within the walls of the castle, not poolside. I'd ask you to remain properly clothed at all times," Ezra says, glaring at Cairo.

"Oh, calm down Ez, I just woke up," he says winking two of his eyes at her. She rolls her eyes before turning to me.

"I will see to it that you are properly packed for your outing." She smiles at me before flying past Cairo without a second look.

"Well, you have an interesting way with the people here," I say to him, laughing.

"I used to date her aunt. Didn't end too well," he shrugs.

"Are there any women you haven't dated in this world?"

"Umm, your mom, and you," he laughs, "I'm working on your mom though."

"Gross, Cairo," I say, shuddering at the thought, "Have you forgotten she could be possessed by some evil demon or something?"

"Sounds like a fun night to me," he says winking, with a smile.

"Cairo, you are shameful," Heqet says, walking into the room, "Ah, I see Asim has finally taught you how to retract your wings. I told her to do it sooner, but she wanted you to adjust to your wings being present."

I nod, "It was a lot easier than I thought it would be."

"She also told me she witnessed you fly at incredible speeds the other day," she says, suddenly very interested.

"Oh, I don't know, I closed my eyes and I just kind of appeared in front of the castle. I don't even know what I did," I say honestly.

"I hear the Pegasus have taken a special liking to you as well. They actually healed you?"

"Yes, Queen used her tears to heal me, when I crashed," I explain.

"Extraordinary. It has been so long since I've heard of such a thing. They must sense Nwt's bloodline in you. A pureness. They trust you," she says thoughtfully, before turning to look at me, "We will have to recreate the scenario where your speed increased drastically later and see if we can trigger something. Your powers seem to be growing with each passing day. I have no doubt they will make themselves known soon," she says, pleased.

"Make themselves known? What do you mean?"

"Since we crossed into our realm, and your magic was activated, it has been building slowly, increasing within you. Soon your body will be fully adapted, and your magic will be at its peak. At that time, we will be able to see all the incredible things you are capable of," she explains.

"Is that true for Isaiah too?" I ask, worried.

"Yes, but I have been working with him daily, trying to coax his powers out, and assess what he is capable of. It is possible his powers will not mirror your own."

"We could have completely different abilities?" I ask. I hadn't thought of that. I assumed I would be able to figure out my own powers, and then teach him.

"It happens here more often than you would think; children do not always inherit exact abilities from their parents. Sometimes it may skip a generation, or both parents' powers may combine and create something new. I have never researched the powers of a direct descendant of a goddess. There is much I do not know."

"I guess I didn't think of it that way. We are a new species," I say, frowning with worry.

"It will be okay; we are all here to help you and Isaiah. Nothing's ever going to happen to y'all again," Cairo says, in a moment of rare seriousness.

I nod, "I believe you, thank you. I appreciate you guys."

Asim walks into the room, announcing herself with a clap, "Okay, you guys ready?"

"For?" I ask, still thinking of my conversation with Heqet.

"For our, uh, little outing today," Asim says, nervously.

"Oh! Yes babe, I'm ready," I say, smiling, ready to solve this mystery surrounding my mother...

"I'm leaving with Cairo and Isaiah to go into town today, to look for Cairo's relatives. We should be back within three days."

"I forgot you were taking him today, where is he?" I ask, looking around.

"He's with the king in the stables. Apparently, your herd of Pegasus have taken up home there. The king has taken him under his wing; I believe he wishes to train him directly. It is unheard of. Isaiah has charmed this kingdom. I'm actually beginning to wonder if it is not a power of his," Asim says amused.

"Hmm, that is an interesting theory. I grew attached to Isaiah quickly in the earth realm, but I have always had a protective nature for children. Since we have come here, it does appear the fairies and other beings are falling over themselves to help him," Heqet says, in a contemplative tone.

"You think one of his powers is charming people?" I ask, confused, "Could he do that?"

"Yes, he could have the ability to sway others' emotions. It wouldn't be unheard of. It would explain everyone's constant need to help or cater to him. Even the king and queen are not immune to it, and they are by far two of the most powerful beings in the realm," Asim explains, "If it is an ability, Isaiah will be quite strong once he learns to effectively use his powers."

"I wonder how it works?" Cairo asks.

"Yes, well, it is just a theory. He is a cute kid, with a charming personality. They could all just be excited to have a new being in child form in the palace," Asim says.

"Still, I think we should keep an eye out as we travel and see if there is something to it," Heqet suggests.

"Please, let me know. Do not let him out of your sight. You know he moves fast," I say, worried.

"Don't worry love, we got him!" Cairo reassures me, "I'm going to go change, and I'll send him up to say goodbye before we take off. It's probably best we all don't leave the castle together. Your mom may have spies outside the castle, waiting."

"That is true. Have him retract his wings when you are on foot," Asim instructs them. They both nod.

"Be careful, huh?" Cairo says to us before leaving. Heqet hugs Asim, and for a brief moment, they look like sisters, afraid for one another.

"The Forbidden Forest is full of tricks and deadly illusions. Do not let your guard down for a moment. There is a very real danger lurking in the lake there. The sirens are cruel. Unlike their peers, they are not bound by their moral beliefs. They are deceitful and savage, and their powers are strong," Heqet says, staring directly at Asim. They are silent for a moment, thousands of years of camaraderie giving them the ability to converse without words. They both nod, Asim briefly kissing the forehead of Heqet.

"Be safe, little one."

After saying our goodbyes and hugging Isaiah until he squeals and begs me to let go, I watch them walk down the hall and turn out of my view. Frowning, I turn to Asim.

"I don't understand why I couldn't send one of the Pegasus with them. You said they were powerful. Wouldn't that be extra protection?" I say, worried.

"No one will harm him, my love. Even if someone was stupid enough to try, Heqet and Cairo are more than capable of protecting him. They are trying to keep a low profile, and a Pegasus following a small child around will draw much-unwanted attention. It could make him a target."

I sigh, "I just don't like him going out into an unknown world without me."

"I know, my love, but Cairo was born into this world, and Heqet has lived here for thousands of years. They know all the dangers. I promise he is safe."

"Okay," I continue to watch the spot I last saw them turn, arms folded in worry, until Asim wraps her arms around me.

"Heqet will check in frequently. We have plans as well, remember? We should get going. I do not want to risk being in the forest after dark."

The flight to the forest is longer than I anticipated. Asim points out the different beings and holds my hand as we fly together. After what feels like hours later, she points to a dark secluded area.

"Do you see those trees?"

I nod, "Yes, they look burnt."

"They may be; the sirens did not take being imprisoned well. We will land there." She points to a field that borders the forest.

We land, and immediately, she takes my hand firmly, "They will attempt to lure you. You will feel an urge to enter the water. Do not give in to that urge. Do not walk to the water's edge. They will try to coax information from you. Do not give them information or mention names. We will only speak of the Queen of the immortals, no one else. Most importantly, do not agree to any deals with these beings. It is always a trick."

I nod, trying to push down the fear that rises as she speaks. She gives me a small smile and gently swings my hand.

"Hey, it's going to be okay. I will protect you. Do not fear."

"I'm not afraid." I lie. She smiles, showing her fangs.

"I can smell it, my love; we will be okay."

"You can smell it?" I ask, shocked.

"You reek of it." She laughs gently.

"What else can you smell? What exactly are your powers?"

"I will share with you once we are safely home. We must focus now. Retract your wings before we enter," she warns me, "Are you ready?"

I nod, as I retract them, and inhale deeply, "Ready."

We walk hand and hand into the forest quietly. The forest itself is quiet, a light fog makes it difficult to see. No birds chirping or insects buzzing. Nature itself has abandoned the dead trees here. I look around cautiously, afraid a monster may jump from behind a tree or pile of branches. Asim looks calm, as she walks her head straight ahead, but from her serious expression, I get the feeling she is listening much further than I can hear.

"It is just behind these trees here; the fog will become dense. Do not let go of my hand." She warns. I hold her hand tighter as we walk past the trees and into a small clearing, the fog so dense it makes it almost impossible to see ahead. The lake seems lifeless. The blue-tinted glow of the Annipe's lake nowhere to be seen. For a moment, I think they must have escaped, or died like everything else in this forest, but the water begins to swirl, and change to a bright red glow. A pair of eyes emerge from the water after a moment. Black and large, much different from the yellow eyes I saw before. I take a step back as the creature swims closer to the water's edge. Asim grasps my hand tighter.

"Proditor, we wish to speak with your leader," Asim says sternly. The siren's eyes flash red.

"You come here into our prison and call us traitors? We are Annipe, even if our people have abandoned us. We are not the traitors here." The siren says, her voice like venom.

"You have murdered thousands, if not tens of thousands. Your obsession with power is why your people have abandoned you."

"You speak of obsession with power, as if your kind was not at war for it. We watched as your kind murdered our people. Slaughtered our families."

"I apologize for the senseless acts done to your people during The Great War; however, I was not present during those times. I-"

"I know who you are! Asim the Great Protector! It was your absence that created that war! You abandoned your duty, when Nwt left, and the beings of this world turned to chaos in the absence of a leader."

Asim puts her head down, ashamed. I squeeze her hand and step forward, "We cannot change our pasts, as you cannot change yours. We mean you no harm now, Annipe. Please, we seek an audience with your queen."

The siren stares at me, looking me up and down, before shock for just a moment crosses her face, "Who are you?"

"I am Ashanti."

"No, I know something as trivial as your name. Why is your past shielded from me?"

I stare at her, confused, "I don't know. The Annipe could see it before."

The siren hisses, raising her body from the water. In place of a fishtail, she has a serpent's body. I step back again, "Thalassa has placed a shield on you. Why?" The siren demands. I think back to the circle she drew on my forehead, Thankful.

"We do not know," Asim lies.

"Do not lie to me. I can sense this one's power. Why have you come?"

"We seek an audience with your leader," Asim repeats. The siren continues to stare at us before quickly disappearing into the water.

"Is she going to get her?" I whisper to Asim, but she doesn't respond as she stares intently at the water. A crown appears first. Small bones and sharp claws decorate the twisted metal crown. The black eyes of the siren appear as she slowly lifts herself from the water. She slithers her serpent-like body close to the water's edge, and for a moment, I think she might leave the water. She is beautiful but clearly deadly. Her pale brown snakelike tail sways in the water. She smiles, showing her sharp pointed teeth.

"Asim! How wonderful!" She says in an unexpectedly cheerful voice.

"Hello, Iteru," Asim says blankly.

"Well, surely that is not a greeting for an old friend?" Iteru says, folding her arms across her exposed chest, "You still have not forgiven me?"

"You betrayed your people and corrupted many."

"I opened their eyes. We allowed our morals to make us weak. We are powerful. So powerful your kind feared us. They tried to exterminate us. You did not witness the slaughter! They murdered our young! Killed our mates!" She yells, her voice thick with emotion, "I wanted to save us! I tried... I did not know... I could not know..." She says, her voice trembling. I want to reach for her, to comfort her, but Asim holds me firmly in my place, far from her reach.

"I was not present for the tragedies that took place here long ago. I live with that guilt daily. I know an apology will not heal what was broken, but I am sorry."

Iteru's eyes flash, and her smile returns, "What is done is done. We cannot undo our past." She looks at me momentarily before returning her gaze to Asim, "I find this one intriguing. She is clearly important, or my sister would not have placed a protection spell on her. I wonder why."

"We have come with a request for your help," Asim says. Iteru smiles, amused by Asim's request.

"My help? We were locked away, labeled savages! You apologize for not being present for the slaughter but make no mention of being present during our imprisonment! I thought we were friends! I pleaded for your help then! You heard only of our transgressions; you never sought to hear our sorrows. You watched as we were imprisoned and never returned. Do not come here now as if you know us. You come full of rumors and myths concerning me and my sisters."

"You sought to slaughter tens of thousands as sacrifice to Apep. You could have brought destruction to the entire realm," Asim says sternly.

"I sought to destroy evil with evil! You did not watch as my child was ripped from me! You speak of my rituals; what of your people? They trapped us! Watched us beg and plead and murdered as many as they could!"

"I understand your anger," I say, stepping forward. Asim tries to pull me back, but I continue forward, "I lost a child too. She was still in my womb. My husband murdered her, while trying to murder me. I have never felt pain so great, but to have her present, in my arms, and watch her ripped from me!" I say, my voice breaking with emotion. Iteru watches me, but does not move, as I continue to step further towards her, the heartbreak overflowing as tears silently fall from my eyes, "As a mother I feel your pain. I do not know where my husband is, but I would gladly see him suffer for the pain he caused me. I understand your anger, and sadness. It can swallow you whole. I was not alive for this war, you suffered through, but I am here now. Please help us. We are trying to save this realm from another war. We do not want anyone else to die from the greed of power."

Iteru continues to stare at me, tears falling from her eyes as she listens to my words. After a moment, she wipes her face and smiles at me, reaching from the water to hold my hand, "You are pure. Pureness has not lived in this realm for many, many years. I will help you, Ashanti."

I smile back at her as Asim steps beside me, worry evident on her face. Iteru drops her hand and looks at Asim.

"Calm yourself Asim. No harm will come to this one."

"Thank you," I say.

"You mean to ask me about the queen's visits?" Iteru asks. We look at each other, shocked by her admission.

"So, the queen has visited?" Asim confirms.

"Of course, she has visited. Is that not why you have come?" She asks.

"We have heard rumors."

"There are no rumors; once she came, I summoned a serpent to send word to the fairy queen. I simply advised not to relay who sent the message, for obvious reasons."

"So, you wished to warn us," Asim says.

"We do not want a war either; this queen is unlike Nwt. She means to take the realm for herself. She attempted a ritual, herself, to gain more power, but it failed. Her attempt caused her soul to split. A battle of good and evil wages inside of her. She came to me, in secret, hoping we could fix her spell, healing her soul, and granting her power. When we refused, she burned our forest. She comes now, with threats. She has threatened our sisters in the Annipe tribe, who have abandoned us. So, I sent word, hoping someone would come and warn our people."

"You want to protect them?" I ask, surprised. She looks at me with sadness in her eyes.

"I know you have been told we are corrupt, and evil. I will admit we have strayed far from our once peaceful ways. My intent has always been to protect my people. I want no harm to come to my tribe."

I nod, "What does she want?"

"She wants to start a war. She intends to conquer all of the kingdoms and rule as the sole Queen. We warned her, when she came years ago. She sought power then as well. She returned from the earth realm differently. A mother. She wanted a glimpse into her future. We warned her of a future where she fell from power, her own child striking her down. She grew enraged and left, returning years later with her request for ritual to heal and empower her."

I gasp listening to her story, "Her child will strike her down? That's what you saw?"

Iteru looks at me, staring for a moment, "Yes, a child born from her will strike her down if her path continues as it is. We warned her of this years ago, and she continues on her path. Desperate to change it. She believes if she is powerful enough, she can defeat her own child and rule."

"She intends to kill her child?" Asim asks.

"Yes. She intends to sacrifice her and absorb her powers as her own."

We stand there quietly, trying to grasp what we have learned.

"That is all that I know." Iteru says, "Leave now. We are not the only dangers lurking in this prison."

Asim nods and pulls my hand to go, but I stop, "Thank you, Iteru. I am sorry for your loss. I pray your child is wrapped in the loving arms of your ancestors."

Iteru smiles at me and nods a thank you as she disappears back into the depths of the lake. Asim squeezes my hand and pulls me along with her as we hurry back through the forest. As we near the forest's edge, Asim stops walking. Her body tenses as she looks around, pulling me behind her.

"What's wrong? What is it?" I whisper, terrified.

"We are surrounded. Do not leave my side." She says, her voice suddenly dangerous and low.

"Ahh, if it isn't Asim! It has been many years!" A tall slender, red-headed man steps from behind a tree, as several others do the same. His complexion so pale at first, I think it might be a ghost. A long red scar trails from his left eye down to his chin. The scar turned his left eye red, as the right one is as black as Asim's eyes. I step closer to her, realizing she is right, we are surrounded.

"Luke," Asim says shortly.

"Come now. We were once on the same team, remember boss?"

"I am not your boss. I relinquished my role on the Queen's guard. I believe you are the head now."

"That is true, that is true. Is this your lovely bride the queen has been speaking of?"

"Do not try my patience today, Luke," Asim says venomously. Luke raises his hand as if surrendering.

"Jeez, calm down. I mean her no harm. I was made aware she is our princess," he says, tipping an imaginary hat.

"What do you want?"

"We heard word, there was someone lurking in these woods and wanted to check it out. Imagine our surprise when we saw you. Tsk, tsk. You know, there is a reason this forest was named Forbidden," Luke says with a smile.

"You heard word? You are pretty far from your kingdom. Why are you lurking through fairy kingdom?" Asim asks.

"What are you doing here?" Luke presses, leaning against a tree.

"That is none of your concern. Speaking to a siren is not illegal. We have freed no one."

"But still, it's a little strange you'd come all this way to what... give your girl a little tour?" Luke says, raising his eyebrow at me.

"As I said, it is none of your concern. We are leaving," Asim says, pulling me close behind her. Luke nods, and his goons let us pass.

"We'll be watching Asim," he calls behind us, "See you Sunday."

I look behind me as we hurry away from them in time to see Luke wink at me. Asim continues to rush from the forest. Once we break free from the trees, her wings quickly sprout from her back, and I follow suit.

"Come, we must hurry to the castle," she says as we take off into the air. She remains quiet the entire way there, lost deep in thought. Once we have the castle in our sights, she finally speaks, "It is good Isaiah has left with Heqet. The queen is watching the castle. We must be careful when we are not within its walls."

I nod, worried for Isaiah, "Is he not exposed? He's outside of its walls."

"The queen's focus will be on me, and you. She has no reason to suspect you have a child, and Thalassa has kindly placed a block on you. No being will be able to see your past, or your thoughts. Isaiah is safe. She must have known you would need it."

I nod, grateful for the mermaids.

After we land, we quickly find Ezra, and she hurries to find the Queen and King, leading us to their private office.

"It is safe to speak here. There are many protection spells around this room," the queen reassures us. "Please speak."

"Yes, what have you learned of the Immortal queen?" The king asks, sitting in his chair at the head of the table. We sit beside each other at the table as Ezra brings in wine and a small assortment of food.

"Thank you, Ezra," the queen says, dismissing her from the room. We wait quietly until the door is secured.

"We visited the forest and spoke with Iteru," Asim says. "She is understandably still angry at some of the tragedies that happened to her people during The Great War. Ashanti was able to calm her and even convinced her to help us."

The queen looks approvingly at me, nodding "Well done, Ashanti."

"Thank you," I say, blushing.

"She was amazing, as always," Asim continues.

"We see where young Isaiah gets his charm from then," the king says. "How is he? Have they made it to town?"

"Ezra advised us shortly after we landed; that they have safely made it to their destination," Asim says.

"Perfect," the queen says happily. "Now, what did Iteru have to say?"

"She confirmed our fears. The queen has visited the forest, apparently many times, long before we suspected. She was warned of her child overthrowing her and has performed rituals that have split her soul. She intends to use the sirens to perform rituals to both heal her and empower her. She wants to start another Great War and become the sole queen of this realm."

The king bangs on the table, "I will not have it! The war was atrocious. My ancestors were forced to commit heinous acts to protect our people. I will not force our people to endure such times again!"

The fairy queen places a hand on the king's arm, "It is okay, dear. No war will come. We must act now to prevent it."

"Aye, we will make plans quickly."

"Did Iteru say when she plans on starting this war?"

"No, but she invited me to a ball on Sunday, and when we were leaving the forest, we ran into some of her guards, and they mentioned Sunday as well," I say. "Iteru said she wants to kill me and absorb my power. Maybe Sunday is when she plans to do it?"

"Clearly, she is aware we know something if she has her guard following you so closely. If you do not attend the ball, she will know we know her plans, but of course, you cannot go. It would be too dangerous for you to go into her kingdom," The queen says, speaking mostly to herself. "Hmmm, I wonder how we can use this knowledge to our own benefit."

"Could the shapeshifter go in her place, perhaps?" The king suggests.

"We couldn't risk harming Cairo," Asim says firmly.

The king shrugs, "I'm sure he'd be fine."

"Honey," the queen chides him, as he waves his hand dismissively.

"I could go," I offer, as everyone turns to look at me.

"Absolutely not," Asim says.

"If I do not go, she could decide to attack the kingdom. She may get scared we will attempt to stop her, and that could put everyone in danger, including Isaiah," I say.

"If you go, she could kill you, absorb your power, and then attack. That would be worst," Asim says.

"I agree, she is already powerful, but with your power, and her own combined. She would be unstoppable," the queen says, worried.

"I keep being told how powerful I am, but I barely have any powers," I say, shrinking down into my seat. "I can only fly."

"I agree with Ashanti. If we have any chance of beating Marienne, she must train, and quickly. I will work with her personally," the queen says, "Beginning today."

"I will work with young Isaiah, if you give me permission. He is quite powerful as well, and at his age that power could be dangerous," the king explains.

"Of course," I nod.

"I will begin as soon as he returns."

"Thank you for your dedication to the realm. I know it is not an easy task to go against a queen you once served, nor your mother," the queen says to us, "I hope we can continue to work alongside each other until we are all safe, once again."

"Of course, your majesty. Our wishes for the realm align as always," Asim says. We excuse ourselves and hurry back to our rooms to discuss our day. I lay in our bed, staring up at the ceiling as I process our day.

"Who is Apep?" I ask, once we are alone.

"Apep is a god of chaos. He enjoys destruction," she explains, lying beside me in bed.

"And the sirens wanted him to destroy the realm?" I ask.

"Yes," she says simply, deep in thought.

"They didn't seem as evil as you described..."

She pauses before speaking, "Before today, I thought of them as purely evil. Corrupted by their worship of Apep. Today, through your empathy, I have realized in a state of desperation, they merely sought to save their family. I wonder what I would do if put in the same situation, to save the family we have created here. Perhaps Iteru is right. I left without thinking of how my choice would affect the others. Nwt trusted me to protect the realm, and I simply left."

"How could you know; that war would spread through a peaceful world? It seems a bit unfair. Nwt left and you were stuck leading a world you did not ask to lead. I mean you deserved to live," I say, holding her hand.

"You are magnificent. The way you spoke with Iteru. It was impressive. You managed to reach the good in her where others could not," she says, squeezing my hand.

"I felt for her. I know what it's like to feel like your child was just taken from you, unfairly, and... I would do anything to protect our family. She just wanted to save hers," I say.

"She was right about one thing. You do have a pure heart."

"What do you think Iteru meant about me striking her down? Am I supposed to kill her?" I ask, worried. While I do not know my mother, I couldn't imagine killing her either.

"She did not specify killing; she could mean simply overthrowing her as well. Although, if I am being honest with you, Marienne will not go quietly into the night if she is defeated. It may come to that," Asim says softly, "If it does, I will protect you. I will not leave your side, ever."

"I hope it doesn't. I know I said I would want Adam to suffer if I saw him, but it's just not who I am," I say. Ashanti tenses next to me, and I look over at her, "What's wrong?"

"I have been keeping a secret from you, Ashanti. I have not meant to keep it for so long, but I feel as though I must tell you before we continue," she says, her voice strained with stress. I reach over and place my hands on either side of her face, turning her to face me.

"Hey, what is it? Whatever it is, we can get through it together. We are a team, right?" I ask. She faces me, but looks downward, unable to meet my eyes, "Oh no. What is it, Asim? Please tell me."

"It's regarding Adam," she starts. I sit up, wondering what she could possibly be hiding about Adam. "Yes? What happened with Adam? Is he causing trouble?"

"Well...no... no, he's not causing any trouble. It's actually, well..." She pauses, nervously looking up at me, then back at her hands.

"Asim, come on. Tell me, what's wrong? What secret could you have about Adam?"

"I need you to understand, after Cairo found you the way you were...after what Adam did to you..."

Suddenly it dawns on me, "Asim...what did you do?"

"We were all so angry. You didn't see how he left you! If Cairo was another minute later..."

"What did you do? Tell me! Where's Adam?"

"He's..." She looks down guiltily, "he's gone."

My body goes cold, "What do you mean? He's gone? Like he disappeared?"

She looks at me, ashamed, and it hits me at once. *She killed him.* I try to calm myself. *I mean he tried to kill me first. I should be happy right? He can't hurt us anymore.* I look at Asim. She has retreated to the far side of the bed, unsure if I want her near me. I fight the urge to reach over and hug her. *Why do I feel so torn?* She just offered moments ago to kill my mother, her queen, and friend.

"I am sorry, Ashanti. I have done many things in my lifetime that I am not proud of. I have hurt many people. I know you still care for Adam, and my intention was never to hurt you further. But if I am being honest, Adam would not have stopped. He would have hunted you. You would have never been safe in the earth realm again. He was cruel, and he tried to kill you. I have no regrets about removing that danger from you and Isaiah's life."

I sit quietly, processing this new information. *I am free. Adam can no longer threaten me, or try to take Isaiah away.* Still, a part of me mourns. *Not for my abuser, but for my husband. The man Adam once was. All those years of waiting for my Adam to come back, and now I'm forced to realize he never will. This is my life now.* I look at Asim. *I truly love this woman, and she has shown me nothing but kindness and love since the day I met her. I have to let go of Adam.*

"I'm not gonna thank you for murdering him. He was an awful human being, but I will never condone murder. I... honestly, I don't know how I feel. A part of me is sad, and the other part feels free." I say sighing and pulling my knees to my chest.

"I understand. I do not expect you to be grateful for anything. I just wanted to be honest with you. I felt terrible holding that secret in all this time."

I nod at her and continue thinking, picturing *Adam holding Isaiah as a baby, or cooking with me in the kitchen. We had such good times.* I picture *the evil I saw in his eyes the night he tried to kill me. Yes, my Adam was gone, long before Asim did anything.* We sit in silence for too long, unsure what to say, or how to comfort each other. I try to make sense of my conflicted emotions, but even as Ezra comes to collect me, *I do not know how I feel.* I quickly change into the training clothes, a pair of loose pants and a shirt the queen has sent for me, and say 'goodbye' to Asim before following Ezra to a part of the castle I have never seen.

"Are you okay?" She asks quietly. I look over at her, as she flies much slower than her usual cheerful, scattered pattern.

"Yes, I am fine, or rather I will be fine. I can't wait to put this all behind us," I say smiling at her.

"I, as well. The queen is stressed much more than usual, I worry for my people."

I nod, understanding. "I'm going to try my best."

She stops flying, looking at me with no signs of her usual amusement. "I know you didn't ask for this responsibility. I like you and Isaiah. I'm sorry this has been placed on your shoulders, but it's important you understand what you are fighting for. All of our lives are in your hands."

"I know, I just, I haven't seen any of my powers. I don't know how I can beat her," I say, wringing my hands.

"Let me show you something," she says, turning down a hall. "This is the castle's hospital wing. The queen insisted on it being built after one of the staff lost a child in child-birth. She wanted her staff to have the best medical care this realm can offer."

I follow behind her, listening intently. I watch as she quietly walks into a heavily guarded room. There, behind a thick curtain, lies a nursery. Tiny fairy babies, swaddled in beautiful blankets, their little faces glowing as they sleep soundly.

"They are beautiful," I say quietly, staring at a little baby girl. Her tiny hand wiggles free from her blanket as she stares up at me, her tiny hand fighting the air. I reach out and allow her little fingers to grip my pinky, barely big enough to cover a knuckle. I think of Isis, gone much too soon. I can't help but wonder how her features have changed. *Will she grow in that realm? Is she smiling?* Tears fall down my cheeks as I think of the birthdays I will never celebrate with her and the tea parties we will never have.

"I am sorry; I did not mean to bring you to tears. I just wanted to remind you of the people who are at stake as well. We may not be humans, but we are your people. You are one of us," she says, wiping her own tears. "Come, the queen waits."

We leave the nursery, careful not to make noise, and make our way to a large set of doors on the basement floor of the castle. The doors are made of heavy metal, and from what I can see, they are the only doors on the entire floor.

"Is this her training floor?" I ask. This floor is bare, and plain compared to the vibrant colors of the rest of the castle. No paintings hang from the walls, or beautiful sculptures are displayed.

"Yes, she takes her training very seriously. In fact, all of her staff must train vigorously. Even the chefs train here. She insists we must be ready to defend ourselves at a moment's notice. The other realms respect our magical abilities, but few see us as a threat, due to our size," she explains.

"I see," I say, feeling the walls that are covered in a strange glowing dust.

"She has reinforced the structure to withstand our training. There was an, uh... mishap when training first began. We almost destroyed the castle."

"It must have been a pretty intense training session," I say. Ezra just laughs and walks towards the doors.

"You ready?" She asks. I inhale deeply.

"Yes," I say, quickly realizing as she opens the doors, I am, in fact, not prepared at all. The transformation of the room seems impossible as we step into a rainforest. I can smell the rain and hear the strange sounds of a beast I have never seen. I look up and see the sky peeking through the canopy of the tall trees of the forest. "How?" I ask, turning to Ezra. She smiles with her eyes closed, inhaling the scents around her.

"The queen has many gifts; it is amazing, right?" She says, "No matter how long I am here, I will never get used to this."

I nod, "This is incredible."

We walk through the forest, along a worn dirt path, until we reach a small field, full of beautiful flowers that seem to dance as if alive.

"Ah, you have made it!" Queen Lotus says. She has changed out of her usual gowns and is wearing loose-fitting pants and a shirt. She claps excitedly, her smile, bigger than I have ever seen. "What do you think?" She says, gesturing around her.

"It is amazing," I say, looking around.

"I enjoy the rainforest so much. After our first training fiasco, I decided the safest route would be to train outside of the castle, but of course, as queen, it wouldn't be the safest for me. So, I decided to bring the rainforest to us. Isn't it lovely? In here, I am just Lotus. I can train as I did as a young girl, and be free from the daily responsibilities as queen."

"It is truly magnificent, my queen," Ezra says. The Queen frowns.

"I've been trying to get everyone to drop the queen stuff in here, but everyone is bound by their rules. I insist you call me Lotus while we train," she says, clasping my hands in hers.

"Sure, Lotus," I say, smiling.

"Perfect! Now, Ezra, please, if you could tend to the issue in the stables while we train?"

"Yes, Your Majesty."

"What's wrong in the stables?" I ask, remembering my Pegasus have taken up home there.

"Well apparently, your friends have eaten all of the grass there. Ezra is a flower fairy. She's going to assist the other flower fairies with growing the garden back."

"I am so sorry!" I say, realizing I have not done the best to care for my herd.

"Please, it is a great honor to host so many powerful beings. Pegasus are a greatly honored species here. I adore the creatures," The queen says. "Now, Ezra, please tend to our guests."

"Of course," she says, waving goodbye to me, and flying quickly off.

"Now. I think our first task will be learning about this super speed you possess," she says, sprouting her wings.

"I don't know how it happened. I was flying with Asim, and I closed my eyes, and suddenly I was at the castle," I say, as my own wings protract.

"Hmm well, let's recreate what happened, hmm? Now stare at the spot over there. At the end of this field," she says pointing at the place. "Now close your eyes and picture it. Flap your wings as hard as you can. Picture me chasing you. I have almost caught you. I am flying faster than you have ever thought possible," she says, describing the scene she'd like me to picture. I envision what she describes, after a few moments I peek my eyes open and realize I am flying at a normal pace. I stop and fly back to her.

"I don't know what happened," I say defeated.

"It is fine, love. That is why we train," she says. "Let us try again."

Once again, I close my eyes, picturing what she describes. I focus all of my attention on my wings, willing them to flap faster, and again, nothing happens. I try again and again for hours, and nothing happens at all. Shame creeps into my mind as I picture Isaiah. *How am I supposed to protect my baby if I can't even get my powers to perform for me?* I remember my dream from long ago, Isaiah in a forest much like this one, the panther fighting the black bear to protect us, as I cower weak and afraid with Isaiah. Then I remember Adam, beating me, watching Isaiah scream and cry as I helplessly lay beaten on the floor.

"Ashanti," Lotus calls to me. I open my eyes, and realize I am much further than I intended to fly. I fly for several minutes until I break through the tree line and back into the field the queen waits for me in.

"That was.... wow," she says, stunned.

"I don't know what happened," I admit

"You were deep in concentration, flying slowly, then you just flew faster than I have ever seen. It was almost as if you teleported out of my sight. I have never seen such speeds, not even by a vampire. Do you remember what you were thinking of when you flew just now?" She asks, her excitement reignited.

"Yes, Isaiah."

"Let's try it again!"

We practice until I have mastered my ability. I fly quickly, circling the entire forest and returning to the queen in minutes.

"Simply amazing, dear," Lotus says, clapping proudly.

"I can't believe I have a power!" I say happily.

"Oh, you have many more powers than that. That was simply the first to appear."

"You think so?" I ask hopefully.

"You are a demigoddess. Your powers could be endless," she says, smiling.

"I hope so-" I stop short. I watch as the queen's face suddenly becomes deadly, like a lioness hunting.

"Shhhh, child, we are not alone," she says, looking around quickly before settling on an area to the east of us. "Come."

We fly slowly towards the direction she looked towards; I instinctively listen carefully, listening for a snap of a twig or footsteps. We fly until we come across a small pond, barely bigger than a store-bought pool, a large rock sitting on the water's edge. I gasp as I notice the large creature drinking from the pond. The head resembles a lion, or rather a giant lion, and the body looks like a hippo, no a bull, with a long lizard-like tail and large eagle wings.

"Queen Lotus," it says, without looking, in a voice so deep it reminds me of thunder. Queen Lotus exhales an annoyed sound, folding her arms across her chest.

"Lionel," she says, her voice dripping with impatience, "Why are you here."

"Now, now, is that how you treat your most loyal subject, your majesty?"

"No, it is not, but I see no subjects of loyalty before me."

It turns around, a look of shock on its face, "Why Your Majesty! Whatever could you mean?"

"Lionel, please spare me your phony emotions. What do you want?"

The creature smiles, a sly smile, "Ahh, you are the one this realm has been buzzing about. The mighty demigoddess that will slay the wicked witch."

"What wicked witch?" I ask.

"Why your mother of course! Surely you know of her misdeeds by now. She has become almost unbearable in her kingdom. Did you know she is demanding sacrifices in her honor now? Dreadful being," he says, shaking his head.

"Ahh, and that is why you have returned," the queen says.

"Well, surely a rare creature such as myself should avoid such a grisly demise. I simply came home."

"You abandoned your home when you left our kingdom and pledged allegiance to the queen of the immortals, Lionel," the queen reminds him.

"Your majesty, surely beings as old as ourselves are entitled to make mistakes. We played together when I was just a cub and you a young girl!"

"How did you get into my castle? I have many protection spells."

"The Annipe have granted me passage, with a message of course," he says.

"Well, let's hear it then. Rarely do the Annipe grant passage without an urgent matter."

"The message is for her," he says, nodding towards me.

"Me? What did I do?" I say, confused. Lionel laughs loudly.

"Ah, you are as amusing as they say, nothing, demigoddess. You have done nothing...yet," he says, licking his paws.

"Lionel, spit out what you have to say," the queen says impatiently.

"Can I stay?" He asks, in a childlike tone.

"If your message is worth the trouble," she says, as Lionel sits up and smiles.

"The Annipe have sent you a warning. They said, 'You must end the war before it begins. If the queen is given the chance, the firstborns will die by the 7th day of the week," he says in a mocking tone. My blood runs cold.

"They said firstborns? As in plural?" I ask.

"Yes, yes, they really wanted me to drill that into you. It is plural," he says, turning away to continue drinking. I feel my legs go weak as I collapse on the dirt floor. Isaiah. *She is coming after Isaiah.*

"Ashanti! Ashanti, please," I faintly hear the queen calling for me. I look up to see her panicked expression, "We must warn Heqet."

I snap out of it and take off, racing through the forest, looking for the exit. Less than a minute later, I'm walking out of the door and flying straight to my room. Asim looks up, startled.

"Ashanti, we cannot fly within the--," she stops mid-sentence after seeing my face, "What is it, love? Tell me?"

"Isaiah," I sob, "She's coming after Isaiah."

Understanding quickly passes over Asim's face as she takes my hand, her wings sprouting before we make it to the window of our room, taking off. We fly in silence for a moment.

"I can get there faster," I say, struggling not to take off and leave Asim. She shakes her head.

"You do not know where he is, and they may attack you alone," she says, firmly grasping my hand, "We need to stay together."

"But Isaiah! He could be hurt!" I cry.

"Heqet would have sent word immediately."

I try to calm myself, but my mind is chaotic as I think of my small child, helpless and unaware of the danger. I turn to Asim, "Which way?" I ask, feeling my skin warm, as the glow around my body brightens. Asim's eyes widen as she points in the direction of the town. I fling her onto my back, yelling "Hold on," as I take off at my highest speed. Within moments, we begin to see the town.

"They should be there," Asim points to a small group of cottages on the outskirts of the town. I slow as we approach them. Heqet and Cairo both come out to greet us.

"Asim?" Heqet asks cautiously, looking around.

"What has happened?" Cairo asks, approaching us.

"She has found out about him," Asim says.

"We have to go," I say, "Where is he?"

"Heqet hesitates for just a moment, pure terror flashing across her face, and then she takes off running, much faster than the human eye could see. I chase behind her, as Asim and Cairo follow. Several of Cairo's relatives in human form wake and come out to see what is the commotion.

"She wants him," Cairo says to them. They all face each other, understanding that the 'she' we are speaking of is the queen of the immortals. At once, they all begin packing things.

"You will fight?" I hear Asim ask.

"We stand with you," The oldest male says.

"Papa, you are not well, you cannot fight," Cairo pleads.

"I will do what is right. I will not die a cowardly old man. I could not protect your brother. I will protect you," he says sternly, "Mary, we must hurry. Grab only what you can carry."

"Isaiah, baby?" I say, gently waking him. He resists for a moment before he hears my voice.

"Mommy?" he says, rubbing his eyes, his tail moving with excitement.

"Yes, little monster, it's mommy."

He sits up, wide-eyed, "How'd you get here, Mommy?"

"I flew! I can fly so fast now. If you hurry and get dressed, I'll show you, okay?"

He nods and scrambles out of bed to put on his clothes. We hurry, a group of ten now. I feel safer with our group expanding, but still, hurry everyone along so we can return to the safety of the castle. As we hurry from the cottage, we stop just outside the doorway. Luke, and 5 of his goons, stand several feet from us. Luke lazily leans against a stack of wood.

"Well, well, well, I didn't think I would see you again so soon," Luke says, winking at me.

"Of course, the queen would send her dog to kidnap a small child," Heqet spits out. Our group begins slowly moving, taking defensive positions surrounding me and Isaiah. I hold him as tightly to my body as I can.

"It's okay, mommy. He's not going to hurt us," Isaiah whispers to me. I look at him and gasp. His eyes have turned blue as he stares at me smiling. After a second, he blinks, and his eyes return to normal. I don't have time to question anything as Luke's goons begin walking towards us, slowly taking small steps at a time, as Luke speaks.

"On the contrary, the queen was quite hurt when she learned of her grandchild. She thought her daughter was beginning to trust her, but she is devasted to learn you would keep her own flesh and blood from her."

"He is my child. I owe her nothing," I say, seething at his mere mention of my mother taking claim of my baby.

"Now, now, I was just sent to escort both you and the child home. The queen looks forward to meeting him," Luke says, winking again, with his horrible smug smile.

"We will return to the castle, and the queen will meet him, when his mother sees fit," Asim says, tensely.

"Now, Asim, you know the queen does not take well to no. We wouldn't dream of refusing our queen now, would we?" Luke says, standing straight up, as if finally interested.

"We will return to the castle," Asim says, saying each word slowly, so Luke can understand.

"Do not make us use force."

"I do not want to hurt you Luke, but I will protect my family," Asim says.

Luke shrugs and nods towards his goons as they suddenly attack. Cairo and his father roar as they quickly shift into great beasts. His father shifts into a large lion, and Cairo into a snake much larger than any snake I've seen, maybe 12 feet in length.

"Ashanti, get back into the house," Heqet calls as she leaps towards one of the goons. I hug Isaiah tightly as I run back into the cottage, Cairo's mother and sister closely behind.

"It's going to be okay," I whisper, rocking him.

"No, you have to fight," he says, shaking his little head.

"No, Mommy is going to stay with you," I say; we have to hide here.

"No, mommy, you have to fight. They need you," he says.

"How do you know that, baby? They are protecting us."

"I can see it," he says, pointing to his eyes.

"You can see what?" I whisper, as a large crash happens outside.

"I can see it happen," he says. I realize this is one of his powers.

Cairo's mother touches my arm as she whispers to me, "Your child is gifted with sight; he can see many things as they will be."

"When your eyes are blue, you see things?" I ask him.

"Yes, I see lots of things," he says, smiling.

"How can mommy fight? I can only fly," I tell him.

"You are a superhero, Mommy; you have to go. Simmy is going to get hurt," he says, trying to climb out of my arms.

"No, Isaiah, please stay here with mommy. Asim will come get us soon."

"No, no, she's going to get hurt! Please Mommy go!" he says, as another loud crash comes from outside. I look at him, his expression much too serious for his little face.

"Ugh, I know I'm going to regret this!" I say, "Go hide, and do not come outside no matter what," I say, "Please protect him." I beg Cairo's mother as she takes his hand, and she and her daughter hurry inside a room to hide.

I inhale deeply, trying to find the courage to open the door. I hear Asim call out in pain, and I run through the door. Looking around, I realize *we are losing*. Luke brought many more people than just the five I originally saw, and Asim is fighting three of them on her own. I watch as she digs her claws into one of them and bites a chunk of flesh from the other. *She looks like she is holding her own, but they are gaining on her.* I look over and see Heqet fighting alongside Cairo and his father; *Cairo looks injured and struggling to stay upright.*

"What am I supposed to do?" I whisper to myself, feeling helpless again. I watch as Luke pummels Asim, over and over as his two goons hold her down. *They're going to kill her!* I feel my skin warm, and glow brighter as I watch, anger building inside of me, until I can barely see past the haze. A feral roar rips from me as I run towards my love. I reach for the man in front of me, holding Asim's left side, and rip him from her. His arm still attached to Asim, gripping her for a moment before falling off. The man screams in pain as I use my claws to tear into him, ripping and clawing the rest of his body. The sight of my brutal attack is enough to cause Luke to pause as Asim kicks him across the yard. The other goon, struggling to hold onto her. I imagine him exploding, his limbs littering the yard, and I freeze in shock as he screams in pain before doing just that. *Did I make him explode with my thoughts?*

Luke, seeing this, quickly retreats, causing his remaining goons to flee as well. I stand there panting, in pure shock at what I have done. My hands shaking as I notice they are covered in black blood. *Had Isaiah seen this? His mother savagely ripping bodies apart? Exploding limbs?*

"Ashanti?" Asim says gently, "My love, I need you to take a deep breath, okay?"

I look up, and see concern on Asim's face, her hand outstretched for me. I look around and notice everyone is staring, unmoving, with concern on each of their faces. I close my eyes and breathe deeply as I feel my skin begin to cool, and the haze covering my eyes dissipates.

"There, much better," Asim says, taking me into her arms as I break down crying. *How could I do that?* I tore a man apart with my bare hands.

"Shhhh, it's okay love. You were protecting your baby. It's okay."

"I don't know what just happened," I say, my voice shaking, as I cry.

"You saved us," Cairo says, limping over in his human form.

"Isaiah, I think Isaiah saw me," I say.

"Isaiah is safe inside," Asim says gently.

"No Asim, I don't think she means now. He has the gift of sight," Heqet says. Asim looks at her, alarmed.

"Since when?"

"He just began showing us today," she says, "We had no idea."

"We should go; they may come back with more," Cairo's father warns. We murmur our agreements as I rush to get Isaiah.

"You did it, Mommy!" He says excitedly, clapping for me. I smile weakly at him. *What has he seen in those tiny eyes of his?*

"Thank you, baby. I did it with your help. You were right!" I say, clapping for him. We fly quickly, as a group back to the castle. As we fly, we notice fairy soldiers appearing to patrol the boundary lines of the kingdom, several walking through the kingdom. As we reach the castle, it becomes evident the king is on high alert. We arrive to find the castle surrounded by fairy soldiers, both inside and outside of the walls.

"Thank the ancestors," Queen Lotus says as she spots us entering the palace, "I sent my best soldiers after you, but they lost you in the skies."

"Luke attacked, your highness."

"He attacked you in town?" She says, shocked.

"He had at least 10 others with him," Heqet says, looking over Cairo's leg.

"Then it has begun," she says, shaking her head sadly, "Well, thank goodness you all made it safely back. It looks like your leg is broken, Cairo; please let one of my medical staff set it before it heals incorrectly," she says. He nods, as he and Heqet follow Ezra to the hospital wing.

"Now please, Asim, Ashanti? Could you follow me to my husband? We must be briefed at once."

We follow her to her private office, Isaiah tightly holding my hand.

"Ah! Isaiah! Hi there, little guy. I am pleased you made it back safely," the king says, as we walk into the room.

"Hi, Uncle Groody!" Isaiah says excitedly, running up to hug the king.

"It's King Grooden," I correct him, reaching for him to come back and take my hand.

King Grooden waves a dismissive hand, "Please let the boy call me as he wishes; it's nice to have a little one in the family finally," he says as he gently nudges Isaiah back to me, "Now let's get to business."

"Umm, perhaps we can find someone to watch over young Isaiah? This conversation may be too much for him," the queen suggests.

"With all due respect, your majesty. My mother and an entire kingdom are searching for him. I'm not letting him out of my sight at all," I say, turning to smile at him. For just a moment, I watch as he stares angrily at the queen. A dark expression I can't place on his face. He looks up at me, and his expression softens, he smiles back, and I realize how paranoid I've become. *Isaiah is scared too.*

"As you wish," Queen Lotus says, interrupting my silly thoughts, "But we will speak plainly."

"Of course," I say, leaning down to talk to Isaiah, "Hey baby, why don't you go sit over there, and I'll see if Miss Ezra can find some toys for you, hmm?"

"Okay," he says happily, skipping over to a seat at the far end of the table.

"Now, what has happened?" King Grooden asks, leaning forward in his chair.

"I've told the king about our visit today to the hidden forest," Queen Lotus says.

"Aye, but what happened in my kingdom? What was the attack?" He asks.

"It was Luke, Your Majesty, Queen Marienne's right hand. He attacked us with less than a dozen men," Asim explains.

"So, she thinks she can attack on my land, without coincidence?" He yells, angrily slamming his fist on the table. I look to Isaiah, but he seems unbothered, busily tracing the lines of the table with his hands.

"Calm yourself, love; we must find a rational method to win this war," Queen Lotus says, placing a hand on the king's arm.

"Now, how did these soldiers fight? Were they trained well?" Queen Lotus asks.

"They were trained in hand-to-hand combat well, but I trained many of the soldiers currently under her rule. I essentially made their playbook when I served as part of the guard," Asim says.

"Great! Then we know what to expect," she says optimistically.

"Yes, but we still were losing in our battle. If not for Ashanti, we may not have returned," she says, smiling at me.

"Ashanti?" The king asks, interested.

"Yes, I've never seen anything like it. She glowed a bright white light, her skin radiated the heat of the sun. She tore through two men in the time it took me to get my footing."

"Really?" The queen says, her eyes widening in surprise, "You showed no indication of such physical abilities at our training session today."

"I don't know how this stuff keeps happening," I say.

"I saw it," Isaiah says, smiling brightly.

"You saw it?" King Grooden asks, "What do you mean, child?"

"I saw Mommy beat up the bad guys, and I told her to go fight them, and she did. Just like I said," he says, pleased with his prediction.

"We believe he has the gift of sight," Asim says.

"Really? We thought only the Annipe were granted the gift. How interesting. And you Ashanti? Do you see things as well?" Queen Lotus asks.

"No, I haven't seen anything," I say, shaking my head.

"Well, it appears Queen Marienne has no intention of backing out of this nonsense. Her attack on our land is a clear act of war, as she is well aware," King Grooden says sadly.

"I doubt the Annipe will get involved, although it is clear they do not condone her actions. They most likely will not get involved unless a direct threat happens to their people," Queen Lotus says, "Ashanti, do you think you could repeat your actions today? Could you fight alongside our people?"

"I would fight for my family without hesitation. I think my powers are triggered by emotion. Whenever I get really upset, I notice my body getting warmer," I say.

"We should explore that closer. I have no doubt this war will progress quickly. I would prefer to be better prepared for the next attack," she says. As she finishes her sentence, Ezra bursts into the room, frantic.

"Your majesty!" she screams.

"Ezra? What is wrong." Queen Lotus asks as we all quickly run to her.

"The castle...It's... It's under attack!" she shouts between gasps of air.

"Under attack?" King Grooden booms, standing from his chair, "Nonsense. No one is stupid enough to attack the fairy castle."

The king flies out of the room, with the queen closely behind. Asim quickly gathers Isaiah into her arms, "Come we must find Heqet, and Cairo."

"Here, let me lead Isaiah, and Ashanti to our keep. She will be safe until you arrive," Ezra says urgently.

"Okay, here Ashanti, take him," She says passing me Isaiah, "Listen to me. Do not fight. Take him and run. I will find Heqet and Cairo, and we will meet you in the castle's keep, and then we will make plans. Do you understand?"

I nod, "Yes. You don't fight either. I need you in one piece, okay?"

She nods as she gently kisses my forehead, and ruffles Isaiah's hair before running from the room. Ezra smiles at us, a sad smile, before gesturing for us to follow.

"Just follow me; we will make it there before there are any breaches of the castle. Queen Lotus has placed enough protection spells on this castle to keep us safe for days under constant attack," Ezra says, flying quickly. I fly beside her, Isaiah tucked tightly against my chest. We make our way downstairs, twisting and turning down hallways and stairs.

"The castle's bunker is in the basement?" I ask.

"Yes, as are most bunkers," she says, looking around as we fly.

"When I was there earlier, all I could see was the room that held the hidden forest. Is it in there?" I ask, confused. I wait for a response as Ezra begins flying faster, as we approach the same door, I walked through hours ago for training. Isaiah taps me, and I look down to see his blue eyes, his face tense with worry.

"She's a bad guy, mommy!" He whispers, fear evident in his voice.

"Ezra?" I ask him, as he nods quickly.

I look up in time to see Ezra opening the doors, her face suddenly so sad it looks as though she may cry, "I am sorry, Ashanti. They have my mother and brother."

I watch in horror as Luke walks out of those doors, that smug smile plastered on his face as he quickly shoots something at Isaiah and I, and my body goes limp. As my world turns black, I hear Ezra scream as Luke shoots her as well. The last image I see is Isaiah's blue eyes as he reaches for me.

Chapter Twenty – Heqet

"How could this happen?" Asim yells, furious.

"It would appear someone let the Queen's guard into the castle, and they waited in hiding," one of the fairy guards reports. I look from the guard to Asim. My thoughts are too chaotic to process what is happening. The only thought repeating itself is that *half my family is gone. Where are they? They were here just a moment ago.* I know Asim looks to me to remain calm, to comfort her in times of turmoil, but I cannot. *Where is my family?*

"We believe they have taken them to the Immortal Kingdom, to the queen's castle," the fairy guard continues, clearly terrified of Asim's rage. Fury rises from the core of my being. It is not Asim they should fear.

"Heqet," Cairo's voice penetrates through my rage like the sharpest sword. I look to him, my eyes blinded with rage, but still, I see his calm, beautiful face. "Heqet, love, please. We must remain calm. It will be okay. I promise."

I listen to him speak as I stare into his eyes. No trace of fear evident. *I believe him.* I close my eyes and inhale deeply, grateful to finally have someone to calm my fears as I calm the others. "Asim."

"Not now, Heqet! We have lost them! How could we lose them?"

I walk beside Asim, placing my hand gently on her arm. "Asim, we must think clearly. They are depending on us."

Asim looks at me, eyes full of sadness, and fear. "I lost them," she says as she gives into her emotions. Unable to cry, she sobs without tears— a heartbreaking sound. I hold her tightly as she falls to her knees, the weight of her guilt bearing down on her.

"Shhhh, we shall find them, and we will punish those that thought us weak. Our family will be whole again," I say, gently patting her back. I look to Cairo, and he nods, understanding passing between us without words.

"The Immortal Kingdom is vast, much larger than the kingdom you have grown accustomed to. The Immortal Queen has become paranoid in recent times," Cairo says to the room full of guards. "It is believed she has begun kidnapping humans of the earth realm and turning them, forcing them into her guard. We can use this weakness to our advantage. She has increased her army from five hundred vampires to a thousand within a few years' time. Most of these new soldiers do not wish to die. They simply want to be free from their captor but remain due to threats on their lives or their loved one's lives. I believe if we offer them their freedom as an alternative to fighting or an eternity of servitude, they will leave without hesitation."

Asim stands, having had time to gather herself. "Thank you, Cairo. If this is the case, then we should have roughly five hundred vampires to grapple with. Make no mistake; an army of five hundred vampire soldiers is deadly. Many of you may not remember the great loss our realm experienced during The Great War. So many of our elders, fairies, vampires, and mermaids, have all gone senselessly. We thought this greed was long behind us. Once again, our people must stand not only to protect this realm but to protect each other. I do not know what is in each of your hearts, but I think it is time we no longer squabble as the humans do for land, for power. It is time for peace. It is time to live as Nwt intended. As one. We will go to the Kingdom of Immortals. We will defeat those who mean to enslave us, and we will free our brothers and sisters of The Forgotten World. Today, I fight for freedom! Who shall stand beside me?"

For just a brief moment, the room is silent, as the fairy soldiers all look to each other. Then, all at once, cheers ring through the castle. I beam with pride as I watch my best friend, my sister, speak words of wisdom into every being within ears reach. Cairo walks over to me, taking both my hands as he squeezes them tightly. Looking into his eyes: I feel hope.

"Come, let us go get our family," he whispers. Asim looks to me, a plan forming in her eyes.

"Yes, sister?" I ask, walking to her, with Cairo in tow.

"I know of a few beings who could help our cause," she says quietly.

"Good, the more soldiers we have, the better our odds," I say, thankful.

"Yes, I think so as well," she says, looking around to ensure no one is listening. *What is she hiding?*

"What beings, Asim?"

"The...the sirens."

"Are you insane? We would be killed for releasing them. They intended to kill our kind. Us! They specifically blame you for the murder of their people," I say, fear renewing its presence. Once Asim has decided, I know there will be no stopping her.

"You do not understand. I watched them. Their queen cares for Ashanti. They will help us," she pleads for my understanding.

"You do not require my permission, Asim. You will do as you please. But I warn you, once they are free, they will not return to their prison," I say.

"I know. Perhaps it is time I take accountability for my own actions that created their actions," she says sadly, "I need you with me, Heqet. Please."

I pause for a moment, thinking of the million ways this will not go well, all of the ways we may die. I look at my sister of so many, many years, her eyes pleading, her spirit broken.

"I am always with you," I say.

We hurry from the castle, as the soldiers prepare to depart. King Grooden will lead them, as is custom. We fly quickly to the forbidden forest, hopeful the sirens will hear our pleas and help. As we run through the trees and burnt debris, we all send silent prayers to our ancestors. When we reach the water, it is already glowing red, as Iteru floats in the water. Her long snakelike body tangled with her tribe as they lay carelessly around the small pond.

"So, my vision was correct. You have come with both audacity and insolence, to plead for our help," she says, laughing without humor.

"I beg you. They have taken my love--" Asim starts, but Iteru's eyes flash, as her features twist into unrecognizable hatred.

"Spare me your sorrows. You have not witnessed love, like a mother to her child," she says.

"They have taken her child with her. The queen means to kill him," Asim says.

For a moment, Iteru's anger falters. She looks to me, surprise crossing her face, "Heqet?"

"Yes, Iteru. It's me," I say, stepping forward.

"Your betrayal cut me the deepest. I thought you, of all beings, would understand the heartbreak of watching a child murdered."

Her face, full of anger, and heartbreak, flashes before my eyes as I remember the day she was locked away. I pleaded for her, but the realm would not hear it.

"I will not help you. I will not put my people at risk again, only to watch them murdered and ripped from each other."

"We will grant you and your sisters' freedom," Asim says. Iteru stops swaying her tail.

"Swear it."

"I swear it. I will release you from your bonds and will leave you free after we have defeated the queen. You can seek your revenge on those who did you and your people harm," she says. Iteru sits quietly, looking to the women of her tribe.

"We must go now," Asim warns.

"Quiet. I must think," Iteru says, holding up a webbed, claw-like hand. After a moment, she clears her throat. "We will assist. However, after this war is over, you will speak to the Annipe on our behalf. We want peace, and to be home with our loved ones. We have suffered enough."

"Agreed," Asim says, already removing the items from Cairo's bag, she stole from the castle. As she begins the ritual, I begin chanting.

"Lage lyezon yo, libere yo! Lage lyezon yo, libere yo!"

Asim cuts her hand, allowing her black blood to seep into the pond. The pond glows brighter as the water swirls and thrashes. The sirens scream out as the water's temperature rises, fighting the ritual.

"Lage yo! Lage yo!" I chant, screaming into the sky. Lightning strikes the pond, and everything goes quiet. The sirens dive under the water, and the glowing stops. The forest becomes so quiet, you can hear Cairo's hearts beating.

"What has happened?" Cairo asks, "They left?"

As he asks the question, the pond glows blue, and the sirens spring from the water, laughing loudly as they hug and sit on the water's edge.

"It has been a long time since I have sat on land," Iteru says, nodding gratefully.

"Will you honor our agreement?" Asim asks.

"Yes. The realm has lost enough children for this lifetime. No more will die for the greed of kings nor queens," she says, "What is your plan?"

"The fairies march to the Immortal Kingdom now. I wish to get there first. To end the war without the bloodshed."

"We must hurry; the Annipe will know our bonds have been broken, and they will come for us," Iteru says, beckoning for us to get into the water, "You must jump in; we will travel by portal."

I pause, grasping Asim's hand, as she walks to the water, "What if it is a trap?"

"Heqet, we do not have time. Ashanti and Isaiah may very well be dead as we stand here. We must trust them."

"You have nothing to fear, Heqet. We will honor our deal. We shall get you there safely," she says, before turning to stare at Cairo, "Well, maybe that one. The dryads told us all about your dealings, before the Immortal Queen burned our forest."

"Seriously?" I say turning to Cairo. *We will be lucky if a war is not started directly with us due to Cairo's transgressions.*

"They enjoyed it at the time," Cairo says smiling.

"Deal with him later; let us go," Asim says, walking into the pond. We follow her quickly, as the sirens all dive under. The pond is hot, a residual effect of the ritual. Despite its red glow above water, it is dark beneath. Only the glow of the siren's skin lights the water. Cairo transforms into a shark under the water, as we swim towards the bottom. Suddenly the pond's floor resembles the day's sky. A portal has opened. We follow the sirens and swim through, down becoming up, as we cross over. As we swim into the pond's floor, our heads break through the river's water edge. We look around, seeing Queen Marienne's castle a few miles downstream. Iteru, barely covered by the water, leads us as we swim towards it. Once we are close, Cairo, Asim, and I pull ourselves from the water. Cairo quickly pulls on his shorts as we crouch and huddle out of sight, eyeing the dozens of tents lining the castle grounds, soldiers patrolling and lazily sprawled around.

"Do not let any soldiers enter this castle," Asim says to Iteru. Whatever you have to do. Do not let anyone enter. Iteru nods before slowly submerging herself back into the water.

As we hurry from the riverbank, hiding amongst the bushes, we reach the castle's gate.

"How do we get past the soldiers?" I ask, as Cairo begins transforming, "What are you doing?

"Don't worry, babe. I've been a distraction or two in my lifetime," he says, winking, before transforming fully into Luke.

"Cairo, no," I whisper, "Cairo!"

I watch in horror as he walks into the gates, the soldiers all greeting him.

"Come. I must inform you all of our new plan," he says in Luke's voice.

"You want us to leave the gate unattended?" One of the guards asks, confused.

"Is that not what I just said, you imbecile? Come now. I don't have all day."

The guards all look at each other confused but follow him, afraid to incur his wrath. As they all leave the gate, we hurry through, rushing to the hidden door feet away from the gate. Having lived in the castle, we know of all the secrets and plan to exploit everyone to our advantage. We hurry down the long stairwell until we are deep under the castle grounds.

I grasp Asim's wrist as she hurries down the passage, "We wait for Cairo."

"Heqet, we are on a mission."

"We wait for Cairo," I say again, fiercely. She nods, as we wait, too far underground to hear anything. After what feels like an eternity, I hear footsteps down the stairwell. I hold my breath as I look up to see Luke running towards us.

"These guys are idiots," Cairo says, transforming back with a smile.

"You are an idiot," I say, smiling back. We continue down the passageway, silently listening for any signs of soldiers. We reach the entrance to the castle's dungeon. Asim quickly runs ahead, overtaking a guard before she knows what is happening, severing her head from her body in one slash of her claws.

"There is only one guard here?" Cairo asks, looking around.

"There are more stationed outside of the dungeon's doors; only one patrols the hall inside," Asim explains.

"Brother?" a voice calls from the other side of the dungeon. Cairo stops in his tracks.

"Caseem?" He calls back.

"Yes, yes, it is me."

Cairo runs, to the cell, holding his younger brother. "Father said you were gone."

"I thought so too, but the queen plans to force me into servitude. She has another of our kind. Forces him to shift into a Pegasus as a show of false power," Caseem explains. "Have you come for me?"

"I thought you dead. I have come to free others and defeat the queen."

"Release me. I shall fight beside you."

"You shall go home. Return to the fairy castle, find father, and our sister. Protect them," Cairo commands.

"I will not leave you here."

"Go, Caseem!" He says, as we pull his cell open.

"No, brother. You will give me this right. I demand to defend our kingdom, our family," Caseem says sternly. I watch as Cairo stares at him, before nodding.

"You shall come, but if I tell you to run, you must listen."

"Yes, of course," Caseem says, clasping his hand on Cairo's shoulder to pull him close, "We shall do this as brothers!"

"Quiet, man! You will alert the soldiers."

We stand quietly, waiting to hear if he has given away our location.

"It is quiet," Asim says.

"Good, let's go," Caseem says, but Asim holds up her hand.

"It is too quiet."

Suddenly, the dungeon door swings open, and soldiers pour in. One of them, being the soldier who questioned Cairo regarding his orders to leave the gate, and lastly, Luke enters.

"So much for idiots," I say glaring at Cairo.

"So, finally! You have returned home, Asim! Queen Marienne has sent me to retrieve you and your friends. She would hate for her trusted counsel to be seen wallowing in the filth of the dungeon," He says with a smile.

"I think we can find our way just fine," Asim says.

"Come now, Ashanti is waiting for you."

I feel the snarl rip from my throat as my muscles tense. My rage boils inside, threatening to tip over. *How dare he!* I feel Cairo gently hold my hand, pulling me back to him.

"Feisty as ever, huh, Heqet?" Luke says, amused. Now it's Cairo's turn to growl. Luke waves for us to follow as he nonchalantly turns his back to us. Asim tenses but follows Luke as the soldiers march behind us. The castle, once cheerful and full of light, has become dark and dreary. Only paintings of the Queen hang on the wall. Statues in her honor decorate the halls.

"Well, it was a fun five minutes of freedom," Caseem whispers.

As we enter the great room, we spot Isaiah and Ashanti, together, their wings tied so they cannot fly.

"Asim!" Ashanti calls, relief in her voice.

"Auntie Heqet!" Isaiah says, and I smile at him. *I will free them. Even if it costs me my life, I have to exchange it for theirs.* As we walk to the middle of the room, the Queen smiles *the evilest, soul-twisting smile I have ever witnessed.* We freeze in place, watching helplessly as a guard raises his sword and cuts the wings from Ashanti's body. The action happens so fast, although it feels as if time has slowed. Ashanti's scream pierces through our minds as we take off running for her. Suddenly, twenty guards appear, and we rip through them, fighting desperately to reach them. Without warning, my limbs go numb as I fall to the ground, held in place by magic. Asim, Cairo, and Caseem all fall around me. *What is happening?*

The queen claps and laughs loudly, "Excellent job, dear! How fun!"

"Thank you, Your Majesty!" Ezra says, as she comes into view, smiling proudly. Luke walks over and kisses her forehead.

"Isn't she amazing?" Luke says, causing Ezra to blush.

"Now," the queen says, clapping her hands and sitting forward, "Why have you come alone? I intended to have more sacrifices than a mere handful."

We lay wordlessly on the floor, unable to move. The queen looks confused, then turns to Ezra, "Oh! Ezra dear, I need to talk to them."

She nods as our hold lessens, and we can suddenly move our heads, although it feels as if a million pounds of pressure is weighing down on us.

"Now, where was I?" Queen Marienne asks, "Oh yes! Where is everyone? Surely, they did not think you could defeat my entire army?"

Asim raises her head and spits in the queen's direction. Luke quickly walks up to her, punching her in the mouth.

"Now, now, Luke. Asim is just a little distracted. Once these two are out of the way, she'll come back to her senses," she says.

"Are you insane? I will never return to your side. Ashanti has no bearing on how I feel about you. You are a vile, selfish woman who has let her greed corrupt her in unspeakable ways. You shall die today, and I will never set eyes on this castle again."

The queen's face distorts into a vicious monster before returning quickly to a pleasant smile, "Yes, well, it appears our guest needs a reminder of her manners... Luke?"

Luke walks up to Ashanti, a small dagger in his hands, as he drags her from the floor, covered in blood and sobbing. He quickly lifts the blade to her throat.

"No, please," Asim begs. Marienne lifts her hand, stopping Luke.

"See, much better. Now, you cannot see it, but Ashanti has a gift of enchantment. Her child has it as well. These feelings you think you have are false. She simply enchanted you," the queen says, smiling, as if that explanation solves everything.

"I've loved Ashanti long before her powers activated, before we ever came to this realm," Asim says.

"Lies!" The queen says, standing angrily, "Do not tell such filthy lies. You love me! Your loyalty is to me! I have shared you long enough. I will remove her enchantment, then rid you of this one!" She says, pointing to me, "Then it can be just you and me, as it should have always been."

"She has gone mad," I whisper with disgust.

"One more word and I'll cut out your tongue and feed it to your dog," she says, gesturing towards Cairo.

"Your majesty, perhaps I can tie them up, and put them into their cells, so that we may make arrangements. I believe the fairy soldiers shall be approaching soon," Luke suggests.

"Fine, tie them up, but put Asim in my room. I would like to continue our discussion."

Luke shrugs and orders his soldiers to take us to our cells, as Ezra continues to render us useless.

"How could you, Ezra?" I ask as they take us back to the dungeon.

"Simply, no one there appreciated me! I was trained as a small child to serve the queen. I deserve to be happy! Then I met Luke, and I won't let anything come between us," she says smiling, as Luke blows her a kiss.

"Luke is incapable of love. He is a soldier, dedicated to his queen. If it comes to you or the queen, he will leave you to die," I try to reason with her, but she shakes her head, unmoved.

"Nothing you say will make me turn against him; just be quiet," she says, and once again, I cannot speak. Luke ensures we are all locked into separate cells before turning to Ezra.

"You did magnificent, my love. I knew when I learned of you, and all your potential, I knew then I had to save you. You are meant for so much more than just a servant of some fairy queen. How could your parents just give you up as a servant? You are royalty to me," Luke says, gently caressing her face. "Now I just need you to stay here a little while longer, Just to make sure they do not try anything until after the sacrifice, hmm?"

"I thought I would be with you? Don't you need me?" She says weakly.

"Of course, I need you, love, but we need to finish this mission. Having you near me, it'll distract me, and I need to focus," he explains, looking behind her at the door, as if he may flee.

"Oh, okay. I understand. I love you," Ezra says. Luke kisses her quickly on her forehead and leaves, closing the dungeon door behind him.

"See, he adores me!" She says, attempting to prove her contentment to me. "He cares about me. He doesn't demand things or expect things from me. I feel free with him," she says, looking into my cell as I lay unable to move, my body crumpled onto the ground. I roll my eyes. She hisses, and suddenly I can move. "What? Why can you not see how much he loves me? If you were smart, you would play nice with the Queen, and she may let you live."

I sit up, stretching my limbs. "Good for you, child."

"What does that mean?" she asks angrily.

"If his love, is so groundbreaking that it is worthy of betraying your kingdom, sending your very people to death, then so be it," I say, examining the wall. *Is it spellbound? Most likely. A spell too strong for my basic magic to break. I need someone stronger.*

"You do not understand! My country betrayed me first! My own parents just gave me to the castle. Not even sold, just given for free!" she says, tearfully, sitting on the floor outside of my cell door.

"Were your parents poor?" I ask, examining the ceiling.

"What?"

"Were your parents poor?"

"Yes, of course, they were, we were just regular villagers. I was born in a small cottage on the outside of town," she says, "They did not want me so badly, they gave me away, not even bothering to trade me for a better life for themselves. If they had done that, I could make reason. They were desperate, they needed the money. But they simply wished to live without me."

"Perhaps, your parents only wished to give *you* a better life?" I suggest, finding the spot, I was looking for.

"What, as a slave?"

"Ezra, you were hardly a slave. You received the best education, and the finest foods. You attended all of the castle balls and banquets. The queen trusted you with her deepest secrets. She counted you as a friend," I say, walking carefully to the back of the cell. "What do you think your life would have been if your parents kept you?"

"I don't know. You know they have never come back to find me. To say hello or check on me? They left me at the castle and disappeared," she says. "Can you believe that?"

"Iteru, if you can hear me, we need help. We are trapped in the dungeon," I whisper into the small leaking water pipe I found exposed through the wall.

"What are you doing?" she asks, peering into my cell through the tiny window of iron bars in the otherwise wooden door.

"Listening to your sorry excuse for betraying everyone who loves you. Maybe your parents died? Maybe they were taken by the very queen you serve, as sacrifice."

"She wouldn't do that. Luke would have told me."

"Yeah, right. Come, child, use your goddess-given sense," I say. She finally gets quiet, thinking of a response. I listen as the pipes behind the walls begin to shake. Water seeps into the cells as the overflow of water becomes too much, cracking the walls. A smile creeps over my lips, as I nod to myself. "There. Always a way out."

"What is happening?" She screams at me, as the water begins to pool at her feet. Losing her concentration, both Cairo and Caseem gain their senses, quickly turning into snakes and escaping through the bars of the cell door. I listen as Ezra screams out when Cairo and Caseem attack her, biting her repeatedly with their poisonous venom. I listen to the one-sided battle as Ezra screams in frustration, the venom causing her limbs to flap lifelessly until her wings give out as well. I walk to the door as I hear the cell slowly open, and Cairo greets me with a half-smile.

"See, I had it under control," he says. I roll my eyes, pushing past him to find Ezra lifeless on the floor.

"You injected her with too much venom!" I scold.

"She wouldn't go down. We had to. She got Caseem good," Cairo says, nodding towards his brother. I look over to see Caseem sitting on the floor, his leg split open at the calf.

"Go tend to your brother," I say before carrying Ezra's body to the now open cell.

"Can you fly, brother?" Cairo asks, checking his bleeding leg. Caseem nods as Cairo instructs him, "Fly home. There is a hospital staff in the castle. Tell them you are Cairo's brother. They will allow you inside. We will meet again once this is done."

I watch as they say their goodbyes, hugging before Caseem shifts into an injured cat and disappears, limping up the stairs. I pause for a moment, watching Ezra's motionless body on the cell bench. Cairo, coming to stand beside me.

"She was just confused," I say, shaking my head, "she was sad, and lonely, and confused."

"It could not be avoided," he says soothingly, "her loyalty was too strong. She would have sought Luke the moment we escaped."

I nod, knowing his words are true, yet they do not ease the sadness I feel for the young fairy. "She had so much potential."

"Let's make these fuckers pay for her, then. No one else will die for this war," Cairo says as he takes my hand. "Come on. I have a plan."

Chapter
Twenty-One – Asim

I pull against the chains locking me into place. Spellbound. These chains must be enchanted, I decide, as I pull harder against them, my limbs tied to the bedpost.

"You are wasting your energy, Asim," the queen says as she enters the room. "Those chains are enchanted. No one could break them."

"What are you doing, Marienne? Have you truly gone mad?" I ask.

"I have clarity. I am tired of playing second fiddle. My own mother would force me to listen for hours each day as she bragged endlessly about her mother, my grandmother. She would tell these incredible stories of all of her feats until my ears felt as though they may bleed, "Marienne says, holding her hands to her ears. "One day, as I walked along the riverbank trying to escape my mother's obsession, I met a small snake. After hearing of all these fanatical stories for years, one day I met a creature not of this world. A reptile that could speak. I was ecstatic. It told me of a magical place where creatures I had never dreamt of roamed freely. A place I could be magical as well. I ran home to my mother, thrilled. Finally, I would be special too." She explains as she climbs into the bed, pulling her long gown back to straddle me. "I ran home and shouted for my mother. I, just a child really, told her all I had found. I thought she would celebrate. I was special too. Do you know what my mother said?" She asks as she caresses my tied arms and face. I struggle to move from her grasp.

"Marienne, please stop this madness," I beg. She digs her claw-like nails into my face.

"Do you know what she said?" She repeats, slowly. "She said I was to stay away from the riverbank and never speak of the snake again. I realized then my mother did not want me to be special; she wanted me to remain a weak child. I, of course, did not listen. I snuck to that riverbank often. I became friends with that snake. For years, he taught me all that he knew. Until one day, my mother found me. I was practicing a ritual the snake taught me. I had no real magic then; I was just practicing. He told me after I crossed into the magical land, I could perform the ritual, and I would be the strongest creature that lived. My mother, she tried to kill him, tried to cut his head off. I watched as he turned into a man and did nothing, as he choked her there on that forbidden riverbank. I came to find out the snake I had befriended all those years ago, his true form was that of the god Apep. He had freed me from my mother. He absorbed her power. Magic I never knew she possessed and released it into me. After years of feeling weak, worthless, living in the shadow of my grandmother, I finally felt special." She said, smiling as though she once again was a young woman, gaining her powers. "Apep told me to flee; the town would see me as a witch, they would blame me for my mother's death. He led me to a small hut in the woods. I lived there for many years, learning that the power he gave me was immortality. I could not age. I lived alone in that hut for so many years; that I lost count. He would visit me, show me rituals, and speak of our plans for once I was ready to cross into this realm." She begins rocking her hips as she straddles me; I try to push her off, to no avail; she laughs as though we are playing a game.

"Please, Marienne, I will remain here. I will stay by your side. Just let the others leave," I beg.

"Do you think me a fool, Asim? Honestly, I know you are still enchanted by Ashanti. I will free you of her soon. Do not fear," she says, laying against me, cuddled beside me. "Where was I? Oh yes, one day after many, many years of living alone in that hut, Apep comes to me. He tells me the realm has been at war and Nwt has vanished. That I must save the realm and begin our plan. It all happened so quickly really. The activation of my true powers, how I enjoyed feeling that magic flow through my veins. Then the imprisonment of the sirens. They tried to take my only friend from me. Just to use him. It was horrid, really. I kept my promise for so many years. Never speaking of the bond he and I have. Never forgetting the plan. Then I fell in love. I realized I could not live without you."

I ignore her revelation of love and focus on the details she revealed to me. "You were immortal when you came to us?" I realize she had to have been. *Granddaughter of Nwt, how could I not see it before?* "You told Ashanti you could not live in the earth realm because you would die, that you would age."

She laughs hysterically. "I lied, silly. Apep told me to find her father, that I would need a daughter in time. It was insufferable living as a human. Having to remain cheerful. I will admit, that Maurice was a kind man. He loved me in a way I had not been loved before. I was tempted to remain, for his sake. Then I found out I was pregnant, and he was thrilled. Apep realized I was staying, and he implanted the cancer in Maurice's body. I renewed my loyalty to him and left. I returned home.

Seeing your face reminded me of my true calling. I knew we could be together. We could remain here. Apep would not care if I married you, a creature of this realm. It would only strengthen my need to remain here. Then you wanted to leave me. You just refused to stay. It hurt me in unimaginable ways to watch you leave, over and over.

One day, Apep came to me; he declared it was time for our plan to move forward. However, he said time had evolved our plans. He had a vision; once Ashanti crossed into this realm, he believed she would be an even more powerful being, and I was to assist her! Can you believe it? So many years of loyalty, of sacrifice! He wanted me to play second fiddle, *again*? I grew enraged. Rightfully so, might I add. I learned of a spell he did not want me to know— the ability to absorb a god. I performed this spell quickly; by the time he realized what was happening, it was too late. I watched as he shriveled and died, and I gained all of his powers. It was such an invigorating feeling. I enjoyed the feeling. What I was unaware of was no being, not even a demigoddess, can withstand the power of a god. It split my very soul before leaving my body. It poured from me and fertilized the realm. I begged the corrupted sirens to help me, but those wretched beings would not. They cursed me out of spite and refused to help. So, I have been sacrificing here to fix what I broke. I hatched my very own plan. I would become all-powerful, and when you returned to this realm, I would convince you. You would see how special I truly am, and we would spend our days here as the Queens of the realm. Then even you betrayed me. Once Ashanti and you came here. Once I saw the way you looked at her, my heart shattered within my soul." She explains all of this to me, a sadness in her voice before her cruel smile returns. "But do not worry, my love; I will fix all of this soon. Soon, you will be free of her, and I will be so powerful, even the Annipe will quake with fear."

I listen to her ramblings, knowing she will not stop. She cannot be reasoned with. She would murder the entire realm to complete her plan. I look around desperately for a way to escape.

"What will happen once you have completed the ritual and absorb her?" I ask. She sits up, excited that I seem to have accepted her plan as fact.

"Once we are done, I will force the realm to bow to me. Those who do not bow will pay with their lives. They will be sacrificed in my honor, and I will absorb their magic as well, making me even stronger."

"Your majesty!" Luke screams as he bangs on her closed door. Marienne exhales angrily before calling out to him.

"I requested to be alone!" she shouts.

"Your majesty, the prisoners have escaped!" he shouts through the door.

"Okay, have the fairy girl take care of it," she says before whispering to me, "Good help is so hard to find."

"Ezra is dead. The dungeon is flooded. We believe the castle's water has also been poisoned."

"What? Fine! I am coming," she says, kissing me on my lips with force before rolling off of the bed and collecting herself. "I will retrieve you before the ritual, my love. I'm afraid I will have to dispose of your friends, though. They have cost me a powerful fairy soldier."

She leaves quickly, slamming the door shut behind her. As the door closes, a lizard crawls from above the door, a small sun imprinted on its back.

"Cairo! You are okay? What of the others?" I ask, relieved to see him. He transforms as Heqet enters, clothes in her hands.

"Why couldn't your clothes transform with you?" She asks, rolling her eyes, "We must hurry before they notice the naked guard."

"Where is Ashanti? Isaiah?" I ask. "They are guarded. It looks as though they are being kept in a room on the other side of the castle. I think it is the room she intends to perform the ritual in," Heqet says, examining the ropes tying my hands and ankles.

"I must say, this isn't exactly how I pictured finding you. It looks like you were having some fun, while we have been doing all of the work," Cairo says, amused.

"Not now, Cairo," I say as Heqet groans at his comment, "It is useless; she has enchanted the ropes."

"Is the bed enchanted?" she asks, staring at the long canopy frame.

"She did not say," I say. I watch as Heqet snaps the frame in two, pulling the tied ropes intact from the frame.

"I fear our boss is an idiot," she says to Cairo with a laugh.

"I could not move to do that; I was tied. Anyway, can we focus? Ashanti may bleed to death, and Isaiah is frightened. We have to find them and get them to safety," I say, rubbing my freed wrist.

"Right, I believe the fairies are here. They will be striking soon; Ashanti and Isaiah need to be free before then," Heqet says.

"We cannot attack head-on; we will not defeat them, just the three of us. Cairo, do you think you could get into the room unnoticed?" I ask.

"Of course, but there are at least five guards in that room alone, even more outside. How could I transform to speak to them? They will not follow a rat," he says.

"Ashanti. She knows your marking. She has spoken to me, of the wolf, with the sun marking. Show her your marking, and she will follow you. We will take care of the guards outside, and once you have freed her, distract the guards so that she may hide. We will enter and help you take care of them from there," I say. They stare at me, unsure, "It is not a solid plan, but it is the only plan we have."

"What if she is tied with an enchanted rope as well?" Cairo asks, worried.

"She will be. I trust you can be as innovative as Heqet here," I say. Cairo sighs.

"Heqet, if I die here today, know I have loved you since I first laid eyes on your beautiful face."

"Cairo, shut up. I will see you after you have freed them," Heqet says, rolling her eyes. She pauses for a moment, pulling him into a quick but intense kiss, "now go."

Cairo, smiling broadly, shifts into a small mouse, scurrying quickly from the room. I look over at Heqet, a smile on my face.

"What?" she says, embarrassed, "you shut up too."

We make our way down the hall, quietly together, knowing in a castle full of vampires, someone will notice us soon. As expected, two guards begin jogging down the hall toward the sound of our faint footsteps. Quickly, Heqet breaks the first one's neck before either can react. The second guard begins to scream for help as I use my claws to rip his throat from his body.

"More will come; let us move," I say as we toss their bodies into an empty room. We hurry down a hall away from the sound of approaching guards and up a flight of stairs.

"She will be down this hall," Heqet says, pointing to a long empty hallway.

"Where are the guards?" I ask, confused.

"We are here," Luke says, stepping from a room at the end of the hall. As he does, a dozen vampires all follow suit.

"Luke, we do not need to do this," I say. "I do not want to kill you, but I will to protect the women I love. I know Ezra--"

Luke spits, disgusted, "Fuck Ezra; I only used that disgusting little insect to secure the queen's plan. Her usefulness was fading. The queen should have sacrificed her like she did her parents and been done with it. I will kill you both. Then Mari- Queen Marienne— will be able to complete her dream."

"Marienne? My Goddess! Are you in love with her?" Heqet says, incredulously, "She is a psychopath. She loves no one but herself. What do you think? She completes her plan, and you run away together?"

"Heqet," I whisper, "What are you doing?"

"She will never want you, Luke! She has a hard one for Asim. She will never let her go!"

Luke snarls at Heqet's words, "Asim will be out of the equation, very soon."

He runs for us, and his minions follow. His anger makes him sloppy, as he runs directly for me, blinded with rage and jealousy. Heqet begins viciously attacking the younger guards, ripping their heads from their bodies, as Luke attempts to attack me. Moving at light speed, he claws at me, snarling, and biting. I dodge each swipe, "Luke, this is pointless. I do not want your death on my hands."

"Your blood will spill before the end of this," he says, increasing the speed of his attacks. He lurches forward, clawing my cheek. He smiles widely at his small victory as my cheek heals itself.

"Very well," I say, hesitating when I hear Heqet scream out as a guard claws her back.

"It looks like your sister won't be here much longer," he says, smiling.

"My sister is capable of wiping the entire immortal army from this earth alone. Your men are simply pissing her off further," I say and begin attacking Luke. I jump over him, quickly landing behind him as I lock onto his back, wrapping my arms around his neck. I pull hard, listening to the tiny bones crack and splinter as I begin ripping his head from his body. A sharp object pierces my back, and I realize a soldier has stabbed me with a sword. Releasing Luke, I pull the sword from my back, using it to decapitate the soldier. As Luke knocks me to the ground, I quickly kick him across the room and run for Heqet, who is now surrounded, angrily clawing at the guards. I remember the day I met her. A tiny, helpless human facing down that group of men. A weapon in her hand, content with dying for those she loves. As I reach her, Luke attacks me from behind, slamming me into a wall before clawing repeatedly at my back. I scream out as the flesh is ripped from my body.

"After I'm done with you, I'll take care of that kid, and his whore momma too," he says. A snarl rips from my chest as I push back, knocking him off of me. Stumbling to my feet as my back slowly heals, I run slowly at Luke.

"The only whore here was your father. He was so far into his debt with the gamblers, he sold you to them. They found you useless and abandoned you. I felt mercy for you. A small, pale, frail child tossed into the river to drown. I saved you. Allowed you to grow in this realm. I trained you, then turned you. You think you could defeat me? I made you who you are, Luke. Even as a vampire, you are useless; your fighting has grown sloppy," I say. He begins to speak, anger flowing through his veins. I pounce, knocking him to the ground, my back finally healed as I rip his head from his body. His mouth twists in pain as his scream gets lost in the air, his exposed neck bleeding as his body limply falls to the ground. I run to Heqet, unable to pause even for a second. I begin ripping through the soldiers, young and ill-trained. We quickly dispose of them once their attention is split between the two of us. We run to the room, hopeful Cairo has managed to free Ashanti and Isaiah.

"Are you ready?" Heqet asks me as I nod my reply. She rips the door open and gasps in horror. Her legs give out as she falls to her knees. I stand in shock, staring at the guard's dead bodies that litter the floor. Cairo's limp body, struggling to breathe, in his original form, too frail to transform or flee. Isaiah, his face contorted into an evil smile, standing in the middle of the chaos, his hands dripping with the blood of the soldiers surrounding him.

"Isaiah?" I call to him, unsure what has happened, as I step closer to him warily, "Are you okay?"

A deep voice that does not belong to this small child responds, "Isaiah is not here right now."

Queen Marienne burst into the room behind me, more guards flanking her sides. Unable to turn from Isaiah, I watch as his eyes glint with pure evil as he focuses on her.

"Ah, my little bumble bee," he says with a smile. She gasps behind me, stumbling backwards into her guards.

"Apep?

Chapter Twenty-Two – Isaiah

I'm scared.

Shhhh, child. I am here. All will be well soon.

But my mom. They hurt my mom.

We will make them pay for what they have done.

I just want my mom.

I can take you to her. I can free you both. But I need you to grant me control. You must let me take over completely.

I can't. You're going to hurt people.

I will only hurt people if they hurt us. Okay?

What are you going to do?

I have to stop these bad men. They want to hurt you, and your mom. I have to stop them.

Will you let me come back?

Of course, little one. I promise.

Okay.

I feel Isaiah loosen his grip on his reality as he allows me control. I break free quickly, pushing him into the small *prison in the back of his mind. Finally, I am in control. I stretch my arms and realize I am still tied in the pathetic enchanted ropes. Quickly, I allow the full force of his power to flow through his tiny body. So much power, for a tiny boy. Even more power than Marienne. A child able to hold me when an ancient queen could not. Pathetic.*

I begin allowing my magic to latch onto the enchantment, feeling the intoxicating power overtake the weak magic, feeling it wither as it fades to nothing. As I work my hands-free, I hear the clashing of metal; the fairies have begun their attack. *An annoyance, but perhaps beneficial. They can keep the castle distracted as I work through my plan.*

As my hands become free, a small mouse scrambles to Isaiah's mother. I watch as it climbs her leg, a small sun-shaped patch of fur on its white coat. *Cairo. Another annoyance.* I smile and shrug; *I love a good chaotic moment.* I watch as Ashanti flinches away from the vermin before recognizing the sun mark. *I'll have to kill them before leaving, I guess.*

No! Isaiah screams, his voice breaking through the prison I had formed for him. *Hmm, this little ant may cause me trouble.*

Fine. I will save your mother if you do not interfere with my plans. I listen for a response, but he has gone quiet again, crying in the darkness of his own mind. I roll my eyes, or rather his eyes. I laugh at the chaos of it all. Finally freeing my other limbs, I stand, shocking the guards in the room.

"Isaiah, please. Sit down. They will hurt us, honey," Ashanti says. *What an annoyance.* I use my magic to render her unconscious, throwing her body into the closet across the room. Cairo, seeing this, transforms into his human figure. I quickly toss him into the stone wall, with such force his bones break with an audible pop. *What a funny sound.* I stop to laugh as the guards, unsure what to do, begin approaching me. *How boring.* I slit their throats in unison, using their blood to paint the ceiling. *Much better.*

Suddenly, I hear fighting outside of the door. *What the fuck could it be now? Ahhh Asim and Heqet. The dynamic duo. Great timing.* I hear Cairo groan from across the room, and I slam his body against the wall again as the door bursts open.

"Isaiah?" Asim calls foolishly. Heqet kneeling like a heart-broken schoolgirl. *How love weakens us.*

I smile at her. *What a fool.* "Isaiah is not here right now."

Much to my delight, Marienne burst through the open door, her pathetic vampires surrounding her.

"Ah, my little bumble bee," I say, calling her the nickname I gave her as a small child. I watch as her face twists in recognition, quickly transforming into fear. Her face pales. She tries to move backwards, retreating from me.

"Apep?" She whispers the question.

"Oh, so you do remember me! How delightful," I say, clasping my tiny hands together.

"Apep?" Asim says, confused, looking back and forth between Marienne and myself.

"In the flesh... well sort of," I say, laughing.

"How?" She says, "You, you died. I saw it."

"I am a god, you imbecile. I cannot die. You did weaken me. I must say that did surprise me. I didn't think you were bright enough to think of something like that on your own. I will not underestimate you again," I say, smiling at her.

"I remained stuck in that awful state as just pure energy, waiting for a body worthy of hosting me. I knew Ashanti, your daughter was strong enough to hold me, but her will was too strong. She would have rejected me quickly. She was much too smart. Could you imagine my surprise when I realized this child was strong enough in this small form? I mean imagine when he grows. Yes, this is a fine specimen," I say looking over my small frame, "Once I absorb his mother's magic, and perhaps you three as well, I will be strong enough to return to my realm, and finally overthrow those other dreadful gods, and goddesses. Chaos will finally reign."

"You have possessed that child since we entered this realm?" Asim asks furiously.

"Yes. It was so amusing. I simply convinced him I was one of his powers. That he would lose his magic if he revealed me and he complied. Until that day those horrible Pegasus came into the stable. Awful creatures. Created purely for my torment. Proof my brother is nothing more than a cruel dictator of the heavens. Those beasts could sense me. The king was growing suspicious. I knew he planned to personally train me to better assess what was wrong. It was pure luck; you attacked the kingdom when you did. So, I thank you, Mari. I knew you weren't completely useless," I say laughing.

"Release that child," Asim commands.

"Release that child!" I mock her horrid voice, laughing hysterically, "You sound insane."

"Cairo..." Heqet whispers as she attempts to approach him. I roll my eyes, lifting her into the air.

"Rise child. I never thought you to be this pathetic. You possessed the brain between the two of you."

"Release me," Heqet says, in a deadly voice.

"Finally," I say, "Some real entertainment."

I drop Heqet to the ground, and she runs towards me. *Amusing.* I throw her into the wall beside her love, pushing her body into the rock until it holds her there.

"Heqet!" Asim screams. *At first, I think she might run for her, but she refocuses her attention on me. Impressive.*

"I am curious, Asim. What was wrong with Marienne? Why did you not choose her? I thought she was impressive at the time. What did you discover that I could not see?" I ask.

"I will not play your game, Apep. I will not add to your chaos," she says. I frown at this news.

"Well, that will not do. Hmmm, I know. What if I tell you where your love is? What if Ashanti was in danger, hmm?"

"Where is she?" Asim asks, searching the room before her eyes land on the closet. *Impressive indeed.*

"I must say, I am impressed with you. I may keep you as a pet," I say, contemplating her future.
"Apep, please. Show mercy." Marienne begs. With a flick of my finger, her mouth snaps shut. *I do not have time for her boring pleas.*

"I know!" I say as the hilarious thought crosses my mind, "I will force Ashanti and Cairo to breed me more powerful beings, an army of immortal transforming beings."

"They would never," Asim says, disgusted.

"Oh, but they would! They would if their love's lives hung in the balance. If I kept you and Heqet as pets to torture for my amusement." I laugh at my own brilliance.

"Isaiah," Heqet says, from across the room. I roll my eyes again. *How boring.*

"He is not here."

"Isaiah, I know you can hear me. You must fight, buddy, okay? He is the bad guy. You can win. You are the strongest person I know," she pleads. "Do not let him win."

I feel Isaiah's mind focus, trying to regain control. She is ruining everything. I flick my wrist, silencing her as well.

"What's wrong, Apep? He's in there, isn't he?" Asim says, suddenly annoyingly hopeful. "Isaiah! Fight back! You can do this!"

I silence her as well. *Fine. Silence it is. What a boring ending to this well-thought-out plan.*

"Kill him!" The soldiers scream as they push past Asim and Marienne.

"I forgot you were there," I admit, slitting their throats as I had done to their peers before. "Okay, well, that was disappointing. Come along, we have much to do.

I lift Asim, Marienne, Cairo, Heqet, and Ashanti, pulling them along as I walk towards the castle's entrance, listening to the battle waging outside. "Perhaps outside will be a little more entertaining to watch, hmm? Can you hear your friends dying?"

As I approach the entrance, I notice the fairies fighting, using their magic to push the vampires into the river, where to my surprise, Iteru and the cursed sirens wait, using their long snake tails to crush them or the sharp teeth to tear them into pieces.

"How exciting! It is so rare of an occasion I am surprised," I say. "I guess this was your doing, hmm, Asim?" I say, smiling at the battle before me. "Here, come watch beside me."

I pull Asim's floating body beside me, laughing as she watches in horror as her friends viciously tear at one another.

Stop it!
Ugh, this little brat will not go away. Perhaps I misjudged his will? He is persistent. Still just another annoyance. I mentally push him back into the darkness. *Stay put.*

"I think we should even the odds, no?" I suggest. Focusing on Iteru, I listen to her screams as she writhes in pain. *Splendid. Now the others.* I watch the sirens all fall back into the depths, sinking to the bottom, as the pain increases. The vampires, confused, run from the river onto land.

"Much better," I say.

"Isaiah?"

The voice pierces through my mind, and Isaiah fights with renewed strength to push through. For just a moment, he wins.

"Mommy?"

I quickly push him as far as he can go into the depths of darkness as I can.

Look, kid. I like you. I do. But do not tempt me. I will erase you from existence and take full control of this shell of a body. I hoped we could enjoy this plan together, but your mind is not a necessary part of this plan.

"Isaiah? I know you are there, little monster. Mommy needs you right now, okay? Come to mommy, please!"

I turn to face his mother, annoyed with her persistence and bored of this plea for Isaiah.

"He is not here," I say, through his tiny teeth.

"Liar! I know he's in there. I can feel him!" She says, "Isaiah!"

"Enough!" I shout, silencing her as well. "I've grown bored with this game. Let's move this along."

I walk to the center of the battle, where the bloodshed has seeped into the earth. Lifting my hands, I silence the battle, forcing all of the beings, aside from my floating friends, to their knees. Slowly, I rise into the air, smiling at my dramatic display of power. *Once again, the god of chaos triumphs.*

"Hello, friends," I say loudly, magnifying my voice. "I am deeply regretful to have to interrupt this amusing display of violence. As much as I enjoy the chaos, I have plans, and this battle is delaying them. Now if you all would, hold tight; I promise you can get back to your savageries momentarily."

I look into their wide, fear-filled eyes, the chaos of the moment intoxicating. *This is perfect*, except for Isaiah's incessant worrying clouding my thoughts. *I'll have to take care of this kid before long.* I bring Ashanti closer to me, taking a moment to contemplate my plans. *I could keep her alive for a while longer, torture her, making Asim watch. That would be fun. Torture never entertains me for long, though.* I would enjoy the look on my brother's face as I return to finally dethrone him and cast the Earth realm into darkness and chaos. I smile, the thought bringing me joy. Yes, I rather like that idea. I bring Ashanti within reach, inhaling her panic.

"Se pou san ou ban mwen pouvwa. Se pou sakrifis ou a ban mwen pouvwa. Mouri epi rete nan mitan dezòd la," I chant, as I slowly slice her flesh, allowing her blood to trickle down her neck. Such a beautiful sight against her lovely brown skin.

NOOO! Isaiah screams, fighting me, as I briefly lose control. I hear another scream, a blood-curdling scream of pain, from somewhere around me, Isaiah distracting me momentarily. I steady myself, pushing him back. I slice faster, no longer able to enjoy the chaos I am creating, as I watch her blood drain from her body, pouring into the ground below.

"Se pou maji san ou manje lespri mwen," I continue my chant. I smile as I feel her life force fade, her magic filling every inch of my body until I feel as though I may explode. Slowly, the glow of her skin dims, and her magic all but empties. I toss her nearly lifeless body to the side, stretching my limbs and enjoying the surge in power.

You promised! Isaiah screams. His rage surprises me, as I again temporarily lose control of his body, crashing into the ground.

Calm yourself, kid. I promise you're better off without a mom. She would have just nagged and nagged. I'll be here with you.

Bring her back.

I can't. It's not within my power scope. Me and the guy in charge of that sort of thing aren't exactly on good terms.

He screeches as he begins fighting against me, forcing me to focus on keeping him at bay. I realize I must choose between stopping him and controlling the mass of soldiers. Angrily, I let go of my hold on them, focusing solely on Isaiah. Too late I realize my mistake as the soldiers charge me, King Grooden in the lead. I watch as Asim flashes to Ashanti's side, cradling her nearly dead body. I hold my hand up, willing the soldiers to the ground once more, as Isaiah bursts forward, once again taking control.

"I did it!" Isaiah yells as King Grooden slits our throat.

"NOOOO!" Heqet yells, as eyes close. The blood loss is too much for our tiny shell of a body.

Chapter Twenty-Three – Heqet

It was as if the world slowed. I watched in horror as *Isaiah, sweet, kind, loving Isaiah, sliced his mother's throat.* I heard Asim's cry of pain, the heartbreak so strong that it broke through the hold this god has on us and filled the air with a heaviness. *A pain so profound that even if you lived a thousand years, you could never comprehend it. My body and mind yearned to comfort her, as I have always done. The pain in her cry broke me as I watched Ashanti tossed aside by her own child. Apep must pay for this, but first, I must save Isaiah.* I listened to Ashanti's faint heartbeat as it wavered, struggling to hold on. *Please. Hold on for a little while longer.* I focus all of my attention on freeing myself from this torture. *Apep must be using his power to hold us captive. I am unable to move, to feel my limbs, as I float through the air, seemingly tied to him. Isaiah must be inside his body still, fighting. I could feel his hold falter after he brutalized Ashanti. I feel the hold weaken again. Finally. As* my body fell to the ground, I heard Asim already running to Ashanti's side, trusting I will save Isaiah. *I will not let her down.* I look to Isaiah, the world around us fading as I watch his face altering back and forth as he fought Apep from inside. *Please, Isaiah, fight hard.* My body tenses, as it prepares to spring forward. *I noticed him too late.* So focused on Isaiah, I didn't notice the king flying right towards him. Isaiah looks at me, his bright innocent eyes gleaming as he stares into my own.

"I did it!"

"Noooo!" I screamed as King Grooden reached him first, his dagger quickly finding his throat. I feel myself crumble to my knees. *No. He won. He fought him and won.* Cairo's strong arms wrap around me as the rage fills my body. Ashanti and Isaiah, gone in seconds. My vision turned red, and I was barely aware of Cairo's whispers, begging me to stay calm.

"Cairo, release me," I said, knowing I am moments away from ripping his limbs from his body.

"No," he says calmly, "You must calm yourself, Heqet. We cannot start another war right now. The king saved us all."

The screech that leaves my body is animalistic. *Saved. He saved us?*

"Isaiah had broken free! He spoke to me! I saw it! He won!" I scream as I began pulling my limbs free from Cairo's hold.
We all heard the laugh simultaneously, freezing with fear. The sudden shift in the air carries a tenseness so thick we

could cut it. We watched, terrified, as Isaiah rose from the ground, his wound healing slowly. Madness returning to his innocent eyes.

"Seriously? You think cutting the neck of a god would kill him?" Apep laughed, "You simply got rid of that little nuisance for me. Sad really, he would have won. He is much stronger than I gave him credit for." Apep said, with a chuckle.

He turned towards the king, still too shocked to move, "Clever though." I watch as he takes the king's dagger from him, licking the blood from the blade before plunging it into his heart. The sound of the queen's screams filled the air.

"Please," Apep said, annoyed, he flicked a finger towards her, and her mouth snapped shut, "much better."

He is. He said he *is* much stronger. *Isaiah is in there.* I froze in place. *Not willing to draw attention to myself. I need to time this just right.* Apep smiled at the queen, eyeing her up and down.

"Hmmm, aren't you a pretty butterfly? I think I'll keep you around," he said, his hand gripping her chin as he examined her face. I hold back a growl, as I watched her tears silently fall. I heard Asim, whispering to Ashanti, begging for her to wake. I say a silent prayer to Nwt: *Please hear our cries and return.*

"Amazing." Apep said, dropping the queen, and facing me, his head slightly turned as if confused, "You're praying? I can sense it."

I quickly backed away, as he approached, "You will not leave this realm, Apep. Your choices now will lead to your own destruction."

"You have always entertained me, Heqet. I find it amusing how persistent you are. Quite clever really. No matter what chaos you endure or witness, you hold steadfast to your purpose. I wonder what tragedy would finally push you over the edge, hmm? Maybe if I left this child's body, and forced you to kill him with your bare hands, or maybe..." Apep stopped, as he scanned the clearing, before his eyes rested on Asim, and Ashanti, "Ah, or maybe if I force you to watch as I relieve your companion of their life? That would be fun to watch... no, no. Asim has always been my favorite. I'm sorry to say. She never does what I expect. I mean falling in love with the child of the very woman she rejected! Ha! I couldn't have even thought that one up!"

"Isaiah... please."

Apep waves his hand, and again, my lips press tightly together.

"No, let's not do that again," he says, annoyed. "I guess I should wrap this up now. It's getting a little repetitive." He waves his hand, and Marienne floats to him. He theatrically dabs his eyes, as if he is crying.

"I may actually miss you, bumble bee," he says, touching his palm to her cheek. "Speak your final words."

"May Ra destroy you."

I watch as Apep takes Isaiah's tiny, clawed hands, piercing through her chest, ripping her heart from her body. He smiles as he chants and absorbs her power. *He's unstoppable. How can we beat him now? The power of a god and three demigods in one small body? How can Isaiah's small frame hold so much power within it?* His eyes glisten with the pure power surging through him. I look to Asim, unsure what to do. *I cannot harm Isaiah, even if I could kill Apep.* She looks to me, *broken*, unable to move from the pain of reliving her love dying in her very arms. *Nwt. We need you. Please.* I beg. I know she will not return. Our cries are falling on deaf ears. Our goddess left us to fend for ourselves so very long ago. *How could she create such a place to abandon us in our time of need? Are all the gods truly this selfish?* My mind flashes over the many years I've spent wandering this universe. The beautiful, majestic creatures we have met, helped, healed. *Healed. Why have I not thought of this before?* I subtly scan the clearing. Cairo beside me, firmly grasping my hand. Asim, engrossed in Ashanti's fading health, The soldiers forced to kneel. Apep ranting and pacing the air. *Now is my time.* I look to Cairo, hoping he will understand what cannot be spoken. We lock eyes for one eternal moment as he stares into my eyes. His body tenses as he prepares to shift. I have never felt as grateful for Cairo's love as I do in this moment. We squeeze each other's hand, the turmoil surrounding us disappearing for just a bittersweet moment before we let go of each other and run away from the chaos together.

Chapter Twenty-Four – Asim

This cannot be happening. I listen to Ashanti's heart, counting the beats. *Please.* I beg to whatever god is listening. *I cannot lose her.*

"Ashanti? You have to wake up, love. Do not stay there," I plead, picturing her in her resting place. I look to Heqet. *She always knows what to do.* Hope leaves my body as I look into her eyes. *She doesn't know.* Apep continues to rant and rave, mesmerized by his own voice. I watch as he paces in Isaiah's small body, occasionally winking at Queen Lotus. *I cannot allow this to continue. I have come to love this child as if he were my own flesh. I cannot allow any further harm to come to him.*

I quickly think over my options. *If I attack, I could hurt young Isaiah, or Apep could attack, killing Ashanti. A head-on attack will not be wise. Apep will not harm the body that hosts him. So, Isaiah is safe, physically at least.*

I can only hope, Isaiah's mind is strong enough, persistent enough to remain. Looking back at Ashanti, fighting to live, I lean towards her, again, preparing to whisper my pleas when Heqet, and Cairo begin to run. *Run? No, they would not abandon us here.* I watch as they continue to run, full speed away from us. Cairo transforming into a falcon, flying quickly away. *Heqet must have a plan.*

I turn to Apep, who's watching them run, a sinister smile on his face. *I have to give them time.* Quickly, I jump to my feet, running for Apep. He frowns at me, annoyed, as he quickly freezes me, mid-stride.

"Come now," he sighs, "was this really the plan? Distract me, and attack?"

He rolls his eyes and raises his hand, flicking me to the side as if I am nothing more than an ant before sighing loudly. For a brief moment, he stares in the direction Heqet and Cairo disappeared, as if contemplating if that would be a problem later. I watch as he shrugs and begins walking towards the castle.

"Okay, I've grown bored of this; let us return to my new home," he says, excitedly before stopping to eye Queen Lotus with an evil smile. "Come along, dear. You shall tell me everything I require to know."

As he approaches the entrance to the castle, he stops, turning around to smile at the being scattered around the clearing. The war that only began hours ago seems like a distant memory. Apep smiles and raises his hand.

"Continue with the savagery." He frowns when no one moves, his eyes glistening. "I said, continue."

A red haze slowly covers the clearing and, with it, a blinding rage. Suddenly everyone begins fighting. Fairies, against vampires, and beings against their own kind. I quickly run to Ashanti, cradling her in my arms as the haze approaches. I turn to run as a group of young, newly turned vampires block me.

"I am not your enemy," I say, slowly putting Ashanti down and stepping in front of her. The sound of their snarls makes their intentions clear. I raise my hands, again trying to plead for their lives. "We need not give in to his cruelty. We can fight this urge," I say, mindful of the oncoming haze, inches away. I look into their black, rageful faces. *I know cannot allow this haze to touch me or Ashanti.*

Sighing deeply, "I am so sorry; I have to save them." I quickly dart forward, ripping the arms of the youngest vampire closest to me from her body before leaping to the next one, tearing her head and tossing it far away. I move quickly, methodically, like I trained so long ago. Seconds pass, and I run to Ashanti as I hear the screams from the disembodied children, no more than twenty or so, piled behind me. *I was careful not to kill them. Once this is over, perhaps they can be reassembled and healed.* I run away from the haze and the vicious killing spree in the clearing. As I run, I realize only one place will be safe from Apep's magic, and I need to get there quickly.

We make it to the forbidden forest as the sun sets, Ashanti moaning weakly in pain. I walk through the dark and suspiciously quiet trees. As I approach the lake in the middle of the forest, I hear two women arguing.

"We must abandon this place! It is only a matter of time before Apep finds us, sister." Iteru pleads.

"We will not abandon our home. Have you forgotten the way the humans hunt us? We will stay," Thalassa says.

"Apep will curse us further. Do you wish me a sea serpent? We cannot win."

"We are the daughters of Tefnut. We will not scurry into the depths of the sea, afraid. Apep dare not venture into the water. We are safe. The remaining enchantments placed on this forest prevent dark magic."

I breathe a sigh of relief, Thalassa confirming my thoughts. I look at Ashanti, her complexion pale, and eyes closed. I hear her heart struggling to pump, and her labored breathing. *I must do something.*

"Come, child," Thalassa calls, "we are aware of your presence."

I walk past the trees and to the edge of the lake. Mermaids and sirens lay scattered along the edge of the water. Seeing Ashanti, Iteru beckons for me to come closer.

"He succeeded then. Her magic is gone," she says sadly.

"He drained her; she survived. I do not know why," I explain, sounding defeated.

"She is fighting. She wants to remain. Come, place her here."

I lay her near Iteru and hover closely by, not trusting the siren. She looks at me sadly.

"I mean her no harm."

"Let us work together, sisters?" Thalassa asks.

"Come quickly," she says, gently touching Ashanti's cheek. I watch as the sirens and mermaids huddle closely together, their hands outstretched as if praying for her. I whisper a prayer to Nwt as I watch their eyes glow a bright golden color, and the lake bubbles and twists as if it were boiling. They continue chanting and praying to their mother, for what feels like hours, but I know no more than an hour has passed.

Slowly, I notice a golden glow trailing from their hands to Ashanti. I watch in amazement as they lend her their own magic. Once they are finished, they turn to me.

"She must rest," Iteru says, "you will be safe here until she awakens."

"Did you give her your magic?" I ask.

"Not all of it; she will survive."

"She will lead us to victory. I have seen it," Thalassa says, turning to her sister. "Come we must rest as well."

I lie beside Ashanti, unwilling to leave her side. I stare up at the canopy of branches, hopeful that she will wake soon. As I lay focused on the individual leaves of the trees, my world shifts, and I feel the smooth dirt near the lake shift to high grass.

"It has been a while."

"Hello, grandmother," I say.

"Everyone has begun calling me that. Isis refuses to stop," Nwt sighs.

Recognizing her voice, I sit up, shocked.

"Nwt?" I say, staring at her.

"Yes, hello, Asim," she says with a smile.

"You have finally come to me! We have missed you!" I say, tears only possible in this realm spilling from my eyes. She reaches over and wipes my eyes.

"Shhhh, child. Do not waste tears on me. I have watched and waited, hopeful you would return to this realm. Ashanti is rather insistent I speak with you."

"Ashanti? She's here?"

"She is safe, resting in her realm. Isis has grown considerably in the afterlife, and she is enjoying the visit from her mother. Ashanti is torn. Her daughter pleads for her, while her son needs her."

"She must return. Isaiah is in grave danger," I say. Nwt nods.

"Come, walk with me," she says. As we walk along the field surrounded by sunflowers, Nwt begins telling me a story, "Do you remember the story of Apep's demise?"

"Yes, of course. The Pegasus held the power to entrap him, but they no longer carry that power," I say.
"Do you know why they were given that power?"

"As punishment, for Apep fighting his brother."

"Precisely. Ra, the creator, has always been a strict god. He enjoys order and peace. His younger brother Apep was a rebellious god. He grew jealous of the strength of his older brother, choosing to idolize chaos and destruction to spite him. They battled often. As their hatred for one another grew, Ra captured his brother, locking him away and creating powerful beings to guard him."

"Pegasus," I whisper. She nods her approval.

"Yes, Pegasus. They guarded this prison and ensured he remained. They had no other purpose beyond this. Now Ra had children, who also became quite rebellious. He assigned everything a purpose and expected his children, most of all, to remain in their purpose. His daughter, whose purpose was to care for the dead, was the most rebellious. She saw these beautiful creatures and felt sadness for them. She would see them daily, talk with them, play, and feed them. They grew to love her deeply. Eventually, this daughter fell in love and sought to have children of her own. Of course, her father forbade it, and so she found a way to have a family regardless. Infuriated, Ra cast his daughter from the heavens, accusing her of creating chaos in her rebellion. Upon hearing of this, the Pegasus were heartbroken and followed her to the Earth Realm, pledging their allegiance to her."

"You were the daughter?" I ask in awe, after so many millennia, finally learning her story.

"Yes, I am that daughter. I was forced to leave my children, my love, and live among the humans. My love would not join me, and thus I lived here alone for many years, hurt and angered, deciding instead of caring for the dead, I would raise them, creating what are today known as vampires. Until one day, I met a brave young man who had a small son; they healed me."

"I do not understand. If the Pegasus were created to guard Apep and keep him imprisoned, why do they no longer hold that purpose?"

"They will always have that purpose. Unfortunately, Ra eventually forgave his daughter, allowing her to return to the heavens, but he did not forgive those creatures he created. They remain stuck, heartbroken, and angry. They no longer serve their purpose," she explains.

"They can defeat Apep?" I say, understanding what she is saying. She nods.

"They can defeat the rebellious god." She nods again.

"Thank you, Nwt! I know what we must do."

I hug her tightly, grateful for her presence. Then said, "Could I convince you to come back? We need you desperately."

"I cannot return. If I return to the living realm, I relinquish my place in the heaven realm. I cannot abandon my children again."

I nod, understanding. I remember the sadness she once felt, no longer being near her children.

"Go, warrior Asim, save our people," Nwt says.

I wake in the dark, Ashanti breathing quietly beside me. I listen to the steady beating of her heart. Their magic is working. Quickly, I cradle her against me as I run towards the fairy castle.

Chapter Twenty-Five – Ashanti

I feel the wind against my back and strong arms holding me. *Asim?* I open my eyes slowly, afraid of what I may see. At first, darkness, and I realize she has me cradled like a small child, my face pressed against her chest. I turn to look and startle her.

"You are awake!" she says, relieved.

"What did I miss? Where is Isaiah?"

"Apep is too strong; we could not defeat him," she explains. I remember the last moments before I was knocked unconscious, before recalling what felt like weeks in my Resting Realm.

"We have to go see Queen."

"I know, we are almost there," she reassures me. "How do you feel? I thought I lost you."

"Better," I say. As we fly, she tells me about the last day.

"A red rage haze? Like an actual mist?" I ask, confused.

"Yes, Apep enjoys his theatrics. He will make a display of all of his actions. He enjoys the fear he creates."

"Do you remember the story you told me? The day we first got here, and you told me about your history here?" I ask. "The Pegasus can stop him. We can convince them," I say, remembering Nwt's conversation with me. *She was so sure I could convince them.*

"We will," Asim says. "Look there, the castle."

We land in the trees along the castle, circling it once before sneaking in. Hurrying to the castle, I realize it is eerily quiet.

"Where are all the fairies?" I ask.

"I'm sure word has spread about Apep; they have gone into hiding," she says sadly as we approach the stables. At first, we hear nothing. Fear creeps in as I realize the Pegasus may have run as well.

"They are here," Asim says confidently, as if reading my thoughts, "I can hear them."

Queen trots out to me first, nervously. She sniffs me, as if she is unsure if it is really me. After a few minutes, she neighs excitedly, and the rest of the herd comes out of hiding. I hug her neck.

"I have missed you too. All of you," I say, petting each Pegasus, stopping at the smallest one, "especially you."

"It is amazing," Asim says, staring at Queen.

"What?"

"She is the Pegasus from the painting. One of the original guards."

I turn shocked, staring at my friend, Queen, "Really?"

"I am sure, the markings are the same."

"Is it true? Are you one of the original guards?" I ask her. She nods, stomping her front hooves, head held high, "All this time, you were trying to warn me?"

"She is thousands of years old, older than me even. More powerful than a god." Asim says in absolute awe.

I think of Isaiah, trapped in his own body, while a psychopath controls him, "Please Queen, imprison Apep again."

She shakes her head, furiously.

"We need your help," I plead. She turns away from us, trotting to the herd, resting her head as if hugging the smallest Pegasus. I look at each Pegasus, realizing I am asking her to risk her friends, and her own children as well.

"I know you mean to protect your children. We can find somewhere to hide them," I say.

Asim steps up," We can take them to the Forbidden Forest. No dark magic can be used there. No harm will come to them. I swear it."

Queen stomps furious at the mention of the Forbidden Forest, shaking her head.

"They could remain in the castle. Think, Queen. Apep is free, it will not be long before he becomes bored torturing us and turns his attention to the only creatures living that could stop him. He is three times as powerful today, but there are more of you now. You could imprison him, ensuring not only your safety but our children's as well. I know it is unfair. You served your purpose for so long, then remained loyal to Nwt, and abandoned your place in Heaven for her, only to be abandoned here. Left to be hunted, and your young slaughtered. You owe us nothing. But I am not my ancestors. I promise you here and now. I will never abandon you. We need you. Please. Don't let him hurt my baby," I beg, crying.

Queen looks at me for a long time, as if thinking. After a while, she takes off, her herd following her, as she flies away. I sink to my knees, defeated.

"We will figure something out," Asim says, kneeling in front of me, wrapping her arms around me.

"Where is Heqet?" I ask, realizing she is nowhere to be seen. Heqet always has answers.

"I do not know. She ran off with Cairo, and I can only assume it is because she has a plan.

"I wish I knew what she was thinking. I feel so lost."

"Me too," Asim admits.
We sit defeated for a while in the grass, holding each other and thinking of plans. As we stand, deciding it may be time to return to the forest, we hear the wings of the Pegasus. Five return, the children and younger ones all gone. I realize they sent their young off to protect them, and I hug Queen tightly.

"Thank you! We will stop him. We will protect all of our young, together," I say confidently.

Finally, after being drowned in hopelessness, a glimmer of hope.

We quickly take flight, flying directly to the Immortal Kingdom. We look in horror as we see the dead bodies littered below.

"Apep must pay for this," Asim says quietly.

The red haze Asim described has dissipated, leaving a trail of blood in its place. We land in the trees near the castle. The Pegasus trot slowly out, walking towards the castle, hoping Apep will see and come outside to confront them in anger.

"It's so quiet here," I say, no signs of the loud battle that took place yesterday. The Pegasus whine and shake their heads as if in pain by what they see.

"Foolish!"

The word echoes through the clearing, as if spoken through an amplifier. We turn in the direction of the sound to see my Isaiah, standing in the opening of the castle doors, a look of hatred in his eyes that doesn't match his innocent face.

"Isaiah," I call and walk towards him, but Asim grabs me, holding me tight.

"That isn't Isaiah, love," she says sadly. I look again and notice Queen Lotus chained behind him, kneeling on the ground.

"He will die," I say through clenched teeth. A bright light distracts us as we turn to see the Pegasus beginning to shift, their bodies growing in size. I watch as their single horn grows into two, long curled horns, and their teeth sharpen, their smooth skin becomes hard as armor. They look like giant war horses. They take off towards Apep, as he laughs.

"You think five of these stupid ponies can stop me? Foolish really," he says, flicking his hand, throwing them backwards. They immediately stand after being thrown and attack again. Again, he throws them backwards.

"They aren't strong enough," I say scared.

"It's all the power he has absorbed," Asim says. We watch as he laughs, as if playing with them, knowing he'll grow bored soon and kill them.

"What can we do?" I ask.

"I do not know," Asim admits, looking around desperately.

"Okay, that is enough," Apep says suddenly, raising his hand. Queen and the rest of the Pegasus kneel to the ground, as if being forced. They cry out in pain as Apep continues his torture. The Pegasus attempt to cover themselves, creating a dome of protection, but Apep quickly destroys it as he continues to press their bodies further into the ground.

"He's going to kill them." Tears spill from my eyes as I hear their pained cries. Asim suddenly looks up.

"I knew it," she says, smiling, relief in her voice. "On time as always."

"What?" I ask, looking around, confused. After several endless moments, I finally see what has lifted her spirits.

Heqet and a giant falcon are flying towards us. Behind them, nearly a dozen Pegasus.

"She found others," Asim says. As they land, we hear Apep's screams of anger.

"No! I will not be defeated again! I have waited millennia for my revenge!" He screams, raising his other hand in an attempt to force the others to the ground. Heqet and Cairo fall to the ground momentarily before the Pegasus raise their glowing light, creating a dome of protection. They quickly reach Queen and her herd, and together they strengthen their dome, allowing the hurt Pegasus to rise. Their long legs shake as they try to stand. Heqet and Cairo quickly run to our side, Cairo shifting to his true form.

"Heqet," Asim says, hugging her sister, "I knew you would return."

"Of course. I always take care of it," she says with a laugh. "It is good to see you awake."

We hold hands for just a moment, a loud crash ending our reunion. We turn to see Apep hurling stones and trees at the Pegasus, but it is obvious they are too powerful. They surround him, their dome covering him too. Slowly, the dome of light begins retracting from them, as if hugging him, wrapping around him tightly. He screams in pain.

"No! They'll kill Isaiah!" I scream, running towards them. I feel my wings expand quickly from my back as I take off towards them. Asim and Heqet quickly grab me, holding me to the ground.

"NO!" I scream. Why aren't they helping? It's Isaiah!

"Ashanti, please listen! They will not kill him. They have to imprison him; once they do, they can extract him from Isaiah's body. They will heal him. If we interfere, Apep will go free," Asim says, holding my arms so tightly they might break. "Please, trust me."

I fight them, using all of my strength to try and break free, but before long, I realize it is pointless; they are simply too strong. My body goes limp as I begin to cry. I listen to Apep's screams, at times I swear I hear Isaiah. After what feels like an eternity, the screaming stops, and they release me. I turn to see Isaiah's tiny body, frozen in the air, their yellow dome of light no longer translucent but solid. His skin looks burned, his face twisted in pain.

"My baby," I sob, his little body looks lifeless. I run to his side, unable to touch him; I kneel in front of him. "I'm so sorry, baby, so, so sorry. I couldn't protect you."

Queen begins nudging me, asking me to move away from him. I refuse until I feel Asim's arms around me, guiding me away. All of my energy is gone as if sucked from my body, as if I am just a shell. I walk several feet away before my legs give out. Heqet and Asim surround me, trying to console me. Their words mean nothing, sounding gargled and impossible to comprehend. I watch as the Pegasus surround his body once again, a light so bright we have to shield our eyes appears above Isaiah. I watch as it acts as a twister of some kind, pulling a dark mist from Isaiah's body; once the mist is completely pulled from his body, it's stored in a smaller solid cube of light.

"They've done it. They have imprisoned Apep," Heqet whispers. We watch as six of the Pegasus quickly take flight, disappearing with Apep's soul or energy. The remaining ones circle Isaiah. I watch as the solid light begins to turn to liquid, melting around him; as it melts, his skin heals. "They are healing him, love; he will be okay," Asim reassures me. I watch closely until he is completely unfrozen, his skin returned to its beautiful rich brown color. He lies on the ground unmoving.

"Come," Asim says, and I run to him. I cradle him tightly to my chest, rocking him back and forth as I cry. The awful, horrible things he's witnessed, experienced, trapped in his own body. *How will I heal him from that?*

"Mom, you're squeezing me too tight!" Isaiah says, pressing his little hands against my chest.

"Isaiah!" I scream before squeezing him tighter.

"Mom!" He squeals.

"Don't suffocate the child," Asim jokes. I loosen my grip as I laugh, happy tears flowing freely.

"We beat him!" He says happily before his expression changes to guilt, "he was a really bad guy. He made me do bad stuff."

"None of it was your fault. He did it, not you, okay?" I say looking into his eyes.

"Okay."

"You did so good!" Heqet says, hugging him, "You were so strong."

"We're all proud of you," Asim says, as Cairo ruffles his hair.

Queen walks up to Isaiah, sniffing him carefully before licking him and nudging him playfully.

"Oh, okay," Isaiah says. I look at him in disbelief.

"You understand her?" I ask.

"Yes, she wants us to hold hands," he says, taking both my hands. We stare at him, unsure what is happening. Slowly, I feel my power flowing from his small body back into mine. A warm wave of power covers my body from head to toe.

"She said grandma's power has nowhere to go, so I can keep it," he says, "she says I am super strong."

I turn to hug Queen again, "Thank you."

She nudges me lovingly before the remaining Pegasus take off into the sky, off to find their own young.

We spend the remainder of the day freeing the few captives in the castle and helping to bury the dead. A process that, even with magic, will take days to accomplish. With so many dead or injured, a new treaty is negotiated. The kingdom will rule under one being, with a being from each species having a representative in the kingdom's counsel. A vote will be held to decide.

We pray for the dead, praying Nwt will escort them to the ancestral realm. It was easy to decide against a celebration. There would be no feast or music. Too much death and sadness filled the air. We instead cry and hold onto each other, mourning the death of so many beautiful spirits. We brought food to the families of the villages of the soldiers. The mermaids and sirens finally forgave one another, deciding to live as one. Thalassa, and Iteru both place protection spells on Isaiah and myself, protecting us from any further possession attacks. We all return to the fairy castle, although the immortal castle is technically our home.

As I lay cuddled with Isaiah, unwilling to let him out of my sight, he looks up at me and smiles.

"Are you okay, little monster?" I ask, gently rubbing his hair. He shakes his head.

"I'm glad Apep is gone. He scared me," he says.

"You won't ever have to worry about him again," I say, hugging him tightly.

"When I fell asleep, Nana Nwt told me a secret," he whispers, smiling sneakily.

"What was that?" I ask, laughing.

"She said she got a special gift before, and she was going to give you the same one!" he giggles.

"Yeah? What's that?" I ask, tickling him.

"She said my sister's coming back, that she's in your belly."

"What? How?"

He simply shrugs and goes back to laying down, as Asim walks into the room shocked.

"Did you hear that?" I ask confused, looking at my stomach. I realize she isn't responding, as I look up to find her staring, mouth up at me, "What?"

"I can hear her," she says, "her heartbeat."

We stare at one another, too afraid to be excited. She gave me my daughter back.

That night as I lay in bed, silently crying happy tears, Isaiah fast asleep in my arms, Asim excitedly whispering with Heqet and Cairo in the next room, making plans to travel to their own home soon. I remember lying in bed, crying a very different kind of tears, what felt like a million years ago, pregnant and afraid. *No, my ancestors had never forgotten me.* So many adventures and tragedies in such a brief amount of time. Hugging Isaiah tightly, I drift off to sleep, ready for this next adventure.

Acknowledgements

This book is dedicated to my mom. Thank you for never giving up on me and supporting me, no matter how many times I have decided to start my book of life over. Every step of the way, I knew you were there. You are truly the backbone of our family. To my sisters, you are incredible women, and mothers. Our father would be proud. To my boys, I live for you. You guys give me purpose. I can never explain how many times you boys have saved my life. Thank you for choosing me. To my best friend, I cannot remember a time you were not there with me. My partner in crime for three decades and counting. Finally, my love, I appreciate you in ways I do not have the words to describe. You make me whole. You breathe life into me. I could not have imagined a better soulmate. I could never thank my village enough. I am grateful every day for your love and support. Thank you, thank you, thank you.

About The Author

Thank you so much for reading my baby, "The Forgotten World." Just a bit about myself. My name is Angela Bastien. I grew up in Reading, a small city in Pennsylvania. I am Haitian American. When I'm not writing marvelous sci-fi books, I spend my days at home, gaming with my girlfriend, or hanging out with the kiddos and my fur babies. I truly hope you enjoy this ride with me while we journey through the chaos of my mind. I love you all lots, and I hope to become one of your favorite authors!

Follow for updates!
Instagram: @official_angye_the_author
Tik Tok: @official_angye_the_author